D0710523

SONS OF BLACKBIRD MOUNTAIN

Center Point
Large Print

Also by Joanne Bischof and available from
Center Point Large Print:

The Lady and the Lionheart

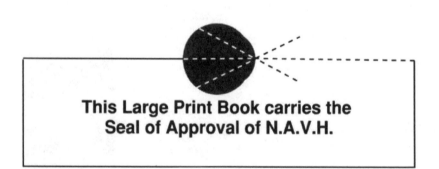

**This Large Print Book carries the
Seal of Approval of N.A.V.H.**

SONS
of
BLACKBIRD
MOUNTAIN

JOANNE BISCHOF

CENTER POINT LARGE PRINT
THORNDIKE, MAINE

This Center Point Large Print edition
is published in the year 2018 by arrangement with
Thomas Nelson.

The text of this Large Print edition is unabridged.
In other aspects, this book may vary
from the original edition.
Printed in the United States of America
on permanent paper.
Set in 16-point Times New Roman type.

ISBN: 978-1-68324-882-8

Library of Congress Cataloging-in-Publication Data

Names: Bischof, Joanne, author.
Title: Sons of Blackbird Mountain / Joanne Bischof.
Description: Center Point Large Print edition. | Thorndike, Maine :
    Center Point Large Print, 2018.
Identifiers: LCCN 2018018093 | ISBN 9781683248828
    (hardcover : alk. paper)
Subjects: LCSH: Mountain life—Fiction. | Deaf—Fiction. |
    Large type books. | GSAFD: Christian fiction. | Love stories.
Classification: LCC PS3602.I75 S66 2018b | DDC 813/.6—dc23
LC record available at https://lccn.loc.gov/2018018093

For my sister

A NOTE ON AMERICAN SIGN LANGUAGE

This story contains American Sign Language (ASL), the most recognized form of communication in the United States for both the Deaf and their community since the early 1800s. Though ASL and spoken English share vocabulary, they are two distinct languages and do not translate directly. Sentences are structured differently in ASL, which uses neither articles such as *a* and *the,* nor "to be" verbs like *am* or *is.*

As is common, the Deaf man in this novel can read someone's lips if the speaker were to say, for example, that "a woman is beautiful." He could also read or write this sentiment as English text. But when communicating with Sign, he would form only the words *woman beautiful.* So simple a phrase, but within the visual exchange of ASL, complexity is at hand. In place of oral tone, facial expressions and manner of movement clarify key distinctions. To drop his jaw on *beautiful* would declare the depth of his admiration. To lift his brows would turn the same phrase into a question. If he were to frown, appearing nonchalant, he would indicate only *somewhat pretty.* Each nuance is key, but ones not widely known among the hearing.

Within *Sons of Blackbird Mountain* I sometimes wrote ASL just as it is signed—including the correlating facial expressions. This is for authenticity and for the reader to experience the language in its purest form. At other times I emphasized only the words. This is for ease of conversation and story flow. In these instances I took great care to express the Deaf character's intent as well as the sentence structure he is familiar with.

Through this, it is my utmost hope to honor the Deaf and their language and to make it possible for a man who neither hears nor speaks to be more clearly heard by those who do.

ONE

Aven peered down at the letter again, noted the address written in Aunt Dorothe's hand, then looked back to the wooden sign that was staked into the ground. The location matched, but with the Virginia summer sun overhead and the shores of Norway but a memory, she was suddenly having a hard time putting one foot in front of the other.

A humble lane loomed—both ahead and behind. Yet if she were to walk on, it would be away from the woodlands she'd spent the morning traversing and into the shade of countless orchard trees. Apple, judging by the fruit dangling from the gnarled branches. A sweet tang hung in the hot air. Aven drew in a slow breath, bent nearer to the sign, and fingered the rough-hewn letters.

Norgaard.

Aye, then. 'Twas the place. The land where Dorothe's great-nephews roamed. Free and wild the boys were, or so the stories declared. Aven minded not. Having lived within the work-house, she'd had to watch from afar as many of the orphans there faded away. The change in

9

circumstance now—in freedom—had her eager to find the house. The family. Most especially, the children.

At a beating on the path, she looked up to see a hound bounding near. The dog's tail wagged as the animal sniffed around Aven's shoes. The banging tail struck her leg, and Aven reached down to pet the glossy brown head that lifted in greeting.

"Hello, you."

The dog gave a few licks, then trotted back along the path as if to show her the way. As it surely knew more of these rolling woodlands than she, Aven clutched up her travel-worn carpetbag. She walked on, brushing dust from her black mourning gown as she did. A dress no longer needed since the two years of mourning had ended before she'd even set foot on this place called Blackbird Mountain. When a stick crunched up ahead, she shielded her eyes. Heavy were the shadows in the grove as afternoon pushed into evening, brighter still the sun that pierced through.

Another twig snapped and a man stepped into the lane, not half a dozen rows up. Aven could tell neither his manner nor age as he knelt with his back to her, stacking metal buckets. The dog circled him contentedly.

Feeling like a trespasser, Aven strode near enough to call a hello. The man didn't turn. It wasn't until her shadow fell beside him that he glanced her way. Slowly, he rose and, using a thick hand, pushed back unkempt hair that was as dark as the earth beneath his boots. It hung just past his shoulders where it twisted haphazardly, no cord to bind it in sight.

His lips parted. Eyes an unsettling mix of sorrow and surprise. A look so astute that it distracted even from the pleasing lines of his face. He spoke no greeting. Offered nothing more than that silent, disarming appeal as if the world were an unfair place for them both.

Aven struggled for her voice. "G'day, sir. Might you . . . might you be able to tell me where Dorothe Norgaard could be found?" Though Aven had been a Norgaard for four years now, the Norwegian name never sounded quite right in her Irish brogue.

The man glanced to the carpetbag she white-knuckled, then to her dusty shoes and up. He ran the back of his hand against his cropped beard. More uneasy, Aven adjusted her grip on the leather handle, reminding herself that she had read the sign right.

The Norgaard farm. This had to be it.

She'd traveled too far and too long to be in the wrong spot.

Seeming displeased, the man shoved back the sleeve cuffs of his plaid shirt, and finally he thumbed over his shoulder.

11

Apparently the lad hadn't the gift of the gab.

And why she was thinking of him as a lad was beyond her. The man seemed more grown than she at her one and twenty. Looking nearly as sturdy as the tree behind him, he had more than a few stones on her as well.

His gaze freeing her own, he angled away and thumbed farther up the lane again.

Aye. She should be moving on . . . that way, it seemed. She gave a quiet thank-you and he nodded, his brown-eyed gaze on her as she passed by. 'Twas but a few steps ahead that Aven halted. This man had the same brow as her Benn. One bearing the noble angles of Norse blood. Though the stranger's hair was a far cry from Benn's pale locks, she saw something in his manner. That same strapping stance and pensive look.

"Might you be one of the Norgaards?" She hoped her accent wasn't too thick for him. It seemed Americans had a hard time with her dialect.

With two buckets apart from the rest, he stacked them. The gaze that landed back to her was apprehensive. He had a wildness about him, and combined with his silence, her unease only grew. But then he nodded. Aven smiled a little. No stranger, but family.

"I'm Aven. Widow to Benn."

The man nodded again as if having known as much.

Perhaps this was an uncle to the children. But why Dorothe didn't mention an uncle . . .

"So . . ." Aven pointed past him, and when a strand of rust-colored hair whipped into her face, she twisted it away. "I'm to walk this way?"

He dipped his head once more, which had her smiling again.

"I thank you, Mr. Norgaard." Clutching the handle of her carpetbag tightly, she continued down the lane, feeling his eyes on her. Strange bloke.

She walked on another few moments, then she spotted a large, red house up ahead. Faded and weather-beaten, it looked more like a giant barn than a home, but with its porch swing and laundry line, 'twas clearly the latter.

Aven glanced back to see she was being followed. From a fair distance, she'd give him that. But it still had her eyeing the man with every few trees they passed until the orchard opened up into a vast yard. Thick, twisted branches giving way to sheds and outbuildings. Two of the structures were massive, a distant one was charred, and around many sat stacks upon stacks of wooden crates and more metal buckets than she'd ever seen in one farmyard.

Her companion stopped and folded his arms over his chest. Hesitantly, Aven continued up the path the same moment a second man emerged from the house. Though as tall as the first, this one's strength was wiry. His hair was a few shades lighter but just as long, judging by the way it was pulled back and bound. Heavy boots stomped down the steps.

Another Norgaard? She glanced around for a sight of the children—but saw nary a toy about, and the clothing pinned to the line was by no means pint-sized. Aven regarded the stranger on the porch and resisted the urge to touch her mother's delicate chain around her neck, as she often did when nervous.

"Hello, sir." She stepped closer and extended a hand, which seemed very small when wrapped in his own. "I'm Aven. I was married to Benn." That seemed odd to blurt out, but she didn't know how many of these introductions were to take place.

"Ah." He studied her a moment. "A pleasure to finally meet you, ma'am." He cleared his throat and gave his name. Jorgan.

She knew that name from Aunt Dorothe's many letters. But Jorgan was to be a wee lad. And this man was no such thing. Aven scrutinized him. Dorothe had certainly not portrayed the sons as men. Before she could make sense of that, another one stepped from the house. Though the third brother's charms had been described in great detail, his great-aunt's praises didn't do justice for who could only be a very grown-up Haakon. The young man's brilliant blue eyes took her in, and though he was clean shaven, his brawn dashed any lingering notion of the Norgaard offspring being children. Even as panic rose, Jorgan spoke.

"And this is Haakon. He's the youngest."

Pear in hand, Haakon cut a slice and used the flat of the knife to raise it to his mouth. Nothing but mischief in that striking face. "We've been wonderin' if you'd show up."

Aven swallowed hard. How had she been so mistaken? She searched her memory of Dorothe's letters. Time and again the Norgaard males had been depicted as anything but adults. *Boys,* Dorothe had called them. Going on to hint at their adventures and mischief, their rowdy ways and their need to be guided. Even chastised. Most often in Haakon's case. The same Haakon who was smiling down at Aven as if he hadn't seen the inside of a woodshed for a good long while.

Hands now trembling, Aven clutched them together, and her attempt at a fervent response came out a mere whisper. "Pleasure to meet you, sirs. You are the . . . the brothers? The sons?"

Sons of whom, she couldn't remember. Dorothe wrote little of the boys' deceased parents. Yet dashed was the image of three children needing Aven to help care for them. Mother them. Aye, Aunt Dorothe had been misleading indeed. Growing stronger was the need to speak with the woman and make some sense of this.

"Yes'm. I'm the oldest," Jorgan said. "Best just

to call us by our first names or you'll be sayin'
'Mr. Norgaard' an awful lot. It seems you met
Thor. He's in the middle." He pointed past Aven
to where the dark-haired man still stood a few
paces back. The one who looked strong as an ox
and who had yet to take his focus off of her.

Thorald. As was written in the letters. Amid
pen and paper, it seemed he held a tender spot
in his great-aunt's heart, but not for a hundred
quid would Aven have put the name and person
together. "Aye," she said hesitantly. "We've . . .
met."

Jorgan smirked. "Sorry. Thor, he don't talk
much."

So she'd learned.

Jorgan glanced past her, then around as if
searching for words. "Did you walk here from
the train station?"

"Aye." And her aching feet were recalling
every mile from town.

"I'm sorry we weren't there to fetch you. And
I'm sorry about Benn."

"Thank you," Aven said softly. She lowered her
luggage to the ground, unsure of what to say in
this instance. Her husband—their cousin—gone.
And now she was here in America.

The dog sniffed at her shoes, and Haakon
snapped his fingers. "Grete!"

The dog retreated to his side.

Aven looked around. With three men near,

she was more than ready to see another woman. "Might you tell me where I can find Aunt Dorothe?"

Jorgan glanced at the brother beside him before rubbing the back of his neck, then it was to her he spoke, eyes drawn up beneath troubled brows. "You didn't get my letter, I take it."

She shook her head.

He cupped his opposite arm just above the elbow. "She's . . . I'm afraid Dorothe's . . . gone. Two months now."

"Where did she go?" Aven's skin flushed. Mourning dress feeling much too heavy and tight.

"To—to heaven."

"Most likely." Haakon slipped another slice of pear in his mouth.

Aven's stomach dipped. Head rushing with a light heat that made the earth tip on its side. "She's . . . *deceased?*"

Jorgan ducked his head sympathetically. "I'm sorry to have to tell you like this. I wrote you soon as it happened, thinking I might be able to reach you." He studied her from her windblown hair to her scuffed shoes. "I can see I was too late."

She needed to sit down but there was nothing other than the dirt, and that she lowered herself to, caring for neither dress nor stockings. Suddenly feeling very small, she blinked up at the

17

clear, blue sky that was a blatant reminder of just how far she was from Norway. Even Ireland. She was here in Virginia. A place called Blackbird Mountain. And there was no Aunt Dorothe.

Though the woman wasn't family by blood and though their letters had formed but a modest friendship, Benn's great-aunt had become all Aven had left of family.

"What do I do?" she whispered to herself.

The man—Jorgan—moved beside her. He knelt in the dirt, touching work-roughened fingers to the ground between them. "Miss?"

Aven drew in a shaky breath and looked up at his face. "What do I do?" she asked again.

"You . . . you just put your arm on mine." He moved to help her. "Come inside. Miss Ida, our housekeeper, will get you something to eat."

Jorgan led her up a few steps, then across a wide porch. Brows tipped up in confusion, the youngest brother held the door open. Jorgan led her into the kitchen where he pulled out a chair at the table and helped her into it. From the pantry stepped a woman with skin as dark as cinnamon sticks. With a gentle smile, the woman brought Aven a cup of coffee and a slice of spiced bread. Aven touched neither. Instead, she clasped her hands between her knees to keep them from shaking.

She vaguely heard the woman speak. "She's mighty pale."

Then Haakon's voice. "She's Irish."

Aven sat without moving.

"I mean to say she's *taking a turn,* Haakon. 'Bout to faint." The cool knuckles of the woman's hand pressed to the side of Aven's temple, and Aven nearly closed her eyes.

Jorgan spoke in a hushed tone. "She didn't know of Dorothe's passing."

With the scrape of a chair, he sat. The woman handed him a cup of coffee. From the corner of her eye, Aven saw Thor leave.

"Are you alright?" Jorgan asked gently.

She nodded, but even the simple motion felt untrue. Despair stung her throat, parching it more than the walk up this mountain. She turned the tin cup in her hand, the sight of the steamy brew tightening her stomach.

"You're still welcome here," Jorgan said, sounding sincere.

"But we don't have anywhere to put her," Haakon countered, none too quietly.

Aven glanced around. Dusk was settling. "Would there . . . would there be other family around?"

"No, ma'am." Haakon's blue eyes—stunning as they were—lessened in charm as they skimmed the length of her. "Just us."

No one moved. All still as the steamy air. A throb pulsing in her chest, Aven placed a hand there. She drew in a deep breath through aching lungs. 'Twas no time to despair. Yet the very tremor rose as a flood. Her vision blurred, and someone spoke words she didn't hear.

The porch creaked, followed by heavy steps. A moment later someone lowered a glass of water in front of her. She peered up to see Thor set it in place. Water dripped down the side of the glass as if it had just been filled from a spring. When she didn't reach for it, he nudged it closer, then dried his hand on the side of his pants.

A small sip sent cool water down her throat as well as a whisper of gratitude to the man who had fetched it.

With a slight limp, the housekeeper stepped near and placed a tender hand on Aven's own. The woman's face was soft with concern. A sensitivity that pressed the ache of tears to Aven's eyes. The woman bid the men to leave them for a few minutes. When they strode out, the housekeeper squeezed her hand again.

Aven closed her eyes and sent up a prayer, nay, a plea, that this day was a dream.

"Now, don't you fret none. We gonna see that you's just fine. Better'n fine. I promise ya. I been keepin' house here for nigh unto thirty years. The boys used to call me Mammy, but now's they grown, they call me Miss Ida. I'll take good care of you." A few stray coils of gray hair framed her glistening forehead, and the eyes studying Aven were filled with such kindness that Aven felt safety edge around the uncertainties.

"You don't need to be afraid of nothin'. The Norgaards are all good boys. Raised 'em up meself, and they's as loyal a lot as comes."

Slowly, Aven nodded.

"Now." Miss Ida motioned deeper into the house, one that seemed to groan with the same emptiness that hollowed Aven from within.

Yet this house was far, far away from the life she'd known, and perhaps this time—in this place—there might be safety and rest. Even a home. Had Dorothe not written of that very thing? The scripture she'd shared had coaxed Aven away from the shadows of the past and onto the gangway of that ship.

"The Lord also will be a refuge for the oppressed, a refuge in times of trouble."

With a ginger grip Miss Ida led them both to stand. She plucked up the carpetbag as if it weighed nothing at all for her spindly frame. "If there's one thing I know about Haakon, it's that he don't always know what he's ramblin' on about." Ida gave a friendly squeeze to Aven's arm and winked. "Let's find a spot to put ya."

TWO

Thor watched from the porch as Ida led Aven into the great room. He stepped inside and followed just close enough to see the way the young redhead skirted around the faded sofa, then an end table laden with books. Her feet slowing, she stared up at the massive antlers above the fireplace. Eyes wide, she lowered them to the firewood flanking the brick hearth on both sides.

Though the logs were neatly stacked, the curtains that had once framed the windows just above were no more—having been used to make clothing during the war. Her attention skimmed to the guns that rested on a side table, then to the boxes of ammunition slung open, freshly rummaged through. His own doing there.

She peered back at him as if knowing all along where he was. It was the same wary look she kept sending his way.

Why? He wasn't going to touch her. And he certainly didn't bite.

Aven's black skirts swayed like a bell as she trailed Ida up the stairs, and that slip of a waistline looked like it needed a month of meals.

Thor had meant to head upstairs himself, but best not to follow too closely. His work in the orchards was finished for the day. The buckets all moved, and with Jorgan's help, he'd hired their extra hands for the coming harvest. Thor had selected three. All of them Negro youths who had been his hardest workers the autumn before. Certain neighbors would be none too pleased with that, which meant there'd be uninvited company soon. Another warning.

With that in mind, Thor went back to his work of cleaning the guns. He lifted a rifle from the side table, closed and locked it. Raising the rifle to eye level, he squinted, centering the bead sight on a pine board in the far wall. He lowered the gun, blew at a few specks of dust, then realigned the sight on the small knot. Satisfied, he set it down.

As if of its own accord, his hand reached for the quart jar sitting there. It was half-filled with the best brew in the county, as always. Already he'd consumed enough to sustain himself until his morning whiskey, but Thor drank a few strong gulps, then set the jar aside, certain he'd be reaching for it again before nightfall. With their guest here, he needed all the liquid courage he could get.

The burnt end of a match went sailing past him, and he glanced back to see his older brother wanting his attention. Jorgan puffed from a freshly lit pipe, then used it to point up the stairs where their new houseguest had gone. Last, and with a sober sincerity, Jorgan made the hand sign for *beautiful,* fanning an open hand downward in front of his face.

Thor turned away. He didn't need to be reminded. Sliding the lid on his jar of cider, he twisted it into place.

Jorgan stomped for his attention again. At the rattle of floorboards, Thor shot a glare at his brother who spoke words Thor could read by sight but never hear. "You know why Dorothe had her come."

Thor closed the box of ammunition, his gaze still on the man who, at thirty-two, was four years his senior.

"Because you never venture out." *Never leave,* Jorgan added. Dangling his pipe from his lips freed him to form the last two words with his hands.

I leave, Thor signed back. He held up his thumb and two fingers for *three.* He'd gone to church on Sunday and twice that week to the pond for a bath. He declared as much.

Jorgan chuckled. Thor saw it in the flash of a smirk and the quick jolt of his chest.

When Jorgan spoke again, Thor couldn't understand. He pointed to his brother's pipe and Jorgan pulled it free.

"You keep to yourself at church," Jorgan said more clearly. He glanced over his shoulder at what had to be a sound. As all those in this house knew to do, Jorgan didn't speak again until Thor could see his moving lips. Harder with Jorgan, whose beard needed trimming. "And there's no women at the pond."

Thor rolled his eyes, and though he tried to exude calm, the way Aven was braided into this conversation alongside him was unnerving. Ida strode down the stairs, seconding Jorgan's declaration about women with a dramatic nod as she fetched the broom. Fresh sheets lay folded over her arm, and her limp was more pronounced in the evening, as usual.

Thor released his breath in a huff. Little eavesdropper. He jabbed the tip of his finger in her direction, and having no hand sign for the word, he had to fingerspell. *M-E-D-D-L-E-S-O-M-E.* Irritation moved his hand so fast the letters blurred.

Ida just smiled. Outnumbered, Thor plucked up his jar and headed for the stairs. Two at a time he took them, then stepped down the hallway. Of the four doors there, he strode past Jorgan's room first, then kept his head down as he passed the room where Aven would have been placed.

There was a bed in there, but last he saw, it had been buried under a mountain of furs as well as two baskets of old canning lids. Judging by the way the pelts and baskets were now stacked in the hallway, Aven would soon be settled. Thor didn't dare glance to find out as he hurried past.

Next was the closed door of Dorothe's room. Strange that Ida hadn't given that one to Aven, but perhaps they meant to preserve Dorothe's memory awhile longer. The final door was up ten twisting steps that led to the third floor—a finished attic he shared with Haakon. It was hot up here in the summer, cold in the winter, but never so miserable that they weren't grateful for the space. Windows were everywhere. Thor's favorite being the pair that overlooked the westward slope where his Baldwins grew, deep and red. Right now, the sun was gone, leaving only its blush behind the gnarled branches.

After easing the door closed, he strode to his bed and sat on the mattress. He reached beneath the bed and slid forward a rough-hewn box. It bore no top, simply a collection of odds and ends, most ordinary save for the one thing he kept there where it wouldn't be noticed.

He didn't need to reach in and pull out the framed wedding photograph to know that Aven's lips curved up so subtly it could hardly be considered a smile. Or that the young bride standing beside Benn Norgaard was seventeen on the month. Plucked from an Irish workhouse to marry a man she had never met. But with her likeness now fresh in his mind, Thor reached into the box and loosened the photograph from beneath two books, the Norwegian titles as well-read as all the English books lining his shelf.

He looked down at the photograph, smoothed his thumb along the frame, and felt a pang at the sight of Aven's wide, uncertain eyes. Benn's proud grip on her hand. Thor had always disliked that about the photograph, which had come by post a few months after the wedding. The unease in Aven's expression. How young and lonely and lost she looked. Perhaps he couldn't hear, but he could see. Better than most. And he'd always seen heartache in her face.

But she'd been the wife of another, so Thor had vowed to push the Irish girl from his mind—the photograph soon collecting dust on the wall with many others. Until news reached them of Benn's death, and Thor had pulled it down and studied once more the face of the young woman who had bound herself to his older cousin.

Who—now widowed—bore the name Norgaard.

He'd stowed the framed image in his box where it was safe. Like the spark of hope forming in his guarded heart.

Now she was but feet away. So near that he need only stride down the hall, rap his knuckles against her door, and find himself peering into those same eyes. See afresh that her hair was actually the color of copper and that her skin was as pale as it was in that photograph of black and white. The shade of buttercream and just as silken, he imagined.

This woman who'd walked up to him but hours

ago in the orchard. Standing there, a reach away, looking bone-weary as she asked questions he could scarcely answer for her. He'd known it was Aven the moment he had turned. His heart so quick in his chest, he thought it would fail him. Even if he had known what to say to her, he had no way to speak it.

Floorboards vibrated beneath his boots. Thor slid the frame away and shoved the box from sight. He straightened just as Haakon stepped into the attic. Pressing his fingers together, Haakon touched them to his mouth.

Time to eat. Thor rose. Haakon spoke, but the phrase was lost in the dimming light. Thor didn't like the dark and the way it made his world shrink in smaller, so he smoothed a palm around his chest, then using his forefingers, circled them toward himself—*please sign*. A freedom he'd never take for granted. Not since the teacher who had bound his wrists together with string, insisting he learn to speak as the others could.

Haakon pointed toward the hall, shaped the letters *A-V-E-N,* then using two fingertips, slid them down his cheeks.

She was crying?

"It's not loud," Haakon said, turning up the lantern. "I heard it when I walked past her door." He backed away because there wasn't a meal in the world that the kid would miss. Haakon paused. "Why do you think Dorothe had her come?"

28

Lifting his shoulders in a shrug, Thor shook his head.

The only answer he would give Haakon.

"Turns out she and I are the same age. Figured that out while I fixed her jammed window." Haakon bobbed his brows as if that wasn't the only thing he wanted to fix for her. Before Thor could even think of a response, his younger brother headed back down the steps.

Not entirely hungry, Thor reached for his jar. He didn't want to, but it was a need so wrought with time and yearning that he unscrewed the lid, lifted the glass to his lips, and drank. No comfort followed as the bubbling cider warmed him, and the liquor did nothing to wash away Haakon's smug expression. Irritated with his own weakness, Thor replaced the lid.

He rose, set the drink aside, and freed the photograph once more. Stiff from a day's worth of work, he headed down the stairs. The hallway was nearly black but for the slit of flickering light beneath Aven's door. He strode with as much care as he could manage. When they were younger and prone to mischief, Haakon had taught him which boards creaked, so Thor stepped over those before slowing in front of Aven's door.

He hesitated, then placed his palm to the wood. Bowing his head, he closed his eyes.

And there it was. The gentle tremor in the slab. It moved against his hand . . . the sound of her grief. Overwhelmed, he pulled away, grateful Ida was here so Aven's tears might fade into sleep easier.

After glancing one last time at the photograph—the beginning of a life he knew nothing about, and one he frankly didn't deserve—Thor knelt, settled it in the nook of her door, and left her with the only thing he could.

THREE

After showing Aven to the bathhouse—a little room nestled on the outside of the kitchen—Miss Ida limped across the board floor to the soaking tub. At the turn of a knob, water spilled in from a reservoir connected to the stove on the other side of the wall, and within minutes the steaming wetness was heaven to Aven's skin. She soaked and scrubbed, savoring the feel of washing the road off her body and out of her hair. Memories of all that brought her here, however, weren't as easy to scrub away. Those she tucked in the quiet places of her heart, thinking instead to simply count the blessings of this day and what it held.

Out and toweled, she dressed in a skirt that had been given to her at the poorhouse. The waistband needed a few pins, so Aven gathered and folded material better into place, then made sure the collar of her somber blouse was fastened snug. The look was a bit severe, especially in the light of a summer morning, but she was aiming for inconspicuous.

Tucked within her carpetbag was a prettier frock of pale-blue bombazine. While outdated with a wide, sweeping skirt meant for hoops, she had altered the secondhand gown to be quite fashionable, modifying the pagoda sleeves to a sparser, more modern style. The dress was one she'd been looking forward to wearing. Just not today.

The smell of hot meat and bread lured her back to the kitchen. Aven stepped in to see Thor sitting at the table. His dark hair was pulled back with a leather cord, and the sleeves of the undershirt he wore had been shoved up past his forearms. He sipped from a cup of coffee, a half-eaten meal in front of him. Haakon entered, moving to the stove where he filled his own tin cup. He smiled at Aven.

"You have very red hair," Haakon said as he handed over the offering.

Aven accepted the cup and peered at the brew, then up into his striking face. "And you have very blue eyes."

He grinned as he pulled out a chair and sat. Aven splashed cream into the coffee, then fixed herself a plate of fried potatoes and ham. Once seated, she eyed the feast before splitting a biscuit in half. To be offered a meal in this abundance— never had she known such a luxury. Her mouth all but watered for the first taste, but the jar of jam sitting in front of Thor was too tempting to ignore.

As difficult to ignore, but by no means tempting, was a bottle of whiskey. It sat beside the jam as if the two went hand in hand at breakfast. Elbows on the table, Thor studied the newspaper spread out beside his plate. His dark, thick lashes moved with the words.

"Might you pass the jam?" Aven asked.

With a lick of his thumb, Thor turned a page. Haakon looked to his brother, then reached out and slid the jar to Aven.

"Thank you," she said quietly, still eyeing Thor.

Haakon shook pepper onto his food. "He can't hear you."

"I'm sorry?"

"Thor. He can't hear you." Haakon tapped his own ear. "He can't hear anything."

Aven looked back to Thor, who was still reading his paper. "He can't?"

After a sip of coffee, Haakon made a face and rose.

Brow lifting, Thor slanted a glance to his brother, then gulped his own brew that was black as night. Haakon fetched a small sugar dish, and Thor rolled his eyes before turning his attention back to reading.

Haakon sat and plopped the dish beside him. "See, look . . ." He knocked on the table near his brother's elbow. Thor lifted his head.

Haakon touched a finger to his ear and then to his lips. Next he pointed at Thor and, after a few more gestures, pointed over to Aven. Thor looked at her, and gone was her confusion from the day before. In its place was a sadness. Rushing to mind was the weighty expression he'd displayed yesterday. The one that befit what Haakon just declared.

Had she really thought Thor so imposing on the lane? Aye, he was a fair height, and the spindly chair he leaned against seemed to be no match for that broad back, but . . .

"What do I do?" she asked Haakon.

"What do you mean?"

Her gaze was still locked with Thor's. "What do I say?"

"Say whatever you want. If he's lookin' atcha, he can read your lips."

Truly?

Thor's focus dropped to her mouth, then back up. Haakon chuckled, and in response, Thor made several motions with his hands to his younger brother. Haakon motioned back. A form of communication, quick and foreign.

"I—I was unaware," Aven said, hoping she wasn't interrupting.

Haakon shrugged. "Sorry 'bout that. We're so used to him this way that we forget others aren't." He picked up his fork and stabbed a chunk of potato.

Thor used the heel of his palm to rub his forehead. After nabbing the whiskey bottle, he uncapped it and poured amber liquid into his coffee.

Such an amount that even Haakon stopped chewing. "Easy, Thor."

Thor gave him a dark look.

Jorgan strode into the kitchen, tucking a small box of matches into his shirt pocket. His smile at Aven was amiable. "Ida said you wanted to talk to me."

"Aye." Desperate was the need to figure out what to do. What her place was here. Would she have one? Or was it best for all if she moved on? If she stayed, tongues would wag—people having their say of her presence here with unmarried men, and that would be no help to this family who'd welcomed her in.

Jorgan slid meat onto a plate. "Lemme get Thor and Haakon off, then you and I can sit down."

"Thank you."

When Jorgan settled at the head of the table, he and his brothers turned all attention to food and drink. Feeling ever so out of place, Aven tried to do the same. After a few minutes of silence, Haakon tapped the table near Thor to get his attention. He made several of those hand shapes again—so smooth and easy they had to be a sentence. Thor watched, face void of emotion until Haakon must have said something about Aven because Thor's gaze slid her way. She sat very still.

With two knuckles Thor stroked the side of his beard. Brown eyes still upon her, he took up the sturdy tin cup that was dwarfed by his fingers and gulped what had to be more whiskey than anything else.

"If it'll set you at ease, you can say good mornin' to him." Plate empty, Haakon pushed it back. "You can say it if he sees you, or you can sign it." With one hand he touched fingertips to his lips, then moved that arm down and up like a rising sun. "Good morning."

Thor was staring at Haakon now. No . . . glaring.

Then he looked at Aven, and suddenly panicked, she rushed out a "Good morning!" Much too loudly. She winced.

Grinning, Haakon tossed his napkin on the table. "You don't have to yell."

Brow stormy, Thor knocked twice on the table and Haakon spoke. "She nearly shouted it."

"Shut your trap, Haakon," Jorgan mumbled around a bite of potato.

Skidding his chair back, Thor stood.

"Have I offended him?" Aven asked, and Thor winced like she'd just made it worse.

"Naw. He's always moody in the morning." Haakon stared at Jorgan as if daring to be countered. "Blames it on the headaches, but it's just his personality."

Thor stomped from the kitchen and into the next room, returning but a moment later with a rifle hitched apart and resting on his sturdy shoulder. He snapped a sharp hand sign in Haakon's direction and strode out into the sun.

Haakon stood and pointed after him. "See,

now if I said that, I'd a gotten my mouth washed out with soap." He stepped onto the porch, and Jorgan fought to hide a smile behind his coffee cup.

Fearing she'd upset Thor, Aven gathered up their empty plates, stacking them. At the washbasin she rinsed the first few dishes. Through the window she saw Thor leading a team of horses from the barn. With Haakon's help, they fastened straps and buckles.

"Where are they off to?" she asked.

"Just scoutin'. Thor's worried about some movement on our land and wanted to have a look around."

"Oh."

"Ida's up in the garden."

Aven hadn't asked, but his mention of her whereabouts was thoughtful. She watched as Haakon and Thor worked without speaking to one another. Realizing the plate in hand was dripping onto the clean floor, she turned away for a towel. Aven made a tidy stack of dry dishes on the edge of the table as she knew not where things belonged.

"Tell me, Aven, about yourself." Jorgan lifted the stack into a cupboard.

She shook the coffeepot to check if it was empty. Aven spoke as she washed it, describing how she'd lived over a bake shop with Benn. "As you know, he worked near the docks building boats. I kept busy by taking in sewing." She'd learned to piece together a window-ready gown in a week's time. If there was something she'd learned from watching her mother work, 'twas efficiency and attention to detail.

And why she'd mentioned sewing as an answer to that, she didn't know.

Perhaps because it was less unsettling than all other aspects of her life.

"And how did you come by such a skill?"

"My mother was in service—seamstress to a lord and his wife. We lived in a manor in the countryside just north of Dublin when I was quite young. I recall very little." Not much beyond her mother's hardworking hands and smiling eyes.

Other memories were frailer. Like the mist that had gathered on the hillside there. Memories of Irish gentry, the clank of tea service, and the glow of downstairs evening parties, when colorful gowns twirled by candlelight to the music of a lone fiddle. "I was allowed to stay so long as I kept out from underfoot and out of sight." 'Twas a rare courtesy extended to the staff.

Who her father was . . . now, *that* she didn't know. She wasn't allowed to play with the other children, and before she was old enough to be told the ways of a man and a maid or how her birth had come about, Aven and her mother were made to leave.

"From there we traveled south to the Limerick

38

workhouse. My mother didn't survive beyond the first month of our arrival. I was there some time longer." She kept her voice steady even as grief and loss grew so cold that Aven whisked her mind back to the present. Standing here, in this place—surrounded by Ida's warm kitchen and Jorgan's compassionate demeanor.

"I'm real sorry for that," he said softly. "And I'm sorry at how misleading Dorothe's letters were in regard to us. My brothers and me. If you're at ease with staying, I have some ideas as to what you might do here but would rather know from you first." He dried his hands on the towel she gave him. "What do you wish?"

A question she'd been asked only once before. In Ireland, a nun had drawn Aven into an office at the workhouse and told her of a man named Benn Norgaard, a boat builder from Norway, who had inquired after the redheaded woman— the one who carried a box of thread spools across the courtyard as he'd stood there on the cobbled street.

Despite Aven's shock of what the man offered, and the tiny gold band the nun unfolded from his handkerchief, Aven had traded in her striped workhouse petticoat and shift for a threadbare dress two sizes too big. Tucked in the pocket was the name for the boardinghouse where the man had secured lodgings for her for two weeks. He was already gone—returned to a ship he was repairing that had struck on the Irish coast. But the Norwegian had passed on the message that he would return in a fortnight to wed her. If the girl could please not flee before then. Aven had no sooner added a pound to her spindly frame and washed the lice from her hair when he'd returned to keep his promise just as she had kept hers.

With his cousin waiting for an answer now, Aven spoke. "I—I honestly don't know. I came with the understanding that I would help Dorothe care for you three. Thinking you were all much smaller, and that she would be here."

Thoughtfully, Jorgan nodded. Yet there was a smile playing in his eyes as if he sensed the mischief Dorothe had been up to. Aven was sensing it as well.

"I've never been one to want for much. All I seek is a way to earn meals and shelter through a hard day's work. For that I would be grateful. Dorothe insinuated I'd find such an arrangement here."

"We'd certainly put you to use." He smiled. "If it's hard work you don't mind."

Not in the least. "Under the circumstances . . ." How was she to phrase this? " 'Twould appear . . . improper, perhaps?"

"To others." He glanced back to the window, deep voice gentle as he beckoned for her to follow him upstairs. "And folks don't miss a chance to speculate."

Nay, they didn't.

Down the hallway, Aven slowed when he did just outside Dorothe's door.

"There may be a way around that, but I'll need to talk to my brothers some more." With a gentle turn of the knob, he pressed into the dim space. Dense floral curtains covered the windows, and after stepping to the nearest one, he shoved back a panel. "For now, there's some things in here I think you could use."

Light seeped into the room, glinting along the stirring of dust motes. Aven walked the length of the nearest wall, seeing framed needlepoints stitched with the tiny signature of *D.N.* The elegant vines and twisting flower petals a taste of Norwegian handicrafts.

Past those, tacked to the wall, hung drawings done by children. Penciled on the bottom corner of each one was a name and age written in Dorothe's familiar penmanship. Noted beneath a mass of pencil scribbles was *Haakon, age 3.* Just under a drawing of a great whale in a roaring sea was *Jorgan, age 10.* And on the last was *Thorald, age 7.* Each one would have been created at a different time, and Aven lingered in front of the last drawing. A boyish sketch of a family. The roughly drawn figures had smiles nearly as big as their faces, and each figure stood beside a tree that was so large it reached the sky. Birds soared overhead. Aven touched the aged corner.

Standing near, Jorgan pushed aside a vase of dried flowers to reach a lidded sewing basket. "You should take this."

"Oh, I couldn't."

"It's no good sitting here. It'd do Dorothe proud for it to be put to use."

Aven took the handle of the basket and the sheer heft of it—from buttons and needles and thread—sent a wash of delight through her. Her own basket was long gone, sold with all else to help procure passage here.

"Anything else you might need?"

"This is the best of starts." And a blessed one. Aven glanced around Dorothe's room, looking more upon the good woman's belongings. Shades of ivory and soft pinks made up the quilt draped over the bed, and the brass headboard gleamed. Scraps of colorful thread rested on the bedside table along with a dainty pair of scissors. 'Twas as though Dorothe had been tending a project up until the very end. "May I ask how she passed?"

Jorgan stepped nearer to the window and peered down. "She was up there in years—nearly ninety—and she went in her sleep. It was right peaceful. One day she was here, and the next she wasn't. We may not show it much—my brothers and me—but she's missed."

"I wish I could have met her."

He gave a sad smile, then glanced around. "She spoke highly of you." Jorgan lifted a square of embroidered cloth that sat folded on a nearby chair. "And I know she'd want you to be comfortable and at home here. So please let us know if there's anything you need. Since you sew, you might like to look in the shed outside. There's piles of fabric and boxes of thread. I can show you if you'd like." He folded the needlepoint and handed it over. As if he knew as well as she did that her carpetbag had stowed very little.

"Thank you." Her embroidery skills were simple at best, but there was something about the deep-blue cloth, its white and pink flowers and vines that made her wonder about placing a few final stitches to finish the job. More so that the arrangement had stemmed from Dorothe's heart and mind.

"Should you ever want to search for work of this sort, we can send inquiries to some of the nearby towns. Though . . ." His smile was friendly. "We'd be awful sorry to see you go."

Aven was about to thank him when gunfire blasted from a distance. She jumped. Another shot fired from the same direction.

When all quieted, Jorgan grinned. "Don't worry. It's just Thor."

"What is he doing?"

"Just scarin' someone off. Sometimes our neighbors get a little cozy. He's careful not to hit anybody."

She swallowed hard.

"Just so you know, Miss Ida stays with us most of the week." He lifted the small scissors from the nightstand and slipped them beneath the padded lid. "She goes to her sister's Saturday evenings. Aunt Cora. You'll meet her. She's real nice. Lives on our land a few acres past the orchards. One of the reasons Thor and Haakon are makin' some rounds—to be sure nobody's pesterin' them."

Jorgan's focus shifted to the window, then back to her. "Ida offered to stay on all week long so it would never be improper. We'd treat you like family. No different from what Dorothe had in mind. We'd pay you for your work. Give you something to make a new life with. However we can help. We have plenty, Aven, and it'd be our right to look after you." Motioning her near to the window, he pointed toward a cluster of outbuildings. "The one with the peaked roof is the one you might want to search through. Has some boxes we moved after Dorothe's passing. Fabrics and such. Use anything you like. And also . . . there's something else I need to show you."

Down the hall, Aven set the treasures in her room and followed him downstairs.

He didn't speak again until they were outside. "What else you should know is how we make our living." He pointed toward the largest outbuilding of all. A barn, as great in size as the house itself.

44

"Some folks find it shameful, so I think you ought to have the chance to know before you decide how long you wanna stay."

Apprehension rising, Aven studied the building with its weathered siding and abundant windows.

"We make liquor. Well, Thor does. Here in the cidery."

At the building, he slid open a heavy door. Within lay dimness and the intoxicating aroma of apples and their juices. Aven followed Jorgan inside the space that was so tall, the angled ceiling soared overhead. Along every wall rose shelves upon shelves of glass jars. If she were to count them, hundreds. Below that, giant barrels were aligned and numbered with chalk. A long workbench stood covered in pencils, paper, and ledgers. From one of the rafters, an owl watched.

"Liquor," she said it softly, not really wanting to.

"It's what Da set out to do when he first came here and why Thor keeps the orchards like they're kin. He brews the best drink in the county."

Aven walked the length of the workbench, awing at the sight of dozens of blue ribbons tacked to the wall. The ribbons grew larger and more prominent as the years drew closer to the present. The man was skilled indeed.

"Folks pay well for it, and he keeps us in a good livin'. Maybe too good, because we want for nothin', and I don't know that it was the best way for Haakon to grow up. But that's already done and dusted, I suppose."

Aven lifted a sheet of paper—noting the rows of square writing and the tidy sums that ran the length of the page.

"Careful where you set that down again. Thor's meticulous. This is his entire world." He smirked, and she took care to set it just as she'd found it.

"His world . . . ," she repeated.

"Yes'm. He couldn't go to school in these parts, so he was Da's shadow here since he was just yea high. It runs in his blood the same."

'Twould explain why the man smelled headier than a pint of ale.

Did they all drink it? Or just Thor?

When she inquired, Jorgan cleared his throat. "I have a share now and again. Same with Haakon. Thor, as you know, is something else entirely. For as much as he consumes, he handles it well. Always has. The man could walk into a room fully stewed and most wouldn't even know it. If it weren't for the scent, that is."

Did he mean that as a comfort? "I only inquire because I was married to someone who didn't handle it so well."

Understanding dawned in Jorgan's face. 'Twas a sobering expression. One of surprise, as if he hadn't known of Benn's addiction. Why would he know? A man's love of the bottle wasn't a pleasantry passed in letters to distant family.

Uncertainty clamoring against all ease, Aven stared out the dingy window to where Ida toted along a basket of clean laundry. If the good woman saw something in these men . . .

Jorgan nudged a tarp aside with his boot, and Aven caught the subtle wink of more glass jars. "Thor. He's wanted—in the past—to cut back. Maybe he'll try again now."

A twinge of curiosity arose as to why he would.

"You'll see wagonloads comin' and goin' plenty. Now and again we get some trouble if we bump in with the wrong sort, but we'll keep a close eye out for you. It'll help us if you stay near to the house." He beheld her as if needing her agreement.

"I will."

"Folks don't usually cross us, but there's rough men in these parts. Some bolder than others. We may have trouble comin' now that Thor's hired some Negro boys for the harvest. There's men around who don't take too kindly to that. Things are about to get stirred up again. Please don't wander from the farm without one of us."

Was he telling her all of this to allow her to decide whether to stay or not? She glanced around the barn. A chill creeping up her arm, Aven ran a hand there. "I promise."

Jorgan motioned her back out into the sun and seemed to search for softer musings. "I'll be marryin' soon . . . by summer's end. Fay." His eyes went alight with the name. "She'll be around before long, so there'll be one more woman in the house. I think you'll like her." He fell in step with Aven as they neared Ida at the wash line. "If you're here, of course. For now, write up any inquiries for work if you'd like, and I'll see them mailed off."

Aven slowed to a stop just on the other side of the hanging clothes. "I thank you." And in the meantime, she'd do all she could to earn her keep.

FOUR

With an early supper roasting in the oven, Aven climbed atop a stool and smoothed a rag along the mantel. A cobweb in the mounted antlers overhead needed swiping, but she'd need a ladder and didn't know where to look for one. She climbed down from the stool and dusted the dark-red bricks of the hearth. The rug beneath her feet was charred in places, as if something had caught flame where it wasn't supposed to. Aven swept lingering ashes into a pan, glad for the kerchief over her hair that caught most of the dust. Feeling a tickle on the end of her nose, she smudged it clean with her fingertips.

The great room befit its name—spanning from the snug kitchen to make up the rest of the first floor. Furniture stood here and there in clusters as though to hold all the lives this house was once filled with. So many hands for much work. And now? The farm seemed quiet and still, the men going about tasks she didn't fully understand. There were no chickens about. No plow or livestock. Just the pair of mares. Though Ida kept a small kitchen garden, there was little more to tend to other than the orchards, and Aven had yet to see anyone other than Thor walk its rows.

The keeper of the trees . . . and now she knew . . .

the maker of the liquor. From what Jorgan had later explained, Haakon saw it all delivered and paid for. Jorgan himself kept the farm running—doing improvements and maintenance so all other things went smoothly. A steady experience that kept everything else looked after, including his family.

Beyond that, the men conducted themselves with care and discretion. A tie of brotherhood she understood little about.

When the fireplace was tidied, Aven moved to the small chess table beside it. The playing pieces rested in odd places, a game unfinished. Rag in hand, she dusted around the board carefully, noting circular stains in the wood from beverage cups. Or mason jars.

Something told her that was Thor's seat.

She swept beneath the table, gathering up pipe ash and two burnt matches. Ida was out at the clothesline, and smelling the aroma of baking bread, Aven went to check the loaves they'd kneaded together. She peeked in on the six pans in the large oven, the tops still pale in color. Aven closed the iron door and latched it since a few more minutes would do the trick.

In Norway, Farfar Øberg had taught her all he could about baking in the few years she'd lived above his shop. The grandfatherly man would have reminded her not to rush the bread with her constant peeking.

She smiled.

With the supper hour drawing near, Aven checked the roast she'd placed to simmer hours ago. It was tender to the touch, juices rich and bubbling. Earlier Ida had shown her the springhouse and the meats available. They'd stood together in the small stone hut wedged into the hillside. Cold water flowed down its center, and built up on stones were shelves that held crocks of butter, meats, and fancy cheeses. A side of beef. Links of sausages and strips of bacon. Not so much as a hint of wild game, and the speckled eggs Ida had taken from a crate were purchased from a neighbor. As was the milk.

Jorgan mentioned they lived richly. Aven was beginning to sense what he meant.

When the loaves were out and steaming on the table, Ida came in. With a spoon in hand, the housekeeper limped back onto the porch and clattered it around an iron triangle hanging from the eaves. The men came in hungry and none too happy about Ida's insistence on washed hands and faces.

Aven took sides easily, nudging Haakon's grubby hand away when he reached for a pinch of tender meat. " 'Tis the least you could do for a hot meal, aye?"

Spoon still in hand, Ida chuckled. "I'm gonna like having you around."

Out they went, washing at the pump while

Ida filled plates with tender roast and garden vegetables. Haakon returned, wet from the shoulders up as though he had poor aim. Jorgan used a rag to dry his slick hands and forearms. Thor stepped in last. His damp hair was as dark as old leather. He pushed it back as he stepped to the stove, inching around Aven as if uncertain how to be in the same room as her.

Aven wished for something to say to him. Some way to say it. But after her blunder at breakfast and how it had harshened his mood, she stayed silent.

With the other men already served, Aven fetched a filled plate for Thor. When she offered over the meal, he seemed confused about the serving. But he dipped his head in a silent thank-you and took the plate in a hand that no longer trembled with need. Though his manner was gentle, she sensed he was as filled with hard drink as Jorgan had alluded to. So different from this morning, when he'd appeared almost desperate for it. As disheartening a trade-off as she knew.

"You best dish up." Ida fetched two more plates.

Aven did just that and carried her own portion into the great room that was aglow with the warmth of a sinking sun. The men sat scattered around, busy forks glinting in the early-evening light.

So they didn't eat at a table. Nor say grace. Might it have been different when Dorothe was here?

Haakon sat on the sofa, and with the opposite end empty, Aven moved that way. Ida sank into her rocking chair and it creaked when she pushed it in slow rhythm. As they ate, Haakon made small talk with both of them, stopping only to fetch a second helping in the kitchen.

Thor fetched another as well, piling up his plate twice as full as Aven had done. Gripping it with one hand, he headed outside. After watching him go, Aven turned her focus back to her meal. 'Twas strange, eating this way. As a young girl she'd grown accustomed to dining alone in her mother's room. Then in later years, amid the rhythmic clatter of scraping benches and dented plates as hundreds of people dined in poor fashion at the workhouse on watery stirabout and stale bread. Never enough to dent the void in their bellies.

The workhouse walls but a recollection now, Aven ate slowly, guilt tapping her shoulder at this fortune. It was so much for one person. Flooding her memory were hollow eyes and faces, especially those of the orphans who had lined many narrow benches. But Aven could no sooner wing them some of this abundance than she could return herself.

She prayed, instead, as she ate—for those faces.

The young ones she'd watched suffer and fade as she had once done until a boat builder had freed her from that place. Benn, with his Norwegian words that she hadn't been able to understand. But she had understood the simple ring he'd slid onto her finger, and the knowledge that it was her freedom.

Ida's voice broke her from the memories. "Don't you think about touchin' a thing when you're done." She rose from her rocking chair. "You saw to this fine meal and I'll see to the rest." Her steps, while sure, were uneven, one of her legs seeming to bear pain she didn't voice. The kind woman took up Aven's empty plate.

"You're certain?"

"Out with ya. Enjoy some of this fine air. Lord knows you've been breathing dust all the day through."

With a gentle summer breeze trickling in from the nearest window, the notion of an evening stroll was tempting enough not to argue. The men had asked that she stay near to the house, so Aven would do just that. She thanked Ida, fetched a lantern from a side table, and carried it out into the growing dusk.

From the massive cider barn came the gentle sounds of a man at work. A tool clanged. Something heavy shifted. Hinges creaked. Thor in his world, as Jorgan had put it. Ducking her head, Aven strode past. Spotting the shed Jorgan had indicated, she stepped that way, coaxed the door ajar, and slipped inside.

Kneeling in the cidery that was more sanctuary than any place he knew, Thor rolled a gallon jar of liquor away from the rest of the two-month-old batch. He uncorked the jug, tipped the mouth of it to a tumbler, and set the glass beside what was left of his supper. After a few bites of meat, he drank. The apple flavor rolled over his tongue with the perfect amount of tannin. Not too sweet and not too bitter. A kick on the back end that told him to sip slow with this batch. Even for him.

Meaning to work as he ate, Thor took another bite, then numbered the top of the jug with a charcoal pencil. His number system would look like chicken scratch to most folk, but Haakon knew all the coding—which customer it was to be delivered to. At the workbench Thor lifted his notes and read, then strode over to the shelving that ran the length of the back wall, pulled a quart of table cider down, and numbered the lid. He slid it into a crate and sprinkled sawdust around the sides.

Next on the list—the O'Mally family. If he wasn't mistaken, their oldest girl was soon to marry, so Thor packed up as much as he thought they'd buy for the occasion. When another crate was filled, he checked his ledgers, eating some of

Aven's oddly seasoned meat as he did. Not that it wasn't tasty. Just different.

Back at his work, it took him several trips to carry over the last eight quarts of his finest brew that was best served with ice when it was in season. Aged in old bourbon barrels that Jorgan had driven all the way to Lexington to procure, the cider fetched the highest price yet, and though the jars were nearly gone, requests always came in. Thor had to be choosy, so he numbered the tops for his best customers and made a note for Haakon to charge at least a dollar apiece. He also made a note for Jorgan to get more bourbon barrels.

Wanting to take extra care with this batch, Thor wrapped each one in newspaper before crating it. He shook out a page and clamped a jar over a printed address given by President Harrison, then rolled it up snug.

At a flash of white, Thor looked up to see the owl settling onto one of the rafters overhead. Jorgan and Haakon sometimes complained that it screeched. Thor had asked his brothers once to describe *S-C-R-E-E-C-H-E-D* and Haakon had said it was a sharp, painful sound. Thor always tried to imagine such a sensation whenever his visitor arrived.

Moonlight seeped in through a missing board high up in the wall, allowing the great bird to come and go as it pleased. Thor didn't always notice the owl, so vast was the cidery. As boys, they used to ride on the rope swing hanging from the center rafter as high and wide as they wanted while Da worked.

Turning back to his supper, Thor broke off a portion of bread and chewed as he consulted his ledger. Another bite and he was glad Aven couldn't see him wolfing down so much food. But perhaps her intentions hadn't been to keep him hungry in the night. Likely, she was used to rationing. From the way the waistband of her skirt was folded and pinned, she'd learned to live on very little.

After tugging down his suspenders, Thor grabbed an empty crate. He set it on his workbench and loaded it with pints of table cider. The common drink had a lower alcohol content but settled well with almost any palate. It was also his least expensive variety, so even the poorest of his customers could secure a jar or two each month. Thor tapped each of the metal lids as he counted. If his sums were right, he needed to pack eighty quarts for the next distribution.

They made deliveries three times a month, and those days always made him uneasy. It was always possible that Haakon would run into trouble with that hot head of his. One of the reasons Thor made it a point to ride shotgun whenever he could. It was easier than unseating

Haakon from the job; he had a canny way of bartering that always lined their pockets with a thick wad of bills. Something none of them were about to complain over.

Thor grabbed six more jars, then finished a crate and blanketed the pints with sawdust. Eyeing his chart, he marked off the recipient. He was just lifting another crate to the workbench when the door swung open.

Haakon rushed near. "We got trouble!" Grete loped beside him, nearly tripping Haakon. "Bolt the door. Come on."

Thor did as told, then followed his brother to the house so quick, he wished he could call after Haakon as to what was wrong.

But when they stepped into the kitchen to find Ida's sister standing there, little Georgie hiding in the folds of her skirt, he knew the trouble. Aunt Cora's homespun dress was streaked with dirt as if having traveled in haste. Her skin, which was a shade lighter than Ida's, was slashed across the cheek with an angry scrape. At the window Cora's grown son and daughter weren't faring much better. The front of Al's shirt was soaked in sweat, and Tess checked a scrape on her brother's neck.

So the warning was here. Confirmed in the way Haakon pulled Grete into the house and shoved her farther toward safety.

Thor turned just in time to see his brother ask how far off the Klansmen were.

"Nearly here," Al said between panting breaths. "They's right on our tails. At least a dozen of 'em. I didn't think we'd make it."

"They hurt you?" Jorgan asked.

Thor glanced between them.

Al shook his head, but his jaw tightened. It had been less than a year since Al's pistol-whipping. Since the night he'd smiled at one of the fair-skinned Sorrel girls in passing on the road. Al had been found half alive in a ditch just hours later. Jorgan and Thor had carried him home, and the women had spent three days patching him back up.

"Did you secure the shop?" Jorgan asked.

Nodding, Thor stepped to the door and peered out into the dark. *A-V-E-N? Where?*

Jorgan shook his head.

Haakon set two shotguns on the kitchen table. Shoving a pile of Aven's mending aside, he dropped boxes of bullets onto the tablecloth. Though Thor didn't see it, Haakon must have asked after Ida because Al answered.

"She's fetchin' water. I'll help her." Al strode out.

Thor ducked into the great room, expecting Aven to be there only to discover it empty. Returning, he hit Jorgan's arm to get his attention. Thor pointed to the others. *They see A-V-E-N?*

Jorgan relayed the question, but Cora shook her head, asking who this person was. Thor ran a hand down his face, already out the door. Beneath the night sky, Al and Ida hurried along. Thor rushed out to help them, and hefting up the heaviest bucket, he took it inside.

Where was she?

To his relief, Haakon was starting up the stairs as if having the same thought. Aven had to be in her room. She had to be.

Ida tugged on his sleeve and Thor watched her mouth move in a rush. "She went for a walk. Check to be sure she's come back."

Nodding, he started after Haakon, but his brother was already returning. "She's not here!"

Thor moved toward the open door. When Haakon got there first, Thor grabbed him by the shirt and yanked him back. Eyes wide, Thor signed *stay* so Haakon would know he meant him no harm. He didn't want his brother out there. The kid was too impulsive, and if outnumbered, it wouldn't end well. Jorgan gripped Haakon by the upper arm, bracing him in place.

Jorgan pointed out the doorway, then made the letters for *D-O-R-O-T-H-E* followed by the shapes of *boxes*—enough for Thor to know where to look first.

Thor motioned for a shotgun, and Al tossed him one. As Thor stepped into the dark, he hitched it open, double-checked for shot, then slammed the barrel closed. He had to find her.

Now. An army of men was coming, and though they had no quarrel with Aven, to them she would be a glimpse of perfection, and that scared him more.

FIVE

Lantern light flickered, stirring the unfamiliar shadows of the small storage shed. Aven sat on the floor in the middle of the snug space where Dorothe's things were arranged. Rather like diary entries, yet in place of words and dates, there were boxes and parcels, all telling of the woman who had collected them. Lidded boxes were filled with patterns, and burlap sacks contained lace and other trimmings. A jar of blue glass kept beads of every shape and color. The large barrel Aven leaned against held piles of fabrics from calicos to upholstery cloth. All would be handy, but for tonight, she was searching for only embroidery thread.

After lifting the lid off another tin, she found small twists of the colored string. Aven arranged several against the embroidered piece Jorgan had given her, matching first the pale green of the stitched vine, then the ivory of the dainty flower buds. The two twists of thread tangled together so she pulled the tiny scissors from the sewing box and snipped them free.

At approaching footsteps she lifted her head. A thud sounded just on the other side of the door. A moment later it swung open.

Thor ducked around it in such a loud rush that

Aven flinched. He beckoned for her to come to him.

"What do you need?" she asked.

His gaze landed on the lantern and he hurried to lower the light.

"Please don't." Aven reached to turn it back up, but his hand caught her wrist.

Startled, she pulled free, but he only blocked her reach again. What was going on? He drew nearer. So close that her upheld hand pressed against his chest. She pushed at the firm, solid strength when he knelt, and her rising shriek was cut short when his hand pressed over her mouth.

Her heart jolted so quickly, pain lanced through her chest. This near, the tang of hard cider seeped from his skin. How much had he drank tonight?

Aven pushed at him as hard as she could, but he didn't budge. After setting a gun across his lap, he lifted a finger to his lips for her silence. He smoothed that same hand against her shoulder, so tenderly her stomach dropped. His face moved nearer to hers, and he peered into her eyes as if willing her to understand his desire.

Dread thickened her throat. Aven grabbed at his hand, but he wouldn't loosen it. How had she been so foolish to think that she could trust him? Fear taking over, she kicked him. As hard and as high in the thigh as she could manage.

He shoved her foot away, and the offended look he flashed her was just too much. Especially when his next breath blew out the lingering flame.

Darkness blanketed them and instinct had her scrambling back. Her head smacked against the barrel, shooting pain across her skull. Her skin flushed with fight, and she barely remembered the scissors as he dragged her up from the floor. Aven wrapped her hand around the metal tool that was small enough to hide in her palm.

When he pushed them both toward the door, she jerked away. His grip faltered over her mouth. She screamed, but his meaty hand clamped it back as though he'd expected as much. She bit his finger. He yelped.

With a growl, he braced her in front of him, gripping so tight she nearly heaved up her supper. He struggled to fetch his gun, wrestling everything out the door.

When he hefted her out into the night, she kicked her feet, hoping to unsteady him. It was enough when he stumbled, taking her with him. They hit the dirt hard, her back against the gun barrel. His crushing weight on top of her shot the breath from her lungs. A sob choked her of air.

The scissors still in hand, Aven gripped his thick arm as it slid back around her middle. With neither time nor leverage, she thrust the pointed end down as hard and fast as she could.

He jammed his mouth against her shoulder, muffling a howl so fierce, her skin prickled.

Tears stung her eyes. He yanked her up and half carried, half dragged her away from the shed.

After a few steps he stumbled, nearly taking them both down again. A warm wetness of what could only be his blood pooled against her bodice. Ahead, the house loomed long and silent in the moonlight. Why was he taking her to the house?

In her side vision came an unnatural glow. One too low and golden to be the moon. It took only a glance to realize the glow was moving. Nay, marching. A steady, eerie bobbing as though from torches gripped by men. Aven's eyes widened when the flickering light revealed masked men.

Thor rammed her against the door, trapping her with the sheer size of him as he struggled to grip the knob.

In the distance the row of tall, ghostly figures walked into the farmyard. Pointed white cloths cloaked their heads with small holes cut for eyes. Those flanking the sides wore only burlap sacks over their heads with rough-cut slits.

She would have screamed again if it weren't for Thor clamping it back. He pressed her harder against the door as he struggled with the knob. Fingers slick with blood, he finally pounded the slab with his fist. It opened in a burst and they crashed to the kitchen floor. He pulled her away from the door and kicked it closed.

Blinking into the dim light of a single candle,

Aven looked up into the stunned faces of Haakon and Jorgan. She scrambled away from Thor and dropped the scissors with a clatter. What was happening?

Ida rushed in and Thor lay back, chest heaving. Blood seeped through the sleeve of his shirt just above the elbow. Jorgan called for a lantern as he knelt beside his brother.

"Was he shot?" Jorgan's voice was sharp as he ripped back the bloodied sleeve.

With a groan, Thor sat up and pointed at Aven. She'd never seen him this angry. He made a scissor motion with two fingers, then thrust that fist toward his bleeding arm.

Jorgan's jaw fell as he swiveled on his knee toward her. "You stabbed him?"

"He grabbed me!"

Jorgan looked to the bear of a man who was still glowering.

Haakon snorted, slid a gun from the table, and left the kitchen. The sight of those masked men still swimming before her eyes, Aven sank back against the cupboard and pushed the hair from her face. Thor sliced a hand through the air, then shoved the tips of his forefingers together. Last, he aimed one at her. He looked up at Ida so earnestly, his desperation seared right into Aven.

"I'll tell her, Thor. I'll tell her." The gray-haired woman knelt beside him and wrapped his arm in a long strip of cloth. She knotted it tightly, and he

66

winced. Thor rose, picked up the gun, and with one last glare at the fallen scissors, walked into the other room.

Turning to Aven, Ida spoke kindly but firmly. "He said he'd never hurt you." She took Aven's hand, holding it tight. "There's some things you need to know about Thor's ways. Now ain't the time, but rest in ease that he done meant you no harm. He meant only to help you along."

Grief tightened her throat. "I'm sorry," she whispered.

Ida lifted a sharp look to Jorgan. "And ya'd all do well to take better care to not be so dad-blasted stubborn and hushin' up so much about this'n that. The poor girl's scared to death. Don't know nothin' of Thor's ways 'cause she ain't been told." Ida smeared a hand back over her forehead in frustration. "Come mornin' this must be set to rights."

Jorgan accepted his chastisement with clear regret.

Ida squeezed Aven's hand, then her focus shifted to the blood on Aven's skin and dress front. "You hurt? Or be that Thor's?"

"His." The admission pained her. "I've only a few bruises of my own doing." She trembled as Jorgan helped her to her feet.

Pulse still racing, she followed him into the next room where two women stood together. Their skin was like coffee with a trace of cream, and they each wore patterned scarves tied around their hair, capping it snug. Remembering Jorgan's declaration that Ida's family lived near, Aven realized the older of the two women had to be her sister. Cora was it? The other must have been her daughter. A young man was there as well. A little girl peeked out from behind him, so small she couldn't have been but six. Her twisted black braids were tied with a scrap of yellow cloth, and Cora worried a finger around and around and around one of the loose ends.

Jorgan motioned them all to sit, leading Aven near to do the same. "Stay low."

She wouldn't have argued even if she wanted to. Settling against the wall, she pulled her knees up. Two small candles burned at opposite ends of the room, keeping the space dim. Back throbbing, Aven arched it gently. Pain shot through her hip, and she stifled a gasp. 'Twould be best not to try and move.

A tall span of windows ran the length of the great room, making up the front of the house. Gun strapped over his shoulder, Haakon climbed onto the desk there. Reaching overhead, he gripped a squared beam and kicked his feet up to clamp on. He clamored over the side of the beam until he was kneeling atop it.

Gun balanced in one hand, he stood and stepped gingerly toward the upper windows. He crouched against the ledge there and lifted the sash on the nearest pane of glass. "They're burnin' the wood crib." The glow of flames lit his profile, and he spoke without emotion. As if the destruction bore no surprise to him.

Jorgan paced with equal composure. Thor stared out the windows without moving. Aven tried to wrap understanding around their lack of fear. Was this cruelty to be expected? Or did the brothers truly feel no threat? Perhaps neither. Perhaps they were simply trying to maintain calm within the room.

Thor moved across the stretch of windows, profile stern in the glow from the other side where a half circle of torchlight was being formed in the yard. He looked Aven's way, but when Jorgan motioned for his attention, Thor switched his gun from one hand to the other, then aimed it at the glass.

Haakon wedged himself into the corner, rifle poised. "Incoming!" he shouted, his voice higher than usual. The other men crouched as a flame arced through the night sky, falling toward the upper windows. Haakon ducked low, covering his head with his arm. Glass shattered.

A rock bound with burning cloth clattered to the floor and Jorgan rushed to stomp out the flame.

"Hold your fire," Jorgan snapped, ducking low again. "That means you, Haakon." He pointed up to his brother.

"I'm not gonna shoot." But after Haakon shook glittering shards from his shirt, he raised his gun as though he wanted to.

A pane above his right shoulder looked patched, and now she understood why the rug was charred in spots. This had happened before.

"They mean only to frighten," Jorgan said.

The hand beside Aven's felt soaked in perspiration, and she squeezed it. The young woman gave her a sad look even as she whispered comfort to the child in her lap. The small girl's crying muffled against her sister's blouse.

Somewhere upstairs, another window shattered.

"Check for fire," Haakon called down.

Jorgan hit Thor's shoulder, and with fingers raised, waggled them like dancing flames. Nodding, Thor started for the stairs. His hand brushed the top of Aven's head as he rushed by as if to make sure she was still down. Blood had seeped through the rag binding his upper arm.

A few moments later, stomping shook the ceiling overhead. When he returned, he set aside a charred stone. Wind whistled through the broken window. Beside it Haakon scanned the room in such a way that indicated something wasn't right. Suddenly he hollered out.

"On the left!"

A shatter came from the kitchen door, followed by three men striding in—each mountainous in height with pointed hoods and white robes. Their faces were covered as though they were figures from the underworld, but behind the narrow holes cut for eyes were the glittering traces of real men.

Fear gripped her, but the brothers stoically faced their company. Thor took a step forward, rifle still in his grip. The disguised men peered around at the room, looked up to Haakon, then down to the huddle of women. The dog crouched down, whimpering.

One man aimed a solitary finger toward Ida's nephew—making it known that he was seen. The dark-skinned lad set his jaw, not flinching.

The forefront of the ghostly figures pulled a fold of paper from within his robe. His hands were gloved, and those giant, angled fingers moved slowly as he opened what he bore. The dusty hem of his robe swayed over patched boots. A trickle of smoke stung the air.

His hooded face lowered to read. "We hereby charge you with enabling those who have been granted undue liberties by great price." The man spoke in a deep, slow voice that disguised his identity, distorting even the drawl of his accent. "Those who were taught hard labor but are now prone to idleness and insubordination."

The stark fabric over his mouth trembled as he spoke. "If you were to turn an honest heart to the cautions of we—a noble assembly—you would find realities to awaken your sympathies of higher attitudes. He who fails to do so remains at risk of having the breath beat out of him and his soul set free from the wretchedness of its cage."

Though he knew not a word that was spoken, Thor paced but feet away from the leader, gaze pegged to the hooded face that inclined to each of his brothers in turn. Bold as brass, Thor was, but when his eyes met Jorgan's, vulnerability lifted the center of his brow.

"We—who are but humble regulators—must appease the call to protect property and preserve law and sanctity. For those who observe this, it would be wise to salute the powers and the superiority that is to be deemed with reverence. A notice to be heeded afore the blood is spilled and dried." The man folded the paper as slowly as he'd opened it and slid it away.

It was silent for several moments, then Haakon called down, "Write that all by yourself, did you?"

Jorgan shot him a warning look.

Suddenly one of the cloaked men shifted toward Aven, angling his hooded face to peer down at her. The white cloth hiding his identity fluttered in the breeze from the open door, stirring the lifeless slits for eyes. Head tipping, he adjusted his stance as if trying to see her better. The man drew nearer, and suddenly Haakon was shouting down.

"Take so much as a step closer, Peter Sorrel, and I'll blow your boots off."

The looming figure looked up to where Haakon was still crouched against the wall in the nook of the ceiling.

The beam creaked when Haakon shifted to set his aim. "Or do you think we don't know you're the only clod with feet that big in twenty miles?"

The man chuckled darkly and looked back to Aven for such a long while that her blood chilled. Kneeling, he drew himself closer to them, casting his attention upon the little girl who was sobbing now. He reached into his robe, then lifted a gloved hand, seeming about to give her something. Ida pulled the child closer. If looks could kill, she would have put him six feet under.

Finally he rose, dropped a tangle of small spools onto the floor beside the child, and stepped away, then ducked into the night. The other two followed. On their way out, one knocked several photos from the wall, sending them to shatter to the ground. A moment later there was a mighty crash as the table was flipped over along with everything upon it.

When silence settled, no one moved.

Finally, Thor stepped across crackling glass and closed the door. He stood at the window for several moments as if to gauge the severity of the fire. Thor watched it without alarm, his calm affirming that the danger wasn't spreading.

"They're headin' off." Haakon clicked the hammer of his gun free. He slung the strap over his shoulder before lowering himself back to the desk where he landed with a thud on its top.

The little girl was quieting, her cries nearly hiccups now. "They's the ones who hurt Al. They's the ones."

"Shh . . ." Soft as moonlight, Ida rocked her. "They ain't gonna hurt him no more. No more." Ida tried to reach for a nearby blanket but couldn't.

Desperate to help, Aven rose, but even as she did, Jorgan bid them all to stay as close and out of sight as possible until morning. "We've time enough to deal with the mess come sunrise."

Sunrise. She ached for it.

Ida's sister fetched blankets from a cupboard, and Aven helped her make a pallet on the floor. Soon, Ida had the child nestled down, stroking that small head of ebony hair. Aven learned that the little one's name was Georgie. Her older sister introduced herself as Tess. Their brother, Al, sat on the floor watching the windows.

When each of them was settled, several blankets lay unclaimed. Aven looked around for Thor. She fetched a wool plaid to offer him, but he was nowhere in sight.

Haakon strode over to where the child slumbered and touched the tip of her nose, then smoothed her shoulder. An affection that might as well have run blood deep. He checked Tess next and Aven as well, giving the pretty-faced lass a gentle squeeze of the arm and to Aven, the brush of his fingertips just below her jaw. "You got a nasty scuff there."

"Aye. And elsewhere."

He smiled as if having witnessed her and Thor's tussle. She was glad he hadn't. She looked into Haakon's blue eyes, but all she could think of was the shattering in Thor's own. The way he'd made those motions—his plea for her to know she was safe with him. Throat as parched as the hour she'd walked here, Aven struggled to swallow.

Haakon went back to the windows and spoke in murmurs with Jorgan.

Beyond that, the chiming of the grandfather clock signaled the late hour. Bruises now staking their claim, Aven ached with every shift on the floorboards, but never had a place to sleep felt so safe. Never with Benn, and certainly not in the workhouse sleeping quarters. The manor where she had lived as a girl with her mother was a blur of memories—like dried leaves crumbled under time. Each precious, but more brittle with every year passed.

Now she was here, and for these people, this place, she was grateful.

Al grabbed a squat, flat pillow from the sofa and lay on the floor. His gun rested beside him, and though he kept a keen angle to that kitchen door, he seemed at peace.

Her own eyelids heavy, Aven closed them. In the stillness she listened to the gentle whistle of the wind. The comforting sound of footsteps as the Norgaard men bedded down. Barely noticing the quietest of the lot settle in beside her as she drifted off to sleep.

SIX

Always would Aven remember the hour she'd learned of Benn's death. She'd been out for the evening buying fish, only to return to their flat and a door that wouldn't open. It took the help of the landlord and his bag of tools before they were able to whittle away the lock, and when they did, Aven stepped into a world that was never the same.

A hot rush slamming her chest, she jolted awake.

Morning was dawning as threads of golden light. Beside her, chest to the floor, Thor lay with no pillow. He had a leg bent up and an arm draped against his face as if to block the day. By the way that broad back was slowly rising and lowering, he was well asleep. Had he truly just passed the night beside her? His nearness confirmed it, but if she was to stay on this farm, she'd do well to look upon these men as brothers. She let her gaze skim back to the nearest one.

The thought would be easier than the doing.

Aven rose and with ginger steps headed to the kitchen. The table had been set to rights hours before, but a vase lay shattered. The air smelled of charred wood and a glance out the window showed the burned wood crib no longer aflame.

Tiny puffs of smoke tinged the air from the blackened boards.

All was silent, so it was with soft strokes that she used the broom to work shards into a pile. After filling the dustpan, and with Jorgan's insistence they all stay near, she fetched a pail from the pantry for the broken pieces. Was this manner of upheaval a common occurrence in these parts? She'd witnessed hatred before, but never in such a precise display. Like soldiers, those men had been. Out to patrol upon this mountain. And now, somewhere out there, women were stirring from slumber after passing the night beside the cloaked men who had stood here under a half-wane moon.

Aven set pan and pail aside and strode to the window, her heart waging a battle. It longed to drift back to that shed and treat Thor differently. But the wish snagged in the treetops because time and actions could not be undone. Only was there the grace of a new day. And just as Ida and Cora deserved a better world for them and their family, those dear women surely sought a better one for Thor and his own distinctions. One where he was seen for his humanness just as they deserved to be.

At the sound of uneven footsteps, Aven turned to see Ida reaching for an apron. Ida gave a sad smile, then set about fishing potatoes from the bin in the pantry. Aven hung up the broom and dustpan. Cora stepped in and, with a soft hymn on her lips, slid a heavy pan onto the stove. Tess joined them and pulled plates from a cupboard. All a gentle rhythm of care and kindness.

They each worked quietly as though a few more minutes of rest was what this house needed. A house that was feeling rather much like a home to Aven. Yet the pleasantness of it wilted when she glanced at the floorboards where droplets of blood reminded her of her mishap the night before. She went in search of a rag to wet.

Ida stopped her. "Them boards won't be bothered to be forgotten awhile yet. Best we set a soak for Thor's arm." Her voice was kind and meant to tend to what needed fixing first. After hefting up the kettle, Ida filled a bowl with steaming water, then sprinkled in salts that turned the water milky. "Best we do it soon."

"May I fetch him?"

"Please."

Releasing a nervous sigh, Aven stepped into the great room. Thor was gone from his sleeping place. Instead, he stood at the front windows, staring up at the broken glass as if he lacked the strength to do anything else. He ran a hand over his thick beard, tugging at the dark whiskers in slow strokes. The moment Aven stepped nearer, his gaze fell her way. His dark hair was as mussed as ever, and he shoved it over the side of his head. Dried blood matted the bandage just above his elbow.

It felt strange—trusting that he could understand—but she spoke all the same. "Ida would like to check your arm. I'm so very sorry that I did this."

His gaze on her lips, he wet his own. Forming a fist, he circled it around his heart the same moment he shook his head.

One of his words? "I . . . I'm afraid I don't understand."

He patted his empty chest pocket, then from the drawer of the desk he fetched a small notebook and stubby pencil. The hand that wrote was trembling. Aven tried not to think of the reason for that as he handed over what he'd written.

Don't be sorry.

She touched the knobby shape of his letters, then looked up into his face. "I shouldn't have been so untrusting. 'Twas unfair to you."

His forehead scrunched as if he struggled to understand her. He withdrew the paper and began a straight line of text just below the first. His hand engulfed the notepad as he held it over. *Me never so well matched.*

Pursing her lips, she slanted a look his way. He was smiling gently.

But when he tucked the pad and pencil into his chest pocket, his hand shook so fiercely, there was no denying his need for something stronger than the coffee being brewed. The scent of it filling the air, she asked if she could fetch him a cup. He nodded, though his focus fell elsewhere. He touched the bandage binding his arm with its dried stains, then lifted her wrist. He slid her sleeve up her arm, exposing her skin where it bore the same crimson streaks.

Her pulse pounded beneath his thumb, but sensing this kind of touch was his usual way, she took care not to flinch. Aven observed his face. Was this what Ida had alluded to?

Brow plunged down, Thor made a scrubbing motion as if to ask her to wash his blood from her skin. His glance to her all but pleaded it.

She nodded, struck by his concern. "Yes." Voice weak, she cleared her throat, and even as she spoke she realized he would have understood her all the same. "But first, let's tend that arm of yours."

Seated at the table, Thor watched as Cora peeled away the bloodstained bandage and discarded it. At her request, he unbuttoned the front of his shirt, then sat still as Ida gently tugged at his crusted sleeve. He set his jaw, determined not to let a sound emerge from his throat.

Ida eased the fabric away from his shoulder and down so his arm was bare. Then her sister wrung out a steamy rag and pressed it there. The warmth soothed but something within it stung. Salt?

With a plume of steam funneling from the kettle spout, Cora rose and quickly motioned for

Aven to hold the rag in place. Aven did, her small hand applying the gentlest of pressure. Her light-brown eyes skimmed his face. Thor lowered his head.

He didn't look up until Cora patted his knee. "I'm gonna have a look at this." She pulled a chair in front of him and sat. He braved a glance at Aven, who had backed away. The woman seemed like she was going to cry. It stirred something in his chest. A desire to assure her, but just as strong was the pleasure it gave him. Of her caring for his distress. It was a warm feeling. One he could get accustomed to.

He winced when a wet sting hit his arm. Aunt Cora had poured brandy on it. Sinking deep into the gash, the liquor burned. Thor had to pin himself into the chair. A groan rose in his throat and must have released because everyone looked at him at once.

Chin trembling, Aven pressed a hand to her mouth.

Pain was lessening the appeal of her compassion. He hated this.

Near the door stood Haakon, and when Thor glanced over, his brother made the hand sign for *drink*. Thor shook his head. He didn't want anything right now. But he—and everyone else in the room—couldn't deny how bad he was shaking. Thor braced his muscles, trying to fight the tremor that was liquor needing more of itself.

Aven paced. She drew near as Cora cleaned the wound, then stepped away when Thor breathed in through his teeth. At one point he thought she was going to faint. When Haakon turned her toward a chair, she sat.

So the woman *could* listen.

Aunt Cora tapped him for his attention. With pinched fingers she made a sewing motion. Thor shook his head. He really didn't want any part of him stitched. Cora turned away to speak to Aven. The redhead left and returned a moment later with a sewing basket. Her face was ashen.

Thor stood, tipping his chair back. Stepping forward, Jorgan restrained him by the shoulder. Thor shrugged him off.

But then Aven was right beside him. She dipped her head, eyes upraised, all but urging him to watch her. Forming a fist, she circled it around her chest as he had done. *Sorry.* Whenever spoken, Thor doubted that single word made much of an apology—he'd seen people say it carelessly many a time. But in his language it was different. Because the way Aven's eyes were filled with wetness as she stood in a room with people she barely knew, using a word she'd remembered from him only minutes ago—it was an apology so sincere, so potent, his skin flushed.

The fight sapped from his body, and Jorgan pressed him back into the chair. Gaze still on Aven, Thor hardly noticed the way Cora unraveled a length of string and set it to boil alongside a needle. Jorgan placed the bottle of brandy closer and Thor tried to ignore it, but it was as hard to look away from as Aven.

Back at the stove, Cora plucked out the needle and thread, shaking her scorched fingers. Thor ignored the rest of the preparations, staring instead at the table. When Cora pressed on his arm, needle poised, he swallowed hard. The first prick was as bad as all the rest, which he counted for no other reason but to stay seated. She was up to six when vibrations in his throat told him he was making sound. Aven swiped a tear.

Finally, Cora knotted and cut the thread. He looked down at her handiwork—his red, puckered skin. Blowing out a breath, he watched Cora's face as she instructed him and Ida how to care for it the next few days.

"I'll be back to check on you," Cora promised.

Touching fingers to his lips, he thanked her, then, to his surprise, she spoke something to Aven, motioning for the young woman to follow her out into the yard.

The memory of Thor's groans still in her ears, it was all Aven could do to stand beside the pump as Cora hefted the handle up and down. Water splashed onto the ground as the good woman washed her hands. She spoke no words. Just took careful attention with the creases and lines of her skin—washing all the blood away. When she finished, Aven splashed water over her own skin, scrubbing furiously.

Cora watched, her brown skin as glossy as the chestnuts Ida kept in a sack in the pantry. "Whatever pain you bearin', child, it ain't gonna come off under that spout."

Aven stilled but couldn't lift her gaze past Cora's hands as she dried them on the side of her skirt.

"Somethin' troublin' you and now's the time to speak it. Lest I misunderstood my eyes and the cause of Thor needin' to be stitched up."

Bowing her head, Aven shook water from her fingers. "I don't know what to do," she finally whispered.

With a cool touch, Cora lifted Aven's chin. "Don't you be hard on yesself. A girl all on her own learns to survive, and I've a hunch you seen a lot in your days. Lord knows you're far from home." She touched Aven's shoulder, and it was a motherly comfort. So tender and sure that Aven's throat tightened again. "He done frightened you last night and you ain't need be ashamed of that."

Aven unwound the bow that tied her apron and pulled it loose.

"And if it's after Thor that you're worryin', rest in ease that the man done been through a whole heap worse." She smiled a little. "He already on his feet again."

Nodding, Aven tried to hold on to that, but it was more than the wound of his body. It was something deeper. "I questioned his character. I made presumptions of his intentions that were far from the truth. He had been drinking . . . and was so forceful that I—I . . ."

Cora pulled Aven near and wrapped her up in a tight hug. The sensation was startling, so rarely had she been held this way. Emotions washed over her until she was crying again. Aven used her apron to wipe her eyes.

"He a good man," Cora said softly. "But as you might'a seen, he a broken man trying to bind himself back up with the one thing that be tearin' him down. It's the same thing that put his pappy in the ground, and it was a loss that shook us all. When Jarle Norgaard lost his wife, he didn't know how to come back from that amount of broken. And Thor . . ." Slowly, Cora shook her head. "He walkin' that same rutted path. He know what the Good Book says 'cause he reads it. He know he ain't supposed to put his trust in anything but the Lord."

The pump dripped as slow and steady as Cora's words.

"But a man gotta want it. Ain't nobody able to want it for him." Her face pinched with sadness. "It a cryin' shame what Thor be doin' to himself, but if you ask me"—a light hit her eyes and a smile of hope played at the corners of her mouth—"he got some fight in him left. It ain't too late yet. He don't have to follow his pappy all the way to the grave."

Aven clung to those words. "You believe there's such hope for him?"

"Yes, child. But he need us. He need people. It may seem elseways 'cause he pushes 'em away. But he do that 'cause most don't take the time to hear him."

So Thor was giving up. And why wouldn't he? When others treated him the way she had. Assuming him a wretch when he'd simply been fighting past a voice that wouldn't work. Twisting her fingers together, Aven glanced to the house, then back to Cora. "Please tell me what I can do."

"Just look at him." Shielding her face from the rising sun, Cora stepped a touch nearer. "Look at his eyes, his face. See him. See him and *be patient*. You'll never wonder." She squeezed Aven's hand, holding it in her cool one. "Spend but ten minutes gettin' to know Thor Norgaard and you'll forget he silent. You'll learn and hear things that most men don't even know how to speak."

SEVEN

Leaning over the edge of the wagon, Thor counted the empty buckets he'd just loaded. Each pail would hold three gallons, and he needed at least eighty gallons of berries today. With the patch nearest the pond drooping with ripe fruit, and with his blackberry wine a favorite in these parts, it was time to cash in on that.

Thor fetched another load of buckets from the north end of the cidery. The pledge they paid on this farm was on 327 acres of Sorrel land. At the cost of $3.25 an acre, no light load. He and his brothers had grown lax after Da's death, so with a few hundred still owed—not to mention eight dollars a month interest—it was time to pay it all off.

With Jorgan to marry next month, he knew his brother agreed.

They still had need of supplies to finish the west cabin, and since Haakon had blown up the chicken coop the year before and Jorgan was building a new one closer to the garden, they'd added more to their tab at the mercantile than they should have. It was high time they learned a little more responsibility. Today it would start with the berry patch.

Fearing he'd forget to secure the cidery, Thor

shoved the heavy door closed, then barred and bolted it. The iron lock used a key that only he and Jorgan had access to.

Thor hefted the next stack of buckets over the side of the wagon, then using his thumb, slid it up the rims to tally each one. Thirty-six. Thirty-seven. Thirty—

A touch at his elbow made him startle. Jerking his arm away, he turned to see Aven.

Her eyes were wide as she took a step back. "Oh dear. I'm so sorry."

He shook his head, though his heart was in his throat. He hated when people did that. Did they think he could hear them coming? Aven swallowed hard, and Thor shot out a breath. With his pulse slowing, he nodded for no other reason than for her to see that it was alright.

Jorgan had told him that her husband had been a drunkard. Much as Thor was. Did that frighten her about him? Thor knew little of Aven. Even less of Benn. But learning of his deceased cousin's struggle was enough for Thor to be vexed by warring emotions. First had come anger that a man would let an addiction rule him even in the confines of marriage. A bond where a woman chose to be wholly abandoned and honoring to her mate, and where a man promised to cherish and care for her. Following that had been a stab of sympathy because Thor knew what a battle it was—the pull of the bottle each and every moment of each and every day.

Who was he to judge? Would he not be the same in marriage?

Aven was still watching him with uncertain eyes. She was walking on eggshells around him, wasn't she? He wasn't helping that just now. Thor reached into the wagon and lifted out his board with the papers clipped to it. After loosening the top list, he flipped it over, then jotted a few words. He handed the board and paper to Aven.

I give you reason say sorry a lot.

Was that a little smile? Visibly easing, she looked from him to the wagon. She gripped the edge and peeked inside. Her eyebrows rose at the sight of so many buckets, but she didn't say anything. A soft chain encircled her throat. So delicate a necklace it might have been missed. She smelled of baking bread just as Ma once had. While Ida baked plenty, this was an aroma Thor hadn't smelled since he was a boy. Cardamom. Part of a Norwegian recipe that Ida never made because Ida didn't know it. Thor hadn't realized he'd missed the scent of Ma's bread until it lifted from Aven's flour-dusted apron.

She smiled at him, and he swallowed hard. Thor glanced around. It was just the two of them. A rare thing for him . . . especially with a woman. What did men usually do in this instance? He thought fast, and it dawned on him—they usually made conversation.

Thinking to try that, he wrote something more, but Aven's head whipped to the left. Thor looked over to see Haakon striding down the porch steps. Haakon spoke to her, and she angled away to respond. The world silent again, Thor scribbled out his phrase and lowered the board and pencil into the wagon. When he glanced at Aven she was watching him again and seemed regretful. Because he'd set the paper aside? Surely not. She had Haakon to talk to.

Thor stepped around the wagon and made sure the backboard was secure. Haakon climbed up to the seat even as Aven moved back. Perhaps she had some things to do with Ida. Thor wasn't sure, but with her shielding her eyes to watch them, might she want to get away from the house for a while? She'd yet to see much of the area, and they could use the help.

He signed the idea to Haakon, feeling more than ever Aven's watch of him. Haakon shook his head and signed back that they were going swimming afterward.

So? They could go swimming with manners.

When Thor mentioned that to his brother, Haakon shook his head again.

Aven's mouth moved with a question. "What are you two saying?"

Thor nudged his brother.

Haakon sighed and turned to her. "He asked if you wanted to pick blackberries with us today." He looked at Thor as if he'd lost his mind.

Thor ignored that, giving his attention instead to Aven. A smile brightened her face, and with his heart pulsing in his ears, he waited to see what she'd say to Haakon.

"I'd love to."

Thor nodded, and when his focus lifted from her mouth to her eyes, he realized that she'd spoken not to Haakon, but to him.

Settled on the wagon seat, Aven straightened the skirt of her mourning dress. Beside her, Haakon drove in easy silence. She reached up to hold Dorothe's wide-brimmed straw hat into place, grateful for the shade on her Irish skin, and glanced back to where Jorgan and Thor sat in the bed of the wagon, legs stretched out, boots crossed. Thor had an arm draped over the sideboard and seemed more interested in where they had been than where they were going. A rifle sat beside him, his hand resting atop it.

From the east came the smoke of a distant cook fire and from the south, the hum of bees in a thicket. The wagon ambled down the road, dipping through a low creek. When it turned at the nearest bend, Aven glimpsed a glittering pond where a dock cut into the water. Beyond that, fields of dried grasses stood still in the heat.

The dog plodded along beside the wagon, her brown head glistened in the sun. Aven had learned that her short fur was as silky as it looked. Jorgan had introduced her as Grete. While the dog often followed anyone around the farmyard, the hound seemed to favor Haakon best. Always there underfoot as he went about his day, or laying near whenever he was still.

Haakon broke the silence, asking Aven if she knew where they were.

She smiled. "Somewhere in Virginia."

Haakon chuckled. "Botetourt County. Not too far out of Eagle Rock—one of the finest little towns there is. There's a checker tournament every other Friday night at the old schoolhouse. And you just missed the monthly quiltin' bee." He winked, then shifted the reins to a single hand. "And, of course, you're on our land. Well, it's sort of our land."

"We're still on your farm?" They'd driven for some time now.

"Yep. It's just over three hundred acres. 'Bout a third of it's orchards, then there's some cabins to the east. Most of 'em are pretty run-down, but there's one near the west side of the farm that we been fixin' up. Just a stone's throw from the house, really. We'll show it to you sometime."

He pointed in the other direction. "Over this way is where Cora and her family stay in a cabin that her husband made real nice before he passed." Haakon pointed in another direction. "Up that way is the Sorrel farm. The men who were here the other night."

Aven shielded her eyes to look that way, but before she could focus on the distant hills and woodlands, Haakon pointed in a new direction.

"Some other neighbors around too, but we get along real peaceable. There's a couple of ponds here and there. Other than that, just fields and forest." He leaned a touch nearer. "Da used to say that a long time ago, the god Thor was in a fight with three giants. Thor, Odin's son that is, not my brother. Though I suppose that's possible as well."

Aven smiled again.

"As the story goes, the giants were a force of destruction so fierce that they meant to turn the land to ruin." He pointed eastward, voice soft for her. "But Thor fought valiantly and in the last blow, he brought his hammer down with such might that it not only scattered the giants, it shaped that valley."

" 'Tis so vast."

"Yeah. I wandered it once when I was a kid. But I got lost, and Da found me two days later. He dragged me home and made me spend the rest of the week diggin' a well near the river. Told me that's what a man looks like when he's a fool." His blue eyes shone a fondness that the hard lesson learned was a dear memory now.

Aven could nearly imagine their father—as braw and bristly as these sturdy Norwegians—pulling them onto his knee for tales and guiding them through life as best he could.

"And how did your family come to be here in Virginia? Dorothe made mention that she left when the potato famine reached Norway. Did your parents arrive then as well?"

"Naw. They came sometime later, just before Jorgan was born. Dorothe was in North Dakota at the time and came to live with them here. Help jostle babies and that sort of thing."

" 'Twould seem she had her hands full with it."

He smiled.

The horses clomped down through a wooded grove. Cheery birds called out to one another as they flitted from limb to limb. The road narrowed, and with a command to the horses, Haakon slowed the wagon. When the wheels stilled, he hopped down and helped Aven do the same.

"Thank you," she said as she righted her skirts.

Thor unloaded buckets. His brothers set to helping, and before Aven could even reach for one, Thor was handing her a pail. He motioned her forward and she followed him.

"Start anywhere you want," Haakon called out, pointing to the thick and thorny brambles that spread every which way.

At the nearest bush she freed a plump berry

that was so warm and moist, juice dripped from it. So tempted was she to pop it in her mouth that she gave in. Heavens, that was good. The next berry slipped from the stem just as easily, and she placed it in the pail. The brothers set to picking. Handful after handful, they all gleaned. Never had Aven seen berries so hearty and plentiful. In mere minutes her bucket was brimming.

With the air stifling, she ruffled the hem of her skirt, stirring a breeze against her stockinged legs. Sweat dampened the black fabric of her dress to her chest. Since the men had long since shoved back shirtsleeves and loosened collars, she unfastened the lace at her own throat. Aven fanned her neck, grateful when a slight breeze moved through the woods.

Underbrush crunched as Thor stepped nearer. He worked quick and steady, large fingers freeing berries with practiced ease. His eyes were focused on his task, and he breathed louder than the others. Aven smiled at the endearing way.

Thor lifted a prickled branch and loosened a cluster of fruit. There seemed a rightness to this work for him. A sureness and satisfaction. Perhaps it was the way he took the lead, his brothers heeding his wordless commands. The men's focus was such and the quantity of buckets so ample, Aven sensed this was no casual picking. Doubtless, Thor would be concocting something a lot stouter than jam in that shop of his.

She tried to ignore the sorrow such a notion lent as she lowered a handful of berries to the top of her mounded pail. She'd agreed to help so here she was, but to think of the tender fruit becoming hard drink upended the gratification of the task. Especially with memories of Benn and the hold the bottle had had on him. The sorrow it had spread over their lives.

Haakon carried over two buckets, giving her the one that was already half full.

With her mind having slipped to life in Norway, 'twas no surprise that her gratitude came out as, "*Tusen takk.*"

Haakon looked at her. "Huh?"

Straightening, Aven used the back of her wrist to swipe her damp forehead. "Do you not speak Norwegian?"

"Not really." He stepped around her, and when her skirt snagged on a thorn, he bent to free it. "I can say our names like I was born there." He stood. "*Yurgan,*" he pronounced for Jorgan. "Then there's the mighty and loud and sometimes clumsy *Tur.*" Last, he spoke his own name, just as it was said in Norway for the kings of centuries past. "*Hohkun.* I can also say potato lefse. But that's it."

Aven chuckled.

"Da spoke it well but not often. Little that I

97

remember. Thor, he reads and writes it, but I never took to it. Just seemed a waste of time."

"And what of your mother?" She knew nothing of their parents except from the glimpses she'd gotten of the photographs in the great room; it seemed Haakon had his father's light eyes and locks while Thor had their mother's dark hair. "Did she speak it with you? There's a lullaby that comes to mind . . ."

"Not to me." Gaze to the ground, he kicked aside a cluster of branches with his sturdy boot. "You'd have to ask Thor or Jorgan. It shouldn't surprise me that you speak it." He cleared his throat as if trying to rally himself. "You lived there for a few years?"

"Nearly four. I only know a little."

"What was it like? For you and Benn?" He yanked at a green shoot harder than necessary.

"Like?" she asked weakly.

He shrugged as if it were easier for them to wade into her deep waters than his own. "Where did you live?"

"In a fishing village called Henningsvaer. Benn was a boat builder." Aven slid the bucket between them with hands as smeared purple as Haakon's own. "We leased a flat above a bake shop. I have eaten many a potato lefse."

Now it was his turn to chuckle. She was glad, as it seemed to tip his mood back to the happier sort. His nose and cheeks, lightly freckled, retained a touch of boyhood, but when he rose to stand beside her, she saw afresh that he was as grown a man as the others.

"You'll make it for me sometime?" Haakon asked.

"Would you like me to?"

"Yes, please."

"Then I shall."

He smiled again and it was the dangerous sort, for with such a handsome face, 'twas a captivating concoction. But he sobered as he carried both buckets off, and Aven remembered the twinge he'd shown at mention of his mother.

At the washtub, Haakon dumped out the berries, then asked Thor if they could be done. Thor's back was to him as he picked from a brimming patch. Haakon nabbed a small stone and hurled it at Thor's boots. Thor flinched, then looked over, a shadow darkening his face.

"We done now?" Haakon asked sharply.

Oh, she'd struck a sharp chord indeed.

Ignoring his brother, Thor turned back to his work.

Jorgan spoke to Haakon. "Why did you have to do that?"

"Sorry. Can we go swimming now?"

Jorgan didn't speak. Hefting up a pail, Thor carried it to the washtub and dumped it in. He took his time. When he finished, he strode to Haakon and gripped a meaty hand to the back of his brother's neck. Thor gave a firm squeeze. Haakon lowered his head. A stern affection that seemed to put Haakon in his place, but when the young man nodded, it also bound the rift between them.

Thor stepped back and loosened the bottom button of his white cotton shirt. Followed by the next. His answer, then.

Suddenly nervous, Aven averted her gaze. The temptation for swimming was beyond bearable. No wonder Haakon had all but pleaded for it. Having grown up within the walls of the manor, she didn't know how such a diversion was done. Never had she been allowed to wander far from the grounds. She was certainly not allowed to play with the master's children. Was swimming something that was segregated between the sexes? She sensed it to be so, but it mattered not, really. Buoyancy was something she'd never learned.

Aven headed toward the wagon. She would wait in the shade and rest her feet until the men had their fun. Yet at a quick whistle, she turned to see Thor motioning her toward the pond. He meant for her to follow?

Confused, she shook her head, but he motioned again before turning away. Thor strode to the edge of the water where he pulled off his boots. His socks went next, then the last buttons of his shirt.

Aven didn't realize she was staring until Jorgan strode past her. "Don't worry. I told them to be on their best behavior. Come on."

Thor pulled his shirt free and tossed it aside. He started toward the dock, back strong and solid beneath the late-afternoon sun. She'd heard many a tale of the Vikings of old—but never did a man rush those stories to mind so vividly as Thor Norgaard. Shed of everything but his wool trousers as well, Jorgan spoke something to his brother. Thor's accompanying laugh was so deep and free, Aven couldn't help but savor it. 'Twas unlike any sound she'd ever heard.

Though she had no intention of shedding an ounce of her wardrobe, to dip her feet in the water would be sweet relief. With damp soil paving the way to the pond, Aven paused to unlace her boots and peel off her stockings. The cool earth was an instant reward.

She glanced around for sight of Haakon but saw nothing other than woodlands stirring in the soft breeze.

Sinking its roots deep beneath the pond was a mighty tree. A long rope dangled from one of the aged branches. Jorgan jogged down the dock, gripped the rope, and swung out over the water where he splashed beneath the surface.

Grinning, Thor pulled the rope back again. After a steadying breath, he ran down the dock just as Jorgan had done. In a burst, he launched himself off the edge. Gripping tight the rope, he arced out over the water. He swung his legs up, head down, then let go, flipping backward into the pond with a mighty splash.

So this was swimming.

Aven treaded down the grassy slope where a short drop-off separated her from reaching the water. She looked around for an easy way down but saw none, and her attempts to scale the little cliff would no doubt send her tumbling. She settled on the grass instead. The distance was just as well, for she felt unstable surrounded by water and the wildness of their play.

After a contented sigh, Aven nearly jumped out of her skin at the sound of Haakon whooping down the hillside behind her. He yanked off his boots and socks as he raced toward the dock. His shirt was last and that he flung carelessly behind him before launching off the edge of the platform in a front flip that landed in a splash so huge, Aven ducked against the stray droplets. He came up for air, only to be dunked back down by Jorgan. The dog ambled in the shallows, head cocked as she hunted for something slippery.

At a different sloshing, Aven looked over to see Thor wading into the shallows. His dark pants were soaked through. He waved Aven nearer and she shook her head. He beckoned her closer again, this time with a quick whistle.

"I'm afraid I don't swim."

102

Unless, perhaps, he was asking something else?

At the sight of his disappointment, she remembered Cora's urging for him to be heard. For that reason Aven rose and paced to the edge of the slope. The earth plunged to the low bank where he stood, his chest just a touch higher than the ledge itself.

"I'm listening," she said with a smile.

Thor smiled back.

Aven knew not his age—only that he was somewhere between Jorgan's thirty-two and Haakon's twenty-one. She pondered the mystery as he stepped nearer and patted the earth where he likely meant for her to stand. The stitched gash in his upper arm seemed to be healing nicely. She nearly apologized again but instead asked, "Is it safe for you to be swimming with such a wound?" She knew little of infection but wondered if this was wise.

Thor shaped a response to Jorgan who spoke for him.

"Said it's gonna take a lot more than pond water to kill him."

Thor patted a hand to the earth again and this time motioned for her to sit. Next he reached up and touched his shoulders, indicating she was to hold on there. Her hesitation must have been clear for he didn't quite look at her as he took her wrists and pulled them nearer until her hands brushed the droplets of water beaded on his skin.

With her palms to his firm shoulders, he gripped her waist.

Remembering the trust that had been hinted at, Aven let him pull her off the ledge. His strength—that which had frightened her only days ago—made her feel safe now. Her feet hit the ground, and his touch fell away as her own did.

Though only a few paces wide, the beach was enough for her to walk on. She stepped forward until cool water splashed at her toes. She thanked Thor, and he nodded before trudging back into the water. Alone again, Aven waded in so that her ankles were wet. Minnows gathered about her feet. They rippled and twirled above the loamy soil. She was all but lost in the decadence of the cool water when she glanced back toward the wagon and the loaded harvest. Though whatever they intended to make wouldn't have been a temptation to Benn, the bounty brought a twinge of sorrow.

Liquor wasn't so much a matter of conscience but a still-raw hurting from her past. Would the men understand if she expressed that? Perhaps she could use the berries she had picked to make into jams and jellies.

With Haakon climbing onto the dock, Aven thought to investigate. "What will you do with so much ripe fruit?"

"Do you want to swim?" he said instead as he clambered up.

"No, thank you."

"Why not?"

"Because I cannot swim."

"You can't swim?" Haakon came around and started down the slope. "What kind of person can't swim?"

"This one, apparently."

"How did you sail on a ship?"

"I prayed it wouldn't sink."

With a wince, he skidded to a stop beside her. "Aren't ya hot?"

"See now." Lifting her hem, she inched forward until the wet coolness churned around her feet again. "This keeps me cool."

"Oh, aye." He sat and leaned back on his hands. "Ye look quite cool, lass."

Aven gathered up the hem of her skirt, keeping it modest as best she could. "It must be blessedly refreshing to be a man."

He squinted over at her. "It'd be more refreshing without my clothes on."

"Haakon," Jorgan snapped from where he was just gripping the dock.

"Well, it's true. I hate swimmin' in my pants."

"I'm sorry, Aven," Jorgan called over.

Unoffended, she angled back to the young man beside her. "Has there ever been a thought, Mr. Norgaard, that you have not voiced?"

Haakon's brow deepened. His expression immersed in matters that looked far beyond this place, this moment. He glanced out to the horizon where the sun was sleepy and low, then to Thor, who was pulling himself up the side of the dock. "As a matter of fact, *Mrs. Norgaard* . . ." Haakon's blue eyes moved back to hers, and when he spoke, she realized he hadn't yet answered her question about the berries. "All the time."

EIGHT

Thor tried to fasten his sleeve cuff as he strode down the hallway. His fingers were shaking, and while whiskey would help, he made it a point not to drink on Sunday mornings. For that reason his fingers were still struggling when he reached the bottom of the stairs.

Ida intervened. She secured both cuffs, and he tipped his chin up when she reached to tidy his collar. His hair was tied in a knot at the nape of his neck, which seemed to satisfy her as she made no complaints. Even his beard passed inspection. He knew well enough to trim it before standing in front of her.

"You look fine, Thor. Right fine."

Ida closed her warm hands around his trembling fingers, squeezing her strength as if it were an offering. He was grateful to have it. For a few hours of sobriety at church, he would ignore his thirst. A battle until they got home and he could give in. Already he was thinking about those wagon wheels returning to the farm. Him twisting the metal lid off a jar . . .

Thor gulped, his need like a leech that was never satisfied.

With a heap of chatter that Thor didn't catch,

Haakon strode in and used the reflection of the window to comb his hair.

"Did you bathe, Haakon?" Ida asked.

A nod.

"And did you use soap?"

Haakon glanced at her. "We're supposed to use soap?"

Thor smiled, and Haakon winked at Ida even as she shooed him from her sight. His nerves settling, Thor stepped onto the porch. They were all waiting on Aven, but she was yet to appear. In the yard, Jorgan stood beside the wagon. The team was already hitched. Thor nodded his thanks before climbing up to the seat to take the reins. He sat there, squinting against the brightness of dawn, cursing the headache that was forming.

At a flash of pale blue, he looked over to see Haakon helping Aven up to the wagon seat. She wore a dress that most definitely wasn't for mourning. The same dusky shade as the mountains that hazed in the distance. Faint embroidery twisted up the snug bodice, accentuating the curve of her waist. She smelled sweet as spice cake as she settled next to him. Thor gulped again, and this time it had nothing to do with cider. Even Haakon seemed awed as he backed away.

Aven gave Thor a small smile, her brown eyes bright. "Good day, Thor." Freckles dotted her nose, and the rest of her skin was nearly as pale as the lace at her collar. A stark contrast to her ginger hair.

He dipped his head in response. With his palms now damp, he ran one and then the other on his pants before adjusting his grip on the reins. The wagon jostled as Haakon and Jorgan climbed in. Miss Ida waved from the doorway and Aven waved back. Dressed in Sunday best herself, Ida would go with Cora to a small church they attended with former slaves and freeborns.

As for Thor and his brothers, Ida made sure they went to the packed service in Eagle Rock at least once a month. Anything less and she would stop cooking again. Everything in the kitchen . . . slamming to a halt. During one of their rebellious stints a few winters back, she'd nearly starved them out until they finally got their sorry hides into a pew. They had decided never to test her again.

They wouldn't have gone this week, but Aven had inquired into church so they thought it right to take her.

The wagon ambled along, and every minute of the drive was harder than the last as Thor's thoughts raced between Aven and the cidery. Each a yearning he had to tamp down. Thoughts of the Lord would be his saving grace, so he tried to draw a scripture—any scripture—to mind as the drive wore on. He was still fumbling through a shaky remembrance of the Twenty-Third Psalm by the time the small, white chapel came into view.

It would have been a fierce relief if the throbbing in his head wasn't threatening to do him in. Thor squeezed the back of his neck and knew he had to be breathing hard when Aven slid him a worried look. She seemed about to touch his hand when he lifted it to tug the reins. The wagon slowed to a halt beside others. It took all his concentration to set the brake. Jorgan helped Aven down.

Thor's next steps were a blur—faces of people he knew hazy as usual as he walked toward the chapel. A deep breath in . . . then another one out. Amid the pain there was only one face he was able to distinguish from the rest. Peter Sorrel.

The young man was deep in conversation with someone, but when Aven strode by on Jorgan's arm, the youth's mouth stilled midword. Peter tipped his head and watched her as if she were spun gold. The same as he'd done the other night when he'd been in his Klan covering. Thor kept nearer to Aven than he might have otherwise, and Peter went back to minding his own business.

Inside the chapel, Jorgan motioned Aven toward the women's sections where the female sort filled the benches that ran along the west and south walls. Along the east and north walls were benches of men and boys, each section four rows deep. Hesitantly, Aven drifted toward her own gender, and when she looked back over her shoulder, it was just Thor there.

He gave her a reassuring nod.

Spotting a bench with enough room for him and his brothers, Thor worked his way there, inching past the crush of men that smelled like sweat and sun-dried clothing. A few were clean shaven and the air bore the woodsy scent of lathering soap. Thor sat, and his brothers settled on each side of him.

It was a noisy operation, church. Thor had decided that long ago in the way people leaned near to speak to one another. Mouths moved rapidly and hands flailed in nonsensical ways. Animated eyes often spoke more than words themselves. All of it an energy of life and movement. People glad to see one another after driving for miles to gather under this roof as one body.

Thor observed as usual. Rarely did anyone try and talk to him. It had been this way as long as he could remember.

When folks settled and drew still, he looked to the preacher, who stood facing the women. Not knowing what was being said, Thor let his gaze lift to the diamond-shaped window high up in the wall. His focus didn't lower until the whole congregation shifted forward to grab hymnals from beneath the benches. Doing the same, Thor handed the leather-bound book to Haakon, who found the hymn that had been called out. Across the page were written shape-notes, but they meant nothing to Thor. It had something to do with *pitch*. Whatever that meant.

Feeling like a fist was pounding against his skull, Thor rubbed at his temple. His mouth was parched as sand. He squeezed his eyes tight and tried not to dislike church as much as usual.

Book in hand, a man rose and moved to the center of the square. The gentleman bent his arm at the elbow and lowered his hand down and up. Everyone followed suit. A way of beating time together that was visual. As a child, Thor had always liked how a manual form of communication could keep a room of people together. It didn't impress him as much now. All around, mouths began to move. It filled the air with a mellow vibration. Normally Thor watched the room in general to follow along, but today he just watched Aven.

She didn't seem to know what to do as she glanced around. Her attention fell to the book when the woman beside her held it nearer. Aven spoke a thank-you and began singing with all the others. Judging by the way her mouth opened and closed, the song was solemn and slow. Thor watched her lips as long as he dared. When she stole a glance his way again, he dropped his attention to the page Haakon braced open.

With everyone lifting and lowering their right

hand, Thor decided it was best to do the same. Elbow at his waist, he raised his hand as everyone else did, then lowered it a beat later. Haakon and Jorgan were singing along, their forearms moving in time with everyone else's. The way Haakon was heaving in breaths, he had to be one of the loudest voices. Probably trying to make up for his behavior since last they'd sat here.

At an elbow from Jorgan, Thor turned the page. His brother nodded his thanks.

Thor didn't dare look at Aven again. Instead, he focused on the words to the hymn.

People said God lived here. Lived in these songs of praise, but Thor knew it only in the text printed and bound. He had different favorites from his brothers and even Ida. They seemed to prefer the ones most often sung. Those that stirred the congregation to sing loudest—deepening the tremble in the benches. But Thor best liked the songs where struggles were clear in the writing. The printed pleas of those who had petitioned for help to a high King.

Those hymns he understood.

When a few more songs had drawn to a close, Thor shifted on the hard bench and watched the preacher best he could. With parishioners spread on every side of the building, the man stood before each section in turn. A quarter of a sermon. That's what Thor always got, and he tried to make it be enough, but with so much of the teaching missed, he never fully understood the lessons. He tried to be grateful for the parts that were preached in his direction, but he missed more than he wished.

Thor bounced his foot. It must have been loud because Haakon hit him in the leg. Thor stopped. He broke his intent not to glance at Aven, and when he did, she was watching the preacher with such a thoughtful expression that the sermon made a sound he had never heard before.

Thor was still looking at her when heads tilted forward in prayer. The closing, then. Thor bowed his head and closed his eyes. The world went blank. He always wanted to watch the preacher to see what was said. That didn't seem proper, though, so with his mouth watering for something strong and wet, he said a desperate prayer all his own, hoping it would be sufficient. He stayed that way for a long time, the plea driving a sting to his throat.

Suddenly Jorgan thumped a fist on Thor's knee. Thor raised his head to see that folks were standing and talking again. It was over.

He could have a drink soon.

Feeling like a wretch, Thor rose and made his way out of the pew, wedging past people until he could stand in the sun. Some gave him wary glances, and he did his best to avert his gaze. Judging by the whispers he saw and the way the congregation inched around him, he made people uncomfortable. It had ingrained in him a habit to keep to the far end of the churchyard. The place he usually waited until his brothers were done visiting; Jorgan with businessmen and farmers, Haakon with girls.

Even now Haakon was speaking to a pair of young women. They were talking and laughing in the shade of the building. When they looked Thor's way, he could tell he was being looped into their conversation. But why? Especially since they were being rather open about it.

Neck vise-tight, Thor gripped it and tried to loosen the muscles, but his body was crying out for what he was denying it. He wanted to go home.

Right now.

Tired of waiting, he strode to the wagon and smoothed a hand up the younger mare's side. He unfastened both of their feed bags and tossed the sacks into the back. By the time he was finished, his brothers and Aven were climbing up. To his relief, Jorgan drove.

The light hurt his eyes, so Thor lowered his head and focused on breathing instead of watching the miles roll by.

Haakon kicked his boot, then held up two small pieces of paper. "This one's yours."

What that?

"It's a ticket. To a dance comin' up."

Eyebrows raised, Thor pointed to himself. Haakon nodded.

"We both have them. It was a fund-raiser for some women's guild, and there's gonna be a raffle too. Or a bazaar. I'm not sure, but I entered us last time I was in town and forgot to tell you. Cost a dollar apiece but I figured it's for a good cause. Jorgan has one too, but they paired him with Fay. Which doesn't seem fair seein' as she's not even in town yet." Haakon handed one of the tickets over. "It's a partner dance, and the guild women paired you with Alice Vogel." Haakon grinned.

The reverend's daughter? Not understanding, Thor was glad when Aven looked back and spoke to Haakon, gleaning more details. On Thor's behalf, he sensed, but the comfort was thin because his skin was on fire. He was to go to a dance? And his partner was already chosen?

Haakon was a dead man.

When the wagon slowed to a stop in the farmyard, Thor shoved the ticket to his brother's chest and hopped down. All he wanted right now was his cider shed. He'd deal with Haakon later. But his brother jumped over the side and passed him. Hands up peaceably, Haakon turned and walked backward.

Not slowing, Thor smacked him in the side of the head, moving past his brother. Covering his ear, Haakon grimaced and ducked away. Thor stormed off, but Haakon clipped his boot.

Thor's stumble only swung him around, and he

grabbed hold of his brother and rammed him into the ground. He pressed the side of Haakon's head into the dirt so the kid squirmed.

Haakon gripped Thor's arm, digging hard to try and be free. Thor ignored the pain.

He was good at that.

From the corner of his eye, he saw Jorgan jump down. Not in the mood to be outnumbered, Thor shoved Haakon away. After rising, Thor strode off and didn't look back to see the disapproving look Jorgan would have for him. Or the utter horror from Aven. He just aimed for his shop, stepped inside, and slammed the door.

He took up a jar of cider and flung it at the wall. It shattered. The amber wetness glistened down the boards to the floor. Wasteful, but he unfortunately had more than plenty. He loosened the lid on a second jar and gulped down desperate swallows. The liquor didn't burn as it had when he was a boy. Now it was a sickening comfort. One he couldn't even get through a morning without.

Drinking more, Thor felt a sob rise from his throat. It escaped and he nearly choked. He spat out the mouthful to heave a breath. With the back of his hand he wiped his beard.

I hate you. The three words he used to sign to Haakon whenever the baby was sitting there on his blanket, the house void of their mother's presence. Thor would sign that wretched oath to young Haakon when no one was looking. At first it was an honest confession. Some way to make sense of why Thor had come home from boarding school to find that his mother wasn't warm and wrapping her arms around him but buried beneath a cross near the woods. Leaving in her place a newborn who flailed his arms and stretched his mouth wide, squalling for a mother who wasn't coming back for any of them.

As time wore on, those three words had been a painful release. Until the day a one-year-old Haakon had peered up at him, and with innocent eyes and dimpled hands, he flicked little fingers in Thor's direction, trying to mimic the shape of *hate*. The baby babbled and cooed like it was a game.

The first thing Thor had taught him.

Eyes clamped closed now, Thor guzzled from the glass rim, but it did nothing to wash away the sight of those little hands or the feeling of crushing Haakon to the dusty ground. Of the pain in Haakon's face as Thor braced him in place with all his strength.

A slit of light broke through the dimness, and Thor looked over to see Jorgan step around the giant door. Hands in his pockets, Jorgan strode nearer, looking first to Thor, then to the splattered cider along the far wall. Last to the broken glass just below. If he'd heard the crash, Jorgan didn't say anything. He didn't need to say anything. Thor's guilt was sufficient, and Jorgan's companionable silence only deepened it.

Thor set the jar aside and twisted the lid back on. The quart was nearly empty—and this was the strongest proof he made. He'd be walking lopsided by dinner time.

Jorgan tugged the shop stool near and sat. "He looks up to you, you know."

Thor shook his head.

"You don't see it, maybe, but it's true."

Well, *he need stop.*

Jorgan glanced out the dingy window to the yard where the scuffle was still marked in the dirt. Hands flat to the workbench, Thor lowered his head. Stared at the floor and the way a thousand glinting jars sent flecks of golden sunlight across it.

Head still bowed, the light spilling in from the window was hot on his hair. His mind was growing fuzzy as the pain subsided, but he felt worse, not better. Thor searched for a way to express what was clawing inside him. Just as it had been for years.

Finally, he looked at Jorgan and pointed to himself. *I need make different.*

Jorgan's brow furrowed, and Thor searched for a way to explain it better. What was the English for what he meant? He pointed to himself again, then hooked his fingers toward one another and twisted them the other way. *I change.* He added a hard *must* at the end to try and make Jorgan understand his desperation.

Jorgan's surprise was evident. "What are you gonna do?"

Thor thought hard and deep of how he wanted—with everything inside him—to wake up in the morning without his first thought being his first sip. How he wanted to drink coffee with nothing else but cream. To be around Aven and not wrestle a headache so fierce that it threatened to break him. Worse yet was knowing that he couldn't care for anyone in the state he was in. Let alone her.

"You thinkin' of tryin' again?"

Yes. Thor had already placed an order for the boards and nails he'd need to seal this place up. When he finished confessing that, his brother's jaw had fallen an inch.

Justifiably so. For many reasons. The last being that it was how they made their living. Thor didn't know how to kick this need for alcohol while still keeping the cidery open. When he relayed that to his brother, Jorgan nodded slowly.

Rubbing at his beard, Jorgan studied the shelves of cider as if calculating. Finally he looked at Thor. "We've always gotten by and we always will. How about you not worry about the earnings for a spell? Lord knows you've carried it long enough. Haakon and I will see to things until you're on the other side. Then we can talk it through some more. If you want to do this, it needs to be done."

The assurance was more freeing than Thor could express. If Jorgan was willing to face the uncertainties, Thor would rest in that.

No tell Aven. Please. Thor didn't want her to know until he'd committed. Until nails were pounded into place, and he couldn't change his mind. Sealing things up wasn't something he'd thought to do with his failed attempt five years ago. One that ended so badly it nearly cost them Haakon and had left Ida on the bruising end of Thor's madness. They couldn't risk that again.

And now with Aven here . . .

Doubts threatened to smother him, but when Jorgan gave a sturdy nod, it felt like a shield going up. One that blocked Thor's nightmares of once again hurting others as the liquor lashed out for being neglected inside him.

"Alright." At the crinkle of Jorgan's eyes, there was a smile blooming somewhere in his beard.

It gave Thor hope. A deeper faith that maybe he could do this. That he could beat back the demons he'd let torment him for far too long.

Jorgan reached out and gripped Thor's shoulder, then leaned closer so their foreheads nearly touched—a way for Thor to know just how sincerely he meant the movement of his mouth. "You can be free of this. And I'll do whatever you need me to do to help."

NINE

Breakfast the next morning was a quiet event. Thor and Haakon didn't acknowledge one another from across the table. Aven tried not to recall the upset from the day before, but it was as impossible to ignore as the silence.

Yesterday Jorgan assured her that his brothers had always been this way. That their row was nothing to worry about. Jorgan had spoken with such ease that Aven clung to the hope that if tension was a regular occurrence, perhaps it would quickly fade. The hope was kindled when Haakon rose, strode out, and Thor lifted a regretful glance after him.

Jorgan stood as well. "Haakon and me are gonna mend a window on the west cabin, then see if the fish are bitin'. We'll be back." He tossed his napkin onto the table, and though he'd scrubbed at the washbasin before breakfast, the creases of his hands were still somewhat blackened. He'd worked with Thor at sunup to tug down the burnt wood crib. With the help of one of the horses and a sturdy chain, they had it pulled down before the coffee even began to steam.

Aven nodded as Thor pushed his way from the table and strode deeper into the house.

With Ida abed resting her legs, Aven set the

kettle to steam and prepared a tray of breakfast comforts. After bringing it to Ida in the back bedroom, Aven returned to the kitchen and hefted up the bowl of berries that had scarcely dwindled. An idea dawned. She went to the pantry and pulled out both flour and sugar. Perhaps a pie was in order. Two, judging by the abundance of the fruit on hand and the tension still in the air.

By the time she finished mixing and rolling dough, Thor had gone outside toward the orchards.

Aven stirred glistening sugar into the dark berries. 'Twas with thankful hands that she worked. For both the bounty and their generosity in giving her a place to be at home.

Using a butter knife, she cut a delicate lattice top. Two pans came next, and she assembled both pies with great care. A few snippets of dough remained, so Aven cut them into dainty leaves and twisted vines. She layered the cutouts into place, then brushed the tops with a beaten egg. Into the oven the pans went. If Haakon and Jorgan were successful, fried fish would be on the menu for dinner, so she stuck potatoes onto the lowest rack to roast.

Her own legs weary, Aven headed upstairs, intent on tending to a project she could settle in for. She pulled her mourning gown from the wardrobe and sat on the bed where she spread out the heavy skirt. It looked as wilted and tired as she had felt upon her climb up this mountain. Which made it all the more gratifying to lift Dorothe's sewing shears and snip through the lightweight wool.

Aven trimmed a large portion from the bottom, then much of each sleeve. Even this simple task reminded her of the kind Norwegian woman. While her letters spanning the sea had been delicately worded, they had been meaningful all the same. Of those memories, the richest were the scriptures Dorothe would pen.

Though raised Catholic as a child, Aven had attended a Protestant church upon her marriage to Benn, and her heart found a home there. The church the brothers attended seemed of a similar make. She was eager to understand more of God's Word in this wilderness. To learn more of grace and salvation as well as devoting one's life to the good Christ. She'd cherished beloved scriptures and Bible stories as a girl, and now she trusted that God had her on a path that would further shape her.

Aven plunged a threaded needle into the dusky fabric. Along one hem she worked, using a running stitch and pulling pins here and there. Before long, a tangy sweetness warmed the air from the pies that had to be bubbling now. Aven took up the gown and sewing basket, then started for the stairs. To work nearer the oven would be wise. 'Twould do no good to become lost in another task and allow her efforts to burn.

So quick she went down that she nearly missed sight of Thor at the table near the stairs in the great room. Back hunched, he pored over one of his books. Not wanting to interrupt him, Aven set her sewing materials down, then stepped into the kitchen. She grabbed a quilted pad and lowered the oven door. Heat wafted out, as did the aroma of melted butter. The lattice tops had darkened to a golden brown, so she slid out the pans and set them on the kitchen table to cool.

Aven gently fingered one of the leaf cuttings. The dough was baked to a honey-hued sheen. The vines twisting around were just as lovely. Perhaps a bit ornate, but that was the result of living over the bakery in Norway, having spent many a lonely night helping Farfar Øberg roll and cut dough just so they would each have someone to talk to. Musing that this handiwork would make the grandfatherly man proud, Aven felt a tickle of homesickness in her chest. His wrinkled face came to mind, and she recalled the way it always brightened whenever she mastered a new technique or surprised him with methods of her own invention.

Aven peeked into the great room and thought a little less of Farfar Øberg at the sight of Thor sitting there. Her sewing basket still rested near him. Should she take it elsewhere? She didn't wish to, so with a small grip of courage she walked over. Perhaps they could keep company until the others returned.

His book sat flat to the table, and the thumb he held atop the page slid along as he read. Beside him on the bench was an open jar of cider. He gave her the smallest of glances as she settled onto the bench opposite him.

Aven pulled the beginnings of the swimming costume into her lap, then reached for a spool of black thread. A snip of the scissors and she gave the thread a little lick before pushing it through the eye of the needle. Though the book was upside down to her, it was clearly in Norwegian. She tipped her head to the side. Her effort to decipher the title at the top of the open page was no use, so faded was the text.

Thor shifted on the bench. His shoe bumped her own, and he slid his feet away. As if noticing where her focus had landed, he used his thumb as a placeholder, then angled the cover toward her.

Aven squinted at the title. *Verdens Grøde*. Something to do with giants. "Are you enjoying it?"

Palm down, he tipped his hand from side to side as if to say *somewhat*. Thor pulled his book away, flipped it open once more, and went back to reading. After a few lines, his gaze strayed to her.

Aven gave a friendly smile as she reached for the tin of pins.

His breathing was soft as he continued to read. Boots shuffling so often, she had to work not to smile again. His feet shifted once more, but this time he cleared his throat. Was he nervous? Perhaps she was sitting too close. With the table between them, it was surely proper. Aven glimpsed his face, wishing for a hint of his thoughts.

Her study of him was cut short when she pricked her finger on the next stitch. She winced and stuck the pad against her mouth. She'd do well to be watching what she was doing. Thor lifted his head, looking concerned.

Finger throbbing, Aven shook her hand. " 'Twas just a prick."

He nudged up the lid of the sewing basket, reached inside, and pulled out a thimble. He set it on the table in front of her.

"Aye, that would be helpful as well." She slid it on and the metal cap fit loosely. With his attention still upon her, she spoke in hopes of bringing some comfort to his newfound situation. "I'm sorry about what Haakon did. About the pairing off of the dance."

Running the back of his knuckles against his beard, Thor made no response.

"If it's dancing that worries you, I could show you how—"

He shook his head and reached for his jar. A gulp disrupted the thin ring of white foam atop the brew.

"Just the basic steps. They truly aren't so hard."

Looking frustrated, he reached into his pocket and fetched his notebook. Next he pulled out the stubby pencil. *Hard for me.*

"Of course." Aven hoped he knew she meant it. "And reasonably so."

He seemed to appreciate that. When he pushed the notebook aside and returned to his reading, she focused on her stitches. It was a struggle not to peer back up at him. She put all her effort into making an even hem, hardly noticing him place the notebook near. A new line of text had been added.

I teach you swim.

"Me?" She pointed to herself. "I don't think I could learn."

In his block script he wrote, *Not so hard.* He touched the word *swim* again.

When she braved a glance, his eyes were smiling. That was fair. It was unnerving the way his gaze immediately focused on her mouth when she started to speak. "You teach me to swim and I will teach you to dance."

With a quick shake of his head, he leaned back against the wall and folded his arms. The wood creaked against his strength. He studied her for such a long minute that she was further unsettled.

Finally, he wrote something more. *No dance. No swim. We fair?* His eyebrows tipped up in question.

He was releasing her, then? To her surprise, disappointment rushed her. Aven glanced around the room. First to the wall of windows where noon cast its glow, then to the fireplace that rested empty on this summer's day, then to the man across from her who was watching her as if her next words would mean much to him.

"How . . . how do I say *please?*" She held both hands out for him to know what she meant.

Thor pressed one of his own flat to his chest and moved it in a small circle.

Aven mimicked the motion, then pointed back to the word *swim*. "You will still teach me? Please?" The thought of him steadying her in the water was a perplexing one. But she trusted she would be safe.

Though his eyes widened, he nodded.

"Thank you."

He smiled, and it was even more captivating than Haakon's. Perhaps because of how rare it was. Or perhaps because she felt sheer delight at being on the receiving end of it.

Before she could make sense of such a thought, the kitchen door opened in a gust. Haakon called out. Aven glanced around the corner. Thor leaned that way as if realizing they were no longer alone. A trice later, Haakon declared utter exaltation over the pies, followed by the clatter of the silverware drawer.

Aven rose and pushed her basket aside. "Do not touch the pies!" She hurried into the kitchen just as Haakon stabbed his first bite.

He lifted it to his mouth, and her cry of despair was enough to freeze him into place.

"Don't touch *which* pie?" He glanced to the bite he had forked out of the steamy center, then back to her, looking as guilty as a person could look.

"Haakon!" Aven stared at the marred pastry.

Heavy boots stomped up the porch and Jorgan ducked in. "There's pie?" He trod nearer, stole Haakon's fork, and shoveled out a bigger mouthful.

Aven gasped. She turned for help, but there was only Thor, who was fetching his own eating utensil. He strode around the table, sat at the head, and pulled the second pie nearer. He stabbed a chunk of crust, then shoved it in his mouth. His approving grunt was her undoing.

"You all are wicked, wicked men." She unlaced her apron and pulled it off. After wadding it up, she threw it on the table.

"You're not upset, are you?" Haakon asked.

"They needed to cool for *after* supper."

Thor pointed to the dessert in front of him, then made several slow motions with one hand.

Haakon glanced at him. "My thoughts exactly."

He pulled the first pan into his lap, then propped his boots up on the edge of the table. He crammed a scoop of blackberries into his mouth.

Outnumbered, Aven sank onto the stool beside the pantry. "Ida would not stand for such behavior."

"But she's not in here," Haakon mumbled around a mouthful. "We didn't catch any fish, and I'm starving. Come have some too." He pulled out a chair for her. "It's not as good if you're mad at us."

Thor waved Aven nearer. When she didn't move, he gestured to Jorgan for another fork, then tried to coax her closer again. She shook her head, and he frowned. Thor lunged toward her, gripped her stool by one of the legs, and dragged her to his side.

Aven stared at him in shock. His arm brushed her own as he accepted the clean fork from his brother. After spearing a gooey piece of crust, Thor held it over. A response stunned right out of her, she took the metal handle.

He was watching her mouth, and there was a wanting in his eyes. One that told her actions spoke so much louder than words to him. When she didn't move, he shaped a phrase with his hands. Aven looked to Haakon for help.

"He said you'll be less upset if you have some. And that . . ." Haakon watched as Thor made several more gestures. "You are like a small bird."

"A what?"

"I'm not sure."

Thor patted the table loudly, and when he signed something different, Haakon seemed to catch on. "Oh. He said you're *thin* like a bird."

Thor circled two fingers around Aven's wrist as if to prove his point.

Haakon rose and reached for the milk bottle. "I think he means to fatten you up."

"So I see. 'Tis a concern for my well-being, is it?"

Thor nodded, and her intention of serving the pie on the lovely china from the cupboard was dying. Especially when he nudged her hand closer to her mouth. His expression ever so eager, she indulged him. And, oh, it was good. A smile twinkled in his eyes as she swiped a finger over her lips to catch the juice. Haakon celebrated with a whistle so shrill, she nearly choked. Thor patted her back much too hard, which made everything worse.

Tears forming, Aven wiped her eyes. "Now may I have a plate?" She rose and plucked one from the glass cabinet.

Thor flicked open his knife, cut a thick wedge, and loaded it onto the dainty dish for her. He licked the side of his blade clean, then stabbed the tip into the arm of his chair.

"Oh." That hadn't quite been what she had in mind. "Thank you . . . Thor."

When Haakon chuckled, Thor smiled at his brother, and Aven felt something between them being stitched back together.

Haakon licked a drop of purple juice from the base of his thumb. "This is the best pie I've ever had."

Aven sampled another bite. It *was* good. Warm and tangy . . . and she'd never had berries so plump and sweet to bake with before. Haakon lifted the jug of milk to his mouth.

Aven reached to stop him. "Be a good lad and pour me a glass before you do that."

He rose to fetch her one. "Can you make more stuff like this pie?"

"Certainly."

"With apple even? How about peach? Oh, and pumpkin."

"I can make whatever kind you wish. Cakes and even turnovers."

Dropping his pan onto the table with a clatter, Thor shaped a thought with his hands. Aven waited for Haakon to explain.

"He asked if you can make chocolate cream." Haakon filled a glass for her, then sat again.

" 'Twould be my joy."

Thor's chest lifted in a satisfied inhale. Aven breathed in deeply as well, savoring this moment and how different it was than her life before.

The breeze that blew in from the open window held the sweet ripening of the orchards. The curtains on the window stirred, and from somewhere in the distance, hoofbeats plodded along. The steady sound grew nearer, and Jorgan moved to the window. Grete barked.

Pushing his chair back, Thor rose. Aven glimpsed a weather-beaten wagon pulling up the drive. In the back was a stack of wide boards. Jorgan was somber now. Looking the same, Thor strode to the doorway, where he leaned a shoulder against the jamb. The wagon creaked to a stop in front of the cider barn. When Jorgan called Grete off, two men hopped down.

With a tip of his head, Thor motioned for Jorgan to follow. They shared a brief greeting with the deliverymen, then reached into the wagon, dragged down two boards apiece, and stacked them just in front of the shop door. The workers pulled down more and piled them there. Board after board after board.

Boots back up on the table, Haakon folded his hands behind his head and closed his eyes. Shooting out a heavy sigh, he looked none too pleased about whatever had just pulled into their lives.

TEN

Holding his pocket watch with a trembling hand, Thor read the time. Just past ten. Nearly twelve hours since his last drink. Over two days since the boards had been delivered. Time enough for him to brace for what was to come and for Jorgan and him to finish closing up the shop.

Morning sun poured through the window as if to mock him and his pounding head. He sipped the glass of water Ida had brought him, but it did little for his parched throat. Bowing his head, he dragged a hand through his hair and gripped the back of his throbbing neck.

During the last delivery, they'd sold enough liquor to keep their customers happy for a few weeks. Beyond that . . . Thor didn't want to think about it.

Now Jorgan was sealing over the last of the windows in the attic where Thor would keep himself. The light dimming, Thor glanced around. He didn't like the way the room was beginning to box him in, but it was safest. With three more swings, Jorgan drove another nail flush. He gave the final wooden slat a firm tug. It didn't budge.

Jorgan looked at him. "You doin' okay?"

Thor nodded as much to reassure himself as his brother. These early hours, miserable as they felt,

135

were just the beginning. He had a good four days of hell in front of him, and he was barely to the fiery gates.

Stomach in knots, Thor tried to remember what he'd sat down for. Oh . . . Aven.

Reaching under his bed, he dragged forward his box of odds and ends and lifted it beside him. He pulled out a tin with a hinged lid. Inside were trinkets he'd collected over the years. A small river rock he'd gathered on school holiday. Three Mohawk beads he and Jorgan had unearthed in the woods one spring. The eagle feather he'd found on the ridge with Da. Thor sifted through the rest of the items until he saw a glinting piece of metal. His mother's thimble.

He turned the thimble that was smaller than even the tip of his pinkie. The smooth shape of it reminded him of things forever lost, so he wasted no time riffling through the box some more. He dug until he found an old leather pouch. Thor dumped out the contents, tucked the token inside, and tugged the drawstrings.

Jorgan thumped the box. Thor looked up, and though his brother's mouth was moving, a wash of dizziness made it hard to understand.

"Haakon . . . wagon . . . time to . . ."

Running his fingers over his eyes, Thor rose. It was time to pick more berries. He quickly shook his head, but it did nothing to right the fogginess that hazed his mind. A final sip of water reminded him of why he was doing this. Of what he was trying to break free from.

Hammer in hand, Jorgan strode out and Thor followed. At Aven's door, Thor bent and set the pouch in the same place he'd left the photo, then headed on until he was downstairs. Stepping out into the bright sunlight, he squinted—pain shot through his forehead. Thor stumbled and, holding up a hand to the sun, blinked to try and right his vision.

Jorgan looked worried. Haakon, just irritated.

Aven was already seated. Thor climbed into the back, in no mood to drive. He closed his eyes and lowered his face into his hands. The wagon lurched forward, teasing more nausea into his gut. His body knew what it wanted—had been so deeply conditioned that going about the most basic of tasks suddenly felt like pouring water into a sieve and expecting it to stay.

The wagon jostled and jolted over the road. Had it always been this rough? Thor's misery grew with every quarter mile. When they stopped, he climbed down and dragged out pails.

Aven was chatting with Haakon. Thor carried several buckets into the deeps of the thicket where he could be alone, but he glanced back—unsure if he'd just seen Aven right. She was wearing an old pair of knickers that had to be Haakon's from years ago and a white shirt covering her that hung to her knees. Cinched at the waist with a belt, the shirt was one of his. He could tell by the pencil lead stains in the chest pocket and the way it nearly drooped over one of her small shoulders.

Her copper hair was pulled up and back. Tied with a strip of cloth, it flounced down her neck in soft waves. Realizing he was watching her longer than was chaste, Thor turned away.

He plucked berries from the hedge until his fingers were stained purple, and thorny scrapes sent his irritation into new realms of unreasonable. Thor drew in a heavy breath that had been one of many. Stretching his neck from side to side, he tried to loosen the tension there.

After a long while, he felt a tug on his shirt. Turning back, he saw Jorgan motioning him over to where Aven had unwrapped Ida's sandwiches for dinner. His stomach was still rolling, so Thor shook his head.

Jorgan nodded his understanding.

It was all he could do not to hurl into the bushes right now. Bread with cheese was not what he wanted. What he wanted was a drink.

Thor glanced at his stained hands. They were sticky and the same color of the wine he made every year. His mouth went wet with longing, and when the sensation turned sour, he held the back of his hand to his mouth. Closing his eyes, he inhaled the muggy forest air and sent a prayer to God for help.

Sweat slid down his temple. Slicked his back. Caring less and less about berries, Thor headed for the pond. He paid no attention to the others as he strode down the hill. Breeze hit his skin as he stripped off his shirt. Boots went next, and then he plunged beneath the cool surface. After holding his breath as long as he dared, he surfaced into the bright light of day. Thor pressed his forehead against the base of the dock and heaved in air.

Time twisted and bent. Playing tricks on his mind because when he felt stable enough to climb out, Aven was walking down the dock to him. Her bare feet were pale as cream, and he felt sicker and more soiled the closer she came. She smiled, and it made no sense to him. How anything about this day could possibly be good. Thor checked his mood, telling himself that it was just his body punishing his mind.

"Would it be a good time for you to show me about swimming?"

Lowering his head, he pinched his eyes closed. He was stupid not to have told her. It was best if she stayed away from him just now.

Desperate to help her understand, he patted his chest in search of his notebook, but there was only slick skin. He looked at Aven, that eager expression of hers, and wished for the countless time that he could speak.

Instead, he watched as Haakon strode nearer. "I

can show you what you want to learn, Aven." He hopped down to the mucky soil and reached to help her.

She looked back at Thor with a trace of hurt. This would look like a snub to her. Made worse in the way he'd distanced himself the last two days.

Haakon spoke, bridging a gap to Aven that Thor couldn't fill. "Besides . . . Thor can't sign and swim with you at the same time, so it'd be confusing. Come with me." He reached up for her again. "I'll get ya sorted out."

"I'm worried for Thor," Aven said. The poor man looked pale.

"He's not feelin' too good."

Thor climbed out of the pond and strode back along the length of the dock toward the grassy slope.

Sparking to heart was the memory of him across the table earlier in the week. Of his kindness and gentle ways. Yet, though he was becoming more and more dear, more a precious part of family to her, his addiction was a broken bridge between them. One that was nearly impossible for her to traverse. No matter how much she wanted to, she could not build it back up stone by stone. The work wasn't hers to do because the choice wasn't hers to make. If he wished it, she would be there to help him, but she'd learned firsthand that—as Cora had said—a man had to want it.

"Is there something that might help him?" she asked Haakon. Perhaps a drink of water or someone to sit by him. The longing arose to do those very things.

"Naw. He'd rather we just leave him alone. He'll take it easy. Come on."

Thor certainly looked like he wanted to be alone. Trying to loosen her worry for him, Aven let Haakon help her down.

He pointed toward a stand of reeds. "On the other side of that is another shallow. A pool of sorts."

She shielded her eyes to better see it.

"We can get to it from the other side but would have to wade through a bunch of mud, and this will be easier. You won't sink. You have my word. But . . ." The sun glinted on his bare shoulders as he looked down at her. "I'll have to swim you over there."

"Well . . ." Maybe this was all a bad idea.

Haakon waded farther out and turned to face her. Water sloshed against his pants. The sight of him made her think of every summer spent in the workhouse. There she had sat, bent over her sewing in the stifling air, dreaming of freedom.

And now it was right here. "Alright." She stepped closer.

When he explained how to paddle and kick, she mimicked his movements.

Something in his face told her he was trying not

to laugh. "I think we're just gonna have to give it a go. Hopefully we'll make it."

"Haakon!"

"We're not gonna drown. But I can see that's exactly what you're thinking. Take a deep breath."

Aye. Deep breath. Aven reached up to touch the chain at her throat but felt nothing, since she'd tucked her mother's necklace safely away for the day.

"Jorgan isn't far," Haakon added. "I'm a very good swimmer, but he'll be nearby if you panic. Also, Thor's a strong swimmer." He pointed to where Thor sat in the grass above watching them. "And lastly, I'm gonna have to hold you around the waist." Haakon wet his hands as he motioned for her to come nearer. "Don't scream or hit me or do anything rash until we get to the other side. Then you can blush all you want."

She wandered farther in. "No hitting. No screaming. I'll even promise not to blush."

He led them farther out until the water was up to her shoulders. Ripples broke against his chest. Thick mud oozed beneath her feet. Aven cringed, but then Haakon took her wrist and slid her arm across his shoulders. His skin was slick, and even as she blushed, he gripped her waist. She wedged her face near his shoulder so he wouldn't see the color that had to be blooming in her cheeks.

"Ready?" His voice was suddenly very near.

When she nodded, he pushed off, tugging her gently with him. All at once there was nothing but water all around. Panic rattled her, and she floundered.

"You're fine, I've got you." He held her against his side. "Just hold on—"

Her elbow bumped his chest, and he grunted but didn't lose his hold. With her free arm, she did as he had directed. 'Twas surely more hindrance than help. Still holding fast to her waist, he used his other arm to pull them through the water with strong strokes. His grip tightened as the water turned colder and murkier.

"It'll . . . help if you . . . kick," he panted.

She did, feeling like a falling fish. When they reached the little pool, he pushed her in front of him and Aven grabbed a handful of reeds, tugging herself into the shallow area. She slipped from the cold murkiness into sun-warmed water that was clearer and almost sandy. He pulled himself in behind her. She glanced back. Jorgan was still on the dock. Thor was nowhere to be seen.

"Was that so bad?" Haakon's eyes were smiling, lashes dark and wet. "You're breaking a promise. All you have to do is hit me and scream next."

Aven pressed both hands to her cheeks to cool them. "You're impossible."

Never had a man moved with more ease as he settled beside her. "This is nice, isn't it? You can sink down some if you want to. Just get comfortable with the water. Do you know how to hold your breath under the surface?"

"I'm afraid not."

He took a deep inhale, then dunked under. Bubbles rose until he came back up, swiping his face.

Aven stepped back. "I think I'd prefer not to do that."

"You're gonna have to."

"I don't know that I want to learn how to swim anymore."

"We've come too far for that kind of talk. Come on, I'll show you." He tugged her lower in the water, and while her knees bent, nothing else moved. "Aven, you're stiff as a dead duck. Try to relax." He shook her gently. "And you're gonna have to get your hair wet, but . . ." Haakon twirled a hand above her head as if to mimic the tie-up she had fashioned. "You're losin' somethin'."

"Oh." Aven touched her hair to feel the strip of cloth falling loose.

"You might want to hold on to it." He tapped his chest. "Maybe in that pocket."

It didn't feel proper to take her hair down, but he assured her it was common for swimming. Not wanting to lose the ribbon, she reached up, tugged it free, and pressed it into the damp pocket of Thor's shirt. Using both hands, she shook the bundle of her hair loose. The ends hit the water and dampened.

Like the ebbing rays of a sunset, Haakon's humor faded, his focus direct and quieted. Gone was the child in him, and in that place was a man. One a few months older than herself. Though youthful freckles lay scattered across his nose, she suddenly felt shadowed by him. A quick glimpse reminded her that his jaw was strong and square, and it took much effort to ignore the braw shape of his chest and shoulders.

Aven cleared her throat the same moment she realized that his hand was still at her waist. "Haakon?"

"Yes?"

"What are we to do now?"

"I—I . . ." He blinked quickly as if to come back from a faraway place. "I want you to practice going underwater. It'll be handy to know how. Help you . . . uh . . . learn not to panic." He seemed to be struggling for direction himself. "Pinch your nose if you want and hold your breath. Hold it for a few seconds, then come back up. I'll go with you. Ready?" After a slow count to three, he heaved in a breath and vanished under the surface.

Aven watched him flounder under the water.

Finally he popped back up, dripping and insolent. "Aven! What are you doing?" He swiped water from his face.

"I wasn't ready." A terrible student she was. 'Twas best that Thor was spared. "Perhaps if we go slower." She rubbed balmy water up her arms, then moved her feet to get used to the feel of the grit beneath. Rarely had she waded into a creek, let alone swam in a pond. There wasn't much water play at the Limerick Workhouse, save for rain puddles for the orphans and a birdbath near the laundry quarters for feathered visitors. Never in her adult life, until her wedding day to Benn, had she been outside its walls.

But this wasn't Benn. This was Haakon. And he looked like summer and a heady dose of freedom. A kind unlike she'd ever known.

Haakon nudged himself around her. Water swirled between them when he stopped. He mentioned trying a different approach. "You alright?"

"Oh, yes." She touched her temple.

Jorgan called out, "Haakon, we gotta go." He thumbed over his shoulder. "Thor's not doin' so well."

Aven looked around for Thor, but the effort was halted when Haakon took hold of her waist again, coaxing her toward the reeds and the dock just beyond. "Can I ask you a question of a personal nature?" He parted the thick grasses and she followed him. "Do you think you'll ever marry someone again?"

Though his inquiry struck the deepest longings

of her heart, she tried to keep her answer light. "I'd like to think so."

Circling his arm around her, he pulled them nearer to the cool pond. Her arm looped around his neck. "If you ever do . . . ," he began softly. Those stunning blue eyes locked with her own as he eased them into deeper water. "Do you think it could be me?"

"Haakon!" Her flounder nearly sank them both.

Sputtering, he tugged her higher above the surface and gave her a reproachful look. But her cry had already echoed across the pond.

"You don't know what you're saying," she whispered. Kicking her feet only seemed to mar his rhythm.

Needing to distance herself from him, Aven's arms moved of their own accord, but she was as buoyant as a stone until he braced her against his side again. Nerves rising, she kicked wrong, paddled wrong, and even seemed to be breathing wrong.

Alarm twisted inside her. "I feel I'm going under."

His fingers dug to grip her shirt as if he worried the same. To her relief, though, his voice was calm. "We'll be there in just a moment. You're gonna have to trust me. Please calm down."

She did as he asked, and he worked them through the water, slow and steady.

Water sloshed as they neared the dock. She

reached out to grab a piece of the under framing. Haakon moved her closer against it, beseeching her to look at him. At the sound of her name and the way he spoke it, Aven faced him. His arm rose above her head, hand gripping a board to hold them in place. Without warning he pressed his mouth to hers. Warm and quick and tender.

Her breath caught. Though having hungered to be kissed for years, she'd set such fancies aside for sheer need to survive from day to day. She'd given no heed to the void, doing all she could to ignore the ache of loneliness until this moment when Haakon's tenderness sang through her. So near was he, so gentle and real, that she indulged in the tiniest taste—kissing him back for the briefest, most sweetest of seconds.

The sound of satisfaction rose from his throat, breaking her from her trance.

What was she doing? Pushing him away sent her slipping beneath the surface without his hold. Water rushed overhead, murky and cold. He grabbed her and pulled her back up. She gasped and coughed and with his help managed to grip the dock. With the back of a shaking hand, she swiped across her mouth.

Ripples lapped against his chest as he leaned to kiss her again.

Aven shifted away. So tight was her hold on the boards that her knuckles went white. "Haakon, no."

A quick call from Jorgan accentuated her plea. Haakon shot his gaze up the dock where footsteps approached.

"Please go away," she said in a rush.

He heaved out a sigh but pulled himself around the side of the dock, then started up the bank.

Aven clung there. Water swirled all around. How to move from this spot? To her relief, Jorgan looked over the edge and spotted her.

"Haakon!" he called over his shoulder. "You just left her here!"

"Sorry!" Haakon snapped back.

Jorgan reached for Aven's hand. He helped her along until her feet struck soil.

The world spun as she climbed to the top of the bank. Aven wiped gritty hands on the wet knickers and fought the urge to sink to the grass. Haakon heaved himself into the wagon and sat as far from Thor as possible.

When Aven climbed up to the seat, she nearly stumbled. Thor gripped her wrist, steadying her. His unbound hair was dried from the sun, but the shadows under his eyes had deepened.

A regret she couldn't make sense of tightened her throat. She thanked him weakly and, settling onto the narrow bench, wished she could become smaller.

Nay, wiser.

ELEVEN

Aven plaited her damp hair into a braid as she left her room. Upon their return from the pond, Jorgan had asked her to meet him on the porch. So while he and Haakon unhitched the team, she'd gone upstairs to change. Best that she couldn't see the horse barn from her room for she couldn't bear to look upon Haakon just now. Her mind still stirred from his words. The tenderness his kiss had borne. Oh, what had she done?

With Jorgan awaiting her, there was no time to sit and ponder it.

Downstairs, she pushed out onto the front porch that ran the length of the house. Jorgan sat on the swing, slowly turning his hat in his hands, gaze on the floor. The swing creaked when she took the place beside him.

"You may have noticed that Thor's under the weather," he said.

"Aye."

"He hasn't had anything to drink today, so he's runnin' a little dry."

Thor hadn't drank today?

"He's doin' it on purpose." Jorgan used his hat to point toward the cider shop.

Aven saw afresh the boards that had been nailed over the door and windows. Was that the reason behind the board-up? She had thought they meant to prevent robbers. Never had she imagined it was to keep Thor out. "Is he going to be alright?"

"He should be. But the worst of it is gonna take about a week. The next few days will be hardest. He's already feelin' it."

Such a challenging choice this was for Thor. Was he truly trying to turn his back on the bottle? Hope stirred in the farthest reaches of her heart. "What can I do?"

Hitching one leg up, Jorgan rested that ankle on his knee. He gripped the top of his boot with both hands. "Just keep doin' what you're doin'. You're always a help, and we're grateful. More than we tell you." With his other foot he nudged the swing forward and back. "Aven, he's gonna be *real* sick. He's gonna be angry and hassled. He's afraid of these days 'cause of how it went last time."

Last time?

"When the terrors kick in, it's different for Thor than for most people. Without being able to hear, reading signs or lips is gonna be real hard for him when he's sick."

She never would have thought of that. There was so much of Thor she didn't understand. A grace that Jorgan was explaining it to her now. Yet gratitude was trampled beneath her sorrow for Thor and all that he faced. All that he lived with.

"Because of that, there'll be almost no reasoning with him. There will be no use explaining much to him or giving words of comfort. We have to keep him as calm as we can and keep him—and others—safe."

She looked back to the boards across the shop door.

"Cora's with him now, keepin' an eye on him. Al's here too. For more manpower."

She was scared to ask what for. Thor's size and strength were answer enough.

"It's real important that you don't go up to the attic."

"I understand."

"Thor made me ask you to promise."

Did he? "I promise. Please tell me what I can do."

He gave her a brotherly smile—muted and protective. "Just seein' after him from down here will be enough. We'll take up his meals and such and be with him through all hours. We'll all be stretched pretty thin. You as well."

To inquire into their past with this felt so personal, but it also felt necessary. "May I ask what went wrong the last time?"

Settling his boots to the porch, Jorgan stilled the swing. "No matter what you hear, or see, or how bad it might seem for us—Haakon or Al or even Cora—I need you to stay downstairs." He looked at her, and she realized that was the only answer he was going to give.

"I promise I will. You have my word."

• • •

It was an oven up here. Gripping the edge of the mattress, Thor bowed his head. Sweat spread along his skin. It made his shirt cling to his back and abdomen. He gave a few quick tugs to try and cool himself down. Even the water he sipped seemed hot. He was tired of drinking it, but Cora had insisted he have at least a few glasses a day. At the rate salty stickiness was beading on his skin, he was going to need it. Using his sleeve, Thor wiped the side of his face.

Cora had taken his pulse, and with worry in her pinched mouth, she wrote down the number before stepping out. She had cause for concern. The way his heart kept speeding up and slowing down was making him uncomfortable. Thor pressed a hand to his chest as someone passed through the doorway.

Cora set a tray on the bed beside him. Next she dipped a rag into a bowl of clear water, wrung it out, and smoothed a cool compress to his forehead. He closed his eyes.

When she rinsed the rag again, he watched her chocolate-brown hands. They were strong and weathered. Shaped by years of doctoring hurts and bringing babies safely from their mother's wombs.

She'd been there the day he was born. Helping him into this world where they say he squalled with such abandon, the neighbors heard. His cord was so thick, it had taken Cora several tries to sever it. She'd weighed him on the farm scale, and with him two ounces over eleven pounds, Ma shed tears of pride and exhaustion, and Da was so proud, he joked that he was going to take Thor to the county fair for the blue ribbon.

Cora often told him the story when he was a boy. It always ended there.

Because then she'd passed Thor into the arms of a mother who wouldn't know it was the last infant she would raise. Or that seven years later when Haakon came along, a bout of seizing would pull her into the dark. Taking her from this life just hours after Haakon's first cries had made her smile.

Cora pulled a small device from her bag and pressed it to Thor's chest, listening through the other end. He tried to hold still. After a few moments, Cora put her tool away. The rag was still near, and she dipped it into the bowl again. Her lean fingers glistened when she twisted it. After a few more brushes of the cool compress to his skin, she gently touched his arm where the stitches still were. A small pair of scissors glinted as Cora took them out of her medic bag. They occupied her palm unthreateningly as her eyebrows lifted in question.

Thor gave a single nod and to his relief, the stitches came out a lot easier than they went in.

She spread fresh ointment over the healing scar and bandaged it snug.

Anxiousness rising, Thor shifted his boots and looked across the room to where Al sat on the other bed. The young man was somber as he watched Thor. Earlier, they'd all agreed not to let Cora in the attic without another man near, and Thor was grateful. He'd already hurt Ida the last time he attempted this, bruising her thin form when she rushed to help during the terrors. When it came to the two women who'd raised him, he couldn't stomach the notion of bringing them harm. Or any other woman.

He tried not to think of Aven and was relieved that she'd made her promise to Jorgan.

Cora folded the rag again and rested the soft coolness to the back of his neck.

She'd cautioned him against quitting abruptly, and while he knew it was riskier, he'd failed at tapering off in years past. Something about being able to have even a little derailed him. Despite her worry—or because of it—Cora was here now.

Except he couldn't shake the notion that if she truly wanted to be of use, she'd put something stronger than water in that glass. Unwanted irritation swarmed his mind. Thor pinched the bridge of his nose.

Thumb to the inside of his wrist, Cora held it there for a minute, then wrote another number. Al shifted his feet, looking as relaxed as a man could look in his position. He glanced to the boarded-up windows, then back to Thor. Worry drew Al's dark brows together. For just reason. The need to tear something apart was putting a crease in Thor's own brow.

Thor gripped the mattress harder when Cora slid the rag down his temple.

Slow breath in, slow breath out.

She wet the cloth again and pressed it to the other side of his face. A few droplets struck the top of his thigh, sinking through his pants where they seemed to sizzle against his skin. What was she putting on him? Confusion buzzed around the edge of his mind, and Thor jerked his head away. So sharply that Cora froze. Slowly, Al rose to his feet.

It took all of Thor's strength not to move. Desperate was the urge to push something. Shove something. Break *anything* to be rid of this sensation. One that ached even into his bones.

God help him, he needed a drink.

Impatience throttling him from the inside out, Thor rose and paced. With a wave of his hand, he motioned them out.

Cora and Al exchanged glances, and she gathered things onto her tray.

Something in the back of his mind told him he should be more polite, but the thought was overwrought with a need to vomit. Ida had placed a bucket beside his bed for that very purpose. He'd be using it before the hour was out.

Thor grabbed up the glass on the table, took a sip, his face skewing at the taste of water. He set the glass aside so fast it tipped over. Liquid pooled across the desk. Furious, he clutched the glass and was about to chuck it against the wall when he stopped himself. Hand shaking, he dropped the cup on his bed and stepped away.

What was wrong with him?

At a tremor in the floor, he looked to see Haakon step in, Jorgan right behind.

Thor drew in a deep breath and hoped he appeared calmer than he felt.

Haakon sat on his own bed and bent to tie a shoelace. When he straightened, it seemed like something was on his mind. Haakon rubbed his hands together. Back and forth. And back and forth.

Sitting, Thor watched him.

Finally Haakon glanced from him to Jorgan. "We try not to keep secrets from one another, so I need to tell you both something."

An itch at his arm, Thor rubbed it.

Haakon ran a hand down his face and must have spoken in that same instant because Jorgan jolted. The man stood straight as a pole, mouth falling a notch.

"You what?" Jorgan asked, eyes wide.

Thor darted a look back to his younger brother, who spoke again. "I kissed Aven."

Thor blinked. Rubbed that itch in his arm again. Haakon . . . did what?

"I'm sorry if that was a stupid thing to do," Haakon added.

Jorgan looked like he wanted to throttle him.

Haakon? And Aven? Thor went to stand, but he couldn't. God help him, he was going to stand. He must have managed because the room started spinning, and Haakon rose as well.

Jorgan made the sign for *when?*

"In the pond. By the dock. When we were all there."

This had to be part of the delirium. It was already kicking in. There was no other way for it to make sense. This sadness that was overcoming him.

Jorgan's gaze narrowed. "Is that what you were doing down there?"

Haakon nodded, and when he looked at Thor, something shifted in Haakon's confidence. It was followed by a wary step back.

"What did she do?" Jorgan asked.

Haakon pointed down the hall to where Aven was, then pursed the fingertips on both hands, pressing them together. He tapped his chest next and made the sign for *same*.

She felt the same? Or kissed him back?

What did it matter?

158

Haakon squared his shoulders. "I also asked her to marry me. I didn't do a good job of it, and I should tell her I'm sorry." He looked at Thor. "But I also won't take it back. She seemed surprised, but she didn't decline either."

Needing to be free of this room, Thor moved to push past Jorgan, ignoring the sight of Haakon trying to talk to him.

Jorgan stepped in his way. Hands to Thor's chest, Jorgan braced him. "You need to stay here."

Thor shook his head and went to push past again, but then Jorgan spoke her name.

Next he signed it. *A-V-E-N.*

The fight to leave waned. Arms limp at his sides, Thor watched his brother's hand shape the letters again, more slowly, and Jorgan might as well have been shaping Thor's ache for her. His sorrow.

Jorgan sent Haakon out, and as Thor watched his younger brother depart, he forced himself to step deeper into the room. Desperate for his jar of cider, he glanced around, but it wasn't there. Jorgan closed the door and slid a chair in front of it to keep watch.

Palm to his forehead, Thor closed his eyes.

He needed that bucket now. He dragged it close as sickness churned his gut. Bending to await it, he tucked his hands in his lap. *A-V-E-N.* His fingers shook as he shaped the name his

159

brother just had. Blinking at the floor, a wet heat dampened his lashes. Thor bowed his head and focused on breathing.

It took all the strength he had. Because now he'd loved two women in his life, and Haakon had taken them both.

TWELVE

Counting by twos, Aven moved fourteen pint jars from the bottom shelf of the pantry to the kitchen table. She washed them with hot soapy water, boiled each one, then spread everything on towels to steam dry. Beside the pot of bubbling water sat another pot where Aven scooped out eight cups of sugar. She dumped in a pail of berries, then went out to the porch for another.

She startled at the sight of a young man standing at the base of the steps. Hat in hand, his brow was dewy as if he'd walked some ways to get there. His hair was flaxen and as closely shorn as a field after a scything. Eyes a light brown and unmistakably familiar. The young Sorrel man from church. One of the neighbors who had caused so much trouble for them.

She took a step back.

"Evenin', ma'am." His gaze drifted to the collapsed, charred wood crib, then back to her. Unlike before, he didn't study her as closely and instead dropped his focus to her shoes. "I'm lookin for Mr. Thor."

"He's . . . uh . . . he's in the middle of something. Will be for the rest of the day."

"Oh, I see." Though clearly disappointed, the young man's eyes finally lifted to hers. "Might you tell him I came by? I was wonderin' if he's still hirin' pickers for the harvest. I could use the work."

Bending, Aven hefted up the bucket with both hands. "I will pass along your inquiry."

"Thank you, ma'am." He slid on his hat as he started away.

"Your name, sir?" She couldn't recall what Haakon had called him.

He turned some. Gave a sad smile. "Peter, ma'am."

She nodded and watched as he walked back down the road.

Haakon was standing at the stove when she returned to the kitchen, and it was a different kind of startling she felt this time. One that sent a surge of uncertainty straight through her heart. How did temptation and caution collide so boldly in Haakon's presence?

"Was someone out there?" he asked, the first they'd spoken since the pond.

"His name was Peter."

Haakon paced to the window. After a few moments he turned back to her. "Did he bother you?"

"No. He was looking for Thor. Inquiring about work." And honest work, at that.

"Thor's not gonna hire a Sorrel."

"I assured him I would pass along the message."

Haakon rubbed a thumb across his bottom lip,

162

making no further response as he watched her. Aven lifted up the bucket of berries, rested it on the edge of the pot, and tipped them in.

"What are you doing? Thor needs those."

She shot out a breath. My, if he wasn't also trying to one's patience. "Your brother is the one who asked me to do this. He's worried they won't keep."

Haakon's forehead pinched. "What are we gonna sell?"

"I'm not sure." She reached for a long wooden spoon and tried to ignore how near he stepped to her.

"So we're gonna live on jam now, huh? That's just wonderful. First there's you, Miss Warm-And-Then-Cold in the water. Then there's a Sorrel knockin' on the door. And if that's not enough, I'm about a day away from gettin' my face smashed in again by my brother."

There was a time to stay quiet and let the hurting express what they needed to say. Perhaps something she'd learned in living life among the broken and the suffering. All crushed into place together by fate and circumstance. So soft came an answer. "I owe you an apology about that. The water, that is. I should not have reacted so hastily."

"I don't want an apology." At a bump from upstairs, Haakon leaned toward the great room.

"Do you need to go up there?"

He listened a moment longer. "I don't think so. Jorgan's gonna sit with him for a few hours. Then I will."

Aven turned to stir the berries. The juices were running now, soaking up the sugar. With Haakon having grown quiet, she thought on his other complaints. One in particular was alarming. "Did Thor hurt you? Some time ago?"

Haakon opened one side of the pie safe and pulled out a biscuit. The pastry flaked as he broke it in half. "I don't wanna talk about Thor."

"I'm talking about *you*."

Vulnerability pulled Haakon's gaze to hers. He set the biscuit on the counter and slid the butter dish near. "I was younger then, so I was smaller." The lid clanged as he lifted it. "I'll be fine now." He opened a drawer, and when he failed in finding a butter knife, Aven handed him one she'd just washed.

He thanked her. Brow pinched, Haakon smeared butter onto the biscuit then, using a spoon, scooped out a dollop of the softening berries. He drizzled the fruit onto his biscuit, looking lost in thought. "It was a couple of years ago. Thor kinda lost his mind. He said later that it felt like somethin' was crawlin' on him. He just couldn't handle it, I suppose."

Haakon pressed the two pieces of biscuit together and licked his thumb. "I tried to hold him but couldn't. He'd smashed my head into

164

the window by the time Jorgan made it upstairs. Even Ida came runnin', and Thor bumped her around more than he would have ever meant to. She'd tried to help Jorgan steady 'im. It's why they boarded up the windows this time."

Aven didn't realize the wooden spoon was dripping in her hand until Haakon took it and set it aside.

Pushing back the short hair at his temple, he ran his pinkie along the jagged white line of a scar. Then he bent his ear forward, showing that the back side was marred. "And this"—he pointed to his nose—"was broke in two places." Haakon chomped a bite, then a second. He mumbled around the mouthful. "Thor's really strong. And when he's scared, it's like herdin' a spooked bull."

Fresh to mind was the way Thor had pulled her from the shed. How hard she'd fought back and how iron his grip had been. Their fall and his crushing weight. How, no matter the ways she'd fought back, he'd dragged her up from the ground like she was a rag doll.

Aven lifted her gaze to the ceiling, and something else tugged at her heart. The memory of him helping her down the bank. Of him sitting across the table from her. His ideas and his books. His words written—the gentle sound of his voice when he put it to paper or shaped it with his hands. The look in his eyes as if he had so much he wanted to say to her but didn't know how.

"He watches you, you know." Haakon leaned back against the wooden countertop.

"He watches many people," she countered, not liking how close he'd gotten to the truth. "It's how he knows what's being said."

Haakon shook his head. "It's different."

At a thump at the door, she was grateful for the need to walk over and open it. 'Twas Ida standing there. At least she was quite certain it was Ida. The gray-haired woman carried a mound of blankets and pillows so tall it nearly toppled. Aven took some.

"These for makin' up beds," Ida said.

"Where do you want them?"

"Jus' downstairs. Cora can sleep on the sofa. Al won't mind the floor none."

Aven followed Ida that way. With the jam needing to stew, she set about helping to tuck and fold blankets and slide cases onto pillows. By the time they finished, the light was so dim that Ida checked the kerosene in the lantern. At the desk there, she slid an envelope from her apron pocket. "Cora fetched the mail in town last she was there. Brought it just now. Somethin' came for you, Aven."

Aven thanked her and slipped the envelope into her skirt pocket.

Ida pulled out a second envelope and placed it

on the desk. "And this for Jorgan. A letter from his Fay." She winked.

Haakon strode past, snatching it from the wooden surface. At the window he pressed it to the glass, but there wasn't enough light to illuminate the papers inside.

"Haakon Norgaard." Ida put her hands on her hips. "I'm gonna swat you."

He sniffed the envelope, then handed it back. "You're no fun."

"And *you* need to go get some sleep. 'S gonna be a long night." Ida limped around the great room, plucking up odds and ends of the brothers' messes.

Haakon grabbed one of the pillows and carried it out to the front porch. He smashed it against an arm of the swing and settled in. His legs dangled over the other end, and folding his arms, he closed his eyes. The sunset beyond was vibrant streaks of rose and gold. A gentle breeze stirred, and a soft rustling came from the orchard where countless leaves trembled.

Back in the kitchen, Aven checked her pots. She stirred the thick, bubbly goodness and added a splash more water. Ida had put up pectin early in the summer—made from the baby apples that had been thinned from the orchard—so Aven dipped into the crock and ladled out enough syrup to thicken the jam.

With time left for it to cook and with the letter

now on her mind, Aven slipped upstairs. In her room she pulled the envelope out and tore off the end. She unfolded the pages and read. It was an answer to the inquiries for employ that Jorgan had helped her post. Mentioned within the folds was a sewing position in a place called Lexington. A victory, aye, but reading on, Aven gleaned that it was almost forty miles away. So short a span in light of the ocean she had crossed, but now that this family had become her own, forty miles felt as far. Visiting would need to be sparse, if at all.

Aven read on. The employment offered room and board. Such a luxury. And with a modest wage as well, 'twas a blessing beyond all hope. Yet sorrow crept in at the thought of such a distance. Aven slid the letter away. There would be time enough in the coming days to form a response.

For now, she adjusted the loose ties of her apron, steadied uncertainties, and forced her mind back to the tasks at hand. She slipped out and turned to close the door when something at her foot caught her attention. Nestled into the shadow of the doorjamb lay a small leather pouch. When had that arrived? In the same spot the wedding photograph had been, no less.

Aven picked it up. She loosened the drawstrings and, peering inside, spotted a glint of metal.

'Twas a wee thimble.

She pressed it to her fingertip. A perfect fit.

There was only one man who would think to give her this. She slid the token back in the pouch where it would be safe and, glancing up toward the attic door, whispered a prayer of strength for the man who was suffering behind it.

THIRTEEN

His stomach was sorrier than an overused barrel. Warped and useless. The ache in his gut throbbing, Thor opened his eyes. Where was he? His hand bumped a pillow. In bed, then. The inside of a working still would have been cooler than his throat. He swallowed but it did nothing for the burn. He looked over to see a clean pail, and though his belly was about to heave again, he just needed to be outside. Now.

Shifting to sit, he saw Haakon in the dim light. Slumbering with his chest to the bed, the runt was draped over the mattress nigh to unconscious. Moonlight seeped through the window as strangely angled slits. Why were the windows covered? It was a struggle to stand, but after he did, Thor crossed to the door.

His feet felt bare, but he didn't look down. If he moved his head that far, he'd regret it. He wobbled, catching himself against the doorjamb with a wince. Though the vise on his skull couldn't be real, he ran a hand there to make sure.

He didn't know how he got down the stairs and through the house, but it was the sheer rolling in his stomach that pushed him toward the yard. He stumbled down the porch steps and fell to his knees in the dark. He'd hoped to get farther, but this would have to do. As his stomach heaved, all he could think about was water and how he was never going to drink the stuff ever again. Finished, Thor swiped his sleeve over his mouth. Not ready to stand, he pushed himself back to sit on the bottom step.

Two moons hovered in the sky, neither holding still.

More nausea rising, Thor stumbled into the yard, gripped his thighs, and bent as his stomach fought to scrape itself clean. Someone was poisoning him with water, that's what it was. A proper drink would set this to rights. Seeing his shop in the dim light, he made it that way and sank against the door, panting.

He reached for the handle. It wouldn't turn. A few choice words came to mind as he recalled that he'd locked it himself. Thor let his hand slip from the knob, and it bumped along the boards. The wooden barricade would keep the cidery barred shut, even if he managed to find the key. But he wouldn't find the key because for some stupid reason he'd slipped it out of reach beneath the door. When had he done that? Bending, Thor squinted to see if the key was near. His fingers fumbled the gap.

If he just had a pry bar.

A flash of white overhead told him the great owl was on the move—fleeing the darkness that had become a tomb for them both. Thor blinked up at the sky that was graying with dawn. The shift toyed with his balance but he caught himself.

Where was Jorgan? And Haakon? Ida? He needed them.

Even Aven.

One of them would help him.

The vise tightened. Thor pinched his eyes closed, a sour stinging his throat. Pry bar. He tried to jam the thought into what was left of his sanity. He kept one in the nearest shed.

He straightened and didn't know how long it took to find the iron tool, but he was sweating by the time he sank back against the door of the cider barn. And itching. Something crawled against his skin. He rubbed at his forearm. It was just his imagination. But it itched mighty bad so he scratched at it. Sweat slid down his spine as he rammed the pry bar behind one of the boards and pulled with all his might.

Which wasn't much.

Something was wrong with him. Cider would fix it. Or wine. He'd even settle for 'shine if he could get some. Thor pulled on the metal bar again, felt the board crack under the force.

But, Lord help him, his skin was itching. He dropped the tool and swatted at his arms— at whatever was on him—heart racing at a maddening speed. Thor sank to one knee, rubbing the outside of his arm against his pants to try and scrub the sensation away.

The sky hazed lighter. He blinked against the splintering brightness as a glow lifted over the treetops. His heart thrashed so hard it hurt. With the rain barrel near—and this itch worsening—Thor rammed his sleeves up and splashed water on his face and arms. It soaked his hair. Sitting, he leaned against the barrel in the shadow of his shop.

Early dawn cooled his damp shirt and he began to tremble. It moved through his body with such force that he could scarcely scratch at his wrists. The back of his neck. His abdomen. But the crawling on his skin wouldn't stop. A sob rose up his throat.

Suddenly a hand was against his face. So soft that he turned his cheek into it. He opened his eyes. Aven.

Her mouth was moving in speech, but his vision wouldn't focus. Gripping the rim of the barrel, Thor pulled himself to stand. The motion made his stomach seize and cramp. Down to his knees, he heaved, but there was nothing left. Those small hands held his shoulders. He wanted to shove her back, but something deep down and far away told him not to hurt her.

She smeared his damp hair from his face. He pressed her hand away. His own was shaking so bad he couldn't shape the words he sought.

He needed her help to get into the cidery.

If he just had the key. All he needed was the key.

He tried to form the word again. Did Aven have the key? Was that why she was here? Thor gripped the fabric of her skirt, pulling her closer. If she had it . . . she could give it to him. Aven. If he could only say her name. Key—if he could only form the word.

Maybe if he could write it. But his chest pocket was wet and empty. He needed to get to the house for some paper. Thor rose and took but a few steps before he fell, knees hitting the dirt hard. He caught himself with his hands before the rest of him collided. He gasped for a breath, needing to slow his heart. He scratched at his wrists. Felt the grit of dirt there. Why was he outside?

Aven was gone. Or had that been his mother?

No, he didn't have a mother. It had to have been Aven. Maybe she was going to bring him something to drink. Maybe if he asked nicely. He pressed a shaking hand to his chest, trying to form the word *please*.

His vision blurred as his eyes rolled back. Suddenly the sky was upside down. A fierce pain split the side of his head, and he knew the ground well enough when he rolled onto his side. Tender hands lifted his head, then his face moved against something soft. A woman's lap. He knew it by the apron pocket and the curve of her waist where he suddenly clutched, desperate for help.

Aven.

She was calling out something—her abdomen

sinking and rising in fast jolts against his temple. She moved, pressing her ear to his chest, her breath warm and soft against him.

Aven could feel Thor's heart thrash along like a raging train. Her cries for Jorgan brought him bursting out of the house, flinging a shirt over his shoulders. Jorgan sank to her side and shouted for Haakon.

"His heart is racing," she said.

Jorgan pressed a thumb to Thor's wrist and waited a few moments. "Aven, there's a sack under your wardrobe with two jars of cider."

"What?"

"Trust me, it's there. I put it there. Run and fetch one."

She shifted Thor to the ground, then ran into the house. Upstairs, she sank in front of the wardrobe and peered beneath. There was the sack. She tugged it out and grabbed a heavy jar, the glass cold to her fingers. Was this wrong? Was this what Thor would want? But when Jorgan hollered her name, Aven rose.

She ran down the stairs and out onto the back porch just as Haakon and Jorgan were carrying Thor to the water trough.

"What are you doing?" she cried.

They dropped him in. He sank below the surface before the two brothers reached down and pulled him back up. Soaked, Thor gasped.

"You're going to kill him!" she screamed.

"He was unconscious! And I need him back." They lowered Thor to the ground. Jorgan loosened the top buttons of Thor's shirt, the plaid sopping and dark.

At a clatter in the kitchen, Aven glanced to the window to see Cora rushing a kettle from the stove. Ida pulled a tin of herbs from the shelf so fast, more tins toppled.

Jorgan shook his brother and lifted his eyelids. "Come on, Thor." As he patted the man's cheeks, he looked up at Haakon. "Get the doctor. Now."

Haakon ran off toward the barn.

"What's happening?" Aven sank beside Thor. Her chin trembling, she gently lifted his head and slid her knees beneath it, holding him up as best she could.

"I need you to get back," Jorgan said.

Aven shook her head.

Cora rushed in, tipping an herby drink to Thor's lips. "This should calm him." She dripped some into his mouth.

His face skewed in disgust. Cora urged him to take more, but he shoved the cup away, spilling it. Defeat warred with determination in the woman's eyes. Aven's hope faltered. Without his wanting it, Thor couldn't be made to do anything.

As if knowing it was a losing battle, Jorgan turned for the cider. Immense sadness in his eyes brought to Aven the burn of tears. Jorgan loosened the lid, lifted Thor's head, and tipped the jar to his brother's mouth. Amber liquid dripped into Thor's beard. Aven gently wiped it away with her skirt.

"Come on, man," Jorgan said, then whispered the same in Norwegian.

He tipped the liquor again. More cider spilled away, but then Thor swelled in a gasp and sputtered. He grabbed the jar, bending forward to drink hungrily. He gulped down half of the brew, then coughed, dropped the glass, pulled himself forward, and heaved it all out. His arms shook so fiercely that Aven reached across his wracking back and held him about the waist.

His weight was more than she could support until Jorgan moved to the other side to bear the most. Thor was heaving nothing but air now, but his body wouldn't stop. Not until he went limp and they eased him back down. Aven cradled his head as Jorgan pressed an ear to his chest.

"Do not fail him." He said it low and urgent as if the heart could be commanded so. When Cora called for Jorgan's help, he stood and hurried back inside.

Aven used the edge of her skirt to wipe the cider from Thor's mouth. She said his name. Tried to tell him that they were with him and would never leave him. But the words flitted right past. Desperate for him to know, she pressed her lips to his forehead. "You're not alone," she whispered.

She kissed his skin again, minding not the saltiness as she slid her hands against his collar, splaying it farther open as if that alone would make the breaths come easier. Water dripped down her fingers. She grazed a hand over his ear and wept his name.

His eyes were closed, and knowing he'd never hear her, she clung to him and cried out to the God who could.

FOURTEEN

Aven paced across the hallway and then back. Faint shuffling and a few thuds sounded from the attic where the doctor was with Thor. Jorgan and Cora had gone up as well. What was happening? Aven wandered back and forth for a few more minutes before the attic door opened.

She moved aside to be out of the way. The doctor came down first. He slid on a black hat, a handled bag of the same glossy color in his grip. The door closed softly as Cora and Jorgan followed just behind.

The doctor gave Aven a polite nod in passing, and she trailed them all down. Haakon was in the kitchen, straddling a chair, and Ida was fresh from the garden with a basket of vegetables in tow. The doctor left, and everyone seemed to be waiting on someone to speak.

Jorgan pulled near his own chair and sat. "The doctor said there wasn't anything else we could be doin' for Thor, but that it's up to him and what his body can handle. And obviously, the Lord."

"And his heart?" Haakon asked.

"The doctor didn't like the sound of it but said there's little that can be done. Said Thor's young and strong and that it should hold out fine. What the doc is more worried about is his liver, which can't be doin' too well just now. Cora's gonna fix something for him to take that should help."

Worry threaded so tightly through Aven that she could scarcely ask the next question. "And for his unease?"

"Doc wants him to keep with the teas Cora suggested. He gave us some medicine, too, that should help him sleep. Gettin' Thor to take the medicine was harder than gettin' him to drink anything we've tried before, so I don't know how much help it will be."

Oh, the state Thor had to be in. Was there nothing she could do?

Weariness and worry stayed companions with them in the kitchen. Cora went out for some air, and Haakon went to see to the afternoon chores. Looking like he was ready to sleep for a week, Jorgan mentioned that he needed to head back upstairs.

"I need another bowl and some rags, though." He opened a low cupboard.

Aven hurried to get a large enamel bowl, and Jorgan fetched the rags that had been washed and dried that morning. When he returned upstairs, Ida watched as Aven resumed her restlessness. 'Twas a relief when the dear housekeeper suggested a batch of crackers for Thor.

"Wonderful idea." Aven rinsed her hands and dried them. Why were they shaking?

Because she remembered this very time in a flat far away.

When it was Benn and not Thor fighting for release.

Grateful for the task, Aven set the jar of flour on the table. A tin cup served to measure out several scoops into a bowl. Next she scraped a hefty dollop of butter from the crock and fetched the baking soda. When the dough was rolled and cut into squares, she placed each one on a baking sheet, pricked them with a fork, and dusted the tops with salt. Into the oven they went. She was tidying up her mess when Haakon went up to relieve Jorgan, who came down a minute later. He sank into a chair at the table.

Aven poured coffee, stirred in cream, and set the hot mug on the table just as Ida slid a plate of stew beside it.

Aven suppressed her wondering until he'd taken a few bites. "How is Thor faring?"

Jorgan lifted his gaze. "He's still thick as thieves with that bucket, but he's hangin' in there all the same. Tonight will be the worst." He stabbed a slice of potato and stirred it in the gravy. "I'm gonna try and get some sleep before he wakes. I'm worried he and Haakon are gonna have a rough time of it."

When Jorgan polished off his meal, he ducked from the kitchen and collapsed on the sofa.

Within moments the man was still as stone, all save his chest that rose and fell in slumber.

'Twas a few hours later that Haakon came down. He dropped a pile of laundry on the porch. Without a word he returned upstairs. Only minutes passed when there was a ruckus followed by a clatter. The attic door opened and slammed. Haakon was back in the kitchen, tossing another bundle of cloths onto the porch.

"He's impossible!"

"I can send up more tea." Ida reached for a tin of herbs.

"There's no point." Haakon took up the bar of soap and wet his hands. "It's just gonna come back up."

"This takes time."

The bar slipped from his grip and onto the floor. "You know what?" Haakon banged the soap into the washbin. "I'm gonna go take a bath." He stormed toward the door. "If anyone needs me, tell them I've died."

"Haakon," Ida said sternly.

He lowered his head, turned, and strode back through the house loud enough to wake all who were slumbering, and a few distant neighbors as well.

Aven exchanged a small smile with Ida, and before either of them could remark, the smell of toasting crackers begged to be tended. Aven pulled them from the oven, lightly golden and crisp.

Cora and Al joined them then, looking rested. Al's tightly coiled hair was closely shorn to his head and he ran a hand over it, making a faint swishing sound as he yawned. Ida heaped two plates with stew for them, and Aven fixed a pot of strong, black tea. At Cora's bidding, she brewed a cup of chamomile for Thor.

Aven set the cup of herbal tea on a tray. Next she added two warm crackers. Oh, that he might be able to take a few bites. Settle his stomach, if not his unease.

"I used the last of what calmed him before he slept. I'll head home and see if there ain't a little left. The medicine the doctor left is decent, but we had a time of it, tryin' to get Thor to take some, and I fear he's on to us now." Cora winked. She ate, sipping her own rich tea with closed eyes.

When she finished, she rose and beckoned to Aven with a lean, work-worn hand. "I gonna fetch them herbs." She pushed back from the table and righted her homespun skirts. "Walk with me, child. It'll spare those floorboards you be pacin'."

On outside study, Cora's cabin was pint-sized, but within were so many nooks and crannies it would take a day to fully discover. Aven stood at one of those nooks as she reached up for a tin on the highest shelf. Dozens of other containers sat in neat rows—the name of seed or herb marking each.

"This here, perhaps?" Aven sniffed the contents and, thinking it right, held it over for inspection.

Cora shifted her finger through the tiny dried pods. "Ah, the fennel. Thatta girl. Now you be lookin' for St. John's Wort. I'll find the milk thistle."

Running her thumb along small glass jars, Aven read more labels. "What is the benefit of these herbs?"

"It a blend to treat anxiousness. Should help settle Thor some. I've a good, strong tincture made up but it's stewed in whiskey. And while it's bitter and don't taste near the same, whiskey be whiskey and I fear offerin' it to Thor just now." Looking like a pair of spectacles would be of help, Cora squinted at the writing on an old tin. "So we'll steep the herbs and hope he might take some." She pulled down a pouch and peeked inside.

Aven unearthed the last herb and carried it over as well. Her skirt brushed against a small bed covered with a quilt of brown and white patches. The bed bowed in the middle, looking near to collapsing, but a little spool doll lay slumped over against the pillow. Georgie's spot.

Earlier Cora had mentioned that her girls were staying with a family from their church. A shelter for them as Cora and Al aided the Norgaards.

Aven righted the doll, grateful to Cora for the time she was giving. All with a smile and spark, no less.

"He kept down some of what I brewed for him near noon." Cora fetched a basket and filled it with odds and ends, last of all the pouch. "But only a few sips. It was enough yet, as he rested. Let's see that he get a good strong cup for the night." She led Aven out, then closed and latched the door.

Pots of herbs grew on the stone stoop, and a hanging basket with flowering ivy spilled shade along with a heady fragrance. 'Twas honeysuckle, Cora declared, as she looped her arm through Aven's. Some years younger than Ida, Cora's hair was frosted with silver strands, but the wiry grip she maintained was as strong as her manner was kind.

Cora plucked a bloom and handed it to Aven. It bore a smell so gratifying, Aven committed the name to heart as she inhaled its fragrance. Over and over she did this until Cora laughed.

"Lawd, child, if you ain't gonna smell the sweet right outta that flower. I'll bring you all you can stand next I come."

Aven smiled her thanks. She placed the white bloom in her palm as they walked, tipping the silken petals over to admire the underside. How often had she held these very blossoms as a girl? They used to bloom just outside her mother's third-floor window where Aven had spent her youngest years. She would sit there in the little gable, watching bees bumble from flower to flower while her mother sewed delicate gowns for the lady of the manor.

In the lifetime since, Aven had forgotten its name. Years later, and alone in the workhouse, there was a vase of this same flower in the office where she met with one of the Sisters of Mercy— the nuns who came to the poor to bring aid. The very Sister who had matched her with Benn that spring day.

Never had Aven thought to ask the flower's name. She was thankful to know it now.

Cora's grip on her arm was steady. As the weariness of the last few days settled into her bones, Aven was grateful for Cora's mellow pace. The woman had to feel as stretched thin, if not more so.

"How did you come to live here?" Aven asked as they walked.

With a flick of her hand, Cora waved off a pesky fly. "Worked on a farm in Louisiana. Me and Ida were the only daughters of our folks who weren't sold off. We was too young, you see. Not much use to nobody 'cept to carry water pails or helpin' our mammy with the missus. When we got older, we decided to run. Scarcely had a feather to fly with, but we got by." She lowered the basket to her side so it swayed among her skirts.

"May I ask what happened?"

"We was runnin' toward freedom, long before the start of the war. We took off before our owner had a chance to sell Ida away. He had plans for her, ya see, as she was grown then. But Ida was wantin' to marry a man who worked the fields. Woulda been only a slave weddin'—not legal to the state—but true in God's eyes, and that be all that mattered."

Aven gently freed Cora of the basket when the woman slowed.

"We got all the way to the south of Virginia when dogs caught up with us and the gang of folk we were travelin' with. It may seem that Ida took the worst of it, but her beau was injured near as bad, then sold off and never seen again. Her heart was more battered than her leg ever was.

"I was smaller so the memories be fragile, but I recall how she bore it well. She learned to let the good Lord mend her, and mend her He has. She ain't bitter none, which is more able than me. Than most. 'Specially with the Sorrels and their kind around. And with their dander still up, no less. Ida be gracious, but it don't mean her heart don't want still. Don't yearn for what was lost."

"I'm terribly sorry."

Cora drew in a slow breath and tilted her face to the breeze. It lifted the tiny hairs that feathered free of her knotted head wrap. "A few years past that, we was sold to the Sorrels, and that's how I was on hand to tend Mrs. Norgaard whenever it was her time. I delivered all three of the boys and eight Sorrel babies. All grown up now. When the war ended and Ida and me was free, we took work from the Norgaards. They paid right good.

"I married my Albert then. Spent some happy years with him before he passed. This place be home. 'S a cryin' shame to think of those boys losin' it. But they know what they be about and they know what they made of. We all know it too, and in that there be hope."

A few weeks ago such words would have been fodder to ponder, but now they provided a sureness beyond measure.

Aven glanced around at the beauty of the evening. The sky was the color of a peach, the glow of the sun much like the place where it was ripest. Birds called to one another from the treetops, and two deer walked slow and lithe atop a distant crest. How vast had Haakon declared the farm? A few hundred acres. A responsibility she couldn't begin to fathom.

"If they're to keep this farm . . . Thor will be needing to make liquor nonetheless, would you think?"

"It a question I been wrestlin' with the good Lord over 'til I realized that the notion be between Him and Thor. In the meanwhile we got our place to pray."

188

Aven nodded. Pray she would. For that man's heart and their beloved land.

The acreage spread out around them now like patches of blue and green and gray . . . all coming together to make up a quilt—a tapestry—of home. Rich in the air was the scent of ripening apples. On the hillside, dried grasses swayed in a wave so vast and gentle, it reminded her of the open seas she'd come across. 'Twas a thing of beauty, and the souls who lived here more so.

Aye, pray she would, and as she did, she would think of a way to help bear the burden. If it would ease Thor's fight—help Ida and Cora and these men keep the only home they'd known—she would give all she could.

It was an old oak—the tree Thor had often climbed while at the boarding school for the Deaf and Dumb. A place to hide amid the velvety leaves. A place to see more of the world. To climb as high as he could just for the chance to look out across the North Carolina horizon and pretend that there, in the distant haze, he could make out the shape of Blackbird Mountain, Virginia. Home.

Nearly eight, he'd only been at the school for two years, but every day of it—every day away from his family—had been more lonesome than the one before. The learning of Sign had been his only comfort, but even that comfort didn't pull him near or tuck him in at night.

So there he'd sat . . . straddling one of the thick branches, battling emptiness. It was then that he'd peered down to see a bearded man in a plaid coat, awaiting him. Da. Thor scrambled down from the tree so fast he nearly collided with the ground, and when he finally ran into Da's open embrace, the tears Thor had spent two years holding back unleashed.

When Da pulled back, Thor peered up into his face to see tears there as well. But they weren't the kind for a homecoming. They were of a sadness so deep, Da's bearded chin was trembling.

Thor felt in that instant the hot fear of knowing that life would never be the same. That a shadow was about to spread over him.

It was such a darkness that threatened to seize him now.

Thor shifted his head. Knew he was lying down, but nothing more. Sleep had taken him for some time. What had Cora put in that cup she kept tipping to his lips? The air was like ice, making him shiver so hard he could scarcely lift a hand.

He managed to grip the back of his head, which was being pressed by a weight so hard it was sure to crack. He opened his eyes. The room was aflame with sunset. Slits of it hit his eyes, intensifying the throbbing.

He was going to die. Right here, he was going to die.

Thor stared at the wall, wrapped his arms around himself, and tried to fight back the cold. It clawed its way through his clothes, prickling his skin. It had been summer last, he recalled, but maybe winter had set in while he was asleep. The knots in the pine walls were small and close together. He stared at them, noticing the patterns to be found—like snowflakes in a blizzard—until he realized that the flakes were increasing. A flurry that was making the walls nearly white.

Thor blinked, feeling the itch on his skin again. Sharp and prickly. It had to be ice. He chafed at his forearms. Shivers quaked him. Did anyone else know a storm was approaching? What of his trees? His brothers? Ida would be out by the line, hanging laundry, only to be caught in the flurry.

Thor went to sit up to warn her. His skull twisted inside his head and he collided with something hard. A burn lashed at his scalp, and he groaned. A warm wetness dampened the side of his head. He'd hit the nightstand on the way to the floor.

Someone knelt beside him and pressed a rag to his head. The hands were like fire. Thor forced them away as he struggled to his knees. He needed to get to Ida. And Aven. She was out in the shed, cutting fabric with her scissors. He'd be ready for them this time—but he had to warn her about the storm. Had to get her and bring her back to the house. Aven needed him.

He'd be gentler this time. He promised.

At a spark of pain, Thor realized someone was dabbing that rag to his skin again. He pushed away whoever it was. Forget the blood. They needed to worry about the storm. Ice was stabbing him. Thor swatted at his skin, but it was so cold it felt like he was hardly moving.

Hands bound his own, pinning them down and away from his shivering body. Thor wrenched free and gripped the edge of the mattress to pull himself up. Someone was beside him. Thor grabbed the person by the front of the shirt. Haakon.

Thor tried to shape the sign for *snow*. The family had to be warned. They needed to make Aven safe. Bring her back to the house. Ida too. Thor stared down at his fingers and forced them to make an *A,* then a *V*. At the *E,* he was shaking too hard to finish. He tried to talk, but the words were like mud in his throat. Furious, he socked the floor. Regretted it when pain shot through his arm. Into his head. Stomach wrenching, Thor lunged for the bowl again.

A moment later a rag wiped his mouth, then those hands were loosening the buttons of his shirt. Why were they taking off his shirt? It was freezing. Thor tried to hold it in place, but Haakon pried it off of him.

Bared from the waist up, a chill slapped his skin. Thor grabbed for his shirt but Haakon twisted away, throwing it aside. Irritation mounting, Thor pushed Haakon into the side of the bed.

Haakon shouted at him—blue eyes flickering with fury. Thor shoved his brother again. This time so hard that Haakon slammed into the wall. Thor was sick of the milksop acting like he owned the world. Was sick of everything he did. The way he looked at Aven. Taught her to swim.

Told Thor he couldn't do it because he couldn't talk.

Stupid Thor couldn't talk.

Thor needed Haakon to warn Aven about the storm—make sure she was safe—but he was fed up with his brother, so he slammed him down with all his might and rose for the door. He'd do it himself.

FIFTEEN

Aven set Cora's basket on the kitchen table. Something knocked above the ceiling . . . then thudded so hard the lantern over the table trembled.

"Jorgan!" Haakon hollered from the attic. "I need you!"

Seated at the table, Jorgan lunged up. His chair slammed back and he stumbled around it.

"Jorgan!" Haakon bellowed. "I can't hold him!"

A crash clattered overhead. The wall of the stairwell shuddered. Too close to be the third floor. Jorgan called out for Al.

Aven turned but saw only an empty yard and a gaping barn door where Al had gone to do the chores. Cora was already rushing that way. Jorgan shouted for Thor to calm down. A heartbeat later there was a slam and Haakon swore.

Two pairs of running feet pounded the hallway, one just behind the other, followed by a crash so hard, the whole house shook. From above, Thor groaned—an agonized, guttural sound that had Aven's heart ripping in her chest. She stepped back only to bump into the windowsill.

The scuffle intensified as did the sound of Jorgan's and Haakon's desperation. Even as panic

194

quickened her pulse, the Twenty-Third Psalm came to mind. Not for herself, but for Thor.

"The LORD is my shepherd; I shall not want."

Aven hurried to right Jorgan's chair when the wall trembled.

"He maketh me to lie down in green pastures: he leadeth me beside the still waters."

Above, boards sounded like they were about to splinter.

"He restoreth my soul."

She lost the rest—pleading to Christ for peace for this man.

Jorgan bellowed a curse and crashed down the stairs. He hit the wall at the bottom so hard, a picture fell and shattered. The whole world seemed to dim when Aven realized that coming down the stairs next was Thor.

Nearly on his knees, he fought against whoever held him. Haakon.

Thor's torso was bare and Haakon clung beneath one of his shoulders, groping at his brother's thick arm to hold on. Like two stags they fought, each clamoring to be stronger.

Al rushed into the kitchen with Grete at his heels. He skidded around the table and into the great room where he hefted Thor around the middle. Grete barked. With Haakon's help, they tugged him up a step. Thor fought and thrashed. He kicked the wall then Al square in the stomach so hard that Al dropped like an empty sack.

When Grete growled, Aven called for the dog. The pup hesitated, looking terror stricken and confused. Aven called again. Whining, Grete crawled nearer. Aven pulled the dog close.

Jorgan rammed Thor with all the force he had, shoving his brother back a step. Then another. Thor punched at him. The sound of his fists colliding with Jorgan louder than even Thor's grunting.

Jorgan ducked against the pounding blows, but still he heaved until Haakon clasped his brother's arms. Al struggled to his feet and took hold of his other side. The three of them forced Thor farther back.

Thor made a sound much like "Av—"

She had to be mistaken. He didn't speak.

"Get down, Aven!" Jorgan shouted.

Was she what Thor was aiming for? Aven dropped to a crouch behind the table. She pulled Grete into her lap. The dog whined in confusion, trembling from nose to tail.

Aven heard a thrashing from Thor. Then a whimper that could have only been his own. A sound so raw and broken that she clutched Grete tighter for fear the dog would scamper after him.

"Av—"

Tears stung her eyes at the sound of him trying to say her name. Aven blinked as her vision blurred.

Jorgan commanded them to keep their grips.

The clamor shook the upper floor like a beating drum, then all at once everything went quiet. All save the panting breaths of three men.

First came Haakon's voice. "He's out cold."

"Let's move him before he comes to." Jorgan sounded wrung out.

Fearing she was going to be sick, Aven sank against the table leg. She tried to heave in breaths, but perhaps that was her problem—they were coming too fast. She struggled to slow them even as the kitchen filled with noise again. This time of that which needed to be done immediately. Cora poured salt into a bowl and rushed for the kettle. Ida drew near to Aven and pressed a hand to her forehead. Aven closed her eyes again.

With Ida's help Aven managed to stand. "I need air," she whispered.

Down the stairs she went. Past the cider barn. All the way around it until she reached the back end. Tall, dry weeds swished as she sank onto a rusted box against the building.

Dropping her face in her hands, her shoulders shook. A sob rose so strong that air was lost to her. Aven heaved in a breath as tears pooled and fell. Because she could still see Thor's struggle . . . and because she could still see Benn's.

The sun was near to setting that day, two years ago. The flat all but golden in the glory of the sunset that streamed in through the windows. Benn had been sitting at the table of their rented room, his profile lit by that soft light. The pale hue of his hair melded to amber and his pensive brow shadowed above his blond lashes. He'd been lost in thought—and she simply watched him. For it had been the calm after the storm. One week after she'd pleaded yet again for him to give up the bottle.

He'd tried—for her sake, he'd tried. Making it into the third day. But by then she'd had to lock herself in the closet due to his panic. A panic taking over that bugs were crawling on them both. He slapped at his skin, at her own. Scratching at nothing. Forcing her to hide away.

Aven had pinned the closet door closed with the broom and tried to stay as still and quiet as possible. Praying that Benn would forget she was there. That their landlord, Farfar Øberg, would hear the ruckus and come to her aid.

Somewhere in the night, Benn had found a bottle of *Akvavit*. He'd finished the spiced liquor off by sunrise. Aven crawled out to find him in a stupor.

So it was four days later, the day of that vivid sunset, that he'd finally turned his head to her and, with a rare smile, asked what she thought about fish for supper. Mused aloud that the market would be open for a few minutes yet. Another bottle of *Akvavit* was in his grasp, turning slowly in his thick fingers.

He'd been a handsome man. Thirty-one to her

nineteen that summer. He had a stoic kind of appeal. Skin gently weathered from hours spent near the docks. Golden hair thick and cropped short. Tidy most days, save when he was lost in thought and prone to tugging it.

When he gave her a second smile, flashing that matchless dimple, Aven had fetched a basket and a krone. Only two had lined the money box since his pub debts had emptied it. She'd stayed up many a night stitching seams in dim light to earn the two coins they had. Lacking powder to cover the bruises on her arms that his panic had borne, she draped a shawl about her shoulders.

She left the flat—that, the last she would see him alive. That smile. The light on his skin. The memory of it was all she had to hold on to as she turned away from the shadows of a life no more. Of a marriage no more due to his choice and the length of a rope.

For months after she was haunted by the sound of it. How could something so still as a taut rope creak yet? 'Twas the breeze from the open window, she knew. He'd opened it after she left because the curtains were spilling in and out as the wind shifted, and he was there—his life no more.

There she had fallen, her basket spilling of its contents, and there her landlord had knelt beside her, urging her to leave the room.

Farfar Øberg had moved a cot into his storage

closet when fear hindered Aven from returning to the flat in the hours and days to follow. He brought her blankets and read to her by the light of a costly candle. Days upon days wore on, and she didn't move from the bakery. Didn't speak.

Until two weeks after the funeral, when Farfar Øberg had announced a letter for her. A message written in Dorothe's hand. One urging her and Benn to come to America. That they would be welcomed to the farm and that there was much work to be had for Benn. After forcing herself to pen news of Benn's death, Aven had tucked Dorothe's letter beneath her pillow.

Months later, Farfar Øberg slipped a twenty kroner in the same spot. How he'd obtained it, he wouldn't relay. But it was hers, he insisted, when he pushed it back into her hand with his gnarled, wrinkled fingers.

Aven held the valuable coin, touching the imprint of the coat of arms stamped into the copper-nickel, repeating the words she'd memorized from Dorothe's letter.

"The Lord will also be a refuge for the oppressed. A refuge in times of trouble."

'Twas nearly a year later when she finally penned a response to Dorothe's bidding.

That, yes. To the Norgaard farm she would come.

SIXTEEN

Aven awoke, vaguely remembering how she'd gotten into bed. A quilt covered her, and a nightgown pressed soft and warm beneath that. She blinked up at the ceiling. By the brightness of the room, it had to be late morning. Her second morning abed. She pushed herself up against the pillows. She knew only because Cora and Ida had tiptoed in and out many a time to check on her.

Had she truly slept this long?

Managing to sit forward, Aven rubbed at her face. 'Twas as clean as her nightgown. All notion of salty tears wiped away. They'd taken good care of her indeed.

It had been Haakon who had found her beside the cider barn. That she remembered, but everything else was a blur as exhaustion had taken over. Noticing a sweet smell, Aven looked to the nightstand where a jar spilled forth with clippings of Cora's porch flower. Honeysuckle. Aven smiled gently. Seeing a plum beside it, she took it and sniffed the smooth purple flesh, but needing to rise, she set it back down.

When her bare feet hit the floor, she pushed herself to a stand, only to feel so light-headed she had to sit again. Perhaps go a little slower. She picked up the plum and took a few slow bites.

When had she eaten last? Or—prior to this—slept? Had she been forgetting to do such things?

Lacking the strength for anything but the simplest of tasks, she reached for her shoes. Aven buttoned them up, for she'd have no luck with them once her corset was on. She fetched that and then a blouse and skirt. As soon as she was dressed, she headed down. The house was unusually quiet. In the kitchen, she set about fixing a cup of tea, taking care to add plenty of cream and sugar. Alongside steamy sips, she nibbled a few of the crackers and a slice of hard cheese.

Jorgan carried boards down from the attic. His own steps were slow, and she couldn't begin to imagine how this had taxed him in both body and spirit. Ida was nowhere to be found, and upon inquiring, Jorgan said she was napping. 'Twas as if this house were healing after a great battle—one she hoped would allow it to heal even stronger than before.

A battle, she prayed, that had been won.

"How is Thor?"

Jorgan rubbed at his shoulder that had to be hurting. "He's restin' well. Through the worst of it now."

All the heartache she'd been bearing melted away into the stirring of joy. "May I see him?"

After balancing the two boards on the table edge, Jorgan pulled out a pocketful of bent nails and set them in a pail. "Yes. And if you don't mind, he's ready for a meal. He's had a few crackers, but perhaps somethin' heartier now. Tess came by earlier and started a stew. She's gone now, and if you're able to dish some up—"

Aven was on her feet before he could even finish.

"Don't wear yourself out again." Jorgan watched her as he pushed the pail aside. "I doubt Haakon minded carryin' you to the house, but I don't think he wants to do it again, for your sake." He gave a brotherly smile then, taking up the boards, strode out.

She owed Haakon a thanks, and even now could still feel the surety of his hold and the steady cadence of his steps as he'd borne her across the yard. As vivid and real was the way Thor had been trying to say her name.

As she checked on the stew, Aven felt a curious longing to hear it again. Carrots and potatoes simmered alongside herbs and hearty meat— just the fare to fortify Thor. She filled a bowl, then turned in search of some bread. A fresh loaf rested on the windowsill, and Aven wanted to weep with gladness to whoever was responsible. Tess, most likely. Jorgan confirmed as much upon his return to the kitchen.

"Tess did that while Ida scrubbed the attic. I don't know how she did it, but a few kettles of hot water and soap and the woman set it to rights again."

'Twas no wonder Ida had needed such a rest.

Aven cut a thick slice of bread for Thor, then steeped ginger and hot water together. After dusting in a spoonful of sugar, she placed the cup on a tray. She steadied the bowl into place, then fetched both napkin and spoon.

Her heart tripped over itself for reasons she wasn't willing to acknowledge, and she lifted the tray and carried it up the stairs.

Near the open attic door, a breeze sifted through the room, fresh and cool. The parted curtains rippled. Skirt lifted in one hand and the tray clutched against her ribs, Aven peeked inside. The room was awash with Ida's handiwork. Every surface scrubbed and righted. But it was the nearest bed that drew Aven's attention. The man lying there.

A wet ring darkened the center of the floor from the tub Jorgan had brought up so Thor could bathe. From his lack of movement Aven surmised that Thor had needed help. He lay on his side now, gaze seeming to rest on nothing in particular. His coloring wasn't as dull as it had been, yet the shadows beneath his eyes were bleaker. His hair was nearly dry. Aven moved in front of him, knelt, and set the tray near.

He looked at her and surprise registered in his eyes. She didn't know why, but a sting of tears gathered and she had to fight them back. Unsure of what to say, she reached out and gently touched his hand. It was nothing, really . . . she simply ran her fingertip along the skin of his knuckles. It was the only hello she knew to form.

He blinked quickly, then his hand shifted on the mattress and the tip of his thick finger grazed her thumb.

She smiled again, and losing the fight with herself, a tear fell. Aven wiped it away. "How are you feeling?" She hoped he could understand her.

He wet his lips but didn't stir. A small cut above his brow glistened with a trace of ointment. His head had to be hurting, and she didn't want him to move unless he wished. His gaze was on her face. Though he was silent, the slight shifts in his expression gave hint to his thoughts. His brow pinched when she mentioned the meal. His mouth parted at the declaration of it being bread and hot stew. When she told him she could make something else if that wasn't appetizing, his gaze roved her face.

"I don't want you to have to sit up just now, so if it seems too much, I can set it here for when you are ready. Or bring more later—"

He gripped the edge of the mattress, trying to push himself up. She moved to assist. So sturdy was he and she weak still, her efforts seemed more hindrance than help. Aven moved aside as he rose to a sit.

His cotton undershirt was snug to his chest and forearms, the sleeves shoved up to his elbows. He wore sable-brown pants—absent of both suspenders and knife sheath. Thor leaned against the wall, tilted his head back, and closed his eyes.

He sat that way for a long while. Not wanting to rush him, she set about tucking his clean laundry away. She'd washed and folded their clothing before, but never had she put it away, so it was by trial and error that she finished the task a few minutes later. Thinking Thor had fallen asleep where he sat, she looked over to see that he was watching her.

Hands slowing, she tucked the last of his shirts into the dresser and closed the drawer. Sweeping her skirt aside, Aven knelt beside his bed again. "Can I get you anything?"

With his eyes on her mouth, his brow furrowed. Something about him seemed unsteady. Then he looked over at the tray, and his hand shifted ever so slightly toward it.

"You are hungry?"

Slowly, he nodded.

Aven perched on the edge of the bed and peeked at him, hoping he wouldn't mind. She offered him the bowl and he took it in his trembling grasp. Thor eyed the spoon warily. He lifted the handle and broth sloshed about as he tried to raise it. 'Twould never do for him in this state. To hold the spoon herself might fluster him, so

Aven took the bread, tore off a chunk, and tucked it into his grasp.

A little sigh slipped from his lips—the sound of relief.

Did he know he'd made it? It was so sweet she found herself swallowing another sting. With slow movements he dunked the crusty piece into the stew, then lifted it to his mouth.

His eyes slid closed as he chewed. Aven watched him, wondering how hungry he had become. Thor struggled to tear off another piece of bread. She slid her hands against his own, broke off a second pinch, and tucked it into his palm. He dipped and ate. They repeated the pattern only a few more times, gratitude heavy in his brown eyes. When he eased the bowl away, she returned it to the tray.

Remembering the ginger water, Aven offered it to him. May that it would settle his stomach further. He sipped and made a face.

She accepted the cup back. "Never have I met a man so choosy about what he drinks."

The lines around his eyes deepened in the faintest of smiles.

Smiling herself, she set the cup aside. "I do promise to make you something else."

He dipped his head in a small thank-you, then seemed to regret it, for he lowered himself back to the mattress. With him lying on his side, Aven pulled his blanket up and nestled it about his shoulders. Her fingers brushed against his arm and she felt a tremor in him. The poor man was chilled.

Aven fetched a denser quilt and lowered that over him as well. His eyes slid closed, breath shallowing. His hair had fallen against the side of his cheek, and as gently as she could, Aven tucked it behind his ear. His eyes nearly fluttered open so she pulled away.

"Rest ye, now," she whispered.

'Twas what the Sisters of Mercy used to say whenever one of them dimmed the lanterns in the orphan dormitory. Aven cast Thor one last glance, then as quietly as she had come, she took up the tray and tiptoed back out.

SEVENTEEN

Never had sleep been so much his friend. It was the balm to his madness. The reprieve that got him to the beginning of his seventh day sober. This hour where the terrors were nearly a memory. It was a small death he'd just died, and he ached with the aftermath. There was a void without liquor—he felt it deeply—but it was a void he had sought, and Thor told himself every few minutes that it was good.

He'd eaten some more, and combined with much sleep, it had given him the needed strength to finally rise from bed all on his own. He pushed his feet into his boots, laced them, and with slow, steady movements headed outside. The air was crisp. It hit his face, and it felt like a new beginning.

His hair wet, Jorgan was returning from the pond. Grete cantered beside him. Jorgan lifted a hand when Thor passed, and Thor did the same—guilt mounting inside him for all he'd done to his brother. As for Haakon, Thor hadn't seen him much in the last few days and that was probably best. A hunch told him that Haakon was at the west cabin, tending to odd jobs as he often did when space between them all was wise. Head down, Thor trudged on, needing the sanctuary of his trees.

They grew in neat rows on the hills and valleys beyond the farmyard. He looked down along his different varieties landing on the Arkansas Black, his best storer. On the opposite side of the road were a handful of Sweet Coppins, just bland enough that he sold them cheap. Past those were two acres of Baldwin, good for cider and a nice apple pie he'd sell to market by the wagonload. Those would earn a pretty penny, but the most acreage was made up of Foxwhelp, an old bittersharp, and Roxbury Russet, one of his sweetest and best. After harvest, he'd press and blend their juices with care, creating palatable ciders that once fermented were irresistible to his customers. Keeping him and his brothers in a rich living. It was for that reason and that reason alone that his pace slackened and he bowed his head, pressing a hand to his eyes.

God help him.

Because none of this acreage was paid off yet. Though he and his brothers were closing in on that day, they had a few hundred dollars left to go. With another eight of interest due every month, there was little time to waste. Yet Thor couldn't think past this day. This hour. Not even this moment to what lay beyond it. He didn't want to think about prying the boards from the cidery. Of stepping into the cool, still air that held the lusty fragrance of his very work and memories that threatened to bring him to his knees even here and now.

Pushing the fears aside, Thor rubbed his sore upper arm as he walked on. Hair unbound, it pressed against his cheek in the breeze. He pushed it back, wishing for something to bind it with, but his wrist was bare of its leather cord.

Reaching one of his favorite spots, the place where an old McIntosh tree grew in the oddest of shapes—like a woman drawing water from a well, Ida had once said—he moved to sit against it. It had rained in the night so the ground was dewy. The air still damp. Thor cared not as he settled down on the orchard floor amid soggy leaves. The world made sense here. It had been the same for Da. Thor had understood that more and more over the years.

When the wind shifted, a few golden leaves tumbled down. He turned one in his fingers. Seeing something on the road, he squinted that way. The team and wagon ambled along, Haakon at the reins. Where was he going? By the way the wagon looked loaded up—and covered with a canvas tarp—Thor had his answer. How had Haakon gotten into the cidery? And what was he doing? Their orders were filled for the rest of the month. Thor had made sure of it.

While Haakon had always had a habit of wandering off, this was different. As the wagon drove from sight, Thor's mind tried to ponder further down that path, but thoughts and worries muddied together until he leaned his head back and closed his eyes.

The world that was gently swaying flushed to darkness. Relief was sweeter than any need to ponder Haakon. No matter how much his younger brother might be undermining his authority just now, it was a dilemma for later.

The late-summer sun and early-autumn breeze were working together to lull him to sleep. Thor nearly drifted off until he felt a brush of wings against his pants leg. He opened his eyes to see two crows hopping about, pecking at his fruit. Picking up a half-rotted apple from the ground, he chucked it that way, scattering them both.

When he turned his head, it was to the sight of Aven strolling down the row, Grete loping alongside her. Aven wore a blouse of cream with tiny, pale flowers. The same make of cloth he'd stacked in one of the old sheds after Dorothe's passing. Aven's patchwork skirt brushed the orchard floor only for leaves to cling to the hem. She glanced down the cross paths with each one she passed, seeming to search for something. When she finally spotted Thor, she slowed.

Was that something *him?*

Grete ran ahead and collided into Thor with licks and wags. Turning his face, Thor pushed her away and the dog circled the tree, then flopped beside him. Aven treaded nearer and knelt a few feet away. The lace at her collar said she'd taken effort with her stitchwork, and he'd never thought that plain fabric could look so fine. Her hair, even more ginger beneath the sunny sky, was braided loose. She pushed a few stray strands from her cheek and looked happy to see him.

That expression giving him a pang, he let his eyes trail the length of her. There was a tenderness within him so severe he wanted to draw himself closer to her and touch the curve of her waist again. To touch the same curving line at her neck and shoulder. Skin that was so soft, he could hardly contemplate it, and knew it wisest not to try.

She'd just seen him at his worst.

Seen his mayhem and unrest. His anger. Even the nausea he'd battled against. She'd held him amid his sickness, only to humble him further by wiping his mouth. Clutching him in the yard even when he'd smelled like a pint gone bad. But there she had been, nearer than she should have gotten. Embarrassment spread a heat just beneath his shirt, and he suddenly couldn't raise his gaze from the ground between them.

When she moved closer and touched his sleeve, he pulled away. His gaze finally lifted. Just in time to see confusion line her face.

Blinking quickly, she glanced around as if trying to rally from what must have seemed a snub. She did so with grace. "As soon as Haakon returns with the wagon, Jorgan and I are away to town." Aven gave him a weak smile. "Fay is due to arrive any day, and Jorgan wanted to ask after the train schedule. We're also going to the mercantile as he's in need of a new part for the cider press. He's wondering if there was anything you needed while we were about. We each set off to find you."

So she was here as a favor. It was small comfort to know the reason for her seeking him out was an indifferent one. Plain and to a purpose. Her gaze skimmed his pocket the same moment he withdrew his pad and pencil. He looked from it to her, and while there were things he had need of, his head throbbed too much to write in English. The language was convoluted enough and right now, well, beyond him. She wouldn't understand his requests in Sign, so he shook his head. The only answer he could conjure up.

Thinking she would rise and leave, he was surprised when she took the little book and opened it to a blank page before she slipped it back in his grasp. The pencil she stole as well, turned it right-side down, and tucked it back in his hands. Blazes, what was wrong with him?

Her eyes flooded with concern as if wondering the same thing. "Are you in pain?"

Desperate to pull himself together, he wrote in Norwegian. And crooked at that. *Ja, litt.*

Her mouth moved with the words as she read. Sadness drew itself across her pretty face.

Recalling one thing he couldn't do without, he added *tobbak*. When Aven's expression went regretful, he realized she didn't know the word. Heaven help him, what was it in English? His mind was a quarry today—a thousand hammers and pickaxes at work within. And for some reason, not much was being unearthed.

Squinting against the pain, Thor did his best to shape the curves and lines with the lead tip. When he finished, the crude drawing looked more like a teakettle than his pipe.

Aven squinted at the figure, tipping her head to one side. Then she seemed to understand. " 'Tis a pipe you're wanting?"

Nei. Thor slid his finger to the rounded chamber.

"Ah, tobacco." Her light-brown eyes were warm when they lifted to his. "I'll be sure to get some."

He made the sign for *gratitude*. When he lowered his fingertips from his mouth, she seemed to understand, for she smiled. Beyond that, she didn't move. Just looked back down the row. Knowing she should be getting back, he put his notepad and pencil away. When he rose it was a struggle, but to his relief she didn't try and help him this time.

Hoping he appeared steady, he stepped on with her beside him. Grete plodded along just ahead.

Aven's chin tipped up when blue jays flapped

overhead, dipping through his orchard in search of a free meal. Cocking her head to the side, Grete watched. Useless dog. Thor wanted to pick up another apple and hurl it at the birds, but he didn't want to startle Aven. Her hands were clutched in front of her skirt, and the way she was twisting her fingers together, it seemed she wanted to say something but didn't know how.

He wrestled with the notion of turning to her, motioning to his eyes, then her mouth—an assurance that she could say what she wished. But his whole body was thrumming with the need to sit down again, so he locked his focus on the porch steps and reaching them, sat.

Aven slipped into the house, and he didn't see her again until Haakon came along the road with the team. She and Jorgan came down the stairs and into the yard, having waited much too long. Shielding his eyes, Jorgan looked about as pleased as Thor felt.

The wagon ambled into the yard. Haakon called a command to the horses. When they stilled, he hopped down, reached for an edge of the tarp, and flung it back. Every crate was empty.

"What did you do?" Jorgan asked.

Haakon tugged a thick fold of cash from his pocket. "Paid a visit to some neighbors of ours. There's forty-six dollars here. And no more interest due for each month we sell 'em more."

They'd never sold to the Sorrels. Granted, a

few of their accounts bought more than could be consumed, and they all knew it was being funneled elsewhere. Matters being what they were, Thor and his brothers had turned a blind eye, but to sell to the Sorrels directly? And without his permission?

Haakon was out of his mind. They weren't selling to those men. Thor didn't even know if he wanted to sell to anyone from here on out.

You not think, Thor signed, but before he even finished, his gaze lifted to the cider barn. One of the windows was uncovered and open, the removed boards stacked off to the side, warped and splintered. His whole body froze. A tingle rose that became warmer and warmer and warmer until his skin lit up with need. His mouth growing wet with it.

He turned to Haakon, who was practically in his face. Bruises flanked the flesh beneath Haakon's eyes, and cuts on his lip and cheekbone told Thor just why his knuckles were sore.

"Did you have something to say to me?" Haakon asked.

When Thor didn't move, didn't so much as blink, Haakon took a step back. "See now . . . I didn't think so." Haakon strode off.

Looking like he wanted to throttle the runt, Jorgan stormed toward the cidery. At the window, he fetched the hammer from the ground, then a board and a bent nail. Thor couldn't hear the blows, but he could see his brother's urgency.

Both shamed and grateful for it, Thor turned away and went into the house, leaving Aven alone beside the wagon.

EIGHTEEN

Rain tapped against the window. A welcome clatter after so many warm days. Upstairs in her room, Aven unfolded a fresh sheet. With Fay due to arrive any day, she spread the bright, clean linen over the new feather tick Jorgan and Ida had made. It rested atop another tick, that of straw. Aven had watched Jorgan over the last three days—the care he'd put into the tasks.

She tucked the sheet into place. The wood frame Jorgan had built was sturdy, and the rope he'd woven across to hold the mattresses made a fine bed indeed. To make room for it, they'd moved Aven's bed against one short wall of the room, pressing Fay's up against the other. In between was just enough space for a braided rug and the dresser with its small mirror. Aven had emptied half of the drawers, which was no effort at all, so little she had. With Jorgan's beloved a child of missionaries, Aven had a feeling Fay would understand that well.

To think of a wedding soon . . .

Her heart soared at the thought. At how two people who had been separated as children went on to form an attachment through letters. A friendship that had flourished into a romance so sincere that a young woman was soon to return.

Aven smoothed sheets into place, then a quilt that had been stitched by Dorothe herself. Fay would be rooming with Aven the few weeks before the wedding, and Jorgan's intent to do things honorably showed in every detail.

With the house quiet, Aven finished her task. 'Twas naught but an unhurried Thursday. The men were out and about, and having visited Cora's family, Ida would be gone much of the day. At the very least, until the rain let up.

At a gentle knock on the doorframe, Aven looked up to see Jorgan.

"May I come in?"

"Of course." She perched on the edge of her bed and he leaned against Fay's.

He considered it. "This is nice, thank you."

Aven smiled.

Falling quiet, Jorgan ran his hand over his beard so many times, she feared there wouldn't be any whiskers left for the wedding.

"If something is on your mind . . . ," she began.

"I'm trying to think of how to ask." He cleared his throat, looking so uncomfortable she sensed what he sought.

"Perhaps 'tis about Fay?"

He nodded and started tugging at his beard again.

Aven checked a smile. "Perhaps marriage as well?"

"Yes'm." Jorgan peered out the window, then looked back to Aven's hands folded atop her lap. "I'm not sure what to ask. But I want to be good to Fay. I haven't spent much time around women . . . apart from Ida, or Dorothe. Or now you. Never in a . . ." He cleared his throat again. "A wooing sense."

Of course. He'd romanced her only through writings.

To set him at ease, then, Aven shifted on the bed, pulling her stockinged feet in beneath her skirt. "A woman simply wants to be loved, Jorgan. Cherished. Seen and, most especially, heard. To be valued. I have no doubt that you intend this."

He nodded firmly.

"But we also don't break so easily that you men need be afraid to stand up to our will if we're heading down the wrong path. Or trying to lead you down the same. 'Tis good for a woman to be given due consideration yet also to trust the wisdom and strength of her husband. And . . ." Aven fiddled with the edge of her quilt, smoothing her hand along a favorite patch. "When it comes to other matters . . ." She cleared her throat, feeling a hint of her own embarrassment. "Being both tender and unafraid will welcome her most assuredly to a joyous union with you as her husband."

The side of his mouth lifted in a smile.

"There are few men I have known who possess those qualities so genuinely as yourself."

After a thoughtful delay, he answered, "I thank you for that." He lifted the smallest of the pillows from the end of Fay's bed and fingered a bow. When he set it back, he spoke. "Ida mentioned that I wasn't the only one to get a letter the other day."

She'd almost forgotten.

"Have you decided what you'll do?"

"Nay." Sewing in a shop in Lexington—a fine offer. With room, board, and a modest wage—a fair living. But the distance . . .

Aven took the letter from the dresser. Good sense told her not to waste the opportunity. A life so near to what she'd dreamed of. Work to be proud of and wages to live comfortably on. What more could she possibly want?

Something that was a matter of heart. One not inside this envelope.

Reaching up, Aven touched her necklace. The chain boasted neither charm nor jewels, but the delicate weaving of the metal threads was pretty all the same. It held little value to most. She'd learned that the day her mother had tried to sell it for food for them both. The peddler she offered it to had turned his nose up at what was only thin steel, declaring it so weightless, he'd not give a halfpenny for it. So her mother slid it back on and took Aven's hand. Farther along the road they'd traveled until they'd finally reached the workhouse.

When her mother had died there only weeks later, Aven unclasped the chain from her mother's neck with the bravest and most frightened hands a girl her age could possess.

She didn't realize how quiet she'd grown until Jorgan spoke. "How long do you have to decide?"

" 'Twould be proper to reply within the week so they're not left to wonder."

When she set the envelope back on the wooden surface, he rose. "We can mail off your answer on our next deliveries. Or deliver you straight to Lexington ourselves should you decide to go. Haakon could take you in. Or I, or even Thor."

Aven nodded, but a sting tightened her throat.

Jorgan was the only one who knew of the opportunity, and she didn't know how to mention it to anyone else. She thought of Thor. Tried to imagine how she would express *leaving*. He would have a sign for it, but the shape was one she didn't want to try and make. Nor did she wish to imagine him being the one who drove her away from this place. For him to be the one to lift her things from the wagon and bid the last good-bye in his own silent way.

Jorgan stepped to the door. "None of us want to see you go. I know that's not fair to say—what with this chance you got—but it's the truth."

"I thank you for that. But I wonder . . . if this is the place for me."

Jorgan leaned a shoulder against the jamb. "Can I ask whatever happened with Haakon? With what he asked you."

"You know about that?"

He nodded.

Aven drew in a slow breath. "Haakon is dear." And charming at that. "But I've been a wife before." She understood both the blessings and trials that came with marriage. While she wished to wed again, it was not a decision to make quickly. "I've known Haakon for only a few weeks. Longer, granted, than I had known Benn, but the situation is different. I'm sorry to tell you that I married your cousin because he offered to feed me. To take me away from the workhouse— where the infirm and insane and unwanted are left to work for survival inside stone walls." Where children often lacked shoes and had only meager meals that came twice a day. Sleeping atop lice-infested bedding and even for that they were thankful.

"I was a child when I went there, and my mother died within its walls. 'Tis a miracle I came out in anything other than a coffin."

Jorgan's face was drawn with sorrow.

Never had she told them how fragile she was upon Benn finding her. "That life is now a world away, and I don't wish to marry for necessity

224

again. But for love, like Fay and yourself."

A resolve filled Jorgan's face as if he knew the man who would offer her such. "Take your time in answering Haakon. It will be good for him to be patient, and more importantly, it's only fair to you." Rain still pattering on the roof, Jorgan looked up to the ceiling, then thanked her afresh for her advice.

When he was gone and with her mind no longer on reading, Aven pulled her sewing near. The black mourning gown was almost transformed into a swimming costume. Only a few more stitches on the waistband to complete it. She threaded a needle as the charcoal sky churned outside. Tipping her work nearer to the window gave enough light to see the stitches. When she reached the end of her thread, she knotted it and took up the spool to cut more.

Would she sew garments for perfect strangers once more?

Her gaze drifted to the letter, but at the sound of heavy footsteps in the hall, she looked over to see Thor step into view wearing a coat and floppy hat pulled low. Her heart lightened at the sight of him, and gone were any thoughts of workhouse walls or marriages of convenience. In its place was a delight she couldn't ignore.

Looking drenched through, he motioned for her to come to him. Aven stood and stepped to the doorway. Dew was gathered in his beard and he ran a hand there, his other braced to his chest as if clutching something just beneath. A smile lit his eyes, but he made no move for his notepad. He didn't even try and shape any of his words. Did he want something?

Aven was about to ask when he tipped his head down, sending drips to fall from the brim of his hat. It was strange—standing so near to him and not smelling cider. Instead, it was the musky scent of rain and the richness of the woods that filled her senses. She hoped he could stay fast to this course of sobriety. 'Twas further than Benn had ever gotten, so Aven wasn't sure what to make of it or what to expect. But she did know what to pray for and that she would continue to do so.

Thor unbuttoned the top of his coat and pulled one side away. There came a soft mewling sound. He angled his body so she could see a tiny face of gray fluff. Peeking out of the front of his shirt, the kitten mewled again. Aven gasped.

Thor reached down and lifted the tiny bundle free. Its little claws clasped into his large hand and he hissed in a breath. Giggling, Aven reached to help him. She took the kitten and eased its paw free from his skin. Thor winced, then sucked the tip of his knuckle.

"Wherever did you find this?"

He pointed back the way he'd come, then gestured the shape of a pointed roof. Perhaps the barn or an outbuilding. With two fingers he made the curving stroke of a cat's whiskers at his cheek, then he rounded his hand in front of his stomach as if to indicate a pregnant mother. Last, he held up five fingers, touching each one in turn before pointing to the gray kitten again.

"Five of them?"

He nodded.

"And this one?"

He pointed at her.

"For me?"

He smiled gently.

"Is it old enough to be away from its mother?" She nestled the warm bundle closer against her chest. It seemed too tiny to be weaned.

He made a gesture she didn't understand. As if realizing as much, he reached in for his notebook and pencil. His brow furrowed as he wrote on a page that was wrinkled from the damp. *Mother gone.*

"Oh no. And the other kittens?"

Cora have.

Never could they be better looked after. "Will you show me how to care for this one?"

Touching her at the elbow, he led her into the hallway. When he released her, she followed him. In the kitchen he pulled off his sopping coat and dropped it on the table. Next his wet hat. Since all would be best hung up, Aven went to take them. Thor shook his head.

"There'll be a puddle on the table." She reached for the drenched items again, but he flicked the side of her hand. Next he took up the jug of milk and placed it in her grasp. His way of saying the coat could wait? Well . . . "You don't need to be such a brute about it."

Smiling, he fetched a clean spoon, then tossed it with a clatter on the table. He took the milk from her and set the jug down with a thud. He motioned to the stove, and she helped him find a pan. Setting it to heat, Aven drizzled milk in.

Thor tapped her arm. She turned to see him holding over his notebook. *Need clean cloth.*

She stepped into the pantry to fetch a piece of cheesecloth. The kitten was warm and mewling in her grasp all the while. The near little life, the tiny heartbeat thrumming against her palm was such a burst of joy that Aven scarcely wanted to let it go. She did, though, when Thor reached to take it.

He sat and placed the kitten in his lap. Having brought the warm milk near, he dabbed the cloth and squeezed white drops onto the kitten's downy mouth. It licked its muzzle. Thor squeezed out more. He kept at it until the tiny, pink tongue had lapped up its supper.

Thor stroked its small head that was dwarfed by his hand. So rough he could be with his brothers or when his wishes weren't understood, but there was a gentleness about him at other times. Aven watched him, enjoying the ability to do it freely. His large thumb brushed a tiny gray ear, then ran down the length of the kitten's thin tail. Lifting one of its scrawny legs, he glanced there, then back up to Aven. Thor stroked his thumb against one side of his bearded jaw.

She shook her head.

He pulled out a chair for her and when she sat, he handed over the kitten. Their fingers brushed, his own warm to the touch and filled with a tremor. He motioned to Aven and made that stroking sign again. Then he pointed to himself and gestured as if pinching the front of his hat. He repeated the two different signs, using one when he pointed to her, then the other when he pointed to himself.

"Oh, 'tis a girl!"

He nodded, his pleasure clear that she'd understood. She was alight with her own kind of contentedness. Of being here with him. Of knowing what was on his mind.

Thor tapped Aven's arm, pointed to his mouth, and made an unmistakable *"Tt—"* sound.

He was full of surprises today.

He slid his notebook near and wrote, *Tis*. After circling the three letters, he crossed them out and added, *Not word*.

She smiled. "I disagree."

Thor rose and strode into the other room. He returned with a thick book that he thudded

on the table in front of her. The spine read
DICTIONARY. He gestured to it as if daring her
to prove it.

Aven laughed. " 'Tis a word to me."

He chuckled, and she savored the sound. Thor
sat beside her again as Aven kissed the top of
the kitten's furry head. He watched them quietly.
When he swiped an arm against his forehead, she
realized it was no longer dew on his brow but
perspiration. Perhaps he wasn't feeling as well as
he seemed.

"What shall we name her?"

He gave a small shrug.

"Let's see . . ." She searched her mind and
thought back to women she had known. Perhaps
one who had been dear to them both. "How about
Dotti? 'Tis short for Dorothe."

Thor lowered his hand for the kitten to see, then
shaped the letters. The kitten reached out to play
with his fingers, and Thor touched its wee paw.

Here Aven sat beside him, her uncertainties
having faded with each day of knowing him. Just
as Cora had promised.

A bead of sweat slid down Thor's temple, and
his breathing was labored. Reaching back, he
squeezed behind his neck and pinched his eyes
closed. Aven clutched the kitten to her front with
one hand and rose to pour him a glass of water.
She handed him the drink, and though he looked
doubtful, he sipped.

Water would be a small comfort to him. 'Twas something much more potent his body was wanting, and as he drank from the glass, his eyes no longer meeting her own, she knew his fight to overcome it was far from over.

NINETEEN

Pack strapped to his back, Thor strode up the hillside, feeling like he was ninety years old. He had to be a good mile from the farmyard now. Panting, he slowed. Sun-warmed evergreens fragranced the air, and it was this piney tang he heaved into his lungs, trying to gentle his breathing. This was a climb that needed to be made in order to hunt.

Haakon would probably pitch a fit to find wild game on the roasting spit, but Thor had a mind to try and bag something today. It was all he could do to sit still any longer, and he had nothing else to keep busy with. At least not right now.

Though Jorgan had let him set off on his own, Thor had been made to promise not to do anything stupid.

Define stupid, he asked.

Not amused, Jorgan had given a warning look. Thor had smiled for the sole reason of it feeling good to smile again.

Jorgan didn't need to worry. Though it was no secret to Thor where most of the stills on this mountain were, and though he could hunt down at least two within the hour, a drink was the last thing he came up here for. No, it was the wide-open space and the need to think clearly. Grete had tried to come along, but Thor made her stay behind. She was handy for small game but didn't like to be far from Haakon, so she would only come up here and fret.

Head still aching, Thor slowed. He sat on a broken log and pulled his pipe from his pocket. Thanks to Aven, there was a fresh quarter pound of tobacco in his pouch. He pulled out a pinch and stuffed the chamber. He patted his pocket for a match, but the small box wasn't there. He looked in his pack. Nothing.

Two curse words and one humdinger of a hand sign came to mind, but he just set the pipe aside and hung his head.

Folding his hands, he pressed his forehead to his knuckles and closed his eyes.

Focused on breathing in and out. In and out. His head pounded like a runaway horse, and there was nothing to take the edge off.

Thor glanced back in the direction of the farm. It was too far to see, but was Haakon still on the porch, Aven trimming his already-short hair? That's what had made Thor decide to get away. He didn't like scissors when it came to hair. Nor when they were in Aven's hand. Even less did he like seeing her and Haakon there together, deep in conversation.

It seemed a good time to load up a pack for a night in the woods.

Shifting his boots, Thor tried not to think about

having a smoke. Or a drink. Or anything else he wanted in life and couldn't seem to figure out. Why was everything so dad-blasted hard? Drinking himself toward the grave had been no picnic. Being sober wasn't either. It was like life was out to corner him. Cram him into a place where he couldn't move and couldn't win.

It had always been this way. He couldn't make himself talk, and he couldn't make himself hear. Not even the traveling preacher with his revival could do a thing about it. Had Da really walked Thor up to the front of the giant tent that night?

Though he'd only been twelve, Thor would never forget how everyone was falling down and carrying on in the name of religion. The preacher saying that Thor's Deafness was a spirit needing to be loosed. But when the old man had put his icy hand to Thor's head and spoke some kind of prayer, nothing had happened.

The preacher chalked it up to Jarle Norgaard and his boy not having enough faith.

Thor walked away from the tent that night still Deaf as a doorpost and fearing neither he nor Da would make it into heaven. Which meant neither of them would see the good Lord or Ma. Thor had crawled up to the highest hideaway in the cidery that night and drank himself to smithereens. It was the first time he'd ever done such a thing. He'd had plenty of sips over the years of tasting with Da, but never so much that he couldn't remember anything of the next day.

It was a numbing he got used to.

Here on the hillside, Thor blinked into the bright light of noon. It pierced his skull so fiercely he had to shield his eyes until his vision righted. When it did, he peered down the slope to see movement in the brush. The tips of antlers. Not fifty yards off, a young buck trod forward, lifted his head, and peered at Thor. Half surrounded by brush, the creature didn't startle. Maybe a two-year-old at most. Those weren't much for wall mounts but tender eating to be sure. Thor dropped his gaze to the rifle that was two feet away. If he moved slowly . . .

Reaching for it, he hoped with everything in him that he was being quiet. His inability to hear himself made him a poor hunter at short range, but from afar, where sound gave way to sharp aim, he was the best shot out of his brothers. Thor closed a hand around the forestock and set the gun across his lap. The creature stepped forward and paused, watching him still.

The rifle was loaded. A quick raise and fire and the animal would drop.

Thor didn't move.

He just watched the young deer lower his face to the ground, sniff, and look back up. Wind stirred the grasses between them, rippling the dried meadow as waves. All glittering and hot this September day. Thor touched the trigger, let the pad of his finger find its place, but still he didn't raise the rifle. Part of him wanted to aim and fire, but more of him wanted that stag to take a step back. Turn away and bound down the hillside. What that creature did was out of his control, so Thor controlled what he could.

He pulled his hand away and just savored the few minutes he had of watching the young deer. When it was gone, Thor's senses kicked in and part of him regretted letting such a prize get away.

A small part of him.

The springhouse was filled with meats, and it was a kill he needn't make. Really, he'd come here to get away—hunting being an excuse. If he trudged home empty-handed, that was alright by him.

Thor hauled his pack near and dug inside. Ida had packed him some bread and jerky. The bread had been sliced down the middle and slathered with blackberry jam. Aven's jam. Thor licked his thumb clean, getting the first taste.

Leave it to Ida to meddle even from afar.

Famished, he went to take a bite when something else in the distance caught his eye. Two blonde heads bobbed into view, a pair of women climbing the hillside. They strolled slowly, burdened by heavy-looking baskets. A second glance showed the baskets loaded with apples. It took a few seconds for his brain to lock and load on that.

Apples.

If their direction was true, they'd come from his orchards. Thor stood. He'd left Jorgan working on the chicken coop, and with Haakon's mind who-knew-where, it would have been easy for the women to slip along the far acreage and glean what they wished.

With the women nearer, the one in front spotted him. Her feet slowed to a standstill so abruptly the woman behind her nearly stumbled. In moments, they were both looking at him. The second went to walk on again, but the first stopped her as if willing to face whatever consequence was coming. Having no idea what he was about to do or how to express it, Thor headed toward them. The gun he left behind.

He ran his hands together, nerves rising. He wasn't good with strangers. Trying to communicate with them was rarely successful because people put little effort into understanding him. The first woman watched him—both boldness and worry traced across her features. He approached unhurriedly so as to send no alarm. Thor gave a friendly nod.

She dipped her head warily in return. With fine lines around her eyes and mouth and threads of silver lightening her already-pale hair, she looked to be in her fifties. The one behind her was just as tall and slender, but only a few years past girlhood. Hair as fair as the rest of her kinfolk.

Sorrel women. He'd bet anything on it.

And now that he was thinking about it, the young one was called Sibby. Probably short for something fancier, but he didn't know. A speaking man would greet her mother as Mrs. Sorrel, the head of the female roost. There were other daughters as well, and wives who had married into the family. Lots of children. Enough to take up several pews if they all were in church, which was rare.

As if knowing that caught was caught, Mrs. Sorrel set the basket at her feet. Thor stepped close enough to glimpse inside. Easily three or four dozen apples in the one. How long had they been stealing from him? He knelt and dragged the basket nearer. It was his right to confiscate it, but all he could think of were the children. The skinny beanpoles from the toddling stage and on up. Children who likely didn't know that the fruit they'd be eating was a few weeks shy of ripe.

He glanced at Sibby and knew hunger when he saw it. The Sorrel men weren't using their income on family provisions. Certain he knew where it was being funneled left Thor with a rock in his gut. Not that selling the Sorrels liquor had been his intent, but turning a blind eye had been a choice all the same.

With a tip of his head, Thor motioned for the

ladies to follow him. He walked to his pack, set the basket aside, and dug among his things. He found a second sandwich that Ida had made and handed both over.

The older woman glanced from the offering, then to his face. Anger sparked in her blue-gray eyes. "What's that gonna cost?" She shifted some in front of her grown daughter.

It was just like a woman who did without to believe that everything had a cost. He wouldn't even dream of touching her daughter and hated the notion of her having assumed otherwise. Thor shook his head.

He shook his head once more as he handed over what Ida had made. When Mrs. Sorrel didn't take them, he set the wrapped meals on top of the apples and hefted up the basket again. Mouth set firmly, Sibby watched with eyes that looked older than her years. Thor couldn't begin to guess all that she'd seen or experienced. On her left wrist were small bruises in the shape of fingerprints. Her mother bore bruises of similar fashion on one side of her neck.

Thor motioned for them to follow. They did, at a distance.

The climb took all he had left. When he reached the top ridge, he was panting again. The Sorrel farm was just on the other side of those trees, so the women wouldn't have much farther to go. Rarely did Thor ever come here. Not to the home of the men who marched into their yard bearing torches. The ones who'd been brutal with Al and would likely not stop there. Thor glanced to Sibby again. Was she the one Al had smiled at?

After striding a few yards nearer to the stand of trees, Thor set the basket down. The women lagged behind. Sibby stumbled, spilling her basket. Thor hurried to help her. He picked up the fruit and placed each one with as much care as if for his own use. Wide-eyed, she watched him. He lifted the basket, settling it in her grasp again, then made the sign for *more* by tapping the pinched fingers of both hands together.

She shook her head. Trying again, Thor knelt. He grabbed a stick and wrote the word. Both women read it. He pointed to the apples. When they still looked uncertain, he pressed both of his palms to his chest, then held them out to try and show the act of giving. It's what Da would have done. Was it not Da who had taught them to look after those who were less fortunate?

To Thor's shame, he and his brothers hadn't given much thought to the Sorrel women and children. So it was with humility now that Thor made the gesture again, pointing to the apples, then to the word he'd written in the dirt.

Mrs. Sorrel's forehead crinkled in surprise, and he knew she understood.

Thor gave a small smile. If he was too friendly it would just frighten them, so he stepped away.

A touch at his arm halted him. The older woman was holding out a small box of matches. She spoke, but he hadn't been watching. Touching his lips, he rolled his finger forward—hoping she'd repeat herself.

"I found these in the grass." Though they were no longer of high society, her speech looked genteel, words shaped with the slow, delicate cadence of a Southern belle. "Are they yours?"

He accepted the box. Dipping his head in gratitude, he started off. Downhill was easier than the walk up, so he made quick time. He didn't glance back until he got to his pack again, and when he did, the women were gone.

Thor sat and pulled his things near, then fetched his pipe. He stuck the end in his mouth, struck a match, and lit the tobacco. Closing his eyes, he inhaled deeply, then shook the flame out. He had fire again, so he could get through for a day or two fine. If he picked off a rabbit or small game, he'd have supper, and while he was finally in the mood for some hunting, that would have to wait. He needed to get back to the farm—and the sooner, the better—because he finally knew what he was going to do. He was going to pay the Sorrel men a visit.

But first, he had to break some bad news to his brothers.

TWENTY

"Oh no you don't." Aven lifted Dotti into the crate filled with sawdust.

The kitten's tail wriggled again, and there was no doubt of what that meant. Aven had cleaned up two puddles already this morning. Time for a success. When it happened, she clapped and the kitten tumbled head over rump out of the crate.

Aven scooped her up. "See now! I knew you could do it." She kissed the downy gray head and dangled the slip of yarn, wondering if their game was at an end. Dotti rolled over, swatting at the tattered fibers with all four paws.

Excitement sounded from the kitchen. Voices, one over another. With Fay due to arrive any day, Aven tied the string to the crate and scrambled to her feet. She hurried out and closed the door behind her so Dotti wouldn't escape just yet. She meant to give the cat free reign of the house but wanted her to be less accident-prone first. That also meant she would need to hurry back to check on her.

Aven made her way downstairs to find Jorgan and Haakon standing on one side of the kitchen table. Opposite them stood Thor. Looking as wind-tousled as a Viking returned from sea, Thor lifted a brace of hares onto the surface and turned one over. Home so soon? As nice a surprise as the day could have brought.

"You're not gonna eat those, are you?" Haakon said. "We got a whole side of beef in the springhouse."

Head down, Thor nodded. He signed something to Ida and she fetched a large tin pan. After rolling back the cuffs of his sleeves, Thor unsheathed his hunting knife and set a rabbit in the pan. He started on the first skin with easy strokes. The pelt began to fall away.

"How does he know how to do that so well?" Haakon asked Jorgan.

" 'Cause Da used to hunt, numskull."

"I know that, dimwit . . ." Haakon stepped to the other side, still watching. "But it was a long time ago."

When Thor finished with the first pelt, he removed the innards. He did the same with the second rabbit and, upon finishing, took the meat out to the water pump and rinsed it all. When he returned, Ida asked if she should start a stew.

Thor made his sign for gratitude. He washed his knife, then his hands. Ida set a pot on the stove and slid her cutting board to the table. She placed one of the hares in the center.

"I'm not eating that." Haakon started for the door.

Thor stopped him with a hand to the chest, motioning Haakon toward the great room. He gestured for Jorgan to go that way as well, even Aven. He signed to Ida, and she promised to be right there.

" 'Twill make a fine meal, Haakon," Aven said, walking beside the young man.

Haakon rolled his eyes, trudged around the sofa, and sat in the center. Jorgan kicked Haakon's boot and Haakon scooted to one side. Jorgan motioned for Aven to sit as Thor shaped more of his words.

When he finished, Jorgan spoke. "Aven, he's asked I explain for you."

She crossed her ankles, curious as to what was happening. Thor waited until everyone was settled, then began in Sign. Some of the thoughts he shaped were intricate, sweeping motions. Others were rapid snaps or the pound of a fist to a palm. Jorgan spoke along with him.

"He's saying he has an idea he wants to run by each of us. It has to do with the cider. I guess it's been a decision a long time in the making."

Ida slipped in, drying her hands on a clean cloth. The rocking chair creaked when she sat.

Thor shaped fluid letters with a single hand. The last resembled an *L* with his pointer finger and thumb both spread open.

"Sorrel," Jorgan said softly. "It's got somethin' to do with them."

Brows dug low, Thor tapped the side of his head, then closing his thumbs and pointer fingers together, pulled his hands down in front of him. Next he dragged a thumb forward beneath the center of his beard and finished by flicking his closed hands away from his body.

"He's saying that—" Jorgan fell silent.

Haakon stood suddenly.

"What is it?" Aven asked.

Thor shaped those letters again. *S-O-R-R-E-L.* He made a face as if he was disgusted.

"He said he doesn't want to sell to them." Jorgan watched Thor explain more. "He's . . . saying . . . that he doesn't want to sell *any* of the liquor." Jorgan blanched.

Haakon cursed. "I knew this was gonna happen." He stepped around the back of the sofa as if needing the distance between him and the man addressing the room. "You don't get to make that call." Haakon jabbed a finger in Thor's direction. "We break our backs at harvest for that money. I been deliverin' for years. You don't get to make that call."

"And livin' just fine for that," Jorgan said. "Calm down."

"Calm down? *Calm down?* There's a gold mine in that shed." Haakon pointed toward the cidery. "What's he gonna do? Dump it all in the river? Oh, I got a better idea. Why don't I just mix up some explosives and we send it sky high? It worked for that chicken coop. Why not do it to all of our savings?" Haakon picked up a book and hurled it across the room. It struck something off a side table, and everything clattered to the ground.

Ida tipped up her chin. "Haakon Norgaard, you pick that up."

Haakon didn't budge. "I'm sick of everybody acting like Thor runs the show. Just 'cause he's cotton to somethin' don't make it the right thing."

Thor held up both palms, then gestured straight at his younger brother.

"Yeah, well, a third of what's in that shop is mine." Stomping out, Haakon opened the kitchen door and slammed it behind him.

Jorgan exchanged a glance with Thor. Wind whistled over the roof. Hanging rose vines clattered against the window. Thor stared out the far window. Though he was silent, whatever weighed on his mind and heart was anything but. Aven watched him and, in that moment, knew that if she were there in that shed again, with him beckoning her to come to him, she would go to him in a heartbeat.

Thor looked at her and was just reaching for his notebook when the sound of splintering wood drew Aven's attention toward the cider barn. Jorgan did the same. Thor followed suit.

Jorgan swiped two fingers in front of his eyes in a sign that made Thor sober even further. Thor headed that way and Aven trailed them out onto the porch. At the cidery, Haakon was prying one of the boards off the door. He threw it aside, dug an iron rod behind the next board, and snapped another free.

Jorgan called for Haakon to stop, but Thor placed a hand on his shoulder. Another squeeze and Thor felt his resolve settle. Holding on to the sensation, he headed to the horse barn. He ducked inside, opened up a lidded box, and rummaged for the largest of the pry bars. The iron rod in hand, he headed back to the cidery.

Thor set the tool between the door and the next board. He pulled the same moment his brother did. The board crashed to the ground. Haakon glanced at him. Wedging the iron rod in again, Thor nodded and waited for Haakon to place his tool. The breeze shook Thor's shirt, pressing it about his waist. Haakon's own lined tight to the shape of his shoulders in the pull of the wind. Together, they tugged down. Nails tapped the dirt. They freed the next board and then the next. All the way down until there was a pile of broken wood around them.

Thor knelt and took up a long splinter of wood. Shoving it beneath the door, he searched for the feel of the key. He finally skidded it out into the sunlight. Thor rose and braced a hand to the door. It was time.

Haakon nearly reached for the door latch when he motioned for Thor to take the lead.

How many times had Thor entered this building? Beyond count. He pressed the key into the iron lock, turned it with a *click,* then shimmied the padlock free. After sliding the heavy door aside, he entered the soaring space that felt as still and hollow as a cave. Having been bound up for over two weeks, the aroma of cider struck him like a speeding train. Thor sucked in a breath. His brothers exchanged glances.

Stepping farther in, he looked from the rows of glass jars to the carefully aligned barrels with their chalk markings. Thor walked the length of his workbench, not touching a thing. When he reached the end, he paused before the blue ribbons, seeing Da's more than his own.

The floor shuddered. Thor looked over to see that it was Haakon who had stomped.

"What are we gonna do?" Haakon asked. "The debt . . ."

Thor hadn't figured that out yet, but there had to be another way.

Hands in his pockets, Jorgan strode the length of the vast barn. He motioned to the product and faced Thor before speaking. "This all holds a high price, Thor."

Aven sought his attention. "I've an idea." She moved to a shelf and pulled down a dusty jar that seemed heftier in her small grasp. "There are recipes that call for flavored liquors. Jams and jellies. Even sauces."

He arched an eyebrow.

She hurried to continue as if sensing his skepticism. "You see, when liquor is cooked, it loses its potency. Becoming delicate enough for even the littlest of children to eat."

Haakon leaned against the workbench. "So you suggest we boil out what Thor has spent years perfecting so it can be baby food?"

"Exactly. Wait, no."

Thor smiled. Curious, he rolled a hand forward for her to say more.

"In Norway I spent time helping the baker who leased his upstairs flat. He made different glazes with mead. Since it has a honey flavor, he drizzled it onto ginger cookies and almond cakes. Once he even made a mead sauce to pour over a pork roast. 'Twas marvelous."

Moving to the workbench, Thor shuffled around for something to write on. Finding an invoice, he folded it on the blank side. Next he nabbed a pencil. *This you make? Know how make?*

Aven nodded quickly, her eyes bright. "It's not hard. If these recipes were to be made and jarred, you could sell them in place of hard drink. Perhaps even set up a farm stand closer to the road to procure income. People would come."

"Who'd watch the stand?"

"You could," she answered Haakon. Her hands moved in excitement as she spoke again to Thor. "Different recipes could be distributed to local shops, or beyond the area. Sold at the county fair. With some experimentation, I think we could come up with a great many . . ."

Her words blurred, so quick she spoke. Thor tapped her arm, touched his mouth, and gestured slowly with his hands, hoping she'd understand.

"Sorry." She gulped a swallow. While her speech wasn't as rushed, her eagerness was as vibrant as ever. "We could create many more concoctions. Dressings to pour over greens. Perhaps a sauce to be drizzled on ice cream or custard. Maybe the cider could be baked into breads. If these items could be sold—who knows what may come of it."

Thor felt a smile lift one side of his mouth. How he loved her.

Haakon straightened. "And what's gonna pay the rent while you're in the kitchen making apple-cider bread?"

"Sell the coming harvest as it is." She peered between them all. "Sell it by the bushel load. Folks around here could use apples in their larder. Set a price for them to pick their own share, saving you the labor."

"They're cider apples," Haakon cut in. "Most are poor eatin'."

"Then press those to sell the cider fresh." She looked back to Thor. "Why ferment it?"

He wrote quickly. *Go bad, not ferment.*

Her countenance fell as she took the paper from

him. Stepping nearer, he wrote more, gripping her wrist to steady the folded page. *Maybe possible.*

"Truly?"

It meant using different methods, but if kept cool and sold off in short fashion, it could be done. He'd just never put any effort to that way because the payoff was significantly less per acre.

Jorgan pulled a stool closer and straddled it. "I like the idea, but fresh cider won't make half as much, and we've got the lease to think about."

In a twirl of her patchwork skirt, Aven left. Thor turned to his brothers. Lacking answers, he expressed as much. Jorgan confirmed his understanding.

"I can't believe you're doing this," Haakon said.

Thor pointed to himself, then hooking a finger struck it down for *need.* He signed *time,* then tapped a finger to the side of his skull. He just needed a chance to think . . . if Haakon could be patient for once in his life.

Aven rushed back in. Her cheeks were pink and her hair windblown. She hurried all the way up to Thor, lifted his hand, and opened his fingers. Shock rushed through him even as he peered down at her freckled nose and rounded ears. He dropped his gaze lower to see her pressing a flash of gold into his palm. A thick coin.

He tilted it to the light of the window. It was

a twenty kroner. Norwegian gold. Why was she giving it to him? It was worth way too much to her. Shaking his head, Thor went to hand it back, but she closed his fingers around the coin again. The rough grooves of the coat of arms pressed into his skin.

"Yours." She glanced to Haakon and Jorgan, then back to Thor. "All of yours."

TWENTY-ONE

Through the bedroom window, Aven spotted Thor walking eastward. He had been scarce the last two days. Ever since the cidery had been opened. He seemed to want to keep busy anywhere but on the farm, and she didn't blame him.

But even when he was around, his eye had been so hard to catch that there had been no chance to even smile a greeting. 'Twas the weight of the world on his shoulders. She could see it in his dogged stride even now. If that weren't enough, over breakfast Haakon had mentioned the upcoming dance, emphasizing Thor's need to learn his right foot from his left. No wonder the poor man made himself scarce.

At her feet Dotti was lapping up a dish of cream. Across the nightstand was spread a mess of papers. Lists of recipes Aven was imagining. Though in the midst of jotting notes for cider marmalade, she rose, stepped over the kitten, and closed the door. Aven hurried downstairs before Thor vanished as he had done the day before and the day before that.

She didn't begin running until she'd rounded the corner of the house to see him nearly gone from sight. She hurried down a shallow hill. Oblivious, Thor trudged onward.

When he glanced to the side, it must have brought her into his line of vision because he slowed and looked back. His eyes widened.

She slackened her pace to a stroll. "May I walk with you awhile?"

He nodded, then took the lead and pushed a branch aside for her. His hair was unbound, the dark twists of it clean but tousled as usual. Each of his steps was loud. No care taken for quiet placement. Aven followed behind, feeling both lost and safe. Liking each in equal measure.

At a fallen log, he climbed over, then reached back to assist her. Her fingers vanished inside his, and never had she felt so steady as that single, blessed step. He released her and pointed up into a sprawling tree. Shielding her eyes from the peeking sun, she saw what looked like a tree house. An adventurously run-down one.

"This is where you are headed?"

He nodded.

Weathered boards had been nailed up the trunk as a makeshift ladder and looked nearly as aged as the tree itself. Thor climbed the first rung and, giving a small bounce, used his weight to test each one. At the top, he motioned for her to follow.

Aven called up, "Are you planning on being there awhile?"

He pinched two fingers close together to show *just a little*.

"Perhaps I'll wait for you to finish."

He vanished from the edge. No longer could she see him, but the platform overhead creaked as he walked across it. Then everything went silent. A few minutes passed and not even a sound came from above. What was he doing?

Aven tapped her foot. Then the other. She paced to the tree and started on the bottom board. Shimmying her foot into place, she climbed atop that one and then several more. She was just scaling the next when the fear of falling pinned her into place. This had to be much easier in britches than petticoats. Panic pricked her insides, but then Thor was reaching down. He looped an arm around her waist and helped her brave the highest rung.

Leaves and branches fanned out in all directions. Just overhead, the tattered remains of a white flag moved limp on the breeze. Birds flittered from perch to perch. Aven nearly gasped at the sudden pleasure of it all. When she was safely on the platform, Thor pressed her beside the tree trunk. She knelt against it. Three names were roughly carved into the bark. In the silence that followed, she traced the middle one.

Thor sat in the center of the platform, screwdriver in hand. All the boards were nailed into place—all save the one he was focused on. He had already loosened three of the screws and was just finishing the last. After setting the hand tool aside, he pressed on one end of the board so the other edge lifted. He worked his finger just beneath and took off the board entirely.

Stilling, he glanced at her.

" 'Tis your hiding spot?"

In answer, he took her hand and pressed it over her eyes.

She parted two fingers to peek through. "Does this mean we are in cahoots?"

When he flicked her leg, she righted the covering, but not before glimpsing the grin that had lit his face. She was smiling herself.

A few bumps and thuds sounded and one strange little rattle, then she heard the board slide into place. Thor tapped her arm and she lowered her hand. He slid the screws back to their holes and fetched his tool. Beside him now sat a medium-sized jar. It kept coins— pennies and nickels mostly. Perhaps his from childhood.

A tiny pile of buttons rested beside the blue-tinted glass. It took a few tries for Thor's fingers to grip a string lying there, but when he managed, he held it up for her to see that the buttons were strung. Aven smiled. More so when he tied the ends together, pulled her wrist nearer, and slid it on.

"Thank you." She grazed a fingertip along the colorful buttons. "A fine collection of things you have."

He dipped his head shyly, using that chance to reach for the screwdriver. He twisted it, securing each corner of the board, then shoved the handle end into his back pocket. He stood and helped Aven to her feet. Scrutinizing the homespun ladder that led to the ground, he seemed to wonder how to get her out of the tree house. She wondered the same.

The jar clanked as he set it near the edge. Then Thor started down. He had only taken a few steps when he inched himself to the side and motioned for her to come down as well. She gripped the nearest branch and lowered her foot to the top board. Thor's hand slid around her waist, his touch gentle but sure. Aven pulled her skirts out of the way and climbed down another. He stayed beside her, taking care to always be a rung lower, and in no time they were on solid ground again.

He squinted sheepishly, then climbed back up and fetched the jar.

Aven giggled as he returned.

They fell in step together and started back the way they'd come. The air was crisper now than when she'd rushed off. Aven folded her arms as they walked. Occasionally Thor glanced at her as if wondering what she might have to say. Not wanting his efforts to be wasted, Aven spoke of the first recipe she had tried.

" 'Twas a batch of cider jelly. I made it this

morning, and it didn't set right as I used too little pectin. I'll try again this evening. Perhaps you can sample a taste when it's done and tell me what you think."

He gave a small smile, followed by a nod.

"Ida mentioned that they are taking donations for the fund-raiser. Haakon said there is to be a raffle before the dance. If I'm able, I'll send along some jars of the jelly and perhaps then we can see if folks take to it."

He seemed pleased by that. And even . . . proud? It shone in his eyes when he looked down at her. When they reached the fallen log again, she climbed over first. He followed, and the jar in his grasp jangled softly.

Aven motioned to the coins. "Though perhaps there is another option as well." She swallowed hard, determined to finally brave this. "I've been offered a sewing position at a shop in Lexington."

Thor's brow puckered in confusion. His gaze lifted from her mouth to her eyes. When he lowered his focus again, she knew he was waiting for more.

"The wage is a fair one, and with room and board provided, I'd be able to send my earnings back here." The jar in his hand suddenly seemed much too small. His efforts, anything but. "My earnings wouldn't be much, but if I could do my part to help you keep this farm, I would go. But I confess . . ." She couldn't look at him as she spoke the rest. "That it would be difficult to do. This has become my home too. You all have become my family. It's for that reason only that I would go. Not because I would wish distance . . ."

He stepped closer and suddenly his nearness was startling. Not because she feared him, but because of what it did to her. Thor shaped four letters. He fashioned two more words, then finished by forming a fist, pressing the tip of his thumb through two fingers, and running his hand beneath his beard.

"I'm so sorry. I don't understand."

He nearly turned away.

She caught his arm. "Please teach me so I can know?"

He shook his head and went to step around her.

Aven followed and turned so he would see her speak. *"Please."*

Thor glanced back to the tree house, then farther down the lane. Finally, he leveled her with a stern look and she knew he was caving. He stepped nearer, took her hand, and opened it. With the tip of his finger, he traced what looked like an *A* on her palm. Her wrist he cradled gently, and his touch had been so soft that she was glad he couldn't hear her quick intake of breath. The pocket at his chest lay flat—the notebook elsewhere.

"A," she repeated weakly.

He traced the letter again, then raised his fist, thumb tucked to the side.

She made the same shape. With both of his large hands around her own, he adjusted her fingers to better match the correct form. When he let go, she held the letter still. He nodded his approval, then moved on to the next. She struggled at the *E,* but he was patient as he guided her fingers in the smallest of ways. It made her sense just how detailed this language was. Even a tiny change in shape would alter the meaning. His care and thoughtfulness—his teaching—took all of her focus until she realized that they had finished her name.

She shaped it once more. *A-V-E-N.* She smiled and his own expression was soft. "Will you teach me the others next? What is yours?"

He made that fist again where his thumb poked through, then traced a *T* on her palm. Next he did the other three letters. By the time she had learned it, she could shape *T-H-O-R* even quicker than her own name. He signaled for her attention. After making the *T* shape again, he ran it under his beard.

He wrote his name on her palm, then slid that *T* beneath his beard again. After a second repetition, she realized the single gesture was *Thor.* She tried it, liking the feel of it.

Thor showed his approval and motioned for them to walk on. Though she didn't fully know what he'd said in response to her mention of Lexington, she meant to find out. Because she now knew that the first four letters of that ardent speech had been her name. The very last word had been his own.

TWENTY-TWO

The Sorrel House stood like a ghost from the past—the mansion only a whisper of its former grandeur. The war had sunk the white antebellum from its days of glory. The once-pristine yard was overgrown with brush and laundry lines bearing sun-faded clothing. The formal drive long forgotten. Artillery wounds near the brick chimney were patched and painted over, but the shattered porch railings still stood in disrepair—both posts and rails missing from its own fight to survive the War between the States.

Unease dwelled on this farm. Hanging in the air even now. Thor tried to decide if he wanted to knock on the front door or try the barn first. Jorgan stepped beside him, and Thor was grateful for his presence. With a toss of his thumb, Jorgan suggested the house.

The stately home wasn't as extravagant as some plantations, but it was sturdy and the land vast. Just a few miles from the James River, the plantation had once been a hub for goods and imports. Or so the story went. While some slaveholders abandoned their plantations or sold them off, Jed Sorrel had limped back here upon the fall of the Confederacy to find his once-immaculate house shaken to the battered floorboards, furnishings all stripped away. His family keeping refuge a few counties over. The basement stairwell cut up for firewood.

Slave quarters empty.

A few of those slaves hadn't gone far. With the Emancipation Proclamation being what it was, the Sorrels hadn't been able to drag Ida or her sister back. Just torment them over the hedge. The pair had sought employment from Jarle and Kristin Norgaard—renters of the upper acreage and freshly arrived from Norway just a few years before the South seceded. Not only had the immigrants leased the acreage from its owners, but upon Jarle's return from his required service for the infantry, they'd given several newly freed men and women work in the orchards with wages. A place to reside in the small cabins.

But just because Lincoln signed a document saying it could be so, sentiments among the Sorrels ran through murkier waters. Their patriarch wasn't the only man to have lost his slaves to the Thirteenth Amendment, nor was he the only Confederate to refuse to sign the oath to the Union.

Forfeiting his right to vote, Jed had taken a stand with the South that some of his fellow Southerners upheld. Some going so far as to join him in the crusades of what had been named the Ku Klux Klan. A group founded by former Confederate generals like Jed himself. All passionate about their cause, making it into newspapers across the country of the terror they inflicted to see the purification of society defended. Though legally disbanded now, that meant nothing in these parts.

Thor strode with his brother up the grand porch steps, feeling with every step the pistol he'd wedged into his waistband at the small of his back. A pair of boys ran past so quick, Thor moved down a step. A barking puppy trailed them across the porch, more interested in the game of chase than the trespassers.

Thor shared a glance with Jorgan, then crossed to the front door. Worried he wouldn't knock with the right amount of volume, he signaled for Jorgan to do the honors. His brother stepped up to the tall door and pounded knuckles with slow precision. Jorgan had his head down, listening. He gave a brief nod, so Thor moved back. Someone was coming.

A woman with pale-yellow hair opened the door. Her belly was swollen with child, and she looked surprised to see them. Turning her thin face away, she hollered out to someone deeper in the house. Thor flexed his hands, recalling what he meant to express to them, all the while hoping he'd be understood. The woman stepped aside, and another wedged forward, this one Mrs. Sorrel, whom he'd seen just days ago.

Jed's wife.

Her hair was twisted up tight, and she carried herself with an air of authority despite the humble cut and threadbare fabric of her gown. While a Southern belle through and through, gone were the hoopskirts and fluttering fans. In their stead was a timeworn determination.

Confusion flitted across her eyes, and for the briefest of moments Thor saw the widening of fear. Did she worry he'd turn her in about the apples? He wasn't here to tattle. Quite the opposite. With the back of his hand, he bumped his brother's side. Jorgan spoke.

When he finished, Mrs. Sorrel shook her head. Thor watched her mouth.

"They're not here. They'll be gone the rest of the day."

Jorgan must have asked where they'd gone because she spoke again.

"You think I know where they're off to? What I do know is that they'll be gone until dusk, as usual." She didn't say it unkindly. In fact, there was a spark of irritation in her eyes for not being more entrusted with her man's whereabouts. At least that's how it appeared.

Thor glanced around. He'd bet every bullet in his pistol that the Sorrel men were on the farm somewhere. No doubt staying from sight in this very house. He nodded to Mrs. Sorrel to show that he understood. When Jorgan thanked the woman, Thor led the way back down the steps. They could come back in a few days.

Jed and his kinsmen couldn't stay out of sight forever.

Thor and Jorgan returned to the house to find Aven rushing out to meet them. Thor worried something was amiss until he saw the cheer in her eyes.

"A new idea has occurred to me." She moved to his side—so near that Jorgan coughed into his fist to hide a smile.

Thor nearly elbowed his brother.

"I'd like to try out an apple butter recipe. Ida was telling me about the recipe she uses, and if we stew the apples and sugar in your cider, it might give an even richer flavor. But I wondered if there was a variety you'd recommend—"

Thor yanked his gaze from her mouth to keep from stumbling into the porch railing. He missed what she said next, but the excitement when she turned to face him again was enough. He offered his agreement, liking the idea. Having tasted the cider jelly she'd stewed up, he'd eat anything she ever set in front of him. But she wasn't cooking up sweets for him. She was doing it for the farm. And that made her efforts all the finer.

He dug for his pencil and notebook, then wrote, *Need fresh apples, apple butter.*

"Yes. When will they be ready? And is there a type you'd suggest?"

Foxwhelp—Sept.

Roxbury—Oct. Sweet Coppins, same. Roxbury best make apple butter.

She read that with care. "Thank you. When the time comes, I'll be ready and you can guide me." She smiled. "But for now . . . there's not much for you to do except await the ripening?"

That was put rather simply. But yes.

"And what are you doing now?"

Nothing pressing. What was she getting at?

"Could you possibly spare half an hour?"

He narrowed his gaze. She was smiling bigger now—almost giddy. Something wasn't right. He nearly shrugged because he'd be more than happy to pass time helping her, but then Aven turned away and spoke to Jorgan. What was going on? Thor tapped her shoulder to try and get her attention.

When she turned back, she pointed to herself, then slowly spelled her name with her fingers.

She did the *E* all wrong, but the effort was such a nice sight that he wasn't going to complain.

Aven angled back toward Jorgan, who showed her the word for *teach*. She faced Thor and made the sign. Then she peeked slyly over her shoulder, fetching the next word. Looking back at Thor, Aven swiped two fingers across her palm in a dancing motion. On her own, she formed a *T* and gently slid it under her chin. She pointed to herself again, to him, then danced two fingers on her palm once more.

So the little trouble maker wanted to dance and was using Sign to soften him to the idea.

Jorgan was nearly laughing now.

Not wanting to be a total brute, Thor tipped an invisible hat for her efforts, then strode onto the porch. In a jiff she was beside him, gripping his sleeve. Her fingers grazed his arm, and he really wished she would stop touching him. It was only making it harder to stand his ground. He pulled her hand away and moved aside even farther.

"Thor!" She whirled the other way to block him and even then, she was giggling. "This dance is only two weeks away. Unless you've told this young lady you're not attending, you'll have to learn a few steps." Behind her, the late-afternoon sun said there was enough daylight left.

He should have walked home slower. And now that he was thinking of it, he had some pencils to hatchet in two and sharpen. He doubted that would impress Aven, though.

"Half an hour. Just half an hour for us to practice a few simple steps. Then you can be done, and I promise I won't bother you again."

Resolve faltered inside him. Thirty minutes? And he could be done with this? It was tempting to cave—to be rid of this once and for all—but Thor shook his head. He really didn't want to dance.

Aven's gaze lifted to his, and there lived in her eyes a final whisper of hope. Her mouth shaped one word. Just one word. "Please."

Breathing out a sigh, he looked from her to the yard where Jorgan was heading off. Thor let out a whistle, and his brother turned.

Thor signed to Aven. *Dance? I not know how.* He looked to Jorgan for help, and his brother spoke for him.

Aven nodded compassionately. "That's why I'll show you."

I not hear music. Did she not understand?

"He's reminding you he can't hear the music," Jorgan said.

Aven stepped nearer to Thor, touching his arm again. He shot out a breath but didn't pry her hand away this time. "Just half an hour. Will you please trust me? I promise I will help you through this."

Thor walked with Aven across the farmyard and to the meadow just beyond. Out of sight of his brothers had been his only insistence. That meant there would be no one to translate, but he figured Aven would do most of the talking. He could write, of course, but his hands were about to be occupied with the Irish lass fairly skipping along at his side. Thor slowed when she did.

"Are you ready?"

He swallowed hard.

Aven stepped back and clasped her hands in front of her. "Some dances are quite quick and animated. A reel or a jig, etcetera. You'll want to avoid those, I'd imagine."

Quite.

"But perhaps a waltz. If you danced even one, 'twould be gentlemanly. Then, perhaps, you could simply pass the time talking with the young lady. I mean, writing . . . or however seems most comfortable with being . . . sociable with her." She stumbled over the words, her eagerness fading some.

Was she jealous by that idea? Thor doubted it, but there was something about her just now. It wasn't as if this other young lady had a liking for him. She'd only pulled his name from a drawing basket for a fund-raiser. Yet Aven wouldn't be attending. The unhappy thought dissipated when she took his right hand and pressed it to the curve of her waist.

Her eyes lifted to his and she gave a gentle smile.

His gaze filtered across the vast meadow. Not a soul in sight. That was for the best. There didn't need to be an audience for this—the first time he ever had a young lady in his touch. Aside from when he'd dragged Aven away from that shed, he'd never had his hands on a woman in any way. Twenty-eight was awful late to just be starting, but it's what it was. He released a slow breath.

Aven fitted her right hand in the crook of his left. Gently, she raised their arms some. "This is the stance. Does it feel comfortable?" So at ease was she that he tried to appear the same.

His smallest finger had a mind of its own, though, grazing against her hip. He hoped she didn't notice. When she patted his shoulder, he shifted all focus back to her face.

" 'Twill help if you're paying attention."

He flashed her a stern look. If he was paying any more attention, he was going to pass out.

"This dance counts by three." Her guidance was gentle, her watch of him even more so. "I'll count as we do each step. We'll go nice and slow so you can get the idea. To begin, you'll step forward with your left foot, then to the side with your right. We'll bring our feet together."

When she stepped forward with her left, he must have moved back with the wrong foot because she landed on his boot. They righted themselves and tried again. The next attempt went better. When she meant him to move his left foot, she tapped his shoulder. When he was to step with the other, she squeezed his right hand. That helped more than she might have realized.

"That's perfect. We're making a square, so now we'll both go to your left and bring our feet together."

He followed her without incident and he could see how delighted she was.

"Look at you. Already a dancer."

That was being generous.

As Aven spoke, "One, two, three . . . one, two, three . . ." He followed in his mind, *forward—side—together. Back—side—together.*

More than a few times he made a mistake, but the instances grew further apart until they were making an invisible square together.

Aven looked breathless by the time she finally stilled them. "You will do better at this than you realize. The only thing we need to focus on next is for you to learn how to lead."

What?

"A help will be for you to watch the other couples. That will guide you in the tempo of the music. If you follow the flow of the room, I believe you could do it, Thor." Her hand shifted inside his. "Now. You step strongly forward and be firm with it. You're to lead. Step forward with surety so the only choice I have is to step back."

He did. And it felt good to guide her.

She smiled. "Well done. Now to the side . . ."

Trying to remember the steps, he pressed her in the direction he wished her to go. Aven was fluid to his every movement. She made it look easy, and even though he couldn't have been doing this full and proper, she followed him. Not an ounce of resistance as he pressed her back . . . led her to the side.

"Now I'm going to turn under your arm."

She was gonna what?

Aven lifted his hand and ducked beneath his arm. She kept turning until she was facing him again. Thor halted, watching her.

"No. You cannot stop. You keep waltzing while I turn."

This was getting too complicated. His face must have shown as much.

Her expression was soft. "Trust me. 'Tis quite simple. All you do is keep stepping around inside the box, and when you want me to turn, you raise your arm. You will find that most men will turn their partner every few squares. Dance is communication without words. Think of it as a straightforward direction. Raise your arm if you want your partner to turn . . . and she will. Truly, 'tis more simple than complicated." Her brown eyes peered up to his. "You're the one leading, and no words will be necessary."

They danced around the invisible box a few more times, and wanting to please her, Thor raised his arm. Loosening her grip on his hand, Aven beamed as she spun beneath it. He'd never seen her so happy. He was pretty sure he did his next step wrong, but she wasn't looking. After finishing her rotation, she slid right into place and they traveled another square. Finally she slowed them. Or was it his doing?

He didn't want to let go, but he did.

Aven laced her fingers together in front of her

skirt. "You've got it now, Thor. A good thing your partner is already chosen. A line would form if the lassies had their pick." She smiled, and to his surprise, it didn't seem like she was teasing.

Sensing the lesson at an end, Thor dipped his head, then touched his fingertips to his lips, and lowered his hand in the sign for *thank you*.

TWENTY-THREE

"Any time now, Haakon!" On the driver's seat Jorgan cradled both reins in his palm.

Sitting beside him, Aven shifted to see what the holdup was. One of the mares stamped a hoof as if impatient herself. Finally Haakon emerged from the house, slamming the door behind him. He fastened the button at his collar, and his short hair was slicked back and combed, the blond color a shade darker in its wetness.

The wagon rocked when he climbed aboard.

Thor looked at him coolly. Jorgan called a command that urged the horses forward. Haakon wedged himself beside the two crates of jelly Thor had packed with care. The arrival of October meant the day of their monthly visit to Sunday service, and the two dozen jars for the raffle would be dropped off while in town today.

With each day a little cooler than the last, gone was the heavy air of summer. In its stead was a cool breeze that swept through the countryside like a welcome friend, making the drive to town more than pleasant.

As the first buildings of Eagle Rock came into view, Jorgan checked his pocket watch. "We'll be late, I'm afraid. But what's that when Haakon has nice hair?"

Haakon chuckled. Even Thor showed a small smile.

Jorgan drove the wagon to a stop amid others parked on the flats beside the church. The fenced yard was empty of parishioners, and chatter spilled from the chapel. When Aven turned to climb down, Haakon was there. His touch at her waist was certainly the Sabbath sort, but it was a gentle startling all the same as he helped her down. The men saw to the horses, insisting Aven not wait for them.

Clutching up the hem of her dress, Aven followed the path that wound inside. So warm and crowded was the small building that she tugged her shawl free. The packed room offered few empty seats in the women's sections, but at the sight of a sparse back row, she edged that way. Aven sat beside a woman who held a babbling baby. The cherub-faced girl sucked on two fingers, and it was no bother when that damp hand reached for her sleeve. Aven wriggled the pudgy fingers and cooed a hello.

The room quieted, and the hymn leader took his place in the center of the open square. He paused when the three brothers came to the doorway and stepped in.

Arriving late, they walked to the empty front pew and sat—a masculine chorus of thudding boots and creaking wood. Their expressions were stoic as light from the overhead windows streamed bright on their sturdy shoulders. Little whispers heralded from the women around Aven.

Norgaards.

Blackbird Mountain.

A woman on her right muttered that they were heathens.

To Aven's left, two young ladies quietly mused as to which they would marry.

Equal measures of protection and jealousy flushed her skin, yet the comments were no surprise. The business ventures of her hosts were not always genteel, and while the room boasted many a robust farmer, these Norwegian brothers were quite possibly the brawest, most strapping of the lot. Aven cast a subtle glance to the lassies who had spoken, wanting to hint that not all of these Norgaards were for the taking. She should have meant the guarding only for Jorgan, but truth be told, it stretched elsewhere.

Feeling Thor's gaze upon her, Aven couldn't bring herself to meet it. Leaning back, Haakon shifted his boots out square, and as he nibbled the tip of his thumb, he stole a glance at the women's side of the room. His focus shifted to Aven, and he smiled at her. She did her best to ignore him as well.

Behind Haakon sat the young man who had inquired for work. Peter was his name. The man slid a tiny fold of paper inside Haakon's collar, then leaned back smugly. Gone was the humble demeanor he'd displayed in his asking for work.

A muscle flexed in Haakon's jaw. Balancing a hymnal with one hand, he reached back and fetched the slip of paper. He set it in the center of the book as the hymn caller addressed the congregation. With slow fingers Haakon opened the tiny paper. His gaze skimmed what must have been written. He smirked and with his blue eyes on the caller's boots, waited for the man to turn before he flicked the folded scrap into the center of the room.

Aven's jaw dropped. Jorgan gave his brother a warning glare. A few folks exchanged glances. Even the preacher looked Haakon's way. Haakon lifted his book some and became very studious of the written songs. Behind him, Peter colored. The hymn leader turned, his boots shuffling over the paper. He looked down but spoke on.

Thankfully, the rest of the service went without mishap. Aven gleaned much from the sermon, and even Thor paid attention when the preacher spoke his way. When the man turned his back, Aven jotted down a few notes to share with Thor later in hopes that it would further bolster him.

At the service end, she was scarcely outside when Haakon mentioned fetching the crates. Aven stood beside the wagon as he lowered the backboard.

" 'Twas a naughty thing you did in church." She reached for a crate, but he slid it toward himself, stacked the second atop, and lifted both. "Ye'd be wise next time to be on your best behavior." Her chastisement felt poorly timed to his kindness.

"I'm always on my best behavior."

She walked on as he did. "Seeing as that's bold as brass, perhaps you should try *not* being on your best behavior now and again."

He glanced down the dusty road before crossing it. "Fair. Let's start with this, then. I've spoken to Jorgan, and he's given me some fatherly advice." Hands full, Haakon used the side of his arm to nudge Aven in the direction he was aiming—a gray, two-story clapboard. "I'm supposed to ask if you wouldn't mind forgetting about what I said. At the pond that day. I mean . . . for now." He slowed at the base of the wide steps and waited for her to reach his side again. "That was kind of a quick thing to blurt out, and I didn't handle myself very well."

Aven pondered that as they climbed. While his offer of marriage had been a ramshackle one, she sensed he had meant it. In the moment at least. Yet it was an offer that was best laid to rest. So unseasoned was he with bearing life's trials that it made his proposition to love and to cherish through all circumstances feel fragile as autumn ice. He had much growing to do yet. Such maturing would be best done without a wife and family in need of him.

She'd been praying for a response that would

be gentle and honest for them both. "At the moment I could use a friend. And family. I'm a bit short on both of those. If you'll be my friend, Haakon, I'd dearly love to be yours in return."

"Of course." At the top of the steps, he ducked into the building first. "You're short on husbands, too, you know."

"Haakon!" The word burst from her the moment she entered and echoed across the empty hall.

Haakon seemed amused by her outburst and not the least bit sorry for his contribution. "I'm just stating what we're all very aware of." He paused to speak directly to her. "Just so as not to take you by surprise . . . I would ask you again. Should the chance present itself." With several other folks coming up the steps, dropping off goods as well, Haakon moved aside.

As fond as she was of this man, she would be wise to take care that the opportunity not present itself. Perhaps in time he would be able to care for a young lady. She prayed it would be so, and perhaps Thor's actions would show him the way.

Aven followed after Haakon to the far end of the hall. She wove around a pile of colorful banners, then past a table laden with lemons and polished punch cups. Beyond that stood another table that was covered with items for the raffle. Carved trinkets and tinware were stacked in baskets, and beside those rested a neat mound of quilted squares. Aven was tempted to lift a jar that held glass beads, but she simply tucked her hands behind her back and waited as Haakon nestled the crates of cider jelly against the wall.

She had wrapped each lid with a pretty round of dotted cloth. From Thor's workbench—and to his chagrin—she'd unearthed a rubber stamp that read *Norgaard Orchard.* Though he'd indicated that it was for marking receipts, she gave the stamp another purpose in pressing dainty paper labels. Those were now tied around the lids with a strip of ribbon, and Thor had seemed a little more impressed then. Especially when she'd put the stamp back exactly where it belonged.

With the splendor of the decorated hall all around, Aven admired each end from the tall, sunny windows, to the colorful bunting that ran the length of the stage, to the plank floor that was so well polished it shone. It took little effort to imagine Thor dancing the waltz in this very room. He would be braw and dashing, of that she had no doubt. To say nothing of how shy and uneasy he would be.

She felt a fierce twinge at missing the evening. The tickets had all been sold, and even if she were to attend, she wished only to dance with the one whose steps had joined hers in the meadow.

When she and Haakon returned across the street, Jorgan shook hands with several men, then stepped to the wagon, thumbing over his shoulder as he did. "Got three families comin' tomorrow for the pickin'."

"Which apples?" Haakon unfastened a feed sack from one of the mares.

"The Foxwhelps." Jorgan loosened the other sack of grain. "Where's Thor?"

"Over there. With the reverend," Haakon answered.

"The same one who saw what you did in church?" Jorgan asked dryly.

Haakon grimaced and rather looked like he regretted his actions.

Aven shielded her eyes. At the far end of the churchyard, small crosses leaned in the same timeworn fashion as the picket fence around them, and just beyond, the clergyman and Thor stood together. The reverend doffed his black hat and held it to his chest as Thor pulled out his notebook and pencil. When Thor handed both over, the reverend tucked his hat under his arm. The breeze stirred his fine, white hair.

The man hesitated before writing. After a few lines, he showed Thor, who nodded soberly and waited as more was written. Aven pinched her hands in her lap, a worry rising at how somber the exchange was. Haakon and Jorgan kicked at the dust while they feigned interest elsewhere.

After reading what the reverend had added, Thor wrote a response. Hesitantly, the reverend lifted a hand to shake. With that done, Thor walked across the churchyard. Though his broad shoulders were squared, a hint of defeat surrounded him. He tugged at his beard, stopping only to grip the sideboard of the wagon and climb in. The wagon lurched with his force.

When he sat, Jorgan tapped the reins. All was quiet until the wagon reached the road.

"Ask him if everything is alright, Haakon," Jorgan said.

Nudging Thor's boot with his own, Haakon signed the question.

Thor looked away and out over the distant hills.

"Guess he doesn't wanna talk about it," Haakon mumbled.

Fiddling with the ribbon in the center of the family Bible, Aven looked out along the road. Stubbs of grass grew up the center of the rutted lane, straight and sure. How she wished life could be as direct. The last of the wildflowers were dry, yet a buxom variety still displayed their golden heads toward a cloudless sky, all but beckoning for her not to despair. But with Thor downtrodden so, 'twas hard not to feel his silent pain.

When the wagon pulled into the yard and stopped, Aven climbed down, careful to tug her skirt clear of the wheel. She'd scarcely entered the kitchen doorway when she spotted a young woman with pale-blonde hair and a rather lost appearance. The stranger was struggling to fasten a petite trunk that rested atop the table. Her form was elegantly tall, slender as a reed, and her wide-set eyes held a sweet innocence in a pale face. Her dress was as modest as it was plain, and the wispy braid that draped her shoulder feathered all the way to her hip.

"Oh heavens, might you be Fay?" Aven laid the Bible on the table.

The woman quickly nodded. "And if you're Aven, I owe you a finer greeting than this. I was to join Miss Ida upstairs, as she was going to show me where I'm to sleep, but this pesky latch came undone and I can't get it closed." She pressed on the snap again to no avail. The poor dear's fingers were trembling, especially when she glanced to the window. "That's Jorgan coming, isn't it?"

Aven couldn't fight a grin. "It is indeed." She scarcely had time to recall that it had been nearly fifteen years since Jorgan and his betrothed had seen one another when heavy footsteps stomped up the porch.

Trailed by his brothers, Jorgan stepped into the kitchen. He tossed his hat aside, wondered aloud about what smelled so good, then halted. His brow lifted—shock dawning. Hands still atremble, Fay folded them in front of her skirt.

"Whoa!" Haakon slammed to a halt beside his brother. "It's Fay," he breathed. He hit Jorgan's arm. Over and over. "Jorgan. It's Fay. Jorgan, it's—"

Thor grabbed Haakon by the upper arm and pressed him back out the door. Grinning, Aven followed. She cast a glance to Jorgan, who stood speechless, staring at his wife-to-be. 'Twas much unfolding between them. All from words on a page that their courtship had borne.

Fay's rosy cheeks were the last thing Aven saw as she slipped away. Best to give them a few moments alone. Aven skittered onto the porch to find Haakon seated on the bottom step. Thor stood a few paces off, signing halfheartedly to him. Haakon responded with much more passion. When Aven drew near, they both stopped.

She settled on the step, and after casting a final glimpse toward the kitchen window, she noticed Thor striding off, his once-steady shoulders looking wilted.

"Is something the matter?" Aven asked softly.

Running his hands together, Haakon finished by sliding one down his face. He let out a sigh that matched Thor's demeanor. "It's just 'cause of his reputation. And I'm afraid I wasn't much help earlier. Thor's a little bruised, but I think he's more relieved. Come the night of it, he'll be happier."

"Night of what?"

"The dance. The reverend said he won't allow Thor to accompany his daughter."

TWENTY-FOUR

She was pretty, Fay. Pretty like wheat. If Thor could compare a woman to wheat. She was tall and thin and golden. He watched as she and Jorgan carried armfuls of picking bags into the orchard where Thor was assembling the pickers. Jorgan's gladness brought Thor the same. To see his brother this happy was something Thor had wanted for a long time. Jorgan deserved nothing less, and in the night and morning that Fay had been here, they'd all learned firsthand what Jorgan had declared—she was good and kind.

With a nod of thanks, Thor helped them hang the canvas bags on a rung of the ladder. He counted twelve thick sacks. With Jorgan having invited several families in from town, it was enough. At Thor's request—and thanks to Aven's idea—the families had come to harvest apples for their own use in exchange for a small fee. One of the families had nothing to pay with, so Jorgan had arranged for the father and his oldest boy to log an extra day of harvesting for the farm as barter for all they would haul away today.

Just past the families stood the pickers Thor had hired. The three boys from last year knew how the bags were to be worn so he handed several over. Abraham, a tall, reedy youth from Cora's church, took one, sliding it on. Jacob, a quiet lad of sixteen, accepted another. Al took a bag, lifted the straps over his head, and settled them about his shoulders.

Days ago Thor had apologized to Al for the rough go he'd given him on the stairs. Al had assured him he'd mended well, but Thor found guilt hard to loose. A reminder he would harness to always take care in avoiding liquor—every hour of every day. Because the cost of his choices hadn't just affected himself, but others as well.

It made this day heavier than usual. An awareness filtering through this orchard as real to him as the breeze itself.

Thor motioned to the stack of empty crates and shaped the sign for *half,* then the letters *B-U-S-H-E-L.* Jorgan spoke for him. Only the apples with the reddest faces were to be gleaned. When Thor's wishes were translated, the pickers confirmed their understanding. Leaning against one of the ladders, Haakon watched, this process as natural to his upbringing as crawling or walking had been.

Thor freed several apples from the nearest tree, taking his time to remind the boys that a gentle twist up of the smooth fruit would break it off. He placed the apples in his bag, and when he'd gathered enough to serve the purpose, Thor demonstrated a reminder of how to unfasten the metal clasps at the underside so the apples could be eased into the bins from the bottom end.

"Be real gentle about it so they don't bruise," Jorgan relayed in English.

Fay stood behind Jorgan, shielding her eyes as she listened on. Her thick skirt was as deep a red as the Foxwhelps, and though her yellow hair was bound up snug, little wisps of it tugged free. Jorgan was taken with her, of that there was no doubt, so the sheer fact that the man had a level head just now was admirable.

Remembering something more, Thor searched the ground for any trace of brown rot. Gnats swarmed around, and he brushed one aside that tickled his neck. Finding a cluster of dark, wrinkled apples, he picked it up and held it over. He sliced a hand through the air for *never,* then made the motion of placing the diseased cluster into a crate.

Thor watched as Jorgan explained. "If you find any that have brown rot, be sure to pile them up separately so we can dispose of them away from the fields. Otherwise more apples'll spoil."

Satisfied, Thor gave a firm nod toward the nearest trees. The young men set to work. He meant to join them, but something irked at the back of his mind. Three additional hands weren't as many as he'd hired the year before. Aven had told him that Peter Sorrel had inquired for a position, but Thor hadn't taken him up on it.

Perhaps he should reconsider that . . .

For now, Thor glanced to the three families who stood waiting along the edge of the row. Little ones played about while strapping sons and wiry boys looked ready to work. Gangly daughters toted infant siblings on their hips. All would doubtless be at work by the end of the hour. If he knew one thing about folks in these parts, it was that even the tiniest of hands were taught to help. To the older children and adults, Thor offered canvas bags. They'd all just witnessed the explanation, so he assumed they knew what to do. Spread around them were buckets and pails of their own to cart home.

If this went well, more folks could be invited in the coming weeks, bringing Thor and his brothers closer to paying off the lease. Thor tried to ignore the twinge he felt at so many apples being taken away from the farm. Never could he recall a time that the bulk of the harvest hadn't been pressed and fermented. It wasn't just about liquor. Hard cider had been an art to him. The timely addition of ale yeast to the choicest juices had been something he'd taken great pride in. The one thing he was truly skilled at.

How many years had he stood in this very spot with Da? Being the one to accept a picking bag and place it over lean shoulders along with Jorgan and Haakon? Da would have guided their work, Ma and Ida would have fixed something fine in the kitchen, and they would have all gathered in the yard for a bonfire. A celebration for the first day of harvest. Pain struck at the memory because neither Ma nor Da would be there when a match was set to wood tonight.

At a little tug on the leg of his pants, Thor peered down to see a boy with two missing front teeth holding a bucket that was full. Thor smiled and, leading the boy by the shoulder, walked him to one of his family's washtubs. With a gentle touch so as not to bruise the fruit, he showed the little fellow how to lower each one into place. The apples would need to be checked every week or so to watch for rot, but these folks would know that.

Just a few steps away from Jorgan, Fay was helping two other children, placing apples into their buckets with words of affirmation. Feeling an absence without Aven here, Thor glanced around for sight of her. Even as he did, he knew she was in the house helping Ida fix the evening meal. With many mouths to feed, he doubted he'd see Aven until dusk.

Taking up a bag, Thor slid the two straps over his shoulders and approached the nearest tree. Lift and break. Lift and break. He took the fruit two at a time, his hands moving in quick rhythm. He'd picked so many apples over his life, he could do this in his sleep. The skin of the Foxwhelp was a deep, speckled red, but if the flesh were tasted, it would be a few days short of perfectly sweet. The best storing apples were always picked a week shy of ripe. In a few days the trees would be further gleaned for first eaters. With proper care and a cool, dark place to pass the winter, this week's harvest should keep through January.

Thor emptied his bag and went back for more. He hefted up a ladder, settled it against a sturdy branch, and climbed three rungs. A few paces off, Haakon was hard at work. The bag strapped to Haakon's chest was already brimming, and he picked with swift authority. Leave it to the kid to rise to the occasion.

By the time the sun was high overhead, Haakon was hefting yet another filled crate into the wagon, and Tess was striding up the row. She bore a pail of water and a basket of tin cups. A striped scarf wound around her hair, covering it entirely. Cora's daughter set her offering in the middle of the grassy lane and divvied up water for the workers. When she came his way, Thor downed his own share and thanked her with a touch to the arm.

Taking up her bucket with a slim, toffee-colored hand, Tess promised to return later with more.

All worked until far into the day when a quick break came for dinner pails to be emptied in the shade of heavy-laden branches. Thor sat with his brothers and ate what Ida had brought them. As Jorgan and Haakon chatted with those gathered round, Thor's gaze drifted across his orchards. This year's offering of Foxwhelp was a good one. Each tree weighted down and drooping. His other varieties had fared equally as well, so barring that an early storm didn't come—or that the creek didn't rise—they'd be in a good position to earn out the lease. Thor lifted his gaze toward the Sorrels' farm, praying it would be so.

A fragile fog had rolled in, feathering the evening air with mist as Haakon wove a tale for the children gathered near him. Supper was soon to be served, and with mothers busy helping in the kitchen and fathers talking in the yard, the children lingered on the porch where Haakon's voice had them all under his spell.

In the yard, Thor was piling up old boards in haphazard fashion. 'Twas a delight to see him for the first time that day. Aven stood in the doorway of the kitchen, pitcher of tea in hand, and though she was to still be filling glasses, she'd paused just long enough to hear the end of the story.

"But because the land was yet to have a name," Haakon continued, "those who settled it argued about what these hills were to be called."

Never far from him, Grete lay smashed against Haakon's leg. Georgie's little hands stroked the dog's glossy coat.

"A carpenter who was tall for his weight thought it should be named for the light that streamed in from the west. A fisherman who had a habit of talking too slow insisted the region be named for the waters that flowed through it. But it was a farmer who had come from the farthest land of all, a Norseman who had traveled by the mercy of the sea, who remembered the tales of his homeland—of a god named Odin, and the many ravens who accompanied him. And so this land was named not for the sun, nor for the water, but for the blackbirds that were a force to be reckoned with."

The children all blinked soundlessly, no one speaking until wee Georgie scrunched up one side of her face. "Did you just make that up?"

"Of course not. Did it sound made-up?" Haakon winked as he sipped from his glass of sweet tea.

Georgie wrapped her thin arms around his own and whispered for another story.

"Yet another?"

"Oh, please!" Georgie cried.

"Alright. One more." He shifted her onto his other knee, looking sore from the day's work. "But you have to help me, missy."

As if jealous by how close Georgie had gotten to Haakon, Grete let out a snort. Georgie resumed her petting, but the dog kept a watchful eye on the pair.

Thor dragged a heavy branch nearer to the pile

he'd been fashioning. The pickers who'd been helping him each gripped a portion. With a heave they clattered it onto the pile. Thor hefted up a jug of kerosene, drizzled it over the wood, and set the canister aside. He pulled a box of matches from his pocket.

The young men drew back. Thor struck a match and dropped it forward. The pile erupted into flames. He stepped aside, squinting against the heat that Aven felt even from where she stood. It pushed back the growing dusk with a warm glow. The menfolk drew nearer and women bustled out of the kitchen, bearing iron pans of round, flat potato lefse. Aven had assured Haakon that she would make the Norwegian flatbread for him, and she saw his look of gratitude as the pans passed by.

Aven was heading inside to fill the tea pitcher when Thor let out a shrill whistle. He motioned everyone to hedge in. Even Ida and Cora came away from their bubbling pots.

When all were gathered, Aven realized that few neighbors had ever visited this farm—these three brothers with their bold occupation. And now . . . to have families standing near. Soon to break bread with the Norgaard men and those they called kin. 'Twas no wonder that Thor bowed his head and others followed suit. Several men tugged off hats. Cora looped her arm through young Tess's. Georgie pinched her eyes closed tight, gripping both of her hands around one of Haakon's own.

Clearing his throat, Jorgan stepped forward. "Lord, we're awful glad to be here this evening and for Your provision. We thank You for what You've given us and in particular for all the folks standing around. We also give thanks that You've delivered Thor to fine health. For walking with him, and with us. Amen."

Aven opened her eyes to see that Thor was watching his brother. His nod of thanks was humble. Haakon watched as well, but a cool shadow filled his expression. As if he wasn't as pleased as the others for Thor's recovery. Oh, that Haakon's spirit might be eased. Whatever it was that ailed him . . . settled and soothed.

"Them cups ain't gonna fill themselves, Ms. Norgaard." Ida hustled back to the kitchen, and Aven trailed her. Even the women who had toiled in the orchard all day came to assist. Ida instructed several to dish out stew as Fay slid another pan of warm flatbreads from the oven. Aven accepted three filled bowls and wove her way through the crowded kitchen.

Earlier she'd diced carrots, celery, and sausage, but it was by Ida's own hand that nearly a dozen herbs and spices had been sprinkled into the stew pot. Aven inhaled the fragrance of seasonings so warm they hailed of exotic lands. Tess followed at her side with a plate of butter, a jar of honey, and that sunny smile she always wore.

"Might you tell me one more time what this is called?" Aven whispered.

Tess leaned nearer. "Be jambalaya, Miss Aven. And in ten minutes it still be jambalaya."

They laughed and together passed out their offerings, then fetched more helpings, not stopping until every set of hands had a hot meal and the large pot was ready to dish out seconds.

Keen on having a taste, Aven carried her own supper down the stairs. People were gathered all around on benches and spread-out blankets. On the outskirts of it all sat Thor. He'd found a spot on a bench alone. Aven went that way, and not wanting to disturb his peace, she perched on the opposite edge. He glanced at her, holding her gaze only moments before his own dropped, as it often did.

It felt strange, the length of an entire bench between them. She wished to move nearer. To find how his day had gone. If he was pleased with the start of the harvest and to know if he bore any worries or wants of mind. She wished to know them, to offer whatever help or insight that came. 'Twas a knitting together of hearts and lives that she wished with Thor. And in that moment, she could no more ignore how much she cared for him than she could deny that he'd been filling her heart and her prayers with a growing affection.

There was love within her—both an offering and a need—and it was for him.

Suddenly overcome, Aven dropped her attention to her meal. Thor reached forward to heft a piece of wood into the fire. The moment he rose, the bench tipped toward her and she hit the ground hard.

Before she could make sense of what had just happened, Al stood and Thor stepped over and bent to circle an arm around her waist. When she was on her feet, he signed a thought, then glanced to Jorgan on the other side of the fire.

Jorgan lifted his glass of tea. "Said you'd do well to sit closer to him next time."

Aye. " 'Twould have been wiser."

Thor picked up the tumbled bench and set it right-side up. He tried to smile at her, but she couldn't bear such smiles just now. Nor the way his sturdy, familiar hand touched her arm as if to steady her. Both of their bowls had fallen, the food spoiled in the dirt. Aven gathered everything up as best she could, discarded the mess, and with her face hot and Thor seeming worried after her, she carried the dishes back to the house.

She meant to scrub everything anew and bring him a fresh helping, but when she entered, Fay was blessedly there.

"Is something amiss, Aven? You're flushed."

"Would you mind bringing Thorald another

meal?" The use of his formal name might have sounded aloof, but it felt anything but.

"Not at all." Fay was clearly the wiser of it.

Aven set the dishes on the table and sought refuge in the dark of the empty great room. The dirt she brushed from her skirt, then swiped a wrist over her forehead. Pain pulsed through the small of her back, and as much as the hurt of the fall already pestered, more startling was a different kind of blooming. One that had been growing from a seed so sweetly, so tenderly, that she'd tried to protect it as friendship in fear of more anguish.

She'd given her heart to a drinking man once. And yet, was Thor still such a man? His efforts were hard wrought and admirable, but his sobriety was yet in its infancy and the pull of the bottle an ardent one.

Was it wrong to long for Thor? To wish for the place right beside him?

She'd learned that to give oneself to a man meant the impending loss of him. Had that not been her own mother's reality? And dear Ida . . . never reunited with the man she loved.

For Aven herself—just as the softest place of her desire had become Benn's, he'd taken himself from this life. Such realities had taught her that a woman's heart was best bundled up and hidden away. But 'twas a path that brought little hope. Surely even Ida dared to dream. And if Aven knew anything about the aspiration inside her, 'twas that her mother would have as well.

And now? This new life? Her own courage to love was small yet, just spreading its blossoms toward the sun. She'd meant to keep such yearning safe. Tucked in the dark and coiled tight. But for weeks now, and without a single spoken word, Thor Norgaard had been its unfurling.

TWENTY-FIVE

"Oh aye, the ivory ribbon is bonny." Having pinned up Fay's hair, Aven arranged the bow above the blonde twists. With one last hairpin, she secured it. "Jorgan won't know what to do with himself." Aven winked as she edged in front of Fay to adjust the strap on the delicate chemise Aven had lent her.

After Fay's confession to dressing plainly for all of her twenty-nine years, Aven had jumped at the task of upending that. Even if just for an evening. Earlier that afternoon Fay had shown her the nicest frock from her trunk, a dress as modest and humble as the woman herself. A dark-blue wool with black velvet trim that harkened back to wartime fashions. With Fay's displeasure scarcely concealed, Aven had assured her that they could spruce the tired garment up.

Aven picked up the dress from the bedstead and draped it over Fay's head, careful not to muss her hair. Fay helped tug it down. Cropping the long sleeves had allowed Fay's slim, delicate arms to show, and Aven had created sleek darts in place of outdated gathers. The trimmings from the sleeves had been just enough fabric to fashion flounces that brought a happy blush to Fay's cheeks as the finishing touch.

"It's an utter shame that you won't be coming."
Fay's soft, blue eyes further declared the
sentiment. "Are you sure you don't want to come
along?"

"I'm sure. Aside from not having a ticket, this
is an occasion for partners."

"Perhaps if Thor were to go with you. He
certainly has a ticket." Fay winked.

Aven helped her settle the capped sleeves into
place. "He was quite the champion in learning
to waltz, but I fear he was miserable. A quiet
evening at home will be much more to his taste."
A true answer, aye, despite her hopes that he
might have asked her. She could have posed
the notion herself but had never rallied enough
courage.

Ida's voice came through the closed door.
"Jorgan's asking after Fay."

Aven swung open the door and gestured toward
the very woman with a dramatic hand. "Have ye
ever seen anything so lovely?"

Ida clapped. "Oh, if you ain't a sight in full
feather!"

Not used to such attention, Fay pressed palms
to her cheeks as if to cool their warmth.

To think of the hours to come and the delight
Fay and Jorgan would share. Aven only hoped
Haakon was as eager for the event, but when
they went downstairs where he stood in the open
doorway, 'twas clear that he was not as pleased

as his oldest brother. He glanced from Aven to the ceiling where Thor had tucked himself away in the attic.

Was their staying behind the reason for Haakon's misgivings? Aven tried to shrug off the wondering. She'd do best not to fret over his frequent shifts in temperament. Haakon had been paired with a young lady who would no doubt shower him with admiration this night. Perhaps good medicine for the young buck who seemed to sink into his darker moods more often of late. With one last glance at Aven, Haakon followed Jorgan and Fay to the wagon. She and Ida wished them a fine evening and soon, they were gone.

Ida's sigh was as melancholy as a lone bird's song. Aven looped her arm through Ida's and gave a tender squeeze. They stood there, watching the dust settle and dark draw nearer.

Finally Ida kissed Aven's cheek. " 'Spose I'll turn in."

"So early?"

Ida peeked in on the supper keeping warm in the oven. "I'm awful tired tonight." She closed the iron door and proceeded toward her room, not looking the least bit tired.

"What should I do about Thor's supper?" Aven asked. "He's made himself scarce."

"Oh, he'll make himself unscarce." Ida opened the door that led to her bedroom at the back of the kitchen. "But he can fend for himself. You enjoy your evening as you wish." The way she said it brought the word *meddlesome* to mind.

Aven smirked as the woman left. Hungry herself, Aven set about filling a plate. She brewed two cups of tea amid the chirping of crickets. A check into the pie safe showed a plate of cookies. She slid them out and onto the table. Next she tested the roasted vegetables, giving the pan a swift jostle before closing the oven door again. She heard Thor stepping down from the attic. The creaking of boards stilled when he paused.

A moment later he went back up.

Perhaps she should leave a trail of bread crumbs to coax him from his room.

A few minutes later he came down, fastening the button of one of his sleeve cuffs. The shirt looked clean, and his hands were freshly scrubbed. There was a roughness about his tousled hair, yet it hung just tidy enough that she knew he kept after it. Thor stepped nearer, attention on the food, and the longer they stood there, on anything but her.

Aven didn't move until he braved a glance her way. She smiled, and he nodded a reserved greeting. Oh, she should stop torturing the poor man and just give him his supper. She hitched the iron door open and pulled out the pan of vegetables.

He brought over a plate, and if the gentleness

of his manner were words, she would have heard *please*.

Aven forked tender ham in the center and smeared on sauce. Thor pulled a crusty piece of bread from the basket. After fetching the tea she had steeped for him, Aven touched his arm.

Thor regarded the steamy drink, then frowned.

Dandelion root, it was. A remedy to fortify his liver, and Cora had insisted he drink at least a cup a day. Though the tea was bitter, he brooked no argument as she settled the mug into his hand. He glanced from the table to where her own drink sat, then into the next room. He seemed uncertain of what to do with himself.

Perhaps to make it easier for him. "Might I join you in the other room?" Dinner in hand, she added two ginger cookies to her tea saucer and balanced it all.

He offered none of his usual tells except to step that way. Aven followed and perched on the edge of the sofa. Dotti was spread across the back of it, purring gently. Thor passed by and, with a pinch of fingers, turned the lantern up so the room brightened. He sat at one end of the chess table. The opposite chair he nudged back. A request for her to join him? When he glanced at her, Aven realized it was so.

A pleasing notion at that. She moved there, wanting to offer a kindness in return. She thought to the reverend's daughter and all the poor dear was missing—the presence of a fine partner. Aven drew Thor's attention, then spoke. "It is my gain tonight . . . your company."

The side of his mouth tipped up.

Aven turned her focus to her meal so as not to make him too nervous. A small space beside the board gave room for her plate and steaming drink. Taking up his fork, Thor speared a slice of meat. Aven nibbled the end of a ginger cookie as she eyed the chess pieces. They were disorderly, a match in progress, but Thor started to arrange everything back to the starting point. He ate another bite, then gestured with his fork toward the board. When she didn't move, he dipped his head toward the game, then tapped her hand nearest it.

When she still didn't move, he took her hand and closed it around a playing piece. Ah. She was to go first. Aven scrunched her nose and tried to make sense of the right maneuver. On a whim, she chose where to set the figure down.

Thor shook his head and put the piece back. Drawing his finger across the board, he showed that it was meant to travel a diagonal.

"Perhaps this one, then." Aven fetched a pawn since she knew what it was called. She slid it up a space, and his only reaction was to do the same with his own. Except he moved his two spaces and reached across the board to do the same with hers.

"Thank you."

While he broke his bread in half, Aven thought on her next move. She shimmied the pawn forward two more squares, and he responded by pushing it back one.

"That makes no sense!"

A laugh glinted in his eyes as he ignored her outburst by moving a piece of his own. The clock on the mantel ticked nearer to seven o'clock, which meant that somewhere in town, instruments were just beginning to sound. Thor reached a thumb and forefinger into his shirt pocket and pulled out his notebook. His pencil was missing, so he fetched another from the desk. Seated again, he wrote, then slid the book forward. His large fingers bumped her own as she took it.

I sorry not ask you go dance.

A rush of warmth started in her chest, and she dipped her head to assuage his regret. A verbal answer nearly spilled forth, but thinking to preserve the companionable silence, she fetched the pencil. *I am happy to sit here with you now.*

He nodded deeply as if to concur. Then his brow dug in. He slipped the pencil from her fingers. *You like dancing.*

Aye, she adored it.

His study of her face was thorough. Brown eyes settled. His chair creaked as he shifted. Gently he tapped the board, then wrote, *You win, us share dance together.*

Aven struggled to conceal her shock. More so her delight. "A wager, then?" She tried to appear composed.

He nodded.

"And what if you are the victor?" As that would be the outcome.

He made a show of scrutinizing her, then wrote, *I win, you chocolate cream make.* He thumbed toward the kitchen.

She laughed and extended a hand "It's a deal."

He shook it.

Thor leaned back in his chair. She waited for him to make a move, and her mind was far too much on her braw opponent because he finally took the notepad and held it over.

Not my turn.

Oh. She slid another piece forward.

He moved a pawn and she matched the step, hoping it looked like she knew how this game was played. With a thud, he took that carved figure with one of his own and set the captive aside.

Drat. Aching to win, Aven poured every effort into the match. Thor did as well, though his strategy was more oft rewarded. Bit by bit her side of the board cleared away of white pieces. Occasionally he guided her in claiming one of his own.

Aven reached for a *who-knew-what* and scuttled it two squares forward, but he stopped her, tapping a different square entirely.

"You're not setting me up for failure, now?"

He shook his head.

She moved the castle thing he'd tapped, only to realize that her queen was now protected. Aven threw him a smile. His own mouth lifted. Thor's supper sat neglected beside him, her tea long forgotten. Dotti wandered over and looped herself around Thor's boot and then Aven's ankle. Aven reached down and pulled the kitten into her lap.

Thor took up the black queen. She watched in dismay as he used it to claim her important-looking pointy piece.

"Rats!" She quickly slid a pawn forward as if that would do *anything* to help.

Thor chuckled and it was the deep, free sound she'd come to yearn for. While she was lost in the savoring of it, he took one of her horse fellows.

"You are an overcompetitive ogre."

He smirked and, after two more turns, gained as many pieces. His decisions had been swift and sure, but when she moved her queen to the opposite end of the board, making him pause to ponder for a full minute, she did a little victory dance in her chair. Poor Dotti went tumbling. Though his focus on the board never wavered, Thor's eyes shone his amusement.

Gently he sobered and tapped the side of the table twice. Confused, she shook her head.

Thor grabbed his notebook. *Check.*

He glanced to the edge of the board and she eyed that very spot. Her king was in a precarious position to his queen. She moved it aside one square, but that seemed trivial. With the turn now Thor's, her loss was all but sealed. Aven's shoulders sank.

Elbows to the rests, Thor leaned back in his chair. He steepled his fingers and pressed them to his mouth. Those steady brown eyes looked from the cornered king . . . to Aven . . . then back. He breathed in gently as his focus shifted around the board. The end would be swift. Yet he continued to study the game spread before them. Was he searching for an alternate move? Surely he wasn't considering losing.

The longer he scrutinized the match, the more she dared to wonder.

"Are you at a moral impasse, Mr. Norgaard?"

The side of his mouth tipped up. He held out a raised finger as if to tell her to be quiet.

Which really wasn't fair, all things considered.

With a soft grunt he touched the black queen, turned her in a slow circle, and amidst the pounding of Aven's heart . . . took her king.

Aven forced herself to guard against disappointment. "Well done."

He showed no gratification in his victory. Instead, he placed her king with the other captives. His large thumb adjusted the board that was already straight. He glanced around again, looking anywhere but at her. Gaze falling to his meal, he didn't seem hungry anymore. He pressed his hands to his thighs and rubbed them back and forth as if to chafe away rising nerves. Slowly he rose.

What was he doing?

He stepped away from the table and motioned for her to stand.

Wait. He didn't mean to . . . he didn't mean to dance?

Her head rushed with warmth when he took her hand, guiding her to her feet. At first he held on without moving, as if forcing himself to decide. Then with a bend of his wrist he brought her nearer to him. He moved her other hand to his shoulder. Instead of raising their arms for a waltz, though, he turned his wrist, cupping their hands against his chest. Next he pressed a gentle hold to her lower back.

Heavens.

With his eyes down, he tapped his chest, then shaped letters slow enough that she understood. *L-E-A-D*. He touched his chest once more. Aven nodded, and he drew them near enough together that the buttons of his shirt grazed her bodice. His head bowed beside hers, the dark twists of his hair brushing her raised arm. The hand behind her waist was sure and strong.

They stood there, unmoving. Then with no warning other than his thumb pressing more firmly against her waist, he moved them from side to side. So subtly, her feet scarcely traveled.

His eyes were closed. A slight pinch creased his forehead—the concentration there so intense, she couldn't look elsewhere. They moved in the smallest of ways, but a sweeping ballroom dance would have been less grand. She traced her gaze past the faint scar over his left eyebrow, down to the ears that let no sound past, then to his mouth that was softly set. Floorboards creaked when his boots shifted his weight. She moved her feet the tiniest measure to follow.

Thor's face dipped lower beside hers. His beard to her cheek was more silken than she'd imagined. His mouth was so near to her own that with the slightest shift, she would satisfy the yearning that was pulling at her every nerve.

Were they even moving anymore?

The rising and lowering of his chest was steady until her hand slid to his neck, grazing the skin. It was then that his breathing changed. Neck bowing as if weakened. When his eyes pinched tighter closed, she feared she'd frightened him.

Loosening her touch, Aven stepped aside.

He adjusted the collar of his shirt, and for one horrible instant she sensed he was about to walk away. Instead, he closed the gap between them, touched his thumb to her jaw, and lowered his sweet, silent mouth to her own. In a scuff of boots, Thor drew nearer. He slid a hand behind her head and kissed her more boldly than she had ever anticipated.

The chess table jostled when his leg bumped it, but he steadied the rattling surface with one hand even as he held her with the other. His mouth never left her own, and Aven laced her fingers into his to ease any worry about keeping everything righted.

The table suddenly forgotten, he drew himself closer in a way that was both tender and sure. Her back bumped against the wall, and he braced himself with a hand to the boards. She slid her touch from his waist to his shoulder and the strength there. His breath against her own hastened, no worry to appear composed as a hearing man might. An uninhibited sound that sent a puddle of warmth straight through her.

Aven slipped an arm around his neck. Rising up onto the toes of her shoes, she leaned into him. The motion sent them off-balance and the table skidded again, this time sending the game stand and all its pieces toppling to the floor.

Though he couldn't have just heard Ida's bedroom door open, Thor pulled away. The sudden loss of him would have been her undoing if it weren't for the need to think quickly. Aven pointed toward the sound of footsteps. Thor fetched up the table, then signed to her in earnest—a handful of words, only two of which she grasped. The very same phrase he'd used near the tree house.

"*Please* . . . I don't understand." A tightness of tears came, for she wanted to know his thoughts as much as she wanted to know him.

But Thor sank down to gather up the spilled game just as Ida poked her head into the great room.

"Everything alright?" Ida raised a lantern.

"Oh, aye," Aven squeaked, certain Ida was peering in on something more telling than a chess match gone awry. She knelt to help. "Just a wee . . . stumble."

Thor set the board where it belonged, then added two handfuls of pieces, letting them clank haphazardly in the center. Stepping sideways, he fetched three more, then placed them with the others. His hair tumbled against his face, and he shoved it back. Nodding a rushed farewell, he turned for the stairs, nearly tripping them both as he did. He steadied Aven beside the bricks of the hearth before heading off, his gait so determined there would be no coaxing him back.

Aven's skin felt as hot as the glow from Ida's lantern. "I'm so sorry it woke you." Such a crash it had been. She was surprised Cora hadn't come running.

Ida watched Thor go. "Just feared that some-thin' had gone amiss. That's the second time this week the pair of ya upended furniture." Her growing amusement was scarcely concealed.

Aven tamped down all embarrassment and forced herself to weave around the sofa to where the housekeeper stood. "Might you tell me what this is to mean?" With hands that were still atremble, she recreated the motion that Thor had made, shaping the first symbol and then the second by closing her hands into fists and pressing her knuckles together.

"That first one is *with*." Ida set the lantern at her bare feet to repeat the second gesture. "Together, it means *stay with*."

That's what he had been asking? *Aven stay with Thor?*

"Thank you so much, Miss Ida!" Aven whirled away, hurried up the stairs, and slipped into her room long enough to fetch the letter that had come from Lexington, then rushed up toward the attic. With no light, she nearly stumbled in the dark.

Would knocking be pointless? She couldn't bear to let morning come without him knowing she understood. Aven rapped knuckles against the wood. Might he see the shudder? When that failed, she rattled the knob, praying that would be more noticeable. After a few more jostles, she heard heavy footfalls and the door opened.

TWENTY-SIX

It took all his composure to peer down at Aven—to see her eyes wide and her stuttering words that didn't make a shred of sense—and not pull her near again. A single candle flickered behind him, and he'd already tugged his suspenders from his shoulders. Thor clamped a hand on the knob to keep himself in place.

Looking as startled as he felt, she was panting from her climb up the stairs. At last Aven managed to string words together that were decipherable. "Did that make any sense?"

He shook his head.

Some kind of envelope was in her grasp. Closing her eyes, she exhaled with, "Yes." She tucked the envelope to her side and clumsily shaped his request as he had, first her name, then *stay* and *with*. Last, she formed a *T* and slid it beneath her chin, the very spot he'd held her so tenderly just moments ago. Had Ida helped her understand? Thor strode down a step, then a few more until he was low enough to look directly at Aven. She appeared taken aback, as if expecting him to do something rash. He wasn't going to do anything—but he sure was thinking about it.

Right now he needed to ensure that she hadn't believed his request for her to stay with him was of a dishonorable nature. Though he doubted that was why she was here, he had to make it clear that he wasn't trying to lure her farther up these stairs.

His notebook was on the chess table, so Thor took her hand, hoping his own was steady. Dipping his head, he pressed a kiss to the inside of her wrist, then placed her palm flush to his heart. He held it there, firm beneath both of his hands, and hoped that said what he couldn't. That he wasn't asking her to stay with him now, this hour or even this night, but that he was asking her to stay with him in this life.

Aven rose onto her tiptoes to press the softest kiss to the side of his face, and he knew she understood. She pulled a letter from the envelope and offered it over. It was the job offer from Lexington. The one that meant to bear her far away from here. Before he could finish reading, she pinched the paper in her fingers and tore it in two.

Thor smiled.

Doing the same, she backed away. At her room Aven spoke a good night and he nodded, wishing her the same. She slipped from sight, and he returned to the attic. Though he'd never felt so peaceful, sleep was hard to come by that night.

When Thor woke, it was to daylight and a kind of contentment that had lingered even through his sleep. He rose from bed, grabbed a work shirt and his boots, and leaving Haakon to sleep longer, headed down. He stepped softly past Jorgan's room. Best not to wake either of his brothers. While he didn't mind learning how their night had gone, it would be harder to explain Aven's and his chess game.

Outside, autumn's chill hung in the air and the orchards beckoned, the acreage needing to be gleaned like a mother in need of her nursing babe. Which made it a relief to see the lads already at work in the distance. Except for the first time, Al wasn't with them. Thor pulled on his boots and laced them up. He finished with his shirt and, still cold, fetched a flannel from the peg behind the kitchen door. He slid it on as he started down the road. When he reached the workers, he wrote *Al?* in the dust with a stick.

Jacob spoke up. "I guess somethin' spooked Tess in the night when she was out fetching water. Al said he'd be along soon but that he wanted to stay around to make sure that everything was fine. Promised he'd be here before it got too late. We told him we'd make up for it."

Thor shook his head so they wouldn't worry and gave Jacob's shoulder a squeeze of thanks. Before the sun got much higher, he meant to help the pickers, but for now there was a different kind of task to be done. With dawn just brightening the horizon, Thor headed east, striding up the hillside that marked the entrance to the Sorrel farm.

The climb wasn't steep, just lengthy. He was breathing hard before he'd even made it halfway. It had him tugging the flannel off to tie around his waist. He rolled back the sleeves of his shirt as well. Thoughts still on Aven, and with him utterly alone, Thor tried to say her name again. He couldn't get past, "Av—" Somewhere in his memory lived the other sounds, but they were too far buried. How long had it been since he'd really tried to speak?

Nearly twenty years.

Thor could still remember the rigorous oral lessons at the school for the Deaf and Dumb in North Carolina and how much he'd hated them. More potent a memory was the day that he'd sat at the end of a hallway there, his hands covered with thick mitts and his wrists tied with string. He'd kicked the wall a few times in anger, but since the hour-long detention was staff ordered and not unheard of amid forward-thinking Deaf schools, few spared him a second glance.

It was just two months after Alexander Graham Bell had visited the school, offering a lecture to the faculty about Oralism and an unhearing child's capability to learn to read lips and speak. Sign Language and fingerspelling were unrefined, Bell declared. Communicating by gestures— coarse and uncultured. How was a person to enter into proper society by such a crude and uncommon form of communication? According to Bell, Sign Language only encouraged deaf-mutes to marry deaf-mutes, thereby continuing a defective variety of the race.

There was a better way, or so the lectures declared. One that kept a child's hands at his or her sides like a young lady or gentleman. And so there, at the school for the Deaf, Sign was outlawed. In its place came arduous lessons on how to shape sounds with the mouth. For hours teachers pressed on the jaws and cheeks of their students, even applying gentle pressure to the windpipe to try and guide the Deaf in the formation of distinct vibrations that were the sounds of vowels and consonants. Every student went through the same lessons. Thor had followed along, and though the teachers patiently guided him, his attempts at speech stabilized at a garbled mess.

So it was in the garden during free time that he'd signed to a friend. Though he knew it was against the rules, he hadn't communicated properly with a single soul in days. He'd been caught by a stern professor and, with it being his third offense, taken inside. There he was placed in the corner where those awful mitts were put over his hands, his wrists tied together with string.

As the detention wore on, Thor decided to do everything he could to get out of the binding. If Da believed that Viking blood lived in their veins, then he meant to test its potency. Maybe it was stubbornness or sheer defiance, but he'd upended the stool and was crying tears of rage by the time a teacher rushed over and snipped the thick strings. His wrists were string-cut, so fiercely he'd been tugging.

This teacher, a Deaf woman like most of the faculty, had bandaged him up and told the other staff that this method of manual confinement was abominable. She declared it all in Sign—turning the entire hallway into a frenzy as she used her beautiful, fluid hands to insist upon a stern letter to Bell. While some of the staff supported her, others reinforced the new method of Oralism, cautioning that her job would be at risk should she proceed in defiance of the new system.

Thor saw her give a letter to the postman the following day.

He never knew what happened to that gentle soul, or if a response from Bell ever came, for it was a few days later that Thor had climbed up into the tree. The day Da had come and everything had changed. Bringing Thor back to the ground where they both sought the end of a different sorrow at the bottom of a bottle.

Thor strode on, thinking that he'd like to meet Bell again someday. Explain a few notions and maybe even make peace with a man he'd been so angry at. If there was one thing he now understood, it was that Alexander Graham Bell had only meant to help, and help he had. Many students had taken to his teachings well, learning to speak.

How freeing that would be.

A victory Thor had always yearned for. If only he could master a few words, maybe even speak Aven's name. The thought emboldened him and terrified him all at the same time. Perhaps Ida or Jorgan would help him.

The air grew cooler as he passed through a stand of tall maples, their rich green leaves feathered with the ambers and reds of early autumn. A flock of ravens soared across the early-morning sky. Their feathers glinted like black silk in the sunshine.

Thor caught sight of the Sorrels' farmyard just beyond. A Confederate flag, tattered and sun-bleached, hung on the side of the barn. Something moved in his side vision, and he spotted Peter jogging through the yard. A little girl with white-blonde braids clung to his back. Thor could see the child's laughter even from a distance.

Peter slowed when he saw that they had company. He gripped the girl by the hands, then lowered her down. With a few words and a brotherly pat on the back of her head, he urged her to run off. The girl obeyed.

Thor headed toward Peter, his presence convenient as the lanky youth was just the man he wanted to see. Thor had seen something in

Peter's display at church the other day. It wasn't animosity toward Haakon that had motivated Peter's behavior. It was an effort to impress the other Sorrel men around him. Which told Thor something about Peter Sorrel. A risk he was about to take on the young man and a gamble he sure hoped he was right about.

This near, he saw that Peter had bruises running beneath his eyes. His lip was split but trying to heal. Red scrapes across his left cheekbone said he'd had a rough time of something. Though introductions were foreign between their families, Thor offered a hand all the same.

After hesitating, Peter shook it. The young man glanced over his shoulder, and Thor followed his line of sight to see that the door to the house had opened. A pair of men ambled out. One spoke, and Peter's response was to motion Thor toward the run-down mansion.

Though unease stretched within him, Thor followed the young man up the battered steps and into a dim foyer. A curving staircase wound to the second floor. A few steps had holes in them, and the ornate banister was patched with rough boards.

Thor followed Peter past a kitchen, where the yeasty smell of baking bread saturated the air. Half a dozen women bustled about within— some kneading mounds of dough, others bearing trays from the oven. A waiflike blonde looked up when Thor passed, as did several others. Though their ages spanned several decades, they were all pretty in gentle measure. Sorrel men never sought anything but that which brought them pleasure. Judging by the thin bands on their fingers, the women were wives, mostly. Little children played under the table with rag dolls, and a baby slumbered in a basket on a chair.

In the center of the kitchen, Mrs. Sorrel flipped a mound of dough over on itself. She gave Thor a cordial nod.

He returned the greeting, then followed the men deeper through the house and to a back room that might have been called a parlor if it weren't for the missing windowpanes, the smell of stale tobacco, and the stuffed game mounted on the wall. The furniture, while worn, would have been grand in its day. A sofa rested at the opposite end of the room, and that's when he saw the patriarch of them all. Jed Sorrel.

The aged man looked up from the newspaper he'd been reading. Three fingers were missing from his left hand, and a leather patch lay strapped over his eye on the same side. From a cannon blast, some had said. Though battered, the general had walked away from the War between the States better than most.

Boots squared wide, the head of the Sorrel family shook the paper closed. His gray hair was skewed in the back, and he looked at Thor coolly as if having long expected this moment. The man stood with the ease of one much younger and with the dignity of one who had once owned over thirty slaves. Though Jed was not tall, his sheer will to survive three years of battle was intimidating enough. Flanked by his male kin, some veterans themselves, added to the surety of his place as leader.

"Mind stating your business, son?" He tossed the paper onto the cushion. "Or have you not found your w-w-words yet?"

Ignoring that, Thor made a quick tally even as two more men edged into the room. Seven total. Peter stood in the doorway still. Overwhelmed, Thor stared at Peter's oversized boots, recalling the way Haakon had shouted down from the rafters, gun poised on the tall youth. Though these men weren't clad in cloaks and hoods, and though they were unarmed at the moment, standing here alone, Thor tried not to wish for his brothers.

Fear. It was the purpose behind everything the Sorrels did. He felt it now, swarming around him. The very reason he'd come on his own; these men would feel no threat. He meant not to risk anything for his brothers over this.

Thor fetched his notepad from his pocket. His business was with Peter, so he flipped to a blank page to inform the general. He held over the notebook, and after a few moments, Jed stepped forward to take it. Thor could have moved closer but wasn't feeling that generous just now. After studying the message, Jed passed it to a man in a sweat-stained shirt beside him.

Each man eyed it in turn, some so quickly they probably couldn't read. A few stole wary looks Thor's way, as if believing the nonsense that his lack of voice truly was a spirit needing to be loosed. Rubbish that, but if it kept them at a distance, he wasn't about to mention as much.

The book reached Peter, who scanned the missive. A hint of uncertainty slipped unguarded through his eyes. The book reaching him again, Thor flipped to the proposition he'd drafted up and handed it back. Peter took a moment to read, then gave it to Jed.

All of a sudden Peter pointed to one of the men, guiding Thor's attention that way. Thor looked to the man who must have spoken—Harlan Sorrel. One of Jed's own sons and Peter's very father. Every angle of his face was tight with the focus of family pride and such bloodlust that the air was colder just looking at him. Harlan smelled of white whiskey. One hundred proof and charcoal mellowed. The only kind of moonshine Thor had ever taken a liking to.

He slammed aside the memory the moment it hit him.

"We heard rumor that you stopped makin' your drink. That so?"

Thor nodded.

A different man spoke. This one as old as Jed, perhaps. His head was bald, but his thick arms belied his age. "Got anything left in that barn'a yers?"

Thor ran a hand over his mouth but didn't respond. They knew as well as he did that there was a hearty stash left. The Sorrels kept a keen watch on everything in these parts.

"How much? For everything? We'll take it off your hands at the right price."

Everything? Thor had at least a hundred quarts of table cider left. Double that amount of his finer two-year batch. His three-year brew was still in barrels, but if he jarred it, that proof would be worth nearly two dollars a quart. If his quick tallies were correct, the cidery still housed about five hundred dollars' worth of product. Well beyond what he and his brothers owed on the lease. Thor tugged at his beard.

Men threw words his way—some excited, others agitated. All seemed to be wondering the same thing. Why was he holding on to it?

The room stilled when a woman stepped in. She toted a tray with full cups of coffee and some kind of baked sweet. Her menfolk eyed her as if surprised by her sudden presence.

Thor didn't like the way she was looking at him. Not for his sake, but for hers. With a subtle yet sure motion, she set down the tray, tipping her head just enough for her yellow hair to slide from her pale neck. Purple bruises speckled her skin. The way Peter's nostrils flared, eyes tightening with a pained sadness, Thor would bet everything that it was his mother, confirmed in the way that Harlan's gaze went hard as steel. The woman straightened slowly, deliberately, and shot a fierce look around the room that Thor feared she'd regret.

A demand for help if he'd ever seen one.

She wasn't going to harbor any of their secrets, that was clear.

Thor swallowed both a sour taste and a rising anger and stepped aside for the woman to slip from the room easier. Peter offered the notebook back over. Thor took it. He almost signed to Peter for an answer but caught himself. He waited, instead, for what the young man would say.

Thor had a hunch the Sorrels would like one of their own on the inside. For some strange reason it seemed a risk worth taking.

Firm conversation tramped around the room, and Thor was torn between trying to follow along and inching aside for a child who was pressing past his leg toward the tray. It was the same girl from the yard. She squeezed by and reached for a piece of sweet bread. One of the men moved to stop her, but Jed shoved the tray nearer, allowing the child a portion.

At a tap on his shoulder, Thor looked over to see Peter wanting to speak.

"When does the harvest start?" The words were a struggle to understand with Peter's split lip badly done.

Thor held up his thumb and two fingers, then moved his hand back to show it had begun a few days ago. The lad seemed to grasp that.

"I'll be there," Peter said.

A curious look flitted through Jed's icy-blue eyes, and Thor pinned it to memory to try and make sense of later. More than ready to leave, Thor stepped back but caught the gaze of the thick-armed man as he did.

"And the liquor?" the man asked.

Thor glanced to the girl who crouched beneath the windowsill, the sun bright on her small form. She nibbled her bread, nose scrunched with delight. She smiled up at Thor as if it was due to his presence that she'd gotten her treat. Did she bear bruises as the other women did?

But blazes, that liquor was valuable.

Now that he'd had more time to put thought to it, he'd yet to factor in the '88 and '89 blackberry wine aging in oak casks. He had four barrels from each year, bringing the value of what he had in the cidery to nearly a grand.

And the debt was a burden he was tired of bearing.

To sell it all in one shot. So clean and easy. Freeing.

His conscience waging its own war, Thor

328

watched the girl even as he thought of the others under this roof. The men waited, all seeming hinged on what his decision would be. On whether or not his cider would continue to fuel their fire.

Thor scribbled his answer. He ripped out the paper and handed it over. Jed read and crumpled it. He threw the wad at the wall and motioned for his men to see Thor out. Because the liquor . . . it wasn't for sale.

TWENTY-SEVEN

Peter came just after sunup. The whole farmyard stilled as he walked onto it. Even Grete's tail ceased its wagging, Thor noticed. The Sorrel glanced first to Aven and Fay, who were oiling the gears of the apple scratter, then to the door that Peter and his kin had once kicked in. Last of all to Al and the other dark-skinned boys who were pulling on picking bags. Al's hands stilled as he spotted the newcomer.

Thor had warned them that Peter was coming, and while Al had confessed to not knowing the identities of the masked men who had pistol-whipped him, something about the wary way Peter glanced at him said enough. A soul-heavy look if Thor ever saw one.

Thor shook Peter's hand, then stepped aside for Jorgan to explain how the operation worked. Peter nodded as he listened—the bruises beneath his eyes had softened to a yellowing, but the scratches across his cheekbone were rougher, as if struggling to heal.

Al hitched up the team while Abraham and Jacob heaped a fresh round of crates into the wagon. Thor nicked two picking bags from a pile, and after Peter had gotten the gist of how this worked, Thor handed one over and motioned for the Sorrel to follow him to the orchard. Once there, he worked side by side with Peter, keeping an eye on him to adjust any skills needed. While the young man seemed to be in pain—gritting his teeth whenever he had to raise his right arm—he was a quick learner and a hard worker.

After filling his third crate, Peter lugged it over to the wagon. Al was already there, sliding one into place. He turned for the next without noticing who extended it. Peter was equally as surprised, and down the crate tumbled. Apples spilled across the row.

Thor strode over, knelt, and helped gather it all up. Sweat glistened on Al's forehead and Peter was red under the collar. Angling to Jorgan, Thor signed Aven's name. He pointed next to the knocked-around fruit so his brother would know those were for her to use up. Better they be apple butter than rot in storage. Jorgan placed the wooden box on the wagon seat.

Thor rose just as Peter spoke. "I'm real sorry 'bout that."

Thor shook his head. He motioned for them to come near, then patted Al's chest and signed the wiry youth's name. *A-L*. He squeezed Peter's shoulder, looked Al square in the eye, and signed *P-E-T-E-R*. Next Thor gripped Peter's sleeve and raised his arm high enough for Al to shake his hand. Al hesitated, then with his gaze strong and squarely on the Sorrel boy, he gave a firm shake.

A start, then. Thor nodded his gratitude to them both. From appearances, Al had lost more than Peter ever had, but Peter knew his own kind of grief. As a grandson of Jed Sorrel, being a member of the Klan might not have been voluntary. To commit acts of violence because it was a family cause was no way to live.

Maybe that's why Peter was here. Maybe that's why he'd knelt in the great room that night and tried to hand Georgie back her lost spool doll. Bold, yes. Especially since no one would put it past the Sorrel men to pistol-whip their own kind if crossed. Son or no son.

Thor didn't envy Peter. Not now nor in the days to come. As the youth grabbed another crate and got back to work, Thor couldn't shake the burden to look after him if it was in his power. He hoped that day wouldn't come, but something told him it might.

They worked until the wagon was brimming, then everyone walked along as Jorgan led the team slowly back to the cidery. Once there, crates were unloaded and carried into the cool storage space. Tomorrow was Sunday, so they'd wait until the workweek to begin grinding. For now, the fruit would pass the night behind closed doors.

Back in the orchard, they began all over again, the cycle not slowing until just before noon when Tess approached with a pail of water. She offered a drink to each of them in turn. When she extended a cupful to Peter and he declined with a shake of his head, she tipped the cup, spilling it onto his boots. Peter's brows shot up, and he looked to Thor as if not sure what to do.

Thor turned away to check a smile. It seemed Al's sister had her own mind about how this was to go. Tess was equally as cool as she helped Ida and Fay serve up the noon meal. Cora wasn't around, and Thor didn't blame her. Some things took time—if they healed at all. He'd leave that up to each of them, but for himself, he needed to oversee that this operation ran smoothly, so it was a relief when Tess simply shoved a plate into Peter's hands . . . as opposed to placing it elsewhere.

With a redhead nowhere in sight, Thor got Ida's attention. *Where A-V-E-N?*

"She's upstairs. Poor thing done twisted her ankle this morning. Stepped funny off the porch. She tried to make it over as nothin', but was hurtin' real bad. I sent her up to bed and she's restin'."

Thor signaled to Haakon to prep the cider press, and Haakon gave a curt nod. Thor polished off his meal as he strode to the house, then set his plate on the table before climbing the stairs.

Aven's door was ajar, so he knocked with a knuckle before touching it farther open. She sat on the edge of her bed, head bowed, ginger braid draping one shoulder. Her bare foot was soaking in a deep pan of water. A coarse bag of soaking salts rested nearby. Aven looked up when he stepped through the doorway.

"Thor. Is something the matter?"

Her cheeks were flushed and her pretty eyes seemed tired. She swallowed hard. Never once had he been in her room, but he doubted that was the cause for her distress. There was a cup on the nightstand, so Thor filled it for her. She sipped, looking grateful. Taking a knee in front of her, he lifted her bare calf and gently felt around the bone.

Aven eased the hem of her skirt out of the way, looking taken aback. Thor took care to keep his focus on the injury so as not to set her ill at ease. The skin around her ankle was swollen and bruised with a spread of purple. He kept his touch as soft as possible as he circled her ankle slowly. Aven flinched some, but to his relief it only felt sprained. Still . . . painful, those.

Thor pulled the hand towel from the nightstand and dabbed her skin dry. He helped her move farther back on the bed. Once she was settled, Aven rested her head into the pillow and closed her eyes. Finished, he bent and pressed a kiss to the top of her head. His thumb grazed her cheek, and with work needing him, he left her.

He returned to the yard to find it empty, everyone back in the orchard save Haakon, who was in the cidery, tugging a tarp from the different sections of the giant press. Haakon shook out the oiled canvas, and Thor moved to help fold it. When they had finished, Thor followed him to where the scratter still sat in the yard from the recent cleaning. Haakon gripped one end of the handled machine and Thor took the other. They slid it off to the side to make room for the press.

The scratter was easier to nudge about than the larger contraption, but by no means less important. Nestled within a wooden box was the cam—a wheel that had dozens of nail heads jutting out of it. Awful to the touch, but it had been grinding apples into mash since Da had built it over twenty seasons ago. Jorgan kept it so well maintained with oil and cloth that it had some years left in it.

Back at the press, Thor and Haakon disassembled and carried the segments out to the yard one piece at a time. They set down the old, white oak crossbeams and went back for the center pivot, which was just as heavy. He and Haakon heaved out the screw next. Made of red oak, it was as massive as all the rest. Wide enough that Georgie would scarcely be able to wrap her arms around it.

It would take grease soon, but for now they just fastened it into place with as much effort as it might have taken to hoist a barn wall. The heavy iron and wood pieces were not made to move back and forth to the yard, but this year Thor couldn't abide the smell of the cidery for days on end. Better the fresh air and moving breeze to sweep the aroma of even the sweetest ciders away.

When pieced together, the press was strong enough to apply ten tons of pressure. Enough to get three gallons of juice per bushel. As for the apple pulp left behind, Ida would use some of it for the garden. Folks would come and take away the rest to feed to chickens and pigs. Others would soak the pulp with water to make ciderkin—a poor man's drink, but not something to be snubbed in these parts, especially since it was good for children.

After Thor and Haakon had carried the center pivot into the yard, they set it up on its end and attached the iron braces. Wrench in hand, Haakon grimaced as he tightened every stiff bolt. Thor spelled him after a time until everything was snug. The surrounding sections went next, but they didn't attempt the larger crossbeams until Jorgan had returned.

As three, they lifted the chunks of white oak into place. The nut of the screw was almost as heavy as the twisted, carved column it rested atop, so it was with much effort that they had it all assembled. Sweat dampened his skin as Thor climbed down from the contraption, only to see that the pickers were returning with another wagonload. The last of the day.

He hefted a crate out before the wagon had even come to a complete stop. While there was no great rush with dusk ending the workday, he meant to check on Aven again.

Inside the shop, Peter stood stock-still, scrutinizing the vast interior. The shelves loaded with jars. Filled casks. Peter's gaze shifted to the many windows as he assessed something. Thor set the crate down harder than he should have. Peter looked at him and headed back out.

When the wagon was empty, Thor bid a good evening to the pickers and headed for the house. He cast a second glance at Peter, who walked down the road with a weary, dogged stride. What Thor wouldn't give to know what would be said among the Sorrels tonight. He tried not to think about it as he climbed the stairs, forcing himself to trust his gut with the boy. If the Sorrels meant to cause trouble, they'd manage no matter what he did. They always had.

In the kitchen, Thor started for the stairs, but Ida signaled that Aven was asleep. Thor came back and accepted the plate of supper Ida handed him. He was so tired, he scarcely noticed what it was. It was good, though, and it filled a void he hadn't realized was clawing for attention. He meant to ask Ida something, but only when no one else was around.

By the time he finished eating, the kitchen was empty and night had fallen. Time had passed like a thief. Had he fallen asleep where he sat? His plate was gone, the dishes washed, and a twinge in his neck confirmed that he'd sat that way for too long. Thor stood and stretched his neck from side to side.

He ached for his bed, but with this rare chance to catch Ida alone, he knocked softly on the housekeeper's door. The floor barely shuddered with her light footsteps. He and his brothers had never been inside Ida's room. They made it a point to give her strict privacy, and it had always been that way. Her room was a world they scarcely knew, but when she opened her door, Thor glimpsed a brown-and-black quilt on the wall, a tintype of a dark-skinned soldier on the nightstand, and an open Bible on the bed.

The Lord had smiled down on them the day she'd come here.

"Figured I'd just letcha sleep." Ida tugged the strap of her robe snug. "Thought I'd find ya in the same spot come mornin'. Y'all did a right fine job today. With all of it."

He offered his thanks in return for everything she did, day in and day out. Would now be the time to ask for more? He pointed to himself, then shaped *need help with question*. He pointed toward Aven's room and fingerspelled her name. How best to phrase this? *Learn speak question, me.* For Aven he would try. Just four words—

surely it couldn't be impossible. *You teach?* With nervous hands he conveyed what that question would be. The one a man rightly took a knee to speak.

Ida's eyes glistened with joy. Leaning forward, she squeezed his hand, and there was a pride in her face that humbled him. "You come find me this time tomorrow and we'll start the first word."

With one arm, he pulled her near and squeezed her thin frame tight. She patted his chest and he left her to rest. Upstairs, he was just passing the middle room when Fay stepped into the hallway. She bore a small basin filled with water in the crook of her arm and a flickering candle.

"She's asleep now," Fay said to him with ease, which was rare for someone he didn't know well. He liked that about her.

Thor nodded his appreciation and headed to the attic stairs. He followed them up to find a faint glow from a candle, though Haakon was nowhere in sight. Seeing an open window, Thor looked out to find his brother sitting on the far edge of the roof. Just as they'd often done as boys.

Gripping the window frame, Thor pulled himself through. A spark flashed as Haakon struck a match. He lit the end of a pipe that Thor hadn't noticed. It was with several quick puffs that Haakon drew in smoke and blew it back out. Exhausted, Thor settled down on the shingles and thought some about what he needed to say. After Haakon's confession of his tenderness for Aven some time back and Thor's request to Ida just now, it was only right Thor give the same clarity.

The words knotted in his mind when he thought of stating them, so Thor went with the simplest approach. He shaped Aven's name, grateful for the moon that was almost full. It lit his hand enough for Haakon to see. Before Thor could finish, Haakon looked away.

Thor thumped his brother's arm because he needed to know this. *Love A-V-E-N.* Thor finished by touching his chest. It was both a desire for her and a decision to care for her. Sliding his hands together, he signed *fervent* so Haakon would understand just how much.

After a few moments, Haakon freed his pipe and offered it over. Thor declined. Was that it? Or did his brother need a chance to ponder? Not wanting to rush him, Thor waited as Haakon peered overhead. With a raised hand, he seemed to be counting the stars. Haakon stopped at just three. The row that made up the story of Odin's wife.

Da had told them that in this country the same stars shaped a belt that belonged to the hunter Orion. While he'd always taught them to put faith not in the Viking gods but in the God who had cast every star across the sky, Da had still woven the fables for them. His way of teaching them of their ancestors. And Da had often pointed out that line of three to them, perhaps because his own wife was as distant.

Thor knew some of that sharp longing. Having wanted a wife for a good many years, it had become harder and harder to be alone. While he wouldn't deny that young ladies had occasionally caught his eye in years past, it was Aven whom he sought to give his life to. It was more than taking a wife for love and comfort. It was about leading, cherishing, and protecting her. A great responsibility and one he felt the Lord equipping him for. He struggled to express that to his brother, but when he finished, Thor knew Haakon had followed along, even in the dark.

"So will you take Aven as your wife now?" Haakon asked.

Thor certainly wanted to. But he was still gauging how best to proceed with her. When he signed that, Haakon seemed surprised.

"She hasn't accepted yet, then? I mean, not officially?"

No.

Haakon tapped his pipe against the roof, then used the heel of his boot to tamp away the ash. He rose to a crouch, bracing himself with a hand. "Best of luck with it, Thor. Truly."

Not certain of what to make of that, Thor

nodded, then watched as Haakon skidded to the edge of the roof. He climbed down to the banister of the porch below as they had so often done. And just like as children, Haakon was gone into the night.

TWENTY-EIGHT

A fire crackled in the hearth each evening. A welcome addition to the cool of nightfall and a reminder that winter was not far behind autumn. Though the crisp evenings beckoned for them, Haakon didn't tell his fables anymore. Instead, he was more and more distant. Usually pulling a chair into the corner where he kept busy oiling his boots or untangling fishing line. He made little conversation except for that which had to do with the harvest.

Rarely did he ever sit completely still. There was a restlessness within him, and it seemed to be growing day by day. A distance that Aven felt in all ways but one, because it was there that she often felt him watching her when he thought, perhaps, that she didn't notice.

By the start of the new week, the swelling in her ankle was much lessened. While the bruising had mellowed, it still smarted to walk on, so she took ginger steps wherever she went. To be up and about was blessed relief, even if Fay and Ida insisted she not do much.

The two women had seen to the laundry, so Aven tucked the folded items away. She was just in the attic putting Thor's and Haakon's things where they went when a clatter sounded from outside. Aven moved to the window. There in the sunny yard, Jorgan and Thor were greasing the mighty screw.

Standing atop the press, Haakon turned the long, wooden arm that twisted everything into motion. Grete paced around the contraption, tail aflutter with excitement. Haakon called to his brothers for more lard. They slathered on fresh handfuls until the wooden pillar was well streaked.

The handle of the scratter hadn't stopped being cranked all morning, and now the pickers lugged over bucket after bucket of ground pulp. There would be fresh cider by days end, if not in mere moments.

Thor set a slatted, wooden frame onto the base of the press and spread cheesecloth over it. The lads layered on pulp. Once covered, that cloth was wrapped up and another frame set over it to repeat the process. Not wanting to miss the grand moment, Aven headed down. Her steps were hindered but she gripped tight the handrail, and sweet victory came when she stepped outside and the crisp air wrapped her in a delicious gust.

Thor replaced Haakon atop the frame of the press. He turned the rod just as his brother had done—one side at a time—cranking the wooden bar around and around. The rotations bore down on the screw, compressing the pulp-filled slats. A few bees buzzed around the press, eager for the sweetness. Thor grunted and tugged the screw a rotation lower. Juice squeezed from the frame. It ran down a spout that filled buckets as quickly as the other men could swap them out. At the grinder, Al turned the handle while Fay and Jorgan dropped in bucketfuls of wet apples. It all ran with such precision that Cora and Ida were able to sit back and observe. If Cora was bothered by Peter's presence, she didn't let on.

Tugging her shawl snug, Aven joined the women on the porch steps. The rod continued to pivot as Thor's grunts grew more strained. Using his shoulder, he wiped at his forehead, clasped the rod, and turned it again. He did that only once more, then let out two sharp whistles. Jorgan climbed up to stand opposite him and gripped the free end of the rod. Together, they cranked it with double the force. Juice gushed from the press. Tess and Georgie strode down from where they had been in the garden. In Tess's lean hands was a basket of green cabbage heads. She set it on the steps beside the women, and Aven watched as they all began peeling off leaves. Ida fetched a board and knife and showed Aven how to cut the stout leaves into shreds.

"What is this for?" Aven asked as she worked.

"Tangy cabbage." Then louder, "Soon as Thorald brings us some of that fine cider."

Thor spotted Ida but his brow furrowed. Ida waved a cabbage leaf overhead. He grinned.

He hopped down, fetched up two buckets, and carried them over. One he gave to Ida and the other he set on the steps. After pacing into the house, he returned with an armful of jars and placed them in a long row across the middle step. He counted them, then tallied all who were around and went back for one more jar.

Gripping up the bucket, he sloshed cider nearly everywhere but into the glasses. Thor shook his wet hand and offered a jar first to Ida, then to Cora. He made sure that everyone had one before taking the last for himself. Grete crawled forward to lick at the damp step.

Thor clanked a jar with his brothers, then with all the others. Last, he tapped his own to Aven's, gave her a wink, and using his glass, mimicked a drinking motion. There was an expectancy in his eyes as he waited.

Aven sipped and it was heavenly. "*Ohhhh, that's good.*" Tangy and sweet—the product of a year's worth of work. As she had been on a ship bound for America, he had stood among his trees as the new spring buds unfolded into promise. And here she was by God's grace. Able to share in it today.

He shaped several words to her.

Ida helped. "Said that Dorothe used to sit here with us and do this very thing." She dropped a handful of cut cabbage into the bowl.

Aven's heart warmed at the thought.

Thor took a hearty gulp, and Aven felt a sudden twinge at the memories of him with more potent brews in hand. With such a claim difficult to conquer, his temptation would surely linger. In fact, she was certain it did, and she respected him all the more because it was a daily choice he was making to overcome.

Cora took another drink. "Best yet, y'all. Best yet."

Thor's head dipped in thanks. Even Al and the lads looked proud. Peter drank his cider, peering at the juice in between each sip as if to make sense of how something could be so good.

Over the course of the morning, the next buckets were poured into jugs and sealed. Fay stood at a makeshift table that had been set up in the shade of the house. With a damp rag, she wiped each finished jug and Jorgan carried them two at a time to the cidery.

While Ida minded her pot of steaming cider and cabbage, Aven tidied up scraps of the leaves from the porch. She filled her apron with the trimmings and carried them all to the new chicken coop. One that was now inhabited thanks to Jorgan's recent visit to a neighboring farm. Despite every effort not to limp, Aven's steps felt far from graceful. After nudging the coop door ajar, she tossed in the offering. The chickens startled, then began pecking at the thin, green trimmings.

Haakon strode up behind her. "Ida's askin' for you."

"Oh, thank you." Aven closed the door and stepped away. Seeing her effort, Haakon offered her his arm. She took it gratefully.

Hands that were nearly as broad as Thor's, circled together, chafing a rough sound between work-worn palms. Even Haakon's shoulders seemed thicker and more spread. Had he grown over the summer? She'd believed him past such years, but when Aven tilted a second glance his way, she could no more deny that Haakon had developed a brawn to rival any man than she could deny how raptly he was watching her. His eyes were such a startling blue that even the sky overhead seemed the wrong color.

"You're walkin' better," he said as they crossed the farmyard.

"Aye. Nearly mended."

"Will you walk with me tomorrow? If you're able?"

"I'm sorry?"

"There's something I want to show you. Something that I could use your help with." They reached the porch steps and Haakon released her arm. "Go for a walk with me tomorrow, Aven."

She laid a hand to the rail. Several responses came to mind, all springing up from her reservation of being alone with him. She meant not to lead him on or cause Thor any wondering about her attentions.

"Please," he added. "It's just a short ways. I really do want to show you something, and I promise you'll be back before you even realize you're gone."

"Might you tell me what it is?"

"That would ruin the surprise. Please. It's not far. Jorgan and Thor and I spent a lot of time working on it. Usually in the winter or spring the last few years."

Jorgan walked across the porch and must have overheard, for in passing he said, "You haven't seen it yet?"

"Seen what?"

But Jorgan had already entered the kitchen and was striding through. His manner was so untroubled that perhaps she need not worry. Perhaps she was overthinking this.

Haakon gave an easy smile. "It's a house, Aven. One my brothers and me have been fixin' up over the years. Come with me, and bring your sewing basket. There's a project I need your help with. Really."

Aven took each step higher and, with little pain, turned to Haakon and gave what she hoped was a sisterly smile. "If I'm able." Dipping her head, she slipped into the house, feeling those brilliant eyes on her all the way.

TWENTY-NINE

Aven went down the following morning, basket in hand, keeping uncertainties in check. She was to assist Haakon with a trace of handiwork. That was all. Even Thor had thought it a fine idea if she wished it. It would be a relief from her recent idleness, and yet the thought of passing the morning with Haakon was an unsettling one. There had always been something very dangerous to her about Haakon Norgaard. He'd burrowed deep into her heart, but the tender place had never felt truly safe in his care.

They met in the quiet of the kitchen, and it was by the fog of morning that they crossed the yard. Fog so thick she could scarcely make out the sight of Jorgan carrying a portion of hay to the horse barn. Ida limped gently toward the coop, basket in hand. In the distance stood the cidery. Tall and imposing—the massive door still fastened with its heavy bolt and lock for the night.

Haakon offered Aven his arm again, but she assured him she was fine. When the lingering soreness in her ankle slowed her before even leaving the yard, he offered again. His flannel shirt was soft to her wrist as she accepted, but it was the steadiness just beneath that was jarring.

The air in the thick of the woods hung cool

and damp. Heavy with each breath she took. They passed the charred remains of what she now knew was their old chicken coop. The one Haakon had blown apart a few years back with a gunpowder concoction. She fought a smile as he assured her that all the inhabitants had been carefully relocated prior to the event.

Her hand stayed snug to his arm as they continued on, and after a few more moments, the trees thinned, the land opening up into a quaint valley where white mist settled sleepy and low. At the far edge of the clearing stood a small cabin. Bent grasses rippled in the breeze, frosted still with dew. While the trees only rustled in the stirring of air, the smallest of saplings quaked and shuddered.

Aven stepped forward as Haakon did. The cabin was aged. Some boards looked ancient while others had been replaced with bright, new cedar. A bird's nest rested in the gable of the upper window. The frames, while showing their years, housed glass panes that had been recently wiped.

"What is this place?"

Haakon slowed to a stop. "It's part of the farm. An old caretaker's cabin. My brothers and I drew straws a few summers back to decide who would get it and which two would share the main house." Bending, he pushed two buckets up onto the porch, then dropped a dried paintbrush into the top one. "It was probably rigged because we can all agree that Thor and Jorgan would live peaceably together. There's room for wives and children in the big house. But over time, that would get crowded with three families."

Aven struggled to make sense of what he was saying. The Norsemen of old lived in communal houses, all gathered with their kinsmen beneath a single roof. While those ancient days were swept away with time, she'd envisioned the Norgaards as the same—wives and children melting into the rhythm of the great house. Something about Haakon's demeanor said that he had once had the same anticipation.

He nabbed up a stick and tossed it away from the yard. "We just do little things now and again." He pointed to the porch where a swing hung. "We fixed that last winter. And these . . ." After climbing the front steps, he tapped the nearest shutter. "These were under the porch. A coat of paint perked 'em right up."

She followed him down the length of the porch. Nearing the swing, she touched the cool metal chain that was rough with rust, and it creaked. "It's a very fine house, Haakon."

"Thank you. Here, I'll show you what I need your help with." He edged around her and pressed past the door. "So in here"—his voice echoed within the empty room—"is where my problem lies."

Aven stepped in to find boards stacked off to

the side and a broken chair resting in the corner. Curtains hung over the windows in haphazard fashion, and it was to these that Haakon led her.

"This was Dorothe's doing a few years back," he said. "But when her health began to fail, I didn't want to pester her with coming over here anymore. The problem is that they either need to all come down or all go up. Do you think you could finish them? Or if it's best they come down, you can have the cloth if you want. I won't need it."

Aven fingered a curtain. The rod it hung on was splintered, snagging the drapes so they didn't slide smooth. "They're in good shape, but it seems like a storm went through here."

"That was just me. I kept tripping over them. Probably best if they come down."

"You won't want curtains?"

He shrugged one shoulder.

"I think these could be set to rights quite well. Maybe not so long, though?" She held up an end. "They could be trimmed back, which might suit you better."

"You wouldn't mind?"

"Not at all. Let's see if we can get them down."

He reached overhead and lifted the wooden rod free from its pegs. With his thumbs, he shoved the snug fabric back and Aven gave a good tug. When they had that length of fabric freed, she folded it and Haakon pulled down more. He offered her a rod to work on.

Sitting in the center of the floor, Aven began to inch the snug fabric from the splintered piece. She bent and folded the hem of the cloth, contemplating how short to make it.

"Does this fashion suit you?" Doubtful, she held up the floral pattern. Elegant curves of red and brown were splayed upon an ivory background.

"Not really. I was hoping it would fade some in the sun. I suppose it doesn't matter so much. Curtains are more for the lady of the house, right? When this house has a lady . . . hopefully she'll like them."

She hoped to bolster him. "There's much to like about this place."

"It's shaping up." He settled beside her and tugged at the piece she was struggling with. "I don't think I'll live here for a while yet, though. We don't want Thor to get lonesome all on his own up in the attic."

Sensing—and dearly hoping—that one day Thor wouldn't have cause to be alone, Aven rose to her knees and fashioned what she needed to ask. What Haakon deserved to say. It hadn't been so long ago when this man had held her in the water, his heart and words right there between them. "Are you happy, Haakon? Even with the way things are?"

"You mean with my life or Thor's life?" His brow furrowed as he focused on his task. Something about the look said drapes were the furthest thing from his mind. "I don't plan to settle down for a while yet." The bent rod grew straighter as he plied the thin wood between his hands. "If that's what you mean. And as for happy . . . I think I will be." He set the wooden rod aside, glancing around at the cabin walls. They seemed to tell stories that only he could hear. "When harvest is over, maybe I'll get away for a spell."

She tried not to think of him leaving but had no right to ask him to stay. "You would be missed." 'Twas a gentle truth. Surely that was alright to say.

He gave her a small smile.

With careful cuts of her scissors, Aven trimmed a portion from one of the panels. "Tell me . . . where would you go?"

"I dunno." His boots shifted nearer to her—the leather worn but solid. The seams dusty. "I like the idea of going to a different state. Maybe up north. Or another idea . . . something I've often thought of is seeing the ocean. Maybe even setting sail somewhere." Haakon reached into her sewing basket for a smaller pair of scissors and chopped off a thread. "If you've crossed the Atlantic, I should probably be able to handle it."

She placed the trimmed cutting between them.

" 'Tis harder than it seems, I assure you." Never would she forget the toss of the sea or the pitch of the ship. The exhausting days and terrifying nights. Of seasickness and worse. But also, there had been the sun on the water and hope in the air due to the direction that the sails were blowing them. To a new home. A new land.

"It would suit you." She recalled the way he'd climbed up to the beam in the great room. How he'd balanced atop it to aim his gun. The way he never backed down from a standoff. How he faced life with little fear. 'Twas a grit that he had, and it would serve him well amid gale and storm. "However, you'd have to learn to listen to your superiors. I've never known a sailor to get by well otherwise."

"I've had a lot of practice at that."

"Without complaining, that is."

Haakon tossed the scissors back into the basket. "Hmm. Maybe I'll just head north."

Aven pursed her lips to fight a smile. "I'll take these with us." She pulled more of the drapes near. "They'll be easy to work on in my spare time."

"I appreciate that." He took up the trimming she'd just cut and absently folded it around his hand. He seemed about to say more but footsteps pounded nearer.

The door burst open with such a crash that they both jumped.

"Haakon! Where are you?" Jorgan stalked into the room. He glanced between them and jerked his head back the way he came. "Come! Now. We've got trouble."

"What is it?" Haakon rose.

"The liquor."

"What?"

"It's gone. Every jar."

THIRTY

Thor stood in the cidery staring at empty shelves. Every level was picked clean, and judging by the state of the floor, not a single one had been dropped. Even the barrels were gone, and a nudge proved the only one lingering to be empty. Overhead, the white owl slept, and though the bird would have seen everything that happened by cover of night, Thor didn't need a second guess to know who had done this.

They all knew.

But how had the Sorrels been so shrewd? While Thor would be the first to admit that he was useless for sounds in the night, it wasn't like his brothers to miss an intrusion. Less likely would have been Grete.

Thor lifted his head. Grete.

Had he seen the dog this morning? Not as he'd come out of the house or even as he'd unbolted the cider shed. Always she was underfoot as he did that. Stepping back out, Thor squinted against the sun. He whistled and waited for Haakon's sidekick to come running. After a minute, he whistled sharper.

Nothing.

Fear slid through him. Thor strode around the side of the barn where Jorgan was looking at the windows that had been removed. Panels of glass sat stacked off to the side, and someone had done a number on the wooden frame.

You see G-R-E-T-E? Thor asked.

Jorgan looked around, then shook his head. He cupped two hands around his mouth and called for her. When the dog didn't appear, Jorgan arched his back, calling with greater intensity. Still nothing. Face drawn, Haakon rushed up to them.

"Why isn't she coming?" Haakon strode along the length of the barn, and judging by the way his shoulders heaved, he was hollering for her. Then Haakon slowed, peering up at the sky. Thor lifted his eyes to see a scattering of crows circle the center of the meadow. Their shadows wove in and out on the grasses where something had to be lying just below.

Thor meant to move—do something, any-thing—but his feet and heart were suddenly leaden with dread. Haakon started into a run. The blackbirds scattered. Reaching the middle of the meadow, Haakon sank to his knees. Hands pressed to the ground, he bowed his head.

A sting clamped Thor's throat. He took a step forward even as Haakon shifted, checking what had to be Grete there. Bending lower, Haakon tilted his head to the side and listened. He held that way for a long while, then bolted upright. "She's not dead!"

Thor broke into a jog, and Jorgan followed. Haakon scooped up the dog, stumbling as he righted her weight. "She's breathin', but barely. Somethin's wrong with her."

"Cora might know what to do," Jorgan said before running off.

Haakon walked toward the house, Grete limp in his arms. Thor tugged the door open, and Haakon swiveled into the kitchen so quickly that he bumped into the table, sending Ida's cake pans clattering into one another. He carried Grete into the next room and laid her on the sofa.

Aven moved in beside them. "What happened?"

Fay was right behind her. No one relayed the story—Thor because he wasn't able to and Haakon because this was his pup. The one he'd gotten for his birthday years back. The one that Cora had tied with a ribbon and plopped into his lap. Grete had flounced about. Chubby and licking him like she'd finally found her way home.

Aven moved to the window, pushing the drapes aside for more light. Fay's long, blonde braid brushed the dog's paw as she leaned down to kiss the top of Grete's head. No one seemed to know what to do, which made it more than a relief when Cora arrived. She set her medic bag beside the sofa, knelt, and took her time examining the dog.

Finally Cora wiped the back of her wrist across her forehead. "I don't know what this is." Snapping open her bag, she pulled out an amber bottle and shook it. Uncapping the vial, she lowered it beneath Grete's nose. The lifting and lowering of the dog's ribs was so subtle, so sparse, that it was almost as if she were gone. "They gave her somethin', that's for sure. All I can think of might be tansy. But I never seen it sedate like this."

Suddenly everyone looked to the entryway. Thor followed suit and saw the last person he expected to be standing there. Peter.

Quite certain Peter had addressed them, Thor snapped for Jorgan's help.

Jorgan ran a thumb beneath his chin for *not*, followed by *T-A-N-S-Y*.

Peter stepped closer. "It was from a bottle that my pa took from a cabinet." He reached into his pocket and held it over. "He told me to douse the dog's supper with it. Said that it would stop her heart, so I just put a tiny bit in."

Cora took the vial and turned it. Thor read *Laudanum* on the label. Opium.

In three steps, Haakon shoved him. "You traitor!"

Peter's head smacked the wall when Haakon shoved again.

"If I hadn't done it, they would have killed her!" Peter yanked Haakon's hands away. "Be glad for that." He tugged his shirt back to rights, flashed Haakon a glare but nothing more.

Peter's eyes briefly flitted to Cora, and catching her cool, stony gaze, he swallowed hard. From the kitchen Ida watched, her expression much as her sister's. Flour dusted the woman's hands that hung limp at her sides. The only hint that she'd had wedding cakes on her mind.

Cora set aside the jar. "If it be opium he gave her, she'll be back to her old self before long."

Peter nodded. "And I know where your cider is." He seemed to take care so as not to look at Al's mother again. As if the sheer weight of being in the same room as her was the worst of it all.

"Why didn't you do something to stop them?" Jorgan asked. "Why didn't you tell us so we could?"

Haakon spoke as well, but Thor missed it.

"Because soon as I started workin' here, they kept me out of their discussions. Always they were behind closed doors. I knew somethin' was stewin', so I looked around your shop to see how secure it was. It seemed solid, so I doubted they could get in." He braved a small step nearer. "But then last night I knew what they were up to. When talk came of doin' away with the dog, I offered to handle it myself. I swear, that's how it went."

Thor bumped Jorgan in the arm and signed a question for Peter.

Jorgan spoke. "He asked why."

"Why? 'Cause it ain't right. What they're doin' ain't right."

Everyone looked to where Aven was standing, but by the time Thor did as well, he missed what she'd said. He wished he knew her opinion even as he looked back to Peter. This was all going faster than he could manage. Moving to the other side of the room, Thor faced them all so he would see more of what was being spoken.

Peter swallowed hard. "They have your liquor stacked in the back end of our barn. It's all behind a dummy wall that hid provisions during the war." When Peter asked for something to draw it up with, Jorgan brought him paper and a pencil.

Thor stepped close enough to watch.

Peter drew out a rough sketch, shading in the area that was the secret storage space. "With this here portion, the boards are loose, and takin' them down makes a doorway. Everythin's in there and sealed up. Nobody can tell that it's a false wall, not even standin' beside it. No one knows this hidin' spot is even there except the family." Peter paused and wet his lips. He drew in a slow breath and nearly set the pencil down. He finished shading in the section that confined what Thor and his brothers and their future wives had of value.

Aven watched it all, her eyes calculating and her tender heart shining there. Thor signed to Jorgan to ask the women what they thought. It would be just like him and his brothers to act rashly, and this was no time for that.

When Jorgan relayed the request, Fay spoke, saying that she was glad Peter had come to help them. Aven agreed, though she wanted to know what Peter would do now that he'd crossed his family.

Peter set the pencil down. "I won't be able to go back after this. Once they find out that I told you." He pushed the paper toward Jorgan with clear resolve. "I been tired of bein' told what to do and what to think for long enough."

"Is that what you call it?" Cora asked.

Though Thor would never know her tone, he saw enough.

And in Peter, he saw a young man who'd been carrying around a heap of brokenness. "I'm only sorry I didn't do somethin' sooner. And as for—as for your boy . . ." He spoke without quite looking at Cora. "I didn't hit him but a few times. Pa handed me the pistol, and they was all watchin'. They don't like us goin' soft on 'em. But I know that even those few strikes was enough to make me no different than my pa or any other body who acts in hatred, and I'm sorry." He finally squared his gaze to Cora's. "It's not somethin' I can undo or make amends for, but I've hated myself for it ever since. I'm sorry to your son and to you. If his pa was here, I'd be sorry to him too."

Cora's eyes narrowed. "And if it's one of my girls walkin' down the road the next time?"

"I'd take a beatin' for them, ma'am."

"How do I know?"

"Because I already have."

The room drew still. Not a single mouth moved. Everyone stared at Peter, and though the bruising beneath his eyes had faded, it was suddenly impossible to forget. The cuts and scratches . . . his fat lip. How it wasn't until recently that he could finally raise his right arm over his head.

Tess had said she'd been uneasy that night in the yard. Thor had since learned from Al that she'd heard footsteps—lots of them—and she'd hurried back inside, but not before hearing the beginnings of a ruckus in the dark.

Ida was the first to move. She stepped forward, took Peter's hand in her floury one, and asked if he'd stay for supper. "Longer, if need be. That's my vote." With that, she turned and walked into the kitchen, mumbling something about a wedding cake to tend to.

Da used to tease her that she didn't like folks seeing her cry.

Fay's eyes were wide. Aven's closed. A softness gentled Cora's face. Her lashes grew damp, and she gave a small nod.

Peter's gratitude was clear, yet worry was just as marked. This wasn't the end for him. To turn one's back on one's family was no small thing.

To turn one's back on a Sorrel was another thing entirely. Thor thought of the little girl who'd been playing in the yard with Peter and of his other sisters and mother. How much would Peter be saying good-bye to?

Thor didn't envy him. But he respected him for standing here.

What did Dorothe used to say? *"The Lord will also be a refuge for the oppressed. A refuge in times of trouble."* That had to count for Peter too.

"They're expectin' ya," Peter continued. "My pa and uncles are ready and waitin' for a fight, and I can guarantee that they'll give you hell. They got enough ammo to baste you boys good. 'Specially if you show up with a fire under your collars."

"So what are we supposed to do?" Haakon asked.

Peter crossed to the window and stood there, hands in his pockets, surveying the land. When he finally turned, there was a steady resolve in his voice. "I have an idea, but y'all are gonna have to sit tight for a few days. If you can trust me, I think I know how to get it back. And how to put a stop to all of this for good."

THIRTY-ONE

It was by candlelight that the men spoke in murmurs around the kitchen table that night. Though Aven wanted to join them, she went upstairs to tend to Fay. The poor lass was weathering this well, but matters of the heart often ran deeper than what met the eye. Especially when Fay's husband-to-be was polishing gun barrels instead of his boots.

When Aven slipped into the bedroom, Fay turned from the dark window. "He means for the wedding to go on, but is it too much?" On the bed beside her was an open satchel, yet to be packed for her night away at Cora's on the eve before the ceremony. "A marriage to happen in just four days' time?"

"It is what's best. You and Jorgan. Your plans and future should not be set aside because of the selfishness of these other men." Aven took both of her hands and squeezed tight. "Take heart, dear one. You are on the right path, and Jorgan loves you fiercely. Life is too short to await calmer waters. Let us rejoice for what is to come. Jorgan is surely doing just that with this uniting with you. Even if his manner is somber, I'm certain the burden he bears over this is for the sake of you and your future. If this is a storm to be weathered, you will weather it more strongly together."

Aven slipped a handkerchief from the top drawer of the dresser, and Fay used it to dry her cheeks.

"Thank you." Fay dabbed at her eyes, then folded the kerchief tight in her hand. "I must look so silly. It's not just the wedding that I'm crying over but a worry about everything else. Something feels unsettled. I'm scared for them and the trouble they could run into."

Aye. She felt the same way. "Then we shall pray. The Lord does not test His children beyond what He thinks they can manage—with His strength. We will pray for the Lord's strength now. To fall upon this place for what is to come." Aven bowed her head, searching for the right words to begin with, but to her surprise, 'twas Fay who spoke.

This sweet child of missionaries. Come from so far into this place of sudden unrest. No stranger was Fay to such matters—of that, Aven had no doubt. For as the woman prayed, it was from a heart for a mighty God.

Aven held on to that prayer through a restless night, and she held on to it more as she sat at breakfast amid the subdued atmosphere. As the men conversed and debated, she tried to rest in the assurance that whether they chose to go after the liquor or not, God saw all and knew all. He saw them even now. If what they had was lost, then God would make a different way.

Though she knew Thor grieved the thievery as his brothers did, she sensed in some ways, he had wished the liquor away.

Was this a blessing in disguise? For it to be finally gone?

Thor pulled Aven's hand into his own, holding it secure in his lap beneath the table. The gesture grounded her, making her wish that he would find peace with whatever outcome prevailed. Though Jorgan and Haakon had unearthed a few hidden jars, even placing them in the kitchen, Aven trusted that the cider no longer held Thor captive as it once had. In fact, he'd scarcely given it a second glance. A stout effort on his part. Made more reassuring in his gentle calm and sober patience even amid this storm. He reached not for a drink but instead seemed to turn to wisdom and something that looked a lot like deepening faith. Aven grazed her thumb against his own, and he lifted her hand to kiss the back of it.

Haakon, who had been finishing the last of his breakfast, looked on. A sea of emotions wet his eyes to a sheen. When he glanced at Thor, it was the closest thing to a good-bye that Aven had ever seen between them. Haakon rammed his chair in, then strode out. Still recovering, Grete stayed in her spot behind the door. Jorgan stopped his youngest brother with a hand to the chest.

Haakon halted and gave Jorgan a muted smile. "Would you like me to help you and Thor patch up the cidery, or should I see to the chores?" Never had he asked to be helpful in such an outright way.

Even Jorgan seemed surprised. "The chores. Thanks."

Haakon nodded and headed out. Going their own direction, Thor and Jorgan did the same, but not before Jorgan pressed a kiss to Fay's cheek. With his hand cupping her head, he promised her everything would be just fine.

Aven stacked and rinsed the breakfast dishes as Ida showed Fay the cake recipes from their tin box.

"The vanilla-almond we tried the other night is a right favorite, but there's other kinds we ought to try." Ida shuffled through the small cards.

Though Aven could see Fay's gratitude, the woman insisted Ida not go to such trouble.

"Nonsense. How often do we have a weddin' in this house? I been waitin' thirty-two years for this day, so we's makin' as many cakes as this oven'll hold."

Fay smiled, and it was a sweet addition to the morning. As the pair of them set to mixing together a new batter, Aven slipped upstairs to steady her hands and heart in the way she knew best. She pulled out her sewing basket and drew the first of Haakon's curtains near. The chore was a simple one: a straight hem and nothing more. By the end of an hour, the first set was finished. Completing the second was just as simple, and soon she laid the finished panels aside.

The smell of baking cake sugared the air, spurring her to tuck the finished items into a basket and carry it all down. Ida was at the table beating together a thick bowl of icing. The faithful woman had a gift for infusing normalcy into this day and these wedding plans. That at such an hour as this, the difference between chocolate and lemon cream was fine medicine indeed.

Fork in hand, Aven helped them sample. Her favorite was most certainly the lemon with the blackberry filling, and while Fay nibbled an entire slice of that one, she noted that the vanilla-almond from the day before was the reason she couldn't decide.

"Then how about I make a tier of each?"

"You're a wonder, Ida." Aven set her plate in the washbin, rinsed her sticky fingers, then dried them on her patchwork skirt. Remembering her basket and the finished curtains, Aven fetched them. She slipped out the door, promising to be right back.

She walked through the thin stretch of wood-land that separated the great house from Haakon's cabin. 'Twas not a far journey—a few minutes at most. Heady in the air was the scent of pine and a lingering sweetness from the kitchen. Aven stepped clear of the woods and into the wind that swept across the meadow. It whipped at her hair in a gust so crisp that she could have been traversing the clifftops of Norway.

"You are lost, Aven."

She turned to see him stride nearer. The shape of him, the sound of him, all beholden to the two distant lands that had formed him. The breeze tugged at his shirt, crushing it to his chest and shoulders, outlining a strength that shadowed her when he stopped at her side.

"Do I seem so?" Lost in thought, perhaps.

But he wasn't looking at her as if that was what he'd meant.

"I brought two of the window coverings—all finished."

"Thank you, Aven. I'll walk with you." He took the basket, carrying it for her. "Did Thor not ask you to stay close to the house?"

"He did. But I didn't think this so far."

He fell in step beside her. When his hand bumped hers, he gave her a wider berth. Aven dragged the hem of her skirt up from the forest floor. Leaves clung to the edge of the petticoat, and the white lace was a stark contrast to the black of her stockings and boots.

At the cabin, he unlocked the door. She hadn't thought of that—the likelihood of it being barred. Good, after all, that he'd joined her. Haakon pushed it open, allowing her to step in first. As he closed the door, she moved to the front windows. He placed the basket between them, and she shook out the first curtain. When Haakon fetched a wooden rod, they threaded the fabric onto it. He reached up and set the long dowel back on its wooden pegs. The ivory sleeves of his winter underwear were snug to his forearms, and the plaid shirt he wore atop it had been folded back to his elbows.

She righted the curtains, closing them at first to check the size, then drawing them open to demonstrate how they would lay. "Nice?"

"Very nice."

" 'Twas so simple, I'll have the others done by week's end."

"How did you find the time?"

She unfolded the second panel. "I haven't the burden you bear right now. You and your brothers. I have my usual tasks. And beyond that . . ." She handed him the curtain and he began to string it on. "Other ways that might help."

"Other ways . . ." His eyes flitted to hers, then dropped the length of her before looking back to her handiwork.

Fingers that were strong and weathered by work inched the cloth into place. Silence rested between them, and it was just the play of light through the glass, of dancing dust motes and his gentle breathing as he finished the simple task.

Always supple his efforts were. Even each step—
so quiet.

How different it was standing with Haakon
than with Thor. Thor's movements rumbled like
the earth, but he was able to bear just as much.
Haakon was agile as a breeze, yet as difficult to
corral.

She wished it were Thor beside her. That it was
Thor lowering a glance to her. That it was he who
had come here. But wherever life took her, for
the rest of her days and years, it would always be
this moment—this hour—that she would regret
having stood in this place with his brother.

"Can I ask you a question?" Haakon lifted the
final rod into place on the front windows. "Are
you gonna marry Thor?"

"I—I don't know."

"Why don't you?"

"Because he hasn't asked me."

He swiped his hands on the sides of his pants.
"If he were to."

"What does that matter to you?"

"It matters a lot."

Something about him was making her uneasy.
It wasn't his words, for those were rarely
guarded. It was the tender way he watched her.
The nearness in which he stood. "Despite the
fact that it's not your concern, I'll tell you that I
would marry Thor. And I hope—with everything
in me—to be able to."

374

"And yet you're gonna sit around and twiddle your thumbs for him, aren't you?" Haakon absently nudged the basket aside with his boot. "It's that way with everyone around here. Jorgan and Fay—waiting an eternity to get to one another. Then Ida, who is waiting on a ghost. Da did the same." He looked at her. "I don't understand it. And so I'm asking you, Aven"—he took her hand—"to come with me."

Had she heard him right? He ran the back of his finger down her arm, and it was softer than any words he might have spoken.

"I'm sorry, Haakon." She turned away, but he stepped backward and into her path.

"I wake up thinkin' about you, and I go to bed at night thinkin' about you." His eyes searched hers as if trying to find a hidden place where she felt the same. "And believe it or not, all day in between I'm thinkin' after you."

She moved away. "You don't know what you're saying."

"I do know!" He followed in one easy stride. "But then there's Thor in the way, and I went through hell for him. We all did. And you know what happened? He beat us all to a pulp, then everybody started actin' like he's Saint Thor."

She swerved toward the door and nearly had hold of the knob when he moved in front of it.

Aven tried to weave around him again, but he blocked the way. "You want to know what's really rotten?" He stepped so near that she shoved against his chest. He caught her hand again. "Havin' everybody act like it's the end of the world every time I have a birthday. Can't hardly conjure up a smile 'cause, dang it, Haakon was born."

Tears stinging her eyes, Aven tugged free.

"And if I hadn't been, Ma would still be here. Ida's always tryin' to rally everybody and poor Cora gets a puppy one year, and I know what she's about and what they're all about and I'm sick of it."

"Open that door."

"What makes it worse is that you don't see me."

"I do see you! But you can't treat people this way just because you're unhappy."

"I'm not unhappy." He stepped forward, forcing her to take a step back.

The same way she'd taught Thor to lead, but this wasn't Thor and she wasn't safe.

Haakon didn't stop until she was in the corner. She shoved against him but was no match for how solid he was. "Move aside, Haakon. Right now."

"I'm not unhappy," he said again. He lowered his head, voice terribly soft and so near that she felt its rumble. " 'Cause there you came. Just walkin' up to the farm. And you're so perfect . . . and so dad-blasted soft." He kissed her shoulder, and she cringed away. Yet there was no place for her to go. His hand gently gripped the side of her neck—thumb grazing her jaw. His eyes on hers were earnest.

His gaze dropped to her mouth, and he moved to kiss her.

She jerked back. "Haakon—"

He only followed. Holding the back of her head, he pressed his mouth to hers. Squirming, she tried to break away. He pulled himself nearer, and his hold tightened. A torment came from within him. An anguish. Whatever brokenness he'd been carrying, now both of theirs to bear.

Aven shoved his chest as hard as she could. It pressed him free enough for her to gasp a breath. "Haakon, stop!" His attempt to draw closer only wedged her into the corner. She shrank away, but he followed, bringing them to the floor. He knelt there—pinning her into place as he did. A wet heat slammed her eyes.

"Get off of me!" Jerking her knee into his leg did nothing, so she screamed. She cried out for Thor. Then again, hoping her voice might reach through the stand of trees. She hit Haakon again, but he caught her wrist.

"Aven. He can't hear you."

She tried to twist free but his hold was solid. Haakon's other fingertips grazed the side of her neck. "And I'm not gonna make you do anything you don't want to do. I *promise*. But if you just took a minute to see . . ." He gripped her waist and kissed her again.

Aven pressed her forearm into his chest, but all the force she bore didn't nudge him, and worse than the clutch of fear was an emptiness of loss. Because her friend was gone. In his place was a being stronger than her and nothing more.

Her heart and lungs fought like the crash of the sea and the beating of the hull into waves. Was she drowning? Had she finally fallen from the ship? Or perhaps the slam of thunder and the clap of sails in the wind was nothing more than Haakon's charged breathing as he tugged his suspenders down. And here she was sinking farther. Losing all hope amid the waters where a thousand souls had been lost to this sea that only God could reach.

She tried to gasp a breath, but Haakon was there instead, so she drew what she could into her lungs—the taste of his skin and her breaking heart. If he meant to entice her, then he knew nothing of a woman's heart or where her own resided. If he meant to have whatever he wished . . .

"The Lord is my shepherd," she whispered when he pulled back to adjust his weight. She spoke the words for her own soul to take courage, but they seemed to touch Haakon because his fingers, which were easing the edge of her blouse from her skirt, stilled entirely.

The next words ached from her parched throat. "He leadeth me beside still waters."

Haakon looked at her earnestly.

If she could do nothing else in this moment, she would trust in truth. The cost of his wrongdoing, perhaps insignificant to him in this moment, was a surety to stand on even when she could not. This moment wasn't her against Haakon. It was Haakon versus a God who was mightier than this man knew. "You may sit in His house and sing His praises, but He will know who you are if you do this," Aven whispered. "And you should be terribly afraid of that."

Haakon pushed a lock of hair from her face. Head falling the tiniest bit lower, he looked at her, his mouth so near, she was certain he would lower it to hers again, but a different kind of intensity settled in his expression. He leaned back, and she peered up into the eyes she'd adored since the day she'd come here.

"And from this moment, Haakon, you will be nothing to me."

He searched her face. "Aven." He swallowed hard, then looked down at her, his gaze taking in the way he had advanced on her.

Feeling the intensity gentle within him, Aven tugged her hand free. She shoved at his chest. "Get off of me!" She tried to yank her blouse down over her corset but it was wedged between them.

He shifted himself farther back, allowing her to move. He grunted when her knee met his thigh.

The door rattled. Then a knock sounded, followed by Al's voice. "Miss Aven?"

Haakon clamped a hand over her mouth.

Al's voice muffled through the door. "Heard you callin' for Thor. You in trouble?"

She cried for help, but it stifled against Haakon's skin. Aven bit his finger. He jerked away, and she screamed. Haakon crammed his hand over her mouth again. The door rattled harder but wouldn't open. Locked, then. When it silenced, Al hollered through that he'd be right back.

Haakon shoved his fingers into his hair, holding them there. "You don't know what you just did."

With the door only feet away, she lunged for it. He grabbed her around the waist, tugging her into him. His heart pounded against her back. Still kneeling, she tried to pull forward, but he held her that way until she finally stilled.

Help was coming.

"You have to listen to me, Aven. Please." He shifted around her, blocking the way. He slid one of his suspenders up, desperation in his wide eyes.

Sorrow rose with such a rush that she had to will herself not to cry. She wanted to strike him, but instead used what little strength remained to try and rise. Her feet felt like weights as she pulled her knees forward so that she might stand. Aven gripped the edge of the windowsill.

He yanked up his other suspender so fast that the clasp snapped from his pants. "Please listen to me. I wasn't going to—"

Voices rushed near. Al. Jorgan.

And Thor—so fiercely the door was rammed.

Haakon cursed as his fingers fumbled to clasp the leather strap against his waist. He glanced around as if for a way out of this when a force slammed the door again.

The pounding rocked so hard the house trembled. Then again . . . and again . . .

Suddenly the door shattered open. And Haakon was gone from her. Nothing left but his shout as Thor slammed him into the far wall.

Jorgan hollered Thor back, but it was for the sound of Haakon's pain that Aven covered her ears. Too stunned to even cry, she simply tried to breathe. Tried to breathe and not shirk away from Al's steadying hand to her arm. Not hear the slam of fists or see that it was Thor whom Jorgan and Peter struggled to hold down as they shouted for Haakon to run.

Haakon finally did. That she knew. Because in a pounding of floorboards, he was gone.

THIRTY-TWO

Thor didn't move from the hallway. Fearing Haakon would return, he sat there, facing Aven's door well into the night, unwilling to go up to bed even when Ida urged him to rest. Grief and anger warred inside him, until sleep finally silenced them both. He woke to a gray light and shadows so cool that he feared for his trees. He needed to rise and tend them. To walk their rows. He needed to keep this place together somehow even as he was coming apart at the seams.

Jorgan and Fay were marrying in two days. He had to rally. For them and for Aven he had to rise.

Stiffly, he stood just as Ida was coming up the stairs. She leaned an ear to Aven's door and gave a gentle knock. Thor stepped back. Ida slipped in and closed the door. It was a few minutes later that she came out again.

"She's wantin' a bath."

Which meant he should make himself scarce.

"And, Thor?" Ida stepped so near to him that he knew her voice was low. "Haakon brought her no harm past what you saw. Aven wants you to know that. She's awful fixed I tell you."

Thor nodded. A relief. Not for himself, but for her.

Gripping his arm, Ida led him down the stairs

and out to the washroom on the side of the house. She turned a knob that released water from the stove's reservoir and into the tub. As steam billowed, Ida drew Thor to the cabinet where she kept ointments. Those steady hands of hers pressed the warm cloth to his own. If she noticed the way his chin set to trembling, she didn't let on. His knuckles were raw—bloodied—and he could still feel Haakon on the other side of them, because as they'd run over, Al had said that Aven had been screaming for him. That Haakon was there as well trying to keep her quiet. Everything beyond that was fragmented except for Thor and his brother and the door that had been standing between them.

Ida shook his sleeve, so he looked at her. "You did what you had to do."

Though he tried to make peace with that, a wretchedness still splintered him from the inside. Knowing Aven would be down, Thor stepped out. She was safe so he need not worry, but it came anyway. She'd witnessed something fierce in him yesterday. Would she fear him? Be it protecting Aven or teaching Haakon a lesson . . . whichever way it was colored, he'd tried to tear his brother apart.

Turning, he faced Ida. *We lose Haakon.* As a brother, a comrade, or as a part of this farm, he didn't know. In some ways it felt like all of it.

Her face shadowed with sorrow. "He made an

awful choice, Thor. But let's not discount what the good Lord may yet do."

Jorgan angry with me?

"No. He as mad at Haakon as you. Said it was hard to hold you down."

Yanking the strip of leather from his wrist, Thor bound his hair back, knotting it tight. Before a response could come, Ida signed Aven's name. She was coming, then. Thor stepped away. With work to do for the wedding, he promised to return to help. He signed *tree* and *house* so Ida would know his whereabouts should Aven have need of him. Should she be ready to see him.

It was hard not to glance over his shoulder as he strode away.

The orchards were empty—no movement other than the flash of birds as they scattered from his path. The pickers were off for the week. With the coming wedding, they had all labored hard to rid the trees of the ready Foxwhelps. The next round of apples wouldn't be blushing until then, and the boys would return. The scratter and press would be at work all over again. Next week the Roxbury and Sweet Coppin storers would be picked as was the way of mid-October. A cycle that would continue until the first snows came and everything was in crates and jars.

When Thor reached the tree house, he sat at the base of the old maple and rested against it. A strength he needed just now. Arms folded on his raised knees, he lowered his head. He meant to keep a watch out for Haakon, but there was a knife at his waist and another in his pocket, so Thor allowed himself a moment of closing his eyes.

Jorgan had said that Haakon looked up to him.

Thor had always known it to be true, and it was like salt in the wound since the time they were boys. The years when Haakon followed him wherever he went, asking a million questions that Thor couldn't really answer for him. So Thor had finally sat Haakon down and, along with Jorgan and Ida, taught them his language. Da learned a few signs but it was harder for him. Haakon had taken to it like a duck to water. If there was ever a word he didn't know, he'd come and find Thor and learn it. Even help Thor make ones up if they didn't know the sign for it.

Until the day that Haakon was seven perhaps. He'd come and found Thor—all knees and elbows and pants that didn't reach his ankles— and with a flick of his hands had asked Thor what a signal had meant. One he had a memory of.

Thor had responded without thinking. Without remembering. *H-A-T-E*. Spelled nonchalantly in his hand as if he were spelling *B-O-O-K* or *C-H-A-I-R*.

Haakon had blinked at him, a bleak confusion filling his face. He'd asked Thor if he was certain. It had to mean something else . . . so often Haakon remembered Thor using it with him.

In his shame, Thor hadn't known how to respond. He'd done what he could to try and make it up to Haakon, like hanging the rope swing. Thor even gave him the better side of the attic and later suggested they build a tree house. Thor had made certain his little brother got to be the one to hoist up the flag. But it had never been the same. Haakon hadn't followed him around so much anymore. Hadn't asked quite so many questions.

Thor had sworn he would never use that word with his brother again. So it was all the harder to keep his hand still right now. To keep his fingers from shaping the sentiment. Arms still folded across his knee, Thor clamped one hand over the other to pin them both in place. But the sensation was still filling his heart. Flooding it because of the sight of Aven there on the floor, dust and tears streaking her cheeks.

Had she walked there with Haakon thinking she was safe?

Why had she gone at all? He fought back jealousy because it wasn't warranted. Not for a moment with Aven. Guilt splayed within him, and his mouth watered for a drink. It had been for the last twelve hours, and he'd been fighting it every breath. He'd fight until he won because going back to that would only be another kind of misery. One that scared him more than facing this pain without a numbing.

Help, Lord.

Thor wasn't much of a praying man, but the plea teemed within him. He pressed an unsteady hand to his chest, circling it in *please*. Surely God knew his words.

A touch at his knee jolted him. It was Aven kneeling there, but so fast she'd startled him that he'd moved his hand to his knife. Hating the thought of instilling more fear into her, Thor released it just as quick.

Her hair was damp from her bath. Braided and draping one shoulder, it was bound with a scrap of lace. He grappled for what to do even as she pulled herself nearer, touching the sides of his face in her small hands. Her fingers brushed against his beard. She gripped tight, lowering her head to press a kiss to his forehead.

Though the burn in his throat was no excuse for not knowing what to say, he was silenced all the same. Fetching his notebook and pencil from his pocket gave him time to rally.

He wrote, asking her how she was faring.

"I am very sad."

I help you? How?

Drawing nearer, Aven nestled into him. For the briefest of moments, Thor couldn't move, then comprehending what she wanted, he wrapped his arms around her, gripping with more assurance when he felt her begin to cry. He smoothed a hand over the back of her head, kissing her hair.

His arms around her made his writing sloppier. *What happen—you and Haakon?* He lowered the notebook so she could see it.

While he'd had no doubt that Aven had wanted Haakon's advance to cease, he hadn't yet asked her how it had begun. Her brow furrowed with thought, then gently she spoke. He couldn't see her mouth, so he touched her jaw, turning her face toward his.

She started again—telling of how she had informed Haakon when they were last at church that she wanted to be Haakon's friend and his family but nothing more.

Her heart had to be all kinds of broken. Thor knew how dearly she'd cared for Haakon. How in a way she had loved his brother. Though Thor believed Aven's affection and desire to be squarely his, there was a piece that she hadn't quite been able to tug free of Haakon's grasp.

Haakon had that way about him, and Thor had watched her every day . . . working to put Haakon in the place of friend and brother. An effort on her part, but he thought no less of her for it. Love was not as simple as it was often made to seem.

If marriage were easy, there wouldn't be vows.

Writing swiftly, he put all that to paper. Aven watched, and when the last was before her, a tear slipped and fell. She sniffed and wiped at her eyes.

Aven gripped his neck, bringing herself high enough to press the side of her face to his own. When she looked at him, he watched her speak. "Such a vow is one that I long to make to you, Thor." Her brown eyes searched his, urgent and honest.

Sitting outside her door last night, he'd ached for the very thing. To be able to hold her close, watch over her in slumber, and not have a barrier between them. While the yearning was a fire inside him, so startling was the wish upon her own lips that he responded in Sign before he realized his error. He took her hand, spread open her palm, and used his finger to slowly draw out the letters. *S-A-M-E F-O-R M-E.*

She smiled as joy filled her face. Aven burrowed into him and moved his arms around her so she was wrapped up. Thor closed his eyes and lowered his forehead to her shoulder. Briefly he clutched tight—and it was a satisfaction unlike one he'd ever known. For it to be just the beginning was a goodness he didn't know he would find.

He ached to ask her now, but he wasn't ready yet. This wasn't the kind of question he wanted to write on a woman's palm. If God could strengthen him through another few nights away from her, he would have a way.

There was a softness to this quilt that she hadn't noticed before. Aven gripped an edge of the calico backing and nestled it beneath her chin. Lying here in bed, she didn't need to turn away from the wall to know that Ida had placed a tray of tea on the nightstand. The aroma of peppermint and honey was as gentle as Ida's footsteps had been.

Warm and purring, Dottie lay against her side. Such comforts. Last of all, the necklace in hand. Aven twirled her mother's delicate chain around her fingertip once more, then let it unravel. It spilled like a dull gray puddle on the crisp sheet and Aven plucked it up. She rose slowly, stiff from having lain still for so long. The light from the window told her that it was nearly midday. Aven slipped the necklace back on and snapped the tiny clasp into place. Ida had told her to rest all she needed and for now, these hours abed, laced with thoughts and prayers, had infused her with a gentle dose of strength.

Sounds and murmurs filled the house below— the planning and preparation for the wedding tomorrow. So as not to be seen by her groom, Fay was to stay with Cora for the night. Aven had volunteered to spend this day at work with Ida in the kitchen. A fine feast there was to prepare, and Aven had been looking forward to the baking of breads and the roasting of meat. She glanced to where her apron hung beside the dresser. To simply rise and put it on shouldn't be so hard. Which made it all the more difficult to keep tears in check when Fay entered, knelt beside the bed, and took Aven's hand in her own.

"I ask you to come with me, Aven." Her blue eyes brimmed with gentleness. "It would be good for you to get out of this house, and I would dearly love your company tonight. Come with me to Cora's. I know it's not so easy to leave troubles behind, but if you let us, we will spoil you fiercely." Fay rose enough to sit on the bed beside her. "And before you fret, Ida has insisted that she has a handle on everything."

Fay went on to explain that Ida had enlisted a crew of neighbor women to help her with the preparations. "There are so many women coming I think Ida might be at a loss for how to keep busy." Fay winked.

These dear women.

Fay slipped a strand of hair behind Aven's ear. "Please come?"

'Twas quite the coaxing . . . one that spurred Aven to dress and, with Fay's help, tuck a few overnight items in her carpetbag. Spread across the opposite bed was Fay's dress for tomorrow, fresh white stockings, new garter ribbons, and her finest shoes, newly polished. All would be waiting for her return in the morning.

Aven had much healing to do yet, but she sensed the first step on that road was to follow

Fay out of doors and down the lane to Cora's. To loop her arm with the bride-to-be and see what fancies the evening held. A little merriment would surely do her spirit good.

Thor saw them along, as much for his assurance as Aven's own, she suspected, and when they reached Cora's quaint cabin, the very woman was standing on the porch, waving. Tess and Georgie were at her side. Al had made himself scarce, so it was the happy chatter of women and the smells of a cooking supper that greeted them.

Thor nodded his farewell, and Aven watched as he headed back down the lane. He had yet to vanish from sight when Georgie took Aven's and Fay's hands and tugged them forward. "Come in! Come in!"

At first Aven feared she'd overcrowd the place, but Cora had made room for them all as though they'd been scheming this since dawn. All through the hours that Aven had been abed, clinging to prayers of hope even as she turned her mother's necklace 'round her hand.

Tess took their satchels and wedged them beneath a cushioned chair, sending two kittens to scamper into a new hiding spot. Aven scooped one up and nestled it close. The kitten stayed by her side all evening, even as Tess and Fay braided ribbons together for the morrow and while Georgie fawned over the notion that Fay was to be a bride.

The girl inquired some as to what that entailed, and conversation of a gentle nature followed. All vague enough of an answer that Georgie then asked why Fay would ever want to share a room with Jorgan. The accompanying giggles it seemed were not to the kitten's liking. But they were indeed to Aven's.

Laughter, it turned out, was rather good medicine, because by the time a comforting supper of broth and bread was dished up and passed around, Aven's heart was lifted.

While Georgie didn't seem to grasp what was so amusing, she did inquire after Thor. "What I also ain't gettin' is that if Mr. Jorgan be wantin' to share a room with Miss Fay, why Mr. Thor not be wantin' to share a room with Miss Aven. Seems to me they like each other about the same."

"Oh, don't you fret over Thor one bit," Cora insisted. "He aimin' to share his room. He just ain't got the nerve to ask her yet." She winked in Aven's direction.

Seeming satisfied with the answer, Georgie followed her mother's bidding to dress for bed. Georgie wriggled free of her outer clothes, then slid a linen nightgown over her shift. Tess helped her button the front, and when the girl was ready for bed, she settled in close to Aven.

"Mama says there gonna be dancin' at the weddin'." Georgie plucked up a downy gray kitten. "Seein' as Mr. Haakon don't have no one to dance with, I thought he might ask me. Or maybe Tess since she be taller. But I hope it's me." Her dark eyes glittered in the lantern light when she peered up at Aven. "You fancy I'm big enough?"

Was this what it was like for Aven's mother? To face the tempests of life and weather them with courage so as to soften the winds for a child's understanding? Aven dug deep for that courage, hoping she might guard the fractures of her heart—and yet give Georgie enough of the bittersweet truth so as not to be misled. Aven ran the back of her finger over Georgie's silken cheek. "I think you're perfect." She slid her legs up, turning some to look the wee one square in the eyes. "But, Georgie, I don't think Haakon is going to be at the wedding. He's gone away for a time. Wherever he is, I'm certain he misses you terribly."

"Oh, but he *cain't* miss it. He ain't never been away from home. He never been from his brothers . . . or even us. Why would he go and do such a thing?"

Aven looked to Cora for help.

Cora pressed a knotty scrap of pine into the potbelly stove and closed the door. "It's time for you to head off to bed, lil missy, but when you say your prayers, I want you to say a special prayer for Haakon, can you do that?"

Georgie nodded, still looking grieved.

Cora freed one of Georgie's little braids from the collar of her nightgown. "Sometime a body need to be away from their family for a spell. It give them a time to learn some things that they might'a missed otherwise. It give them time to remember what the Good Book say on the matter."

Slowly, Georgie nodded.

"I'll pray for Mr. Haakon. That he not be scared right now." Georgie hopped down off the bed and sank onto her folded blankets near the stove. "And I'll pray for the rest of us not to be so scared neither."

THIRTY-THREE

Looking into the small mirror hanging beside Haakon's bed, Jorgan tied back his hair. When he finished, he turned to Thor and held out his arms. "This alright?"

Thor stepped closer, flicked a finger against his brother's beard, and bobbed his eyebrows.

"I know. Ida made me trim it some." Stepping back, Jorgan adjusted his suspenders. He looked as nice as Thor had ever seen him, and if he was nervous, it wasn't showing.

Thor glimpsed his own reflection in the mirror. He was a sight—fresh from seeing to the horses and tending the chickens so no one else would have to. It was time for his own bath, but he needed to wait until the water heated again. With time yet for that, Thor sat, pulled his boots nearer, and picked up the rag he'd fetched. He spit on the leather and scrubbed it. There was polish in the house, but it hadn't been used for so long that neither he nor Jorgan could find it.

Jorgan sat on the other bed and looked from it to the wall, then around at Haakon's things. Thor watched him, hating the twinge it brought. Haakon's pile of laundry sat untouched. The map of the world he'd tacked up on the wall unmoving, all save a loose corner that fluttered beside an open window.

Jorgan spoke, but Thor missed all but the tail end. "So, about Aven. You do realize that the preacher is here today, right? On our farm. All day. A whole preacher. The kind that can marry people."

Right.

Thor stood. He took up the clothes that Ida had pressed and headed downstairs. In the kitchen, he strode past the housekeeper so quickly that she thunked him with her spoon to get his attention.

"If you don't hurry and wash up, I'm gonna do it for you."

Thor held up the clothes, and she nodded her approval. He headed outside and around to the bathhouse. After bolting the door, he set his clothes aside. A turn of the knob on the hot water reservoir sent steaming water into the tub.

A rattling of the door caught his eye. He unlatched it to see Ida standing there.

"Use soap!"

Thor shut the door on her. He knew that!

When it rattled again, he gave her a stern look as he opened it.

"Did you ask her yet?"

After heaving out a sigh, he motioned to the filling tub, then out to wherever Aven was.

"Right. Might as well look your best." She shut

the door, and he waited to make sure she was done before locking it again.

When he finally braved the hot water, he dumped it over his head with both hands. Eyes closed, he scrubbed with more force than even Jorgan had used after that awful week in the attic.

Once dried and dressed, Thor combed his hair, then bound it back with its leather cord. At the foggy mirror he worked to get the collar of his shirt perfectly straight. Satisfied, he checked that his beard was tidy. Running a few drops of oil into it made it look rather fine. Soft to the touch and as well trimmed as Jorgan's. One of his sleeve cuffs was more problematic when it wouldn't fasten right. Something Ida would fix, but when his search for her unearthed an empty kitchen, Thor fetched his boots from upstairs so as to make the most of the time.

Coming back down, he crossed the length of the hallway. The girls' bedroom door was ajar. Several women bustled about within, all working to right the hem of Fay's dress as she stood there in the late-morning light. Thor glimpsed her in passing before a lady hurried to shut the door.

He smiled at how happy Jorgan was going to be. The moment his brother laid eyes on his bride, his knees would want to buckle. Not any different from how Jorgan had looked when he'd first spotted Fay that day in the kitchen. Thor had seen even then that his brother could hardly catch a breath.

He knew the feeling.

It had been the same sensation when Aven first walked into the orchard that day in her mourning gown and with more hope in her face than she probably knew. Her hands had trembled as she clutched her luggage. And he'd stood there, watching her pretty mouth move for the first time. Him struck dumb not because of a birth condition but because she was the one he had been waiting for. The sheer memory had him all the more eager to find her now. Thor pushed past the back door and onto the porch. His boots scraped the boards as he halted.

Tables and chairs sat scattered around. Lace cloths and jars of the late wildflowers as yellow as the meadow beyond covered rough surfaces. Aven and Fay had gathered enough that jars with flowers even gleamed along the porch banister and on the table where Ida's cake had been freshly iced. But Thor's attention wasn't on the cake as he stepped across the porch. It was on the Irish lass who stood in the yard, working with Tess to tuck a few flowers into Georgie's coil of braids.

"There." Aven nestled a final stem into place. "You look like a wee sprite now." When Aven spotted him, her eyes widened. She straightened the airy folds of her skirt as she rose, and the lace hem fluttered in the breeze. She spoke to him, but by the way her head dipped shyly, he wasn't able to understand. He saw her pleasure with him, though, and that was enough.

He tugged at his collar some. It seemed too tight, but Ida said that it was the proper way. Since he was to stand with his brother, some suffering was only reasonable. While other folks would be in attendance, Thor was to be a witness for their marriage. Aven, the other. So it was no wonder that she looked as lovely as she did with her ginger hair twisted and pinned. Little wisps of it making her look like a sprite herself.

Remembering his troublesome cuff, he showed it to her. Aven's brow pinched as she worked to slip the stubborn button into place, her small hand holding his as she did. His heart was banging in his chest because when she finished, he took that hand and led her across the farmyard. He didn't know if he was ready for this, but one thing he did know—that even if he stumbled his way through, Aven would be there beside him.

She tapped his shoulder and spoke when he looked down at her. "Where are we going?"

He shook his head. She was going to have to wait. Her freckled nose scrunched as she smiled. Though he was leading them, she followed willingly. It settled his nerves. Grete dashed by and up the hill where she'd probably spotted something more interesting than coming wedding guests to be greeted and licked.

When Thor and Aven reached his favorite tree—the one shaped like the woman drawing up water—he slowed and turned. He'd prayed for this moment upon learning that Aven was alone across a sea. It had felt a thin hope then. One that had doubled in fervor upon learning that the woman from the photograph—the one with the face that looked like it wanted to find home—was coming.

He had a sense that Dorothe knew his desires then because she always seemed to notice the way he would slow in front of the photograph on the wall, taking in the sight of Aven's face longer than he had cause to.

He owed Dorothe a great thanks.

For penning the letter he was too afraid to write. The one that had set Aven on a course to them . . . and now beside him. And here he stood, wondering why God had seen fit to bless a man such as him. One who had spent his life looking for a way out or a reason why. Always wondering and questioning why the Lord had picked him to live this silent life. This tucked-away existence where he hurt apart from people. Where they didn't know and couldn't see because he had let it be that way and had even worsened it.

Now Aven was here and had helped change all that.

Thor squeezed the hand that was still inside

his as Ida's voice filled his head—sure and comforting. Through their nights of practice, Ida believed he could do it, so it was with that homespun faith of hers that Thor lowered himself to one knee. Whatever reaction Aven had to that, he couldn't look up to find out. Swallowing hard, he reached into his pocket and pulled out the slip of paper. He had no ring to offer her yet, so this would have to do.

Tamping down every last fear, he looked up at Aven and thought, as Ida had said, that a spoken "w" was the same effort as stifling a yawn, but with his lips close together.

"W—"

The shock that flooded Aven's face was potent enough to derail him, so Thor forced himself to concentrate on the next sound. He was to pull the "i" into his throat. Tuck it up high, Ida had said, and so he did. "Wi—" Then his tongue to the roof of his mouth, and he pressed out the sound. "Will."

One word done. He had no idea if it had come out right, but Aven was already crying.

She wiped her eyes with her sleeve. The wind up here on the hillside tugged at her hair and tidy attire, but she didn't seem to mind.

His attempt at "you" felt wrong, but if he knew anything about Aven, it was that she had learned to hear him. She'd always heard him because she knew how to listen.

He loved her for that.

Lips pressed together, Thor made the "m" vibration, feeling stuck on it as he stuttered—searching for "a." It was a hard one. He was to pull the vowel far back into his throat, but not as high up as the "i," and he was to tuck his tongue to his bottom teeth. Or was it his top teeth? He glanced quickly at his notes and, thanks to God above, finished "marry." It had to sound like gibberish, but he was almost done, and the last one was the shortest.

"M—" Thor wet his lips. "M—" His hand holding her own was sweating now.

Blast it. What was the "e" sound? He'd practiced it with Ida, but it was gone from his mind. He looked to the end of his notes. They'd smeared beneath his thumb, but there was the lingering trace of an arrow from the "e" to the "y" above it. They made the same sound? Slamming his eyes closed, Thor searched his memory.

And it was there that he saw her face. The kind teacher who had helped him that day in the hallway. The one who had tried to teach him his vowels. Her touch soft to his cheek and her smile sincere as she showed him how to breathe out an "eeeeee." Over and over they had practiced and over and over he had failed, so it was on a wish and a prayer that Thor made his mouth create the sound.

It came out wrong. He could feel it. Rough as sand and nothing like he'd practiced.

Aven's left hand came to join her right. Tender and soft around his own. She gave a firm squeeze, then bending, kissed his knuckles in a comfort he couldn't describe.

Thor tried again, and the small word felt smoother. He peered up at her.

Using her palm, she wiped at her cheeks. She nodded so quickly that he couldn't help but smile. With a tug, Aven urged him to his feet. He'd thought this part through as well, so he pulled a different slip of paper from his pocket with one more question. This one he simply showed her.

Now? As Jorgan said, there really was a whole preacher here.

Covering her mouth with her hand, she slid him a look that took any wondering right out of the inquiry. Eyes glistening with joy, she nodded again, giving him a response that he didn't have to work to understand. But he wanted it from her lips all the same. He wanted her to have the chance for her voice to be heard with him. It mattered more than he could explain.

Adding pencil to paper, Thor wrote, *You need say answer.*

Her laugh had to be one of the loveliest sounds. The sight of it was the real treat, though. "Yes. I would very much like to marry you, Thor Norgaard." Pulling herself higher, she pressed a sudden kiss to his mouth, and while it ended sooner than he wished, she took his hand, walking backward so he could see her. "And, aye. Now, if you please."

With Fay still in the house and guests just finding their seats along the benches, Thor gave his brother a nod. Grinning, Jorgan stepped down the center row to press a kiss to Aven's blushing cheek. He embraced Thor next, and Thor gripped tight to his brother's neck with all the thanks he felt. After sharing a few words with the preacher, Jorgan set the rest in motion. Before Thor knew it, Aven was stationed beside him even as Fay took her spot next to Jorgan.

With the cool of evening sweeping over the farm, stirring the very last of the porch roses, Jorgan and Fay shared their vows. Her family had come from afar, and as they sat there, they watched their daughter become a wife with pride shining in their faces.

Next the preacher shifted toward Thor and Aven with a nod of assurance to them both. Thor held Aven's hand, watching the clergyman state the vows he was to repeat. A holy decree that he'd put a lot of thought to. Not just because Aven was lovely or good or wanting him as he wanted her, but because God had saw fit for Thor to bind himself to her. To care for her and to be faithful to her. It wasn't an oath he took lightly.

Thor released her fingers long enough to repeat his promise. With Jorgan deciphering, Thor trusted that the preacher, the guests, and most importantly, Aven knew the depth of his pledge.

In answer, she spoke hers, and he was torn between watching her mouth and her eyes. Both were saying the same thing. It was like coming home for him. Staggering, since this was the place of his birth, but now, with her, it was suddenly lit all different. The fields were more open, the mountains steeper, and the hollow swollen with all the places he wanted to take her.

And yet it was she who took his hand first and, with a gentle nudge, seemed to be showing him that they were all done. That, along with Jorgan and Fay, they were to be the first to step away from this hallowed place and toward another.

Well wishes came from all around. Pats to his shoulder, firm grips to his hand, and many, many kisses to Aven's cheeks. He stayed close to her, overwhelmed with the flurry and not understanding all that was spoken. But he knew joy when he saw it. Made all the finer as the soft of Aven's shoulder stayed nestled to his chest as if she meant to be as close to him as possible.

Thor didn't realize the size of the feast that Ida had prepared until folks were settled and savoring it. He took his share, and though his heart was beating faster with all that was to come, he tried to eat as the others did.

Cake came next, and that meant the tail end of the meal—and soon—the evening. But to his surprise, dancing followed. He'd forgotten all about such things, so few weddings he'd attended. Aven didn't urge him into it and instead sat cozy at his side. He wanted to please her, though, so he signaled for Jorgan to tell him when it was a waltz. Sometime later, Jorgan caught his eye over the crowd and gave a nod. Time, then.

Taking her hand, Thor led her to the outskirts of it all. To his surprise, the steps weren't as difficult when a swell of people were doing them all at once. He turned her under his arm enough times that she looked breathless with delight. She beamed up at him. Would one dance satisfy her? He wished it wasn't such a struggle for him. It seemed she could do this all the way until dawn.

But the decision need not be made, for as the bow still pulled slow across the fiddle, other instruments were set away. A gentle sound, he imagined. Guests began to bid farewell. Contented and waving toward the wagons that would bear them home.

By the light of the moon, Jorgan bid a good night and took his bride inside. To sidestep an awkwardness on the stair, Thor waited a few minutes, then led Aven out of the evening air.

The kitchen was dark. Strange without Ida in it, but she had already seen to every last detail. The remaining fixings of supper were tucked away to make life around here rather easy, and she'd made plans to stay with her sister for the week.

Aven's shoes were dainty beside his on the stair, and he tried to take temperate steps so as not to *"thunder about,"* as Dorothe used to say. In the attic, Thor closed the door. Aven clasped her hands together, not straying from where she stood in front of it. Was she anxious of him?

With sunset having come and gone, the light was dim, but not so dim that he couldn't see enough to light a candle. The single flame was sparse, so he tipped the match to one more. Thor glanced at Aven, hoping she wouldn't mind. He needed something to see her by. To know what she was thinking or wanting or wishing to say. Otherwise it would be dark, and she would be lost to him. Perhaps a pleasure for her in time, when he was surer, but for now, he hoped this would be alright.

Rubbing his hands together, he tried to think of what would be the right thing to do next.

Aven's red hair was coming loose of its pins, or was she working it free? She lowered another slip of metal and set it aside. Of her own doing, then. Piece by piece, her coiled hair tumbled. The color striking against her pale neck. Overcome, he watched until she finished.

He hadn't thought enough of this through. Not formally as Jorgan would have, who had weeks to prepare. The curtains weren't even drawn, so

Thor moved to do that. As soon as he finished with the last window, he feared he might appear too eager. Perhaps they should make conversation for a while. Give Aven time to acclimate to being in this room alone with him. Of him as her husband.

He reached for a chair, thinking to draw it near for her, but when she touched his hand—stopping him—she didn't seem the slightest bit interested in conversation. Not of the talking variety. Instead, he came to realize a language that he understood much better. One of action instead of words, and as the moon made its arc in the night sky, she was his undoing with it.

THIRTY-FOUR

Thor was still asleep. Lying on his stomach just as she'd found him the morning in the great room when he'd slumbered beside her. Only then, he'd been a man she scarcely knew. Now the broad back that rose and fell was hers to touch. Aven wanted to slide her hand there. Feel his skin and strength all over again. But with this her first morning at his side, she feared she would startle him. Eyes still closed, his world was silent and dark. If she didn't take care, he'd be in for a jolt that he wasn't ready for.

She nestled in as gently as she could. Chilled, Aven tried to ignore the cold, but as Thor slept on, she braved a careful tug on the blankets, pulling them gingerly toward her chin.

Not gentle enough when he lurched upright.

A flash of silver filled his hand as he pulled a knife from beneath his pillow.

With a screech, she tumbled over the side of the bed, glad to have tugged a quilt with her, for it softened her fall. She bundled the blanket up around herself, and suddenly Thor was leaning across the bed to look down.

"Did you forget I was here?" Aven asked.

The side of his mouth lifted, and all at once there was a world of understanding in his eyes.

So sparse sleep had been that if he'd forgotten about her, it had only been in that still place of dawn between dreaming and waking.

"Perhaps we can agree that I didn't sneak up on you?"

He reached over the edge of the bed, pulling her and the bundle of bedding back up. The knife he closed before sliding it from sight. In what she knew as the word *sorry,* he circled a fist around his chest. Thor settled back in when she laid to face him. He worked his thick arm beneath her and pulled her near. As tender an apology as she could feel. Perhaps startling him hadn't been such a bad thing after all. His eyes closed again, and his fingers began to play with a twist of her hair.

Aven tapped him so he'd look at her. "You'll be keeping the knife under the pillow, then?"

He nodded sleepily.

She poked him this time. "Since I'm going to be around rather often, 'twould be better in the drawer, perhaps?"

He looked up at the ceiling for a few moments, then reached over her. The drawer opened and closed. In lying back down, he kissed the far side of her neck. Then the tip of her nose.

"Thank you, husband." And apparently the apology was continuing. Aven giggled.

He moved the kiss to just below her ear, and it was some time later that she finally coaxed them both from this place with the promise of breakfast. One so late that it might as well be deemed teatime. 'Twould be easy to linger longer, for it was his nearness she craved and nothing more, but if she didn't eat something, she would faint away. More selfish, she meant to keep his strength up. After checking the button on the waist of her skirt, Aven whispered that to him in the hall, and with his eyes on her mouth, she was rewarded with one of his gentle laughs.

She tiptoed past Jorgan and Fay's room thinking not to disturb them.

To her surprise, the kitchen was already bustling as Fay pulled a steaming kettle from the stove to fill two mugs and Jorgan stirred a sizzling pan of sweet meats. It seemed they weren't the only ones who had forgotten about breakfast. There followed a few moments of smiles and attempts at small talk, but finally, they all had to laugh. Thor rustled his brother's hair, signing what looked like an impish little phrase.

"Yeah, well, you slept through church too," Jorgan said with a grin.

Chuckling, Aven went to fix two more cups of coffee. A moment later, Jorgan and Thor stepped out onto the porch. She carried the cups out to find the mood much shifted, everyone quieted and watching the near end of the road. She lifted her gaze to see Peter striding close, a limp in his normally strong gait.

Thor stepped out to meet him. Jorgan followed. Even from where she stood, Aven could see a nasty gash across Peter's ear and a fresh bruise along his jaw. He was staying in one of the old cabins on the farm. Not too far from where Cora lived. Had he wandered back home? Or had his family come to find him?

Peter didn't speak until he'd come to the edge of the porch. "Ammo's gone missin', and they think you done it. I told 'em you didn't."

Aven looked to her husband. He circled Peter, tipping his head some as he considered Peter's injuries. She'd seen Thor angered before, but this was different. He was collected, but underneath was an enmity for who had done this that she could feel from where she stood.

Looking at Aven, there was a hint of regret in Thor's eyes as he gestured a request for a compress for Peter.

She minded not a bit. "Certainly." Aven stepped away, but not before hearing what Peter said next.

"Pa and the boys'r talkin' of comin' this way. Somethin' tells me this ain't the time for that, but they'll be comin' all the same. Prob'ly tonight."

There was no sense waiting around like sitting ducks. It helped that Thor's desire to head out matched Jorgan's own. Before leaving to see the women along to Cora's, Thor chose two pistols, checking that they were loaded. He set the safety

413

on each and tucked the first pistol snug at his back in the waistband of his pants. It was a cold day, so his plaid coat covered it well. Jorgan had the other. He could tell by the lump beneath Peter's shirt that he was armed as well.

Peter said little as they took the road. Grete trailed them, sniffing the ground as if on the trail of something she didn't like. Once to Cora's, they relinquished Fay and Aven to stay with Ida and the others. Aven's eyes were wet, and sensing her fears, Thor pulled her to him and held her as tight as he could.

With only a few moments to spare, Jorgan explained what was going on. It was safer for Al to stay, and there couldn't have been a better man to aid the women. Grete they pushed into the house, then fastened the door snug.

Peter finally spoke. Explaining a few things as they headed to the Sorrel farm. How many men there were. Who was the best shot. Just how angry Jed was.

They'd taken mere steps up to the old mansion when men poured out of the house. Six . . . seven . . . eight. Two hopped over the railing and another climbed out a side window. The wind shifted, fluttering the white cloaks and hoods on the clothes line. A taunt.

With Peter's father speaking, Thor shifted to better see him. ". . . so tell your little brother to stay off our land."

Haakon?

They'd seen him?

Jorgan had a heck of a poker face, and Thor hoped he did as well. Jorgan took his time in answering. "We ain't got a thing that's yours. You're welcome to a search, though. Come now if you want. A good place to start"—Jorgan casually shifted his stance—"would be the cidery. You know how to find it, I imagine."

Sorrels exchanged glances.

An odd scent tinged the air. Thor inhaled deeply. There. A smell that wasn't right. One that tainted his awareness even above the stink of their sweat and his cider on their breath. Thor's sense of smell was sharper than others, so he signed to Jorgan to see if his brother noticed it as well.

Jorgan shook his head.

Thor fingerspelled *S-U-L-F-U-R*.

His brother gave a slight nod.

The men watched, looking both puzzled and irritated. Thor's focus on them fractured when a little girl bounded from around the back of the house. About as young as Georgie, her ears were large and round where they poked through her straw-blonde hair. She was the only movement on the farm. Her faded red dress bounced above her bare ankles as she skipped along in the direction of the massive barn.

No one paid her much mind, and even Thor's

attention was short-lived when every head whipped to the east. He followed suit. Nothing showed out of the ordinary, which meant they'd heard something. Then he saw it: a tumble of leaves and dirt down the steep hillside . . . running boots . . . then a man—Haakon.

Haakon barreled down the slope, using his hands for balance as he skidded around a fallen log. His face was panicked, and he was shouting something, gaze locked on the little girl. Haakon smashed through branches at the base of the hill and charged toward the child who had slowed just in front of the barn door.

Her small hand seized the latch. Haakon stumbled again, righting his stance just as he reached her. He grabbed her up and ran straight for the Sorrels.

The girl's eyes pinched tight, mouth open in a scream. Still Haakon raced forward.

Several charged him, but Haakon slammed past, shoving the crying girl into Thor's arms.

Thor grabbed her, and his brother's face was so close. Greenish bruises flanking eyes that were wet with grief. Despair and shock crashed through Thor's numbness, and even if he wanted to put words to the thousand things that needed to be said, there wasn't time.

Collar open, Haakon's chest heaved, glistening with sweat and dirt. His gaze tore from Thor's as he turned. Slipped. Caught himself. And ran back the way he'd come. He had stolen but steps when the earth shook. A heat exploding into the air as timbers of the great barn shattered outward.

The men crouched, Thor included. He hovered over the girl, using one arm to wrap her head as another section of the barn blew. Then another. Suddenly, the earth shook again as the whole building came apart in one great ball of fire.

Thor draped the girl best he could, and another man pulled her beneath him. His arms free, Thor wrapped his own head even as he worked to help shield the child. His skin stung through his clothes.

As quick as it had seared, the air cooled enough for them to unfold. A cloud of black smoke billowed from the barn, chased skyward by angry flames. Sorrel men struggled to their feet. Mouths moved in shouts.

The missing ammunition. The smell of sulfur. A potent explosive. Something Haakon knew how to do.

The nearest man lifted the girl to her feet and sent her running for the house. If this had been Haakon's plan, he must have been watching from the hilltop, hidden from sight. He'd blown his cover for the child. A great price when Jed pulled a gun from his hip.

The man set aim on Haakon and fired.

Thor lunged for the general, slamming into the

wall of Sorrels that surrounded him. Thor fought to get forward but couldn't reach Jed as the gun fired again. The bullet hit just feet below Haakon, who was clamoring up the base of the hill.

The heat from the fire slicked Thor's skin with sweat as men shoved him to the ground. Thor kicked and swung, but still they slammed him down. He couldn't find Jorgan.

Jed's gun jerked again . . . shot hitting wide. At the steepest part of the slope, Haakon ducked against the off spray and struggled to climb higher. Dirt spilled from beneath his boots, waterfalling down the hill. Another gun reeled, its bullet ripping through a sapling.

Desperate, Thor pummeled the nearest man, striking with all he had to get free. Haakon was nearly to the top now, but Jed's aim was surer and surer with each trigger pull.

A tree limb shattered with the next shot. Haakon stumbled. Thor's heart tearing in two as his brother hit the ground. Someone reached for the pistol at his back, and Thor turned to sock the man in the shoulder.

Haakon scrambled up and kept running.

Thor thrashed with everything he had. He kicked a man in the gut and elbowed another in the face. It gave him way to break free enough to scramble to his feet. He reached Jed as the man was pulling the trigger on the final round. Thor grabbed the hot barrel, jerking it up.

The bullet should have swept high, but Haakon stumbled.

Dropped.

A cry choked Thor of air. Another man drew a gun, and more shots pierced through branches and leaves, shooting bark and dirt. Thor freed his pistol, cocked it, and pressed it to the Sorrel's head. The man stopped firing, and the gun fell limp on the crook of his finger. Reaching over, Thor took the firearm, aimed it to the western sky, and emptied it. Smoke stung his mouth, filled the air. Tinted blue by liquor, flames ate at the barn.

Jorgan rose to his feet, spitting out blood. Peter was still down, but he was moving. Sorrel men were down as well, some struggling to rise. No more guns fired—the traces of ammo gone as all the rest.

Desperate for Haakon, Thor surveyed the hillside but couldn't see anything in the thickening smoke. The wind shifted, pushing the smoke aside, only for the sky to darken again. Thor ran forward. A burn in his chest tugged at his pulse. Then a figure moved amid the smoke.

Haakon was scampering higher, gait hunched, but not that of a wounded man. One of a man trying to stay alive. Haakon cast them one last look, then bolted into a run.

Thor sank to his knees at a wrenching behind his ribs. His heart wasn't made for this.

A wagon barreled down the road at full speed. Beyond that, neighbor men were running. All coming to help. Thor didn't care if they were here to aid him and Jorgan or to put out the fire. All he saw was Haakon.

There comes a time in a body's life when they learn their name. But Thor learned his twice. His brothers did too. Two fingers pressed together in an *H*—arcing across one's eyes—that was *Haakon*. Thor had spent hours coming up with it for Haakon's third birthday and could still recall the joy on the kid's face when he'd taught it to him. Little Haakon smiling up at him as if there were a newness to the world. A gift Thor could give among Da's brokenness.

At first glance, the motion meant eyes so blue that people spoke of them, but anyone who knew Haakon would note the line of indignation often found between his brows. Or the laughter that sparked there, able to charge the very air. Thor had meant to never use that name again. Not ever. But with Haakon climbing the crest— disappearing amid the thick plume of smoke—his hand shook with the desire to form a good-bye.

Ida didn't let the men say much as their cuts and bruises were tended to, but once Jorgan, Peter, and Thor were patched up as well as they could be, each of the men told the story a little differently.

First Aven listened with the others as Jorgan described how men had come from all over the area, seeing the smoke. The Sorrels had pleaded for aid in putting out the fire but not so much as a person volunteered. Instead, a freedman from Ida's church said that should the Sorrels wish for help in rebuilding it, they would be there to aid them. As much a kindness as it was a challenge.

The way Peter relayed it, his ma and the other women had come out of the house. That not all the ammunition had been consumed. While no more shots were fired, a rifle in the hands of Mrs. Sorrel made it evident that she meant to aim it at no one other than her Jed.

Outnumbered, the general had limped off then, taking some of his men with him, and even a few women had followed. The other men had divided away, stating that they didn't want to be part of the unrest anymore. Mrs. Sorrel allowed those she trusted to stay.

Thor explained it last. Slowly, by paper, describing that both stories were true and that there was more yet. That he believed Haakon had blown the barn to free them all from the burden of the liquor. Though Thor didn't put as many words to it, Aven knew what that meant. That for his brothers, Haakon had given up his share of the profits he had so desperately wanted. Thor also relayed his sense that Haakon bore regrets. It was only a glimpse Thor had gotten, but the way he described it silenced any further conversation from Aven. She didn't know what to make of all this, but it landed in her heart in that lonesome place called bitter and sweet.

Though unable to tell any stories of her own, Grete was aimless. Pacing almost as much as she whimpered. The door ajar for her to roam, should she wish, said what they all knew—Haakon was gone.

THIRTY-FIVE

"Pardon me, miss!" Haakon steadied the young woman he had just bumped into. She bore an armful of parcels but didn't drop them, which was good because he didn't have time to help her pick them up.

He panted as he hurried around her. With a salty breeze drawing him closer to the wharf, he rushed along, dodging workers and shoppers and everyone in between. A priest stood on the corner of a church, trimming a hedge where just above, bells chimed the noon hour.

Masts and sails could be seen along the horizon, obscured by buildings. Haakon stepped around a wagon to cross yet another street that he didn't know the name of. He had no idea where he was going except to find the ship called *The Grel— something or other,* in a place called Norfolk. A bustling Virginia port with so many docks and harbors he had been lost all morning. He only hoped he was getting closer because a glance at that sun said nearly as loudly as those bells did that he was going to be late.

For weeks he'd been searching for a way off

of this hunk of land, and his luck had struck two nights ago when he'd spent his last twenty cents at a portside pub. While slowly drinking a lukewarm ale, Haakon had heard talk that the huddle of men seated in the far corner was a crew bound to ship out soon. He worked his way through the rest of his pint slowly, weighing what to do with such information. By the time he reached the bottom of his mug, he had just enough courage to cross the smoky room and inquire as to when they would be setting sail. He discovered that they were bound for Morocco to procure oranges and olives. Dates by the ton.

"And from there?" Haakon asked.

The man who answered was a stately one. Dark hair neatly kept and threaded with the faintest trace of silver. The brass buttons on his open coat gleamed in the lantern light. He quirked a brow as if none too pleased with the interruption. While his answer had been charitable, there was authority in his manner that made Haakon realize this was no average seaman.

Confirmed when a serving wench sauntered past, asking, "Another for you, Cap'n?"

The captain gave the lass a nod, then looked back at Haakon. "From there . . . Portugal. If the weather holds."

"And the maidens are willing," a fellow at a nearby table said with a guffaw.

Other men laughed, and judging by their

ruddy skin and weathered clothing, they were all part of the crew. A mismatched lot. Rough and coarsened, but with a confidence that Haakon respected. More so because they had what he sought. Passage out of here.

With this his chance, Haakon had stepped nearer. "Are there other ships leaving Morocco? Bound for other places?"

"Bound for Davy Jones' Locker with you on it if you don't shut up, Squidlet." That came from a stocky man who sat across from the captain. The gray-haired lout was shuffling a deck of cards in roughed hands. A scantily dressed woman sat beside him, nestling in despite his sweat-stained collar. She whispered in the man's ear, and he smiled.

The captain didn't answer until he was dealt five cards. He opened them slowly, moved two around, then spoke without looking up. "Some ships will disembark to England. Others, the West Indies."

The young serving wench returned with a filled tankard. She set it beside the captain, who lifted his gaze long enough to give her a gentle smile— one that said just how long these men would be at sea.

Lace trimmed the straps of her chemise that settled so low on her upper arms, the lantern over the table illuminated all of her pale shoulders. Unlike the other women about, she didn't fawn and giggle or flutter a fan. She simply sat on the bench beside the captain, her ivory arm brushing the gentleman's sleeve. She spoke nothing else as if she, too, knew her place in his presence.

The captain grazed a hand against her corseted waist and, after he drank from his pint, spoke to Haakon again. "Some will be bound for Brazil. With the demand for ice in London, others will venture to Scandinavia."

Scandinavia.

Home.

Hitching his pack higher up on his shoulder, Haakon braved his next question. But first he introduced himself.

At the words *Haakon Norgaard,* the man eyed him. "Norse?"

"Yes, sir. Norwegian." Which meant the sea was in his blood.

It was then that the captain invited him to pull up a stool. They spoke more of it, and the next thing Haakon knew, he was signing his name in a worn ledger along with the promise to be to the dock at noon sharp.

"Ship won't be waiting for nobody," said the stocky man as he plunked two gold coins onto the table, raising the stakes.

That was why Haakon was sprinting just now.

Though he'd meant to be on time, he'd spent the morning lost in the giant port city that boasted so many inlets; dozens upon dozens of ships had sailed across its waters already that day. He ducked beneath a traveling trunk that was being hefted onto a wagon, then skidded around a pair of mules that waited a lot more patiently than he for the train roaring past. When the caboose dashed by, opening up the road, Haakon ran across the tracks and closer to the wharf that he hoped was the right one.

That's when he saw the ship. The same one the captain had described. *Le Grelotter* was painted in fine lettering along some of her boards, and sailors shouted commands to one another as they hoisted lines. The great anchor dripped as it rose. Haakon ran faster.

In his pack was a letter for home, but the chance to mail it off vanished.

He raced ahead, nearly crashing into a cart loaded with sacks. The cart owner shouted at him in French and he shouted back in English, finally skidding to a halt at the bow of the ship where he jumped aboard, panting. The urge to drop to his knees was so overwhelming that he gripped the wooden railing to steady his shaking legs. He'd scarcely caught a breath when someone yelled at him to move.

He ducked as a rope was tossed from one man to another. Haakon turned, searching for a face he might recognize.

"You'll fare better if you stop looking so lost."

The voice came from a young man striding

toward him. Tall and broad of shoulder, the man was suntanned as if having sailed across the Atlantic more than a few times. He scrutinized Haakon through thin-framed spectacles. This one hadn't been in the pub. "You the greenhorn?"

"I'm sorry?"

"You the new one?"

"I think so."

The stranger stepped around wooden crates that kept clucking chickens. Brown hair askew, he crunched the last of a green apple before pitching the core over the side. "Come with me. And thank you, because I just won a bet on whether or not you'd show."

"I got lost." Remembering the letter in his pack, Haakon pulled it out. "Is there any place to leave this? I need to get it to my family."

With a sigh, the man snatched it, jogged back the length of the ship, and called to a group of workers on the dock. With a flick of his wrist, he flung the envelope to someone who caught it.

The fellow strode back to Haakon. "That was addressed, right?"

"Um . . . yeah. It'll get where it needs to go?"

"Possibly."

Gripping him by the shoulder, the young man aimed Haakon forward. Haakon glanced back for sight of his letter, but it was as gone from view as the person who had caught it. He supposed there wasn't much need to worry. What he'd written wasn't profound. Just a few simple lines to say that he was leaving and that he was sorry. That felt like a weak way to do it. Insufficient in light of what he'd done to Aven, but he couldn't fight the urge to at least try, and maybe one day he would know how to do better.

"Name's Tate Kennedy," the young man said. "I was told you're looking for Norway."

"Yes."

"That's where I'm bound, so I'll show you the way." He smiled as he extended a hand, and Haakon shook it, grateful. "What brings you aboard our fine vessel?" Tate grabbed a length of rope, pulled it taut, and knotted it around a metal hoop that was secured to a part of the ship Haakon had no name for.

"I . . . uh . . . needed to get away." Haakon ducked when another coil of rope went unfurling past.

The man tugged his knot tight, then moved to form another. He panted as he worked. With a snap of canvas, a sail unfurled overhead. Haakon peered up as more men tugged lines that hoisted it higher and higher and higher. It snapped in the wind and he watched, awestruck.

"What do I do?" he called out.

"Stash your kit belowdeck, and we'll find the first mate. He'll get you a task."

"How do I do that?" Haakon didn't even know how to get belowdeck.

Tate chuckled. "Lemme finish this, then I'll show you." He moved to climb a stretch of netting, and Haakon backed out of the way.

The surface of the water rolled and glittered. Seagulls swooped. A pelican dove for a catch. Otters bobbed on their backs, turning their whiskered faces to the ship as it dipped and creaked over the surface spraying back seawater. The mist of it hit Haakon's face, and he knew it was just the beginning, this calm, welcoming sea.

Sails continued to rise and ropes slithered into place, all mixed with languages he didn't understand. Save for one he knew as a memory. A whisper. Norwegian. Two men shouted commands to one another in it as they worked. The burliest of the pair tossed Haakon a line and showed him where to coil it. The man's thick hands moved in quick precision as he fastened a knot that Haakon didn't understand but wished to.

The stranger's hair was pulled back with a leather cord, and his sun-bleached shirt was strained around strong arms. He worked silently with Haakon, motioning to a second line. Haakon knew enough of gesturing to grasp what was being asked. Unfurling the rope, Haakon twisted it around the next iron clip.

The bearded man stepped in again and, without words, reshaped the knot to his liking. When the large man gave a friendly nod, Haakon touched fingertips to his mouth, then lowered his hand in the sign for *thank you.*

The suddenness of it startled him. What was he doing?

This man wasn't Deaf. Haakon stepped away, but all he could think of now was Thor and how they had done that same exchange ten thousand times in the past.

Haakon turned to try and lose the memory of his brother.

More desperate was the need when thoughts of Thor brought forward the vision of Aven's smiling face. Sharper to his soul, her tears. He glanced out over the bay, glad for her sake that there would be an entire sea between them. When it came to his wanting of her, he feared nothing else would suffice. They were married—Aven and Thor. That he knew, for he'd watched from the hillside where no one would see. Grete had been at his side.

Aven was free of him now. She would have her peace.

He could only hope that God would do him the same favor.

Were there any reaches of this sea that were far enough away to escape this guilt? Were there tropical beaches so distant? Icy fjords deep enough to pull him in and tuck him away? Haakon wasn't sure, but he meant to find out.

Sunlight glistened on the water as the ship

gained speed—air whipping by so fast that Haakon almost closed his eyes as he breathed in the scent of freedom, holding tight for what was to come. Wind gusted so powerfully, it was nearly deafening, but over that rose the steady shouts and commands of a herd of seamen all working as one.

Behind, the Virginia port grew smaller and smaller and up ahead, the Atlantic spread out before them—vast and bold. Stunning to behold, but suddenly all Haakon could see were the hills and meadows of home. All he could feel were cool pond water and the prick of blackberry brambles under the hot sun. Could only hear Thor moving about in the great room, loud as an ox as he settled at his chess table. An unfinished game waiting between them.

Haakon cast a glance back to land. Though he knew he couldn't see home, he strained his eyes all the same, wishing for sight of the mountains where the blackbirds flew. Where Thor had taught him to swim, and in return, he'd taught Thor how to whistle. The place where walls had often trembled with their brawls. Both in play and in anger.

Where Da had told stories of the kings of old.

The place where everything began and the place where everything had changed.

Haakon blinked quickly to push the past where it needed to stay. The ship sailed ahead with such speed that gusts pounded the sails. It was a freeing feeling, the past growing farther and farther behind. The strength of canvas and wood bringing the future nearer. Freedom. He would stalk it until he found it, and even if it was never meant to be his, he would try all the same.

"Hey! Squidlet!"

Jerking from his thoughts, Haakon turned to see a stocky sailor storming his way. It was the same one who'd been playing cards with the captain. "This ain't a passenger ship!" The man flicked a dull-looking knife to Haakon, who caught it by the handle. "There's potatoes to peel."

The man strode off. After casting a glance up to the young man who was still busy in the rigging, Haakon followed. The ship struck a rolling wave and Haakon stumbled. "Shouldn't I be helping with the sails? Hoisting them . . . or something?"

The man gave a gritty laugh. "You so much as touch one of my sails before I say and you're gonna find out what life is like with just one hand." Reaching an opening in the deck, he stomped down a steep set of stairs.

Haakon followed into the dim space just as the man told him to watch his head.

Smack! Haakon rubbed his forehead and ducked beneath the beam he'd walked into.

Belowdeck, the rocking of the ship intensified. Planks creaked and everything swayed. The air was stale and reeking. Haakon swallowed hard as nausea struck both his head and his stomach. Made worse at the way a large sailor with stringy hair was cutting the heads off of fish.

Haakon gritted his teeth to fight a sour taste— his idea of heaven suddenly a lot more like hell. Grimy benches sat shoved up against a rough table, and barrels and sacks were stacked in every available spot. The ship swayed again, and Haakon fought to keep his stomach from wringing itself out.

A bucket of potatoes was shoved into his grasp. He looked at them, then back to the sailor who plunged his knife into another fish. The man ripped out the guts and dropped the dripping mess into a rusted pail. Using the blade, the man pointed Haakon to one of the benches just as the sailor who had brought him here started back up the stairs.

"Are you sure this is my job?" Haakon asked.

"Yep."

"How often will I have to do this?"

"Every day. Morning, noon, and night."

"For how many days?"

The man turned and strutted back down until his ruddy nose was an inch away from Haakon's. "Until I say you're done."

"How long will that take?"

"Only time will tell, *Squidlet*."

"And what if I want to do something else?"

The ship rocked and Haakon adjusted his stance,

but his stomach was still moving in the other direction.

"Then I'll inform the crew that they'll be eating raw potatoes tonight. That will be thirteen hungry sailors who get the bad news that there's a beardless tadpole on board who isn't feeling too domestic just now."

Haakon swallowed hard. "I'll get to peelin', sir."

"I thought that's what you'd say." Stepping back, the man smiled, and to Haakon's surprise, it wasn't unkind. "Welcome aboard *Le Grelotter*. Work hard and do not irritate me. I'm your first mate and you will call me that. The captain you will call Captain or Shipmaster. He's your Master Under God so long as you're aboard, and if you even think about giving him the sass you just gave me, you'll be peeling a lot more than potatoes."

Haakon nodded.

"The ones in the bucket will do for a start. And while you're at it, you can *say thank you*." He nodded to the knife in Haakon's hand. "There's your ticket across this water, so gratitude would be sufficient."

"Gratitude."

The first mate started back up the steps. "A whole heap of it, I suggest." Herring gulls swooped over the patch of blue sky, and Haakon squinted as the man climbed toward the sun.

"The captain is not your mother, and I am most certainly not your friend. We did not have to let you on this ship. But because we did, you, little Squidlet, are about to see the world."

EPILOGUE

"This'll do?" Jorgan asked.

He and Thor hefted the new table to the base of the porch. The men had spent a whole week fashioning it within the open space of the cidery, and just in time for the Thanksgiving feast. Made of clean pine, it was sanded and oiled to a silken sheen.

"Oh, it's beautiful!" Aven hurried down the steps and smoothed a hand along it. "So fine!"

"And large enough for many," Fay exclaimed.

Suddenly everyone focused on her. She held up her hands, face pinker than the plum sauce she'd spent half the morning making. "I have nothing to share."

Jorgan chuckled, and Thor elbowed him.

After gripping one end of the table again, Jorgan nodded toward the house. "If one of you'll prop the door open, we'll get this inside."

Fay hurried to do just that, and with much effort from the men, the table was brought into the great room. Furniture had already been moved about; the sofa nudged nearer to the fireplace—a need for such cold weather. Ida's rocking chair

437

had been slid to its side. The changes allowed for a table that would hold them all. A place where many family meals could be had.

Ida limped in and dropped a folded lace cloth in its center. "And not a moment too soon."

With company due upon the hour, they had much to finish. Aven helped Ida spread the cloth, then Fay placed a large jar of autumn florals in its center. Feathery Yarrow, dainty Heart-of-the-earth, and pretty Nodding Ladies' Tresses with their white bell-blossoms.

The men brought in chairs—Jorgan setting them into place much quieter than Thor. When her husband passed by, Aven caught him by the shirt hem and, giving a gentle tug, nudged him nearer for a kiss. He smiled against her mouth, pulling away a moment later, ever reserved in front of others. When they were alone, well, that was another matter.

Aven smiled even as she fluffed the flowers.

Perhaps a little too cheerfully when Fay tapped her shoe. "And have you something to tell, missy?"

"If you're asking what I think you're asking—I must answer no." Though how Aven wished it were so. For some, eight weeks of wedded life would be cause for a baby to be coming. But for Aven, hope told her that such a wish would take time, if at all. She'd born no children to Benn, even amid two years of marriage. If she was meant to be a mother, it would happen in due course, and if it wasn't to be, she would better love those who crossed her path.

Fay leaned nearer to whisper, "I must confess that I was being coy in the yard." Her blue eyes were full of both joy and worry over what Aven's reaction might be. "It's too soon to be certain. A few weeks at most. But I'm becoming quite convinced."

Aven stifled a gasp and nearly knocked over the vase to pull Fay into a hug. " 'Tis a wonder and a secret I shall keep most carefully," she whispered. To think . . . a baby in this house. Aven pulled back just as the men returned with more chairs.

Jorgan smiled at his wife in a way that told the secret wasn't one from him.

Fay hurried to change the course of the conversation. "Perhaps we should splay out the desserts. They're so pretty."

"Aye," Aven answered as abruptly.

Together, they fetched the sweets. Aven brought in the tart she'd baked that morning and set it on the small side table. Made with apples and dusted with sugar, 'twas a new recipe. The last of Thor's cider was in the brown butter sauce that she drizzled on top.

Cookies and doughnuts followed, both sprinkled with cinnamon and nutmeg. Last was the crowning glory. A pie made of pecans that Cora brought in.

A hundred-year-old recipe, she declared, and it was a wonder to look at. Tess brought in freshly-baked rolls, Al two pitchers of creamy eggnog, and Georgie flounced in with her sunny smile. It faded some as they all sat, and the girl's dark eyes seemed to take note that someone was still missing. Georgie didn't say anything, though. She just looked up at her mother with a sorrowful appeal, and Cora squeezed her tiny hand.

Aven felt a twinge in her throat and was grateful when Jorgan blessed the meal, drawing Georgie's focus off of those who were gone. He prayed a thanks for the days that had passed. Prayed in trust for the days that would come. Most of all, he gave thanks for this day, for those gathered 'round, and for the gift they all had been given from the Sorrel women.

The deed to the farm.

'Twas a thanks that went beyond what words could say, so Aven and Fay had delivered a basket of doughnuts and another of cookies that morning. Jorgan had carried over the rest of their earnings that they'd saved to pay toward it. And Thor—well, Thor had given a gift of thanks that told the remaining Sorrels the trees were theirs for any need. To take all the apples they could possibly use, and for any need beyond that, to come calling. The arrangement was friendly, but there were Sorrels yet unaccounted for, and she knew it was the reason Thor watched the land with more care than ever. And why he slept with a rifle never farther than a reach away.

When Jorgan finished his prayer, Ida stood to slice into her roast turkey. She served up thick helpings, and Fay followed along with steaming baked potatoes. To Georgie, she gave the smallest of all and a kiss on the wee girl's head. Georgie smiled again then—sorrows forgotten for a little while.

The meal was a merry affair and they took their time with it, letting the clock tick away its reminder that change would blow in with every passing season, while they feasted and celebrated what it meant to be family and for the freedoms of this land. The latter was not always easy to come by, but an effort they'd never give up on.

When dusk crept in, Jorgan stood. "If you'll all follow Thor and me outside, we've got somethin' to show you."

Napkins were tossed aside, and Georgie hopped up to grab one more cookie before running out into the evening air. The breeze was crisp, so Aven pulled snug a shawl and clung even tighter to Ida's arm that looped around hers. Tess kept sweet company with Grete as they strode up ahead. Al fetched a stick and gave a good fling. Grete bounded to reclaim it.

Cora and Fay walked side by side, and at the gentle manner that Cora was speaking—and Fay listening with shining eyes—Aven had a hunch that a secret was being unearthed by a faithful midwife.

Jorgan and Thor led them all the way down to the end of the lane. To the place where Aven had once stood, letter in hand, reading the sign.

Norgaard. Blackbird Mountain.

And yet she saw in that instant that the sign was gone. In its place was a new one. Thor touched her waist, gently drawing her around so she could read it.

Norgaard Family Orchard.

His other hand joined the first until his arms circled her from behind. Aven leaned her head back even as he bowed his own to kiss her shoulder. " 'Tis a fine name for this place." Pride and gratitude surged through her that she was a part of it.

She clasped her hands over his, holding tight. His fingers grazed the button bracelet around her wrist. No ring she wore yet, so this gentle circle that he'd fashioned was one she savored in its stead. Ida blew a bit of dust from the freshly carved letters, then smoothed the edge of her apron over it.

Aven smiled, but rising up was a different sensation. She had tried to ignore it all day. And really, for weeks now. She'd been handing all worry and all wonder to the Lord—as was right— but in this moment, He seemed to be handing it back.

For her to *feel* it.

Because there was a piece of her that wouldn't die away. One that couldn't imagine going through this life without ever seeing Haakon Norgaard again. The notion pinched at her heart, reminding her she had a reason to despise him. A right to wish him far away from here. But if there was one thing she knew of him that day, it was that a broken man had walked with her to that cabin. A broken man had closed the door.

And a broken man had thought she would be able to fix what wasn't hers to repair.

It was God's. Haakon needed a tending-to that only the Lord could complete.

Eyes growing wet all over again, Aven swiped at them, grateful for the dimming light. No one seemed to pay her damp cheeks any heed. The others stepped away, returning to the glow of the house. Thor took her hand in his while they walked. He held it safe and secure as though his spirit was wandering its own complicated path. One not much different from her own.

While he was often quiet, she'd come to know his thoughts in the hours they spent cuddled up, a candle burning beside them as Thor wrote his words to paper. Aven always read with care, answering with pencil in like fashion, and together, they carved away his silence.

She saved each slip of paper, for in them lay his desires. His hopes. Even his worries. His wishes for her, and how he meant to care for her in return. Though she'd once thought him a shy man, he wasn't shy in that place. Nay, there was a boldness to Thor Norgaard, and it was a guiding light in the weeks that had passed and would continue to be one in the years to come.

She clutched tight to his hand as they walked the same road they had months ago. Except this time, instead of him trailing behind as a stranger, he was at her side as both husband and friend. Even those months back . . . on that hot summer day . . . he'd been there for her in the same tender way. His love had simply borne a different shape. One of quiet protection. Of patience.

How thankful she was for the man beside her. Tempests would still come and the waters would not always be calm, but she was beholden to this place—where body and heart knew the love of a husband so sure and so strong that even the coming winds of winter seemed to fall at bay.

Aven breathed the cold air in deep.

And as for Haakon . . .

If she ever stood before him again, she knew not what she would say, but there was the gift of time. God was giving it, that she knew. For how long or for how far, *that* she didn't. Come tomorrow or come years from now, she would say to that man—the one who had once been her friend—that no, she didn't hate him. Hate wasn't hers to bear justly and if she tried, it would leave her wrecked upon the rocks she hoped to navigate safely around. So instead, she would seek to forgive Haakon. Perhaps in time she would come to even pray for him. While such notions felt steeper than this mountain had been to climb, she longed for both, and as they walked toward home, she trusted in the Lord, who would provide the way.

A NOTE FROM THE AUTHOR

It began the week I met the young Deaf man and his sister at summer camp. I knew very little Sign Language beyond the alphabet, and when I first observed this sibling pair communicating, I was fascinated. In an auditorium holding hundreds of teenagers, this quiet brother sat watching as his sister translated the worship music and preaching. Her hands shaped sweeping words, and I longed to know how to shape them too. More importantly, how to understand the people behind this language. During that week, both brother and sister showed me some of these words, and it became a comradery and a tradition that I looked forward to every summer.

Years after those camp adventures, after I had taken several semesters of Sign Language, I pulled up a blank document and wrote down a title for a new Appalachian romance—*Sons of Blackbird Mountain*.

Beyond those four words I knew nothing of the tale. I knew not who would walk its pages or where the journey might lead, but it seemed destined to hold the taste of summer because just like that, so rose the tree house in the woods with its white flag flickering on the breeze. I heard the thundering footsteps of Thor, the contagious laughter of Haakon, and the calm, steady wisdom of Jorgan. Ida's smile beamed from where she sat in her rocking chair, and thousands of trees rose up from the earth, branches twisting into place, filling the air with the fragrance of ripening fruit. Viking legends whispered in on the wind even as the days of boyhood faded into memory.

Then I saw Aven trudging up the hillside with her carpetbag in hand where she first met the man who watched—instead of heard—what she was saying.

So began the journey of writing a character that challenged me in heart-deep ways as a writer. When it came to writing a man who had almost no traditional dialogue, each scene offered new and intriguing challenges. As a writer, I considered alternate ways to get his voice onto the page. Thor's humble, unassuming ways made it an absolute pleasure to think outside the box, and in truth, he rather showed me the way.

To do his character justice, I expanded my study of ASL beyond the modern courses I'd taken and began an investigation of the Deaf in the nineteenth century. This included documented testimonies of students who were taught Oralism, to the history of Deaf education in the late 1800s. All of this led me to an 1883 memoir written by Alexander Graham Bell, whose life's work not only involved the invention of the telephone but, as the son of a Deaf woman, a zeal to teach the Deaf to read lips and speak. Bell's methods and opinions remain controversial to this day. Some students responded well to the teachings and rigorous lessons, while those who didn't were known as *oral failures*. This was one of the reasons Thor was up in the oak tree that day, longing for home, his words rooted only in his hands when his Da came to fetch him. It was a tragic day that propelled Thor into a new realm of pain: one he tried to allay with a jar of cider only to discover the emptiness was unquenchable.

For some of us, our pain is similar to Thor's. In other ways, we're not so different than Aven as she climbed up that mountain, holding onto a budding hope. Isn't it just like the promise of God to not give us one without the other?

Oh the joy that lies around the bend if we open our hearts, deepen our trust, and jump into the brave unknowns knowing God awaits. My heart fills with hope as I imagine the young sailor who still yearns to do the same. His journey has just begun, and I hope you'll join me and the rest of the cast as it unfolds in the sequel to *Sons of Blackbird Mountain*. Oh yes, friends, there is more to come! More romance, more redemption, and a new unfolding of the bond between brothers.

Thank you for spending time with me and the Norgaard family in these pages. I would be honored for you to visit me (and this bunch of colorful characters!) at www.joannebischof.com, where I stay connected with readers on upcoming books, faith, and the writing life.

Thank you for being a part of it,

Joanne

DISCUSSION QUESTIONS

1. New beginnings are everywhere in the story. Which new beginning is most relatable to your own life?

2. Aven came to the farm believing that Thor, Jorgan, and Haakon were children. Would you say this was an accidental miscommunication or an intentional mis-informing on Dorothe's part? If Dorothe was matchmaking, what do you think her motives were and do you believe she had a particular brother in mind for Aven?

3. Each of the Norgaard men has much in common with his brothers, yet each is distinct in his own way. What similarities do you see in them? What differences? What role do you think their birth order and upbringing served in the way their personalities developed?

4. Aven first learns that Thor is Deaf while we are in her point-of-view. If we were in Thor's head during that scene, what do you think he might have been thinking? Most Deaf Americans in the 1800s lived in rural areas, separated by distance, with little communication with people around them. What do you think life was like for a person such as Thor in these days?

5. By looking at Aven's history together, how was she shaped by her past? Her mother taught her sewing and love, her time at the workhouse taught her determination and compassion, while Farfar Øberg showed her lessons of baking and kindness. How did each of these elements come to play in the molding of who she was in this story?

6. As a freedwoman working for wages, why do you think Ida chose to live in a room off of the kitchen instead of living with her blood-relatives, Cora and the children? What do you think were her reasons for becoming such an integrated part of the Norgaard family? Why do you think the Norgaards cherished her so, seeing her less as a housekeeper and more as a member of the family?

7. When Aven offers the brothers her twenty Kroner, she is giving her most costly possession. What does this say about her character? In what ways did Farfar Øberg lead by example when he first pressed it into her hand? Has there been a time in your life when you received an act of kindness that breathed hope into your heart?

8. The 1870s were known as the dark ages for the Deaf due to the frequent banning of Sign in Deaf schools. Young students such as Thor who were unsuccessful with Oralism

were known as "oral failures." What do you think a label such as this would mean to a person? In what ways did Thor overcome the idea of failure? How did reading his story change your viewpoint on the Deaf? If you are Deaf, what sorts of connections did you make with Thor? Did this book offer you new insights into the thoughts and behaviors of hearing people?

9. Why did the Norgaard brothers value their Viking heritage as they did? Having been raised primarily by their father, Jarle, what role did this serve in their reverence for the Viking tales of old? How did such a heritage shape them as men living in the wilds of Appalachia?

10. What sort of lessons do you think await Haakon at sea? Do you foresee him maturing during his time aboard ship? How do you see his character being challenged?

11. What's a book club chat without a wee bit of fun? If you were sitting in that church in Eagle Rock, Virginia, and you noticed the Norgaard men come in, what is the first thing you would whisper to the woman beside you?

12. With the second Blackbird Mountain novel just around the bend, what sort of lessons, changes, or adventures do you imagine might await the cast?

ACKNOWLEDGMENTS

Never has my mailbox been more filled with cards, greetings, packages, and notes of encouragement. Never have people so tenderly offered up words of hope and wisdom. That yes, this mountain can be climbed and that my children and I are not alone. To every dear soul who has bolstered us along this journey these last few years, truly making the writing of the Blackbird Mountain novels possible, you have my utmost gratitude.

A sincere, heartfelt thanks for being the light along the road and for filling our sails with wind of the sweetest kind. You lent me the courage and strength to finish this book and never have I seen God's people move in a more wondrous way than you have moved in our lives.

Much like with Aven, thank you for being the letters beneath my pillow and the ones who took my hand, pressed your kindness and wisdom into it, and helped me to rise.

ABOUT THE AUTHOR

JOANNE BISCHOF is an ACFW Carol Award and ECPA Christy Award–winning author. She writes deeply layered fiction that tugs at the heartstrings. She was honored to receive the San Diego Christian Writers Guild Novel of the Year Award in 2014 and in 2015 was named Author of the Year by the Mount Hermon conference. Joanne's 2016 novel, *The Lady and the Lionheart*, received an extraordinary 5 Star TOP PICK! from *RT Book Reviews*, among other critical acclaim. She lives in the mountains of Southern California with her three children.

Visit her online at JoanneBischof.com
Facebook: Author, JoanneBischof
Instagram: @JoanneBischof

Books are produced in the United States using U.S.-based materials	Books are printed using a revolutionary new process called THINKtech™ that lowers energy usage by 70% and increases overall quality	Books are durable and flexible because of Smyth-sewing	Paper is sourced using environmentally responsible foresting methods and the paper is acid-free

Center Point Large Print
600 Brooks Road / PO Box 1
Thorndike, ME 04986-0001 USA

(207) 568-3717

US & Canada:
1 800 929-9108
www.centerpointlargeprint.com

Due
10-6

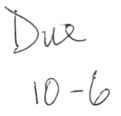

COEUR WHARF™